The Devil's Scribe

ISBN: 978-1-939156-72-3

Ink Smith Publishing
P.O. Box 361
Lakehurst, NJ 08733

The Devil's Scribe

By Rod Baker

Ink Smith Publishing

www.ink-smith.com

Acknowledgements

Loving gratitude to my wife, Pattie, who knows all the reasons why.

Thanks to my family for their support: Corinne, Cass, Duane, Edythe, Linda, Deanne and Kent--and much appreciation to the following institutions: the Westminster Preservation Trust, Baltimore Police Department, George Peabody Library of the Johns Hopkins University, College of Notre Dame of Maryland, The Peale Museum, University of Maryland College Park, Baltimore Area Convention and Visitor's Association, Baltimore City Archives and Records Management Office, and the Enoch Pratt Free Library.

Prologue

● ● ●

"Let's do it in a graveyard!" Marsha Mayfield suggested excitedly, her voice competing with squeaky windshield wipers and hammering rain on the auto's roof.

Chuck Nash cocked his head. "Which one?" he asked, steering his van on a watery city street.

"The Westminster Burial Grounds."

"Why there?"

"It's more Gothic than the others," Marsha replied simply.

"Whatever turns you on," Nash chuckled quietly.

Marsha peered through the windshield at Baltimore's rain-slick streets. Torrents of dark water rushed down the curbs, carrying the city's grime out to sea. Against the day's last streams of sunlight, the skyscrapers shined wax-like against the rapidly darkening sky. And whenever the lightning streaked, Marsha knew the rolling thunder would be heard throughout the city.

From the corner of her eye, Marsha caught Nash leering at her deep cleavage that pressed against her low-cut blouse. She gave him a nettled look. "Eyes on the road, Bozo!"

Nash quickly withdrew his gaze. He refocused on the

street, tightening his grip on the steering wheel.

Marsha leaned back in the passenger seat, recalling how she had been ogled by men since her high school days. She was twenty-seven now with a playmate face and body. No matter what she wore, she looked alluring and sparked men's primal interests.

"I can think of dryer places to do it," Nash said, running a hand through his long graying hair. His crooked nose and the puffy crescents beneath his eyes made him look older than his thirty-nine years.

"So can I, but I want to do it at the Burial Grounds," Marsha said with no room for argument. "We need to hurry before they lock the place up for the night."

"Okay, you're the boss," Nash said, stepping on the throttle.

The van lurched forward and broke through sheets of driving rain, toward Baltimore's oldest graveyard.

● ● ●

Nash eased the van toward the curb at the Westminster Presbyterian Burial Grounds. As he parked, a sword of lightning stabbed the cemetery. A peal of thunder followed with a deafening rumble.

This storm could raise the dead, Marsha thought as she climbed from the van and glanced up at the ominous, black clouds roiling in the sky. She had never seen a storm with this much unbridled power.

Marsha lifted an umbrella above her head, but the sharp wind whipped it from her hands and blew it over the graveyard's spiked fence. The icy chill of the rain penetrated her clothes, knotting her nipples against her thin silk blouse.

Jumping from the van, Nash met Marsha at the side doors where WRTV Weather Center was stenciled in royal blue letters. His heavy pullover, already soaked, clung to his body like a wet chamois. "You sure you want to do this?" he asked, looking up at the flashing sky.

"We need the ratings, Nash," Marsha reminded him pointedly. "Our careers need a jump-start in case you haven't noticed."

Nash nodded. He opened the van's door and dutifully retrieved a broadcast HD video camera wrapped with a rain cover.

Marsha stepped toward the cemetery's heavy iron gate, remembering that most of Baltimore's founding fathers were buried here. This was Baltimore's glorious past stranded in the future, she mused as she glanced upward in time to see a streak of lightning hissing through the wet air. As the local Meteorologist for WRTV, Marsha knew millions of volts of raw power split the sky above her. With a temperature five times that of the sun, the bolts would destroy whatever they hit.

Marsha pushed open the cemetery's gate and noticed that the clouds had clustered over the graveyard. *The storm is really weird*, she thought.

Marsha and Nash leaned into a howling wind as they walked down a long row of marble monuments with clashing designs spanning more than 200 years. Several Egyptian sarcophagi and obelisks were near Greek and Roman statues. Some burial chambers, Marsha observed, were like small concrete dog houses while others featured tall lotus figures and winged hourglasses.

"I have a distant relative buried here. A war hero," Marsha said as she and Nash hiked deeper into the burial grounds, their wet clothes offering no protection against the icy, huffing wind.

"World War Two?" Nash asked.

Marsha glanced sideways at Nash. "I'm talking about the Revolutionary War. No one's been buried here since the 1940s."

"Oh, right," Nash mumbled.

Marsha could see in Nash's expression that he was embarrassed by his own ignorance. "Edgar Allan Poe is here," she explained, her words almost swallowed by the rumble of thunder.

"Whatever," Nash replied.

Driving streams of rain whipped Marsha and Nash as they walked farther onto the grounds. A shaft of lightning broke from the clouds and hit a tombstone near them, disintegrating the marble. Stony shards flew into the air.

Nash cringed. "That was like bomb!" he blurted.

Marsha nodded, also shaken by the blast. "A hundred million volts will do that. But don't worry. It's a million to one chance we'd be hit," she added, attempting to regain her composure.

Suddenly, another bolt pierced a tree near Marsha and Nash. The tree's sap boiled instantly, exploding the trunk and causing the tree to burst into flames. Marsha ducked to avoid a flying branch. Nash stumbled in the mud when he tried to dodge the hot sap that sprayed the area. He glared at Marsha. "Million-to-one my ass! To hell with ratings! We're gonna get fried out here!" Nash's voice was barely audible over the sounds of the storm.

"Storms like this are rare, Nash. We can't pass it up!"

Marsha argued, hoping her tone masked her rising fear. "Let's do it right here, right now."

Without a word, Nash hurriedly hoisted the camera onto his shoulder and checked the settings. He then aimed the camera at Marsha and pressed a button. "We're rolling."

As Marsha began to speak into the camera, several fingers of lightning streaked down from the clouds and hit a grave twenty yards from her and Nash. A pile of muddy earth flew skyward. A dark round object and several pieces of worm-eaten wood landed near Nash's feet. He lifted the round object from the wet earth.

"Shit! It's a friggin' skull!" Nash yelled, throwing the bony head to the ground as though it carried the plague. "That's it! We're outta here!"

Nash set the camera on a marble monument and rushed to Marsha's side. "The camera's running," he said quickly. "It'll tape the storm. You can do a voice-over later. You look like shit anyway," Nash said, his eyes sweeping Marsha's body. Her chestnut hair was wet and stringy, her makeup was streaking down her face and her clothes were spattered with mud.

A bright, jagged ray struck a marble tablet near Marsha and Nash, splitting it in half. Then another shaft blasted a smoking hole in the soaked ground nearby.

Suddenly unnerved, Marsha's eyes darted about anxiously in an urgent search for shelter. She saw the cemetery's high-towered, brick church about a hundred yards away. "We'll be safe in there!" she shouted to Nash, pointing at the church.

Without hesitation, Marsha and Nash dashed forward, sloshing through the mud toward the church. Lightning cascaded into a grave near them, blowing up the plot and knocking them down into the mud.

As Marsha and Nash pushed up from the slimy earth and sprinted forward, a lightning shaft hit a tree behind them. Marsha turned and watched in horror as the electricity shot down the trunk and broke into multiple strokes. It splayed across the wet grass and shot directly toward her and Nash. It climbed their legs in an instant.

Nash's tremulous scream was choked off by death. His body twisted and his limbs curled grotesquely just before he fell silently into the sludgy earth.

Marsha's body jerked rigid when the voltage surged through her. Her eyes bubbled from their sockets and dripped down her cheeks. Her stiffened legs held her upright for a few seconds, then she tipped and fell like a piece of lumber. Her body hissed in the wet grass.

Part One
Resurrection

• • •

Would God I could awaken!

For I dream I know not how,

And my soul is sorely shaken

Lest an evil step be taken—

Lest the dead, who is forsaken,

May not be happy now.

Edgar Allan Poe

ONE

• • •

Rolling on his torn and dirty sleeping bag, Leonard Ravnik drifted in and out of sleep. Closing his small dark eyes was little help in bringing unconsciousness against the storm's loud and penetrating rumblings. Even the thick church floor above him could not silence the thunder. It echoed from above and rippled along the rows of marble body vaults in the musty catacombs below this house of God.

Ravnik's clothes and heavy jacket also kept him awake. They were stiff and slick with grime and offered little insulation against the cold. He had collected the filth from many states and scores of cities where he had lived in fields and empty houses and sometimes had to sleep on sidewalks, alleys or vacant lots. These were the only homes he had known for over a decade. He was always on the move, running and hiding. Wanted for murder in several states, he had already been profiled on several of the cable television crime shows.

Ravnik twisted on his sleeping bag again, breaking from his tenuous nap. He sat up and collected his thoughts, realizing that trying to sleep during the storm was impossible. Ravnik pushed his matted shoulder-length hair back from his face, allowing rivulets of dirty sweat on his heavy brow to slide down over his high cheekbones and long Roman nose. Ravnik knew his primitive features made him look much older than his twenty-six years. His fugitive life had carved his face into an unsmiling smirk and permanently cast it with hostility. He liked the power his look gave him, though. People shied away from him like frightened sheep when he approached them. And few people ever tried to make friends with him. Those who did sometimes went missing.

After wiping yellow curds from the corners of his eyes, Ravnik stood and stretched his limbs. He was over six feet tall but seemed shorter on his feet because his chest was stout as an oak barrel. His arms rippled with biceps as large as a thin man's thighs, and his legs were as powerful as a gorilla's. Unlike others on the run, he occasionally supplemented his robberies and muggings by working for construction labor crews or traveling carnivals. The no-questions-asked work was rigorous enough to build and sustain muscles and provide food that kept his body strong.

Ravnik walked down a row of the darkened marble crypts, in the church's catacombs, toward the arched opening that lead to the graveyard outside. The flashes of light from the storm penetrated the opening and guided his way. Moving past two centuries of the dead, Ravnik realized the departed souls surrounding him once sang hymns about everlasting life in the church above him. Now they had journeyed to the afterlife to harvest the promise of Christian scriptures.

Reaching the end of the catacombs, Ravnik stopped under the archway and looked out at the cemetery. Lightning crackled down from the dark clouds and illuminated the graveyard's destruction.

Scattered in the muddy earth were skulls, bones and pieces of coffins and tombstones. Craters left by the lightning made the graveyard resemble a war-torn battlefield.

Ravnik was surprised to see a man and woman lying on the cemetery grounds about fifty yards away. What appeared to be steam, coiling from their bodies did not dissipate into the cool, wet air as expected. It remained thick and lingered. It was smoke, Ravnik realized. He studied the lifeless forms for a moment and surmised these people were dead. Hit by lightning, he guessed. Ravnik contemplated the money he might find in the man's wallet. He also noticed the faint glint of gold hanging from around the woman's neck. A large necklace, he hoped. It would be a profitable night, he assured himself as he stepped into the storm to collect the easy bounty.

Ravnik walked just a few yards when he saw a blinding flash of light in the sky. He was suddenly aware this bolt was not like the others. It was massive, hissing and crackling as it streaked down toward the cemetery—and him. In amazement, he noticed a blue glow surrounding his arms and legs and in the same millisecond, the hair on his head
spiked. But before he could react, Ravnik's world suddenly turned black.

Ravnik opened his eyes and looked upward into the stormy clouds above him. They were still filled with streaking blasts of lightning. The thunder rolled downward and swept the graveyard, vibrating Ravnik's ribs. Ravnik noticed his vision was blurred and he felt a jackhammer of a headache. His ears rang and his mouth was parched, the taste of copper on his tongue. He felt the wet grass and mud beneath him soaking into his clothes. It was then he was fully aware he was flat on his back in the cemetery just like the man and woman he planned to rob. He started to rise but his muscles were flaccid and lacked the strength needed to lift his body from the earth.

Ravnik moved his head from side to side, hoping to alleviate the painful pounding in his temples. He could not remember what had happened, just a hot burning sensation in his body and the feeling of being hit by a cannon ball. His best guess was he had been struck by lightning.

Ravnik rolled to his side and tried to climb to his feet again. With his strength sapped, however, it took him a full minute before he stood, wobbling like a drunk. He raised his hands to his ears to stop the ringing but the fingers of his right hand became stuck in hot, smoldering, clay-like flesh. It took a few seconds before he realized his right ear was missing!

Ravnik looked dizzily ahead and retreated slowly to the exterior wall of the catacombs and leaned against the bricks, sucking in deep breaths. He waited several minutes while the numbness left some parts of his body, and he began to feel some control of his senses.

Ravnik pushed himself from the wall. With unsteady strides, he made his way toward the man and woman sprawled in the graveyard mud. Ravnik studied the bodies for a moment. They were black in places, cooked like barbecued steak. The stench of the cooked organs assaulted Ravnik's nose. He tried to compare the odor to the smells in the catacombs but this was much worse.

Ravnik yanked the gold chain from around the woman's neck. He studied its large opal stone. He was sure the necklace was worth a hundred dollars in a pawnshop. He rolled the man over and removed his wallet. There were two twenties and a five inside. Ravnik removed the twenties and pocketed them. He left the five and put the wallet back in the man's pocket. He rolled the man back into the position he found him. Ravnik figured if there was still cash in the wallet, the police, who would eventually be notified, wouldn't add robbery to an accidental death report and search the grounds for clues to a graveyard thief.

Ravnik cracked a slight grin, congratulating himself for his cunning. As he started back toward the catacombs, a guttural male voice interrupted his thoughts. It muttered something about checking the dead man to find out if he was wearing a money belt.

Stopping, Ravnik panned the graveyard, expecting to see someone—but no one was there. Ravnik figured his brain was misfiring and had created this voice. After all, he had just been struck by lightning.

"*Why would you not examine the man's belt for paper money?*" the invasive voice seemed to come from nowhere. This time it was clear and distinct.

Ravnik studied his surroundings carefully, expecting someone to step from out from the shadows of the headstones—but no one came forth—only the wind howled through the graveyard.

Where had the voice come from, Ravnik wondered. And why was it talking about a money belt? From all of his muggings, Ravnik knew they were not common anymore. Over the years credit cards had replaced the need to carry cash.

"Who's there?" Ravnik shouted against the rumbles of the storm. "Show yourself!" he challenged the darkness.

The only response Ravnik received was a gust of icy rain

against his face. Ravnik thought his mind was still playing tricks on him—or was he hearing voices like a crazy person? The voice had been close and clear, and Ravnik was sure he did not imagine it. He listened, waiting to hear it again. Moments passed. No voice. Ravnik was relieved, hoping whatever triggered the life-like voice was gone.

Ravnik, still shaky on his feet, moved back into the catacombs. He settled back down on his sleeping bag and dropped into a deep sleep.

TWO

• • •

"Stay down on the ball, Alex!" Renee Holland shouted, standing in the backyard of her two-story Victorian home. She swung a baseball bat from her shoulder and hit a grounder to her twelve-year-old son. Renee was an attractive woman with a face molded from smooth, unblemished skin. She had a slim nose, full lips and penetrating green eyes. Her firm, full breasts pushed against her sweatshirt and her jeans were stretched tautly over her shapely buttocks and thighs. A modeling agency had once invited her to walk the runway but she declined. She never wanted to be as thin as a professional model. She liked the way she was with perfect proportions for her body size. Although thirty-five, Renee could still pass as a college student.

Wearing an Oriole T-shirt, baseball cap and faded jeans, Alex charged the baseball. He squatted to catch the ball, but it rolled under his glove. "Darn it!" he exclaimed, blinking his blue eyes and shrugging.

"Stay down on the ball or the Orioles won't think you're ready for prime time," Renee warned with mock authority.

"Yeah, I know, Mom," Alex replied, picking up the

baseball and throwing it back to his mother, bouncing it at her feet.

Studying Alex, Renee felt maternal pride. She was delighted she shared a warm relationship with her son. Even though Alex was approaching the rebellious teen years, few civil wars erupted in the Holland household. Renee knew it was because they trusted and understood each other. And most important, they respected each other.

"Hit me another one, Mom," Alex shouted. "Harder this time." He thrust his head forward, bent with determination.

Without a word, Renee tossed the ball into the air and whipped the bat into it. The baseball cracked off the oak and bounced toward Alex on the lawn.

Alex crouched and stayed down on the ball this time, but it jumped from the ground, hit the heel of his glove, and clipped him on the mouth. "Ouch!" he exclaimed, reeling back slightly.

"Are you all right, honey?" Renee asked, concerned Alex had chipped a tooth.

Alex rubbed his mouth. His freckle-splashed cheeks were aflame with embarrassment. "Yeah, I'm okay," he answered, exposing a complete set of enamel. He snatched the ball from the ground and tossed it to his mother. "One more, Mom. This time I'll show you how they do it in the Majors."

"Fly ball?" Renee asked.

"Go for it," Alex replied, crouching slightly.

Renee threw the baseball in the air, swung the bat from her shoulder and hit the ball solidly. The baseball shot straight ahead, a line drive instead of a fly ball, and headed toward a large picture window.

Alex turned and sprinted toward the baseball. He pushed

off the ground with his strong legs and snatched the ball out of the air before it could hit the glass. He landed on his side and slid to a halt, painting his jeans with grass stains.

"Great play! Sign him up!" Renee shouted, dropping the bat and clapping.

Alex, despite the impressive catch, only muttered, "Oh, shit!" He pushed himself up from the ground with a long frown on his face.

Renee gave Alex a stern look. "Alex, we don't use that kind of language around here!"

"I know, but—" Alex lifted his arm and revealed the glob of dog manure smeared on his elbow. "It's the real thing."

Renee fought the urge to laugh and only allowed a private smile to surface. "Go wash up. Dinner's almost ready," she said, her grin lingering.

Alex trotted toward the house, holding his elbow in the air as if it had leprosy.

After Alex had gone inside, Renee walked up the porch steps, then stopped and let her vision sweep the neighborhood. She felt fortunate to live here. Her street was beautiful, a garden suburb of leafy trees shrouding homes that were truly snapshots of history. Her house, with its fine woodwork, was built in the Queen Anne style that prevailed during the 1800's Gilded-Age. Its Victorian elegance—a high turreted roof, fish scale shingles, a columned, gingerbread trimmed porch, and arched windows—were the reasons she bought it.

Renee's thoughts were interrupted when she noticed a large burn mark on the edge of her second story bedroom window and the glass was broken. The paint was bubbled and cracked.

Beneath it, Renee could see blackened, charred wood. It looked as though her house had been hit by a blast of high heat. But how this happened, Renee had no idea. She made a mental note to call a carpenter to repaint and repair the window.

● ● ●

Renee walked through her living room, passing furniture bridging the Colonial and Victorian eras. She had Original Windsor chairs surrounding a Colonial pine dining table. Her hardwood floors were covered with colorful Victorian carpets. Dark rich woods were evident in her Queen Anne highboy. She had a carved mantle, wooden archways between rooms and Chippendale fret work on the stairwell leading to the second story.

Renee entered her kitchen and withdrew a modern baking dish from her jet-black ceramic oven. Nothing in this room was antique. Even with her fondness for heritage, Renee believed in modern cooking conveniences. She placed the dish on the table next to several others and sat down. Renee inhaled deeply, allowing her nose to savor the appetizing aromas.

Alex walked into the kitchen and sat next to his mother.

Renee reached out and lifted Alex's arm, looking at it closely. "That's the cleanest I've ever seen your elbow," she grinned.

"Don't remind me," Alex replied. "It was gross. It had—"

"We're at the dinner table, Alex," Renee interrupted, then casually spooned pieces of chicken onto her plate. "When I picked up the mail today, I saw that you received a letter from your father."

"Yeah, he wanted to know how I was doing in school," Alex replied, half interested, filling his plate. "I already told him last week when he called, but he never listens to me."

"Of course, he listens to you, honey," Renee tried to comfort Alex. "He's probably just busy with work and forgot."

"He's always busy with work," Alex said.

Renee heard the disappointment in her son's voice. She set her fork down and studied his forlorn expression. "I'm sorry the divorce was so hard on you, honey," she said, feeling guilty for not providing Alex with a complete family. "I didn't mean for it to happen."

"I know, Mom. It's not your fault."

The pain in Alex's face was clear to Renee. She wanted to tell her son why the marriage had broken apart, but he was too young to understand the downward emotional spiral of a man and woman locked in a bad marriage.

Alex forked a piece of broccoli into his mouth. After he swallowed, he asked, "What really happened between you and dad? One word is okay."

"It's not easy to explain in one word," Renee said, lifting a small piece of chicken from her plate.

"Make it a sentence then. You're a writer," Alex joked.

Renee ran the question through her mind, trying to simplify it before she answered. She found some glittering generalities. "You could say your father and I just went sour together. Some people call it *bad chemistry*. Two good people can make one very bad marriage," she said, not wanting to tell Alex about the string of secretaries who accompanied his father on business trips. Renee could still remember the faint odor of perfume on his clothes when he came home. When the divorce was final, Renee had worried about her son not having a male role model in the house. But she realized her ex-husband's cold insensitivity and philandering ways were not traits she wanted passed on to her son anyway.

Alex looked somberly at his mother. "I'm just sorry your time with dad was bad, Mom."

"It wasn't all bad," Renee answered with a grin. "I had you, didn't I?"

Alex's lips curled into a half circle. "I love you, too, Mom."

THREE

● ● ●

Ravnik awoke on his sleeping bag in the catacombs of the Westminster Presbyterian Burial Grounds. Still suffering from the effects of the lightning strike, he felt the vice-like pain in his head but was thankful the pounding and ear ringing had faded. His vision was clearer but not quite normal yet. The burned flesh on the right side of his head had hardened and only blood oozed from the hole where his ear had been.

Ravnik sat up, suddenly remembering the dead couple in the graveyard. He knew the police would come to the cemetery to remove the bodies once they were discovered. He was also aware he would have to find another place to live. If the cops found him, he could either face a long stretch in prison or the death penalty for his past crimes.

Ravnik stood up and walked rigidly to the archway. His muscles were still stiff and sore from his encounter with lightning.

When Ravnik looked out into the night, his expression drew taut with confusion. The sky was a clear, cloudless landscape of bright stars. No lightning and no rain. The burned bodies of the man and woman were no longer lying in the cemetery. Many of the tombstones that had been split and shattered by the lightning had been removed, evidence of a clean-up was already in progress.

Ravnik stepped back onto the dark catacombs with an uneasy mindset. He wondered how long he had been asleep. Twenty-four hours? Or was this the second night after the storm? Either way, he needed to leave this place. Someone was sure to venture into the catacombs during the restoration of the cemetery and find him.

Ravnik moved to his sleeping bag, kneeled at the end of it and began to roll it up. He figured he had enough cash to rent a cheap place somewhere in the city. He knew he could lose himself in the dense urban population.

Before Ravnik could form another thought, he suddenly felt very cold, like he had stepped into a meat locker. The hair on his neck stood out like small cactus spines and a crop of goose bumps filled both arms. He felt a strange presence.

"*It was possible the man's belt had a hidden money compartment.*" The words seemed to materialize from thin air and then reverberate in Ravnik's head.

Ravnik froze. He could not mistake the deep, theatrical tone of the voice he had heard in the graveyard during the storm. He slowly rose to his feet. His eyes strained at the shadows between the body vaults near him—but he saw no one.

"*I wondered when you would awaken from your profound slumber,*" the mysterious voice said.

"Who's there?" Ravnik asked angrily, his vision tracking the shelved dead stacked against the walls.

"*There is no need to raise your voice,*" came the instant reply. "*I can hear you quite clearly.*"

"Come out and show yourself!" Ravnik called out again, watching the tombs. "Where are you?"

"*As close as your next thought,*" the voice explained.

The response didn't make sense to Ravnik. He paused a moment, then: "Show yourself!" he demanded again.

"*I cannot,*" the voice admitted. "*I am confined to the inner chambers of your brain.*"

"That would mean I'm hearing voices!" Ravnik argued with an attitude. "That only happens to crazy people!"

"*I do not fully understand my circumstance either.*" Ravnik hesitated. This was all too weird. He told himself he was not crazy and he was not hearing voices in his head! Someone must be in the catacombs, trying to scare him.

"Come and out and show yourself," Ravnik snarled. "I'll send you straight to hell!"

"*I have already been there my friend,*" the voice answered in a grim tone. "*Just like many of the dead who repose around us.*"

Ravnik picked up a flashlight near his sleeping bag and shined it at the many dark passages of the catacombs. He saw no one. It was evident he was the only person there—but the words sounded too real to be coming from his head. Maybe it was just an after-effect of being struck by lightning? Or maybe this was a dream and when he woke up, the voice would be gone?

"*You will find no one here but me,*" the voice said.

"Who are you? And what do you want with me?" Ravnik asked, still trying to determine if the voice was real or imaginary.

"*I am someone who Providence has given a second chance,*" the voice replied. "*A freak of fate has bound us together.*"

"What are you talking about?" Ravnik asked, not

believing he was having this conversation.

"*From your state of existence, it appears you have led a misspent life much as myself,*" the voice stated matter-of-factly. "*We are both miscreants. I know you are a slayer of men.*"

The statement snared Ravnik's attention. "How do you know about me?"

"*I am in a place where my senses are extraordinarily acute. My insights are well beyond your mortal grasp. I know your inner soul, and I have been given the mastery of your mind.*"

"You sound crazy!" Ravnik said. "What's a mis, mis—kreeant?"

"*A criminal,*" the voice replied. "*But that is not troublesome to me. We have a common goal—killing people. We can do fine work together.*"

"Why would I need you?" Ravnik retorted.

"*I can help you elude the authorities. I loathe them as you do.*"

"But you're not real. I'm only hearing you because I was hit by lightning," Ravnik countered. "By morning you're gonna be gone. So, fuck you!"

"*Spare me your distemper!*" the voice fired back. "*You should be cautious as to whom you curse.*"

Ravnik felt these words came in a dark, threatening tone. He decided to humor what he considered was a temporary delusion. "Okay, let's say you're real. How can you keep me from being arrested by the police?"

"*I can make you stronger and more intelligent with our murderous deeds. People will have charnel apprehensions when you strike,*" the voice professed.

"Charnel?" Ravnik repeated, not understanding the word.

"The same fear as if they stepped into a vault of dissected corpses."

"Why should I believe you?" Ravnik asked.

"Because I have knowledge of your world that I never had when I lived the life of a mortal."

"Well, I'm not interested," Ravnik replied. "Now get the hell away from me!"

"I do not know how to do that," the voice answered. *"That is why I need you."*

"Need me? Well, I don't need you," Ravnik advised. "Besides, you can't really make me any stronger than I already am. You're just words in my head," Ravnik challenged, glancing at one of his large muscled arms.

At that instant, Ravnik's head jerked back violently and his eyes slid high in their sockets. He groaned and fell back on his sleeping bag. He quivered and twitched then rose again and turned toward the catacombs opening. He moved outside, striding woodenly, moving into the graveyard with no conscious control over his movements.

● ● ●

A short time later, Ravnik opened his drowsy eyes and discovered he was lying on his sleeping bag again, still in the darkened catacombs. A tremendous weight pressed down on his chest. He could hardly breathe. Unable to see clearly in the dark, he raised his arms and felt the scrolled edges of a very large marble headstone, realizing someone had put it on his chest while he was asleep. But who could lift such heavy weight without a forklift or a crew of men?

Ravnik grabbed the edges of the marble and tried to push it off—but the weight seemed elephantine. He tried again, but still it would not budge. Ravnik's breathing became more labored. His oxygen-starved body was beginning to lose its strength.

"*Do you believe me now?*" the voice asked, breaking into Ravnik's thoughts.

"You did this to me?" Ravnik muttered in nervous bewilderment.

"*No, you did it.*"

"I can't lift this much weight," Ravnik gasped.

"*Until you made my acquaintance,*" the voice said.

"No," Ravnik rebutted weakly. "This is some kind of trick."

"*Look to your right, on the ground.*"

Ravnik turned his head and noticed a deep furrow in the dirt floor leading from the catacombs' archway to his sleeping bag. Alongside the groove, Ravnik saw the unmistakable waffled pattern of his own boot prints. "Okay, okay, I did it somehow… Now get this fucking thing off of me!" The sentence barely made it past Ravnik's labored breaths.

Suddenly, Ravnik's eyes shot up into his head and trembled in their sockets. He grabbed the heavy piece of stone and pushed it aside like balsa wood. Then, he stood and lifted the headstone above his head and tossed it against the brick wall that separated the catacombs from the graveyard. Ravnik's eyes snapped down in time to see the marble headstone as it broke into four sections and dropped to the dirt floor. He noticed the dates 1798-1847 on one of the pieces.

"*Hiram Berenson. I hated that despicable man,*" the voice growled in Ravnik's head, referring to the broken tombstone. "*That is one of the reasons why I killed him.*"

Ravnik was so amazed by the inhuman strength he had gained from the mysterious voice that he paid little attention to what the voice said. He had never felt so powerful. "How did you do that?" he asked excitedly.

"*My nether-land connection to you allows me to accomplish this somehow. And, ere long, I will need you to assist me with an important undertaking.*"

"Undertaking?" Ravnik repeated, glancing at his muscled arms, still in wonderment over this newfound strength.

"*A mission I began a long time ago and was not given enough time to finish.*"

"What if I don't want to help you?" Ravnik asked, casting a defiant expression at the darkness as though he were speaking to a person.

"*Apparently you have not given me your full attention,*" came the impatient reply. "I thought I made it quite clear that you have no choice."

With those words, Ravnik's eyes locked upward. A tremble flashed through his body. He staggered back against the wall, then slid down helplessly into a sitting position. After a moment, his eyes unlocked and dropped back to their normal position in their sockets.

Ravnik lifted himself from the ground. The chill was gone and he did not feel the voice's presence. Relieved, he mulled over what he should do. If this thing lived in his head, perhaps he would find some gratification in the voice's mission if it involved killing? Ravnik's inner rages always burned like wildfires. When he murdered, the flames died. But when time passed, the fires rekindled and he had to kill again to extinguish them. Maybe he would find the same release with the voice's undertaking? Besides, as the voice had proven, Ravnik had little choice in the matter. All he could do was wait to find out why the voice needed him.

FOUR

● ● ●

Early in the day, Renee had walked the grounds of her Alma Mater—Baltimore's University of Maryland campus. She came here often to mentally work out her story ideas, characters, and chapters for her best-selling novels. The campus buildings held many memories for her, and she appreciated their architectural beauty. Each one was like a historical landmark. Their Georgian style was a reflection of an older European era; brick set in white lime mortar, carved wood surrounding sash windows, gabled roofs, multi-paned dormers, and Tudor chimneys. If it were a different century, she felt the college could be the home of English royalty.

Renee was behind a podium in a classroom full of creative writing students about to give a lecture. She had been nervous when she accepted the school's request. She knew students were the most critical audiences. If she was to live up to her fame, she was aware her talk would have to be flawless. Renee tried to appear more dignified by wearing a business suit with a high-necked, lacy blouse. She had swept her shoulder-length hair into a sophisticated coil.

As she spoke, Renee only occasionally glanced at her

notes. She told the students how she developed and structured plots and created characters and stories by drawing from the famous and infamous historical characters and events of Baltimore's past.

"What is the event you're using for your next novel?" a bushy haired male student asked.

Renee smiled. "Don't you know it's bad luck for a writer to divulge what they're writing until they're done?"

"Oh," the student muttered. "Sorry."

"But in general terms," Renee began again, "this city owns a huge piece of U.S. History. So much has happened here. There are thousands of springboards for story ideas and characters."

A dimpled female student raised her hand. "I'm new here. What are some examples?"

"Well, it's the small events and the not so well-known people of the past that interest me—so you may not be familiar with them. But to give you an idea of the more well-known people, we can start with Babe Ruth. He was born here and so was Frederick Douglass and Billie Holiday. We also have the final resting place of Edgar Allan Poe, and Francis Scott Key wrote 'The Star-Spangled Banner' here," Renee said with patriotic enthusiasm. "But let's talk about being first. We all like to be first, right?"

Several of the students nodded in agreement.

"Well, many first events occurred right here in Baltimore. The first commissioned U.S. Navy ship was built here. So was the first passenger and freight train depot," Renee explained. "We have George Washington's first statue, we received the first telegraph message, we built the first suburb and worshipped in the first Roman Catholic Cathedral. Not to mention we constructed the first skyscraper and created the first museum."

Renee sipped from a glass of water on the podium before she continued. "I know you're going to think I'm crazy when I say this, but I feel living here in Baltimore makes my mind more fertile for writing. I mean, we are surrounded by some of the most dramatic and important moments of U.S. history—and that comes in handy when you're a writer of historical romances like me," Renee said in a modest tone.

After Renee had covered several more writing tips, she concluded her talk with a warning—a writing career entailed long hours of hard work, incredible self discipline, self denial, and the ability to maintain long periods of concentration on tedious detail. It also required perseverance, a creative mind, a dash of insanity, and egocentricities not found in the average person. If anyone in the class possessed these traits, she added, they had a chance to become a successful writer.

When Renee concluded, the students erupted with hearty applause. Many lingered to shake Renee's hand and thank her personally for an enlightening morning.

Once the classroom emptied, sixty-five-year-old Professor Scott Winfield approached Renee. He was a cerebral man with a confident gait. He was trim for his age and worked out regularly. He changed his lifestyle several years ago to stay as healthy and as youthful as possible for as long as he could as he grew older. And so far, Winfield had been successful.

Throwing his arms around Renee in a patriarchal embrace, Winfield kissed Renee on the cheek. "Bravo!" he said into her ear, smiling pleasantly when he released her. "The mere fact I brought you here will keep me at the helm of the Literature Department for at least another year."

Renee smiled, obviously fond of Winfield. "Thanks, Scott, but nobody really believes that. Especially me."

"You're wrong, my dear," Winfield rebutted. "Your novels are known throughout the world. *The Times Book Review* calls them historical epics with characters that live and breathe in the reader's mind."

"You taught me everything I know," Renee reminded him as she planted a kiss on Winfield's cheek.

"How long ago was that anyway? Twelve years?" Winfield asked.

"It seems like yesterday, Scott," Renee said.

"You look the same as the day you graduated. While the rest of us wither away, you remain the eternal Venus. Damn you anyway," Winfield grinned, then looked at his watch. "Well, I've got a class in five minutes. More fertile minds to harvest. How about lunch next week?"

Renee nodded. "Just give me a call, Scott."

Winfield turned and exited the classroom, leaving Renee alone to think about her lecture. As near as she could tell, it had been a success.

Outside the classroom, Renee moved into the flow of students as they passed down the corridor. She walked only a few feet when forty-five-year-old Martin Zeller blocked her path. A short man, Zeller wore a toupee that looked like a small explosion of hair on his shiny crown. He was impeccably dressed in an expensive European suit. His stomach, however, hung over his belt and tarnished his dapper look.

Renee stopped, surprised by Zeller's appearance. "Marty, what're you doing here? Why aren't you in New York?"

Marty's eyebrows lifted as he slid his arm through Renee's. "Because I have a client who's so rich and famous now that she doesn't have time to return her agent's calls!" he scolded, ushering Renee from the stream of students. They found a less crowded place in the corridor to talk.

Renee averted her eyes from Zeller's. "I'm sorry, Marty. I was going to call today."

Zeller knew Renee was lying. "Have you found new representation?" he asked matter-of-factly.

Renee's eyes shot toward Zeller. "Of course not, Marty. You know I wouldn't do that to you."

"Then what's going on? Why haven't you called?" Zeller asked from beneath a deep scowl. His years invested in Renee had been instrumental in grooming her career. He assumed their bond was strong enough for them to be honest with one another.

"I guess I didn't have anything to say," Renee answered weakly.

"Then let me get to the point," Zeller said brusquely. "I've got a reputation, and you've got a reputation. And both of them are in the shit house right now."

"I know," Renee muttered, avoiding Zeller's probing gaze.

Although sensing Renee's uneasiness, Zeller knew he had to press on. He needed answers; answers that would help him understand why his client was faltering. "We've already got a six-figure advance on your new book," he said, applying pressure.

"You had a deadline to meet last week, and the publisher hasn't seen one page! What's going on for Christ's sake?"

"I'm having a problem."

"No shit. What's the problem?"

Renee sighed heavily. "I don't know."

Zeller wrinkled his brows.

"I really don't, Marty," Renee replied. "Every time I try to start the new book, I get this urge to write about murder. It blocks out my thoughts. My mind freezes."

"Oh, Jesus," Zeller mumbled with visions of a blown deal. "C'mon, let's walk while we talk."

Renee and Zeller moved down the corridor returning to the traffic of students.

"Let me tell you the true meaning of the word angry," Zeller began. "Your publisher wants to lop off my nuts and yours, too, and you don't even have any! Now what's this about you wanting to write about murder? Murder as in a murder mystery?"

Renee shrugged. "Yes."

Zeller twisted his head. "But murder mysteries aren't your forte."

Renee snapped her eyes on Zeller's. "Now it's my turn to say no shit."

"I deserved that," Zeller said. "You know I'm not one to use big words, Renee. I like the four-letter ones better. But indulge me—what the fuck is going on?"

Renee shrugged without argument. "Maybe I've got writer's block?"

Stopping, Zeller glared at Renee who also halted. "Give me a fucking break! You with writer's block?" he repeated loudly in amazement.

The reply drew curious stares from nearby pupils. "Sorry, Renee," Zeller said in a hushed tone, realizing the attention he was drawing. "But you don't get writer's block. That's something psychologists dreamed up for novices who can't concentrate."

Zeller noticed Renee's eyes were about to spring tears.

"I'm at a loss, Marty," Renee confided. "You know I always meet my deadlines, but now every time I try to work, I get this obsession to write about murder. I think the headaches have something to do with it."

"Headaches?" Zeller asked as he and Renee began walking in the flow of students again.

"Yes, I've had a lot of them lately."

"Have you gone to the doctor?"

"I've got an appointment tomorrow morning."

"Good. That's the Renee Holland common sense I've been missing in this conversation," Zeller said. "Meanwhile, I'll call your publisher and down play the advance we've already banked."

"I could pay it back."

Zeller frowned instantly. "Why not write your own obituary in the *New York Times Book Review*?"

"Stupid idea," Renee said.

"I could think of stronger words," Zeller said. "Just remember you're in the highest literary circles with half a dozen best sellers and two movie deals in the works. You have thousands of fans you can't let down."

"I can feel the pressure. Believe me."

Zeller stopped and tugged on Renee's sleeve. Realizing he

had hammered Renee enough; he felt a rare moment of compassion and tenderness. "Forget the money, Renee, and forget that the publisher wants to kill us, but please think of yourself. Don't let yourself down. You're too young to end a brilliant career in its prime."

"Thank you, Marty," Renee said, delicately wiping a tear from her eye with a handkerchief she had withdrawn from her purse. "And thanks for caring. I know you wouldn't be here if you didn't really care beyond the money. If the headaches go away, I'm sure I'll get back on track."

Studying Renee's sad look, Zeller knew she considered him a true friend no matter what came from his mouth. "Call me as soon as you're finished at the doctor."

"I promise," Renee agreed through a tiny smile.

Zeller glanced at his watch. "Well, I've got a plane to catch. I'll talk to you tomorrow afternoon." With that, Zeller turned and walked away.

Zeller flowed into the tide of students. He knew his conversation with Renee had rattled her. She had been holding things back from him. This was the first time he heard about the headaches and Renee's strange desire to write about murder—and how these strange thoughts had interrupted her normal writing process. Zeller was aware this was hard on Renee because she realized this could end her career if it continued. Renee knew fame was a transient condition. And Zeller didn't want Renee's career to be as fleeting as a flavor of the month. He hoped Renee's visit to the doctor would help solve the mystery.

FIVE

• • •

The middle-aged man in Leonard Ravnik's dream wore scuffed boots, threadbare pants, and a T-shirt tanned with a mix of sweat and dirt. His crooked grin, set deep in an unshaven face, had all the warmth of the Alaskan tundra. His arm suddenly swung out with a slapping motion causing a sharp, stinging pain against the cheek of a five-year-old Ravnik.

The blow broke through Ravnik's sleep. Sitting up quickly in his bed, Ravnik waited for his head to clear, realizing he had just escaped from a tormenting childhood memory. He ran his forearm across his brow and wiped away beads of sweat. He raked his fingers through his matted hair, then pulled it down to hide the scar tissue where he lost his ear. The sight of his familiar surroundings reassured him he was completely back to reality and in his new home—a small one-room apartment. Wallpaper, yellowed with age, curled from the walls at the edges. A scaly toilet and sink in the corner looked like they hadn't been scrubbed in ten years. Ravnik knew his living conditions were shabby but it was an improvement from living in the catacombs of the Westminster Presbyterian Burial Grounds.

Moving from the bed, Ravnik looked into the cracked mirror above the sink. He pulled back his hair to study the scar tissue around his ear canal. The flesh had healed into a fiery, rippled circular scar, much like the folds in a weld of steel.

After splashing his face with cold water, Ravnik moved to a door where his coat hung from a hook. He slipped on the coat, pulled dark gloves from its pockets and pushed his hands into them. He opened the door, and stepped out.

Trotting down one-story of creaking, wooden steps, Ravnik passed through another door and stepped into the early chilly night. Above him, the flashing red neon light of Huan's Massage Parlor illuminated his face. The sign reminded him of the aging, plump, ex-hooker who had rented him the room above her business.

Ravnik walked down the sidewalk in Baltimore's infamous *The Block*. The Block was a landmark of libido for several decades, Ravnik had learned, consisting of many sex shops, peep shows, strip clubs, and topless bars. Over the years, The Block had shrunk in size—and Ravnik knew he was walking on the two blocks of it that remained—from South Street to Gay Street. A few pimps, hookers, adult entertainment entrepreneurs, and panhandlers populated the sidewalks.

Ravnik didn't mind the garishly painted windows and blinking neon signs that named the shops and bars. They attracted his victims—military men, college students, straying husbands, and out-of-towners who wanted a night of voyeurism, titillation, or more. Ravnik grinned, thinking: if any of them crossed his path, they would lose their money and any other valuables in their possession.

The cool night air nipped at Ravnik's cheeks as he stopped near a liquor store. He glanced inside and noticed an elderly woman working a cash register. The woman handed change to a droopy-eyed young man who clutched a six-pack under his arm.

The sight triggered a memory for Ravnik. His face glazed over as he remembered a time when he hiked through the Louisiana farmlands to a small town where he planned to rob a liquor store. He pretended to buy a six-pack while the owners, an elderly couple, served him with friendly, small-town hospitality. When they asked for their money, they looked into the muzzle of a double barreled, sawed-off shotgun Ravnik had hidden under his coat. Their fearful expressions excited Ravnik. He shoved the couple around and spat obscenities in their faces. After he emptied the register, he ordered them to lay face down on the floor. The elderly gentleman sensed what would follow and pleaded for his wife's life to be spared.

Ravnik didn't listen. Tightening his finger on the shotgun's triggers, he felt an inner rage building. It was hot and explosive, as fiery as the shotgun's barrels when he pulled the triggers. The double blast splattered blood, brains, and bits of skull against the wall. He recalled staring at the bodies without a blink of remorse. He had felt powerful and understood the uncontrollable rage that surfaced in him from time to time. When he jerked the shotgun's triggers, he had imagined he was killing his father.

Later, after running through several crop fields with the sheriff on his heels, Ravnik hopped a freight train and escaped from Louisiana. He knew he was lucky. In small towns, he stood out like a grave digger at a christening. Ravnik figured he'd head for a large Eastern city where he could lose himself in an ocean of faces. And so far, in Baltimore, it had worked.

Ravnik pulled his eyes from the old woman in the liquor store and moved on. Paying little attention to the panhandlers and prostitutes chattering near him, he focused on his search for visitors to The Block. Married men were the easiest mark. They rarely went to the police when they were mugged in this part of the city. They didn't want to chance a costly divorce or losing the respect of their family and peers. Ravnik looked for gold rings, Rolex watches, fine clothes, or other indicators of wealth. Prowling the streets, he felt he was a lion among lambs. If a victim resisted, he would kill them.

Ravnik tilted his head and rubbed the back of his neck. Another headache, he mused unhappily. Ever since he had been hit by lightning, he was plagued by these weird headaches. Beginning as small annoyances, they soon escalated into migraines, feeling like jagged screws being twisted through his skull. No over-the-counter or off-the-street drugs could stop them and Ravnik knew why. These were not caused by a physical problem. They usually announced the arrival of the voice.

"*May I ask what your plans are for tonight?*" the voice asked quietly.

Ravnik could feel the words dropping into his brain like weights. "I'm just gonna roll a tourist. He won't know what hit him," Ravnik replied in a hushed tone. He didn't want anyone to notice that he appeared to be talking to himself.

"*Yes, being the impudent rogue that you are, I cannot envision you having a problem with one of these out of town gentlemen,*" the voice agreed. "*But remember what I told you. If I need you, I will call upon you at a moment's notice."*

"Yeah, I know," Ravnik mumbled back, wishing the voice would leave him alone tonight.

"In return, I will help you elude the police and make you strong and powerful whenever you need me," the voice repeated what he had told Ravnik in the catacombs a few nights earlier.

"Yeah, I like the extra muscle," Ravnik admitted openly. "But what is this undertaking and unfinished business you've been talking about?"

"Nothing I wish to explain presently," the voice advised. *"But when my mission is concluded, you and I will have added a murderous chapter to this city's pristine history, Mr. Leonard Ravnik."*

"How did you know my name?" Ravnik asked guardedly.

"I am not sure," the voice said. *"I seem to be attached to what I would categorize as an astral knowledge bank. I am positive I will decipher the mystery that binds us soon."*

"How do you know you'll figure it out?" Ravnik asked.

"I am a firm believer in ratiocination."

"Ratiocination?" Ravnik repeated. "What's that?"

"Exact thinking," the voice clarified. *"It always brings one to the truth if the will of the mind is great enough."*

"Yeah, or shit always floats to the top," Ravnik grumbled. "Now can you leave me alone for awhile? I've got one of those headaches I get whenever you start talkin' to me."

"You will have your wish but I cannot guarantee for how long," the voice replied. With that, the voice went silent.

While Ravnik felt a softening of the painful pressure inside his head, he remembered what the voice had told him in the catacombs. It said whenever Ravnik needed extra strength in his body, it would be delivered. The voice had given its word about that and said that its word was more dependable than any promise Ravnik would ever receive from a mortal who walks the earth.

Ravnik liked the prospect of having super-normal strength. He would be the most unconquerable bad-ass on the streets of Baltimore.

Ravnik washed his mind of his thoughts when he noticed a man in a pin-striped suit bartering with a mini-skirted hooker. The man's clothes looked expensive. His diamond Rolex gleamed under the street lamp.

Ravnik crossed the street and headed toward the man.

SIX

• • •

It was about seven o'clock in the evening when Renee returned home from the campus. She tossed her keys on a table by the door and slipped out of her coat. She felt tired, realizing her lecture and unexpected encounter with her agent had drained her. She wanted a night of relaxation. A light meal, a snifter of brandy, and a hot bath were well deserved.

Alex stepped from his room onto the second story hallway when he heard his mother. He leaned over the second story railing.

"Hey, Mom. How'd your lecture go?"

"Pretty good, I think. How was your day?" Renee asked, opening the closet door and hanging her coat inside.

"Not so good. I have too much homework," Alex replied. "I might be up to midnight."

"Nice try, Alex," Renee said all-knowingly. "You need to be done by your bedtime."

"Aw, Mom," Alex muttered.

"If you keep working on your homework and because I'm late, I'll make your favorite dinner."

"Meat loaf and mashed potatoes?" Alex asked in an

upbeat tone.

"You got it," Renee replied as she turned and moved toward the kitchen.

After Alex had gone to bed, Renee took her bath and retired to her living room bar where she poured herself a brandy. She sipped from a snifter, surrendering to the warm sensation as it spread through her body. The drink seemed to calm her and made her feel creative. She felt ready to work on her overdue novel again. This time, Renee promised herself, she would not succumb to the inexplicable urge to write about murder.

Taking her brandy with her, Renee climbed the stairs and entered her den. She approached her century-old oak desk and ran her fingers across the carved oak leaves on its drawers as she sat down behind her computer.

Renee logged into her computer and opened her word processing program. She typed a few sentences then decided she didn't like what she had written. Renee began again. But after a paragraph, she knew she hated this passage also. On the third try, however, Renee liked what she saw on her monitor. She began to tap the keyboard as though she were playing piano. Her thoughts flowed freely and filled the computer's screen. A great sense of relief overcame her. She was truly writing again.

Renee's light mood was cut short, however. A sudden pain sliced through her thoughts, making her feel like her skull had split. Her fingers went limp on the keyboard, her eyes rolled upward and became sightless white marbles. Suddenly, Renee's fingers sprang to life again and danced energetically on the keys and the screen began to fill with words.

After several minutes, Renee's fingers sputtered to a halt and her eyes unlocked from the zombie-like stare. Confused, she glanced at her watch. Five minutes had passed, five minutes she couldn't remember. She must have blacked out. But why? she wondered. The idea of losing consciousness unexpectedly and inexplicably terrified her.

Massaging her temples, Renee tried to relieve the stabbing pain in her head. But it would not stop. She knew it would be useless to take aspirin. When these odd migraines struck, nothing ameliorated them. They would end as abruptly as they began with or without the miracles of modern-day medicines. Renee recalled how powerful the headaches had become—and now she had lost consciousness. Renee feared these were the symptoms of a brain tumor. What a horrible way to die. A destructive mass eating its way through the brain, destroying the body and obliterating the personality. Thankfully, she had a doctor's appointment for tomorrow.

Renee glanced at the monitor. She was amazed to find it filled with what appeared to be sentences. She started to read them but what she found was not what she expected. She was staring at a stew of letters and punctuation that made no sense. It was clearly the work of a disconnected brain. Renee's expression darkened as she considered the blackout and the fear of having a brain tumor. They were crushing blows against her optimism to write again. Rising from her chair, she rebelled in an unexpected fit of angry protest. She threw her brandy snifter against the wall. It shattered, spraying the carpet with pieces of glass. When Renee glanced at the broken glass, it reminded her of how her life was beginning to break apart.

SEVEN

● ● ●

Sitting at her desk, Renee tapped her agent's phone number icon on her cell phone. While she waited for Marty to answer, she reflected on the last forty-eight hours of her life. The time had been a living hell as she waited for the final results of her physical exam. Convinced her physician would discover a brain tumor, fatalistic worries had occupied Renee's mind from the moment she left the doctor's office two days ago.

"Hi, Marty," Renee greeted into the phone. "All my tests are back."

"I can hear your smile. Good news, huh?" Zeller's voice filtered through the cell phone.

"Yes!"

"Well, Jesus, give me the details!"

"My CT scan showed no tumors," Renee reported with a sigh of relief.

"So, what'd the doctor say was causing the headaches?"

"Migraines," Renee said. "He gave me a prescription. Said it would stop any kind of pain."

"Terrific. Now you can get back to work," Marty said.

"Yes, I can hardly wait."

"Just keep me posted, Renee, and call me if there's anything I can do."

"I will, Marty," Renee pledged.

Renee leaned back in her chair. A soft smile traced her lips. With a new lease on life, she regretted the anxious moments she had created for herself. She knew they had taxed her body. She wanted to work on her book now. It would be her way to reclaim her old self. Renee was determined to write the best novel of her career.

Looking through haggard features at the clock on her desk, Renee noticed it was two o'clock in the morning. Glancing at her blank monitor screen, she suddenly realized she had been nodding off at her computer for most of the night and hadn't produced one watt of creative energy. Renee thought the migraine that struck her earlier might have been the cause. Despite taking her new prescription, the headache had pounded her head relentlessly and triggered that unnatural desire to create a murder mystery. This time Renee noticed the impulse had been much stronger than ever before. Renee's heart quickened as she remembered the frightening image she had seen in her mind—a savage-looking, one-eared man. She didn't know who he was or why he had popped into her head, but he was more vivid than any character she had ever created. His primal face was all she could remember of the night.

Renee's thoughts drifted back to the dark computer screen. She wanted desperately to write again. Leaning forward, she dropped her fingers on the keyboard for one last attempt. When she tried to focus on her story, however, she felt an electrical jolt beneath her skull and her vision suddenly darkened. Her face went rigid and her body jerked in a spasm that almost threw her out of her chair. Renee's eyes rolled upward until only white orbs filled her sockets.

Her fingers splayed as if they had a life of their own. They felxed toward the keyboard and tapped on the keys, placing words and sentences on the monitor's screen.

● ● ●

Breaking from another childhood nightmare, Ravnik sat up in his bed, sweat dripping from his face. He could still see his drunken father, staring angrily at him with his hand outstretched ready to slap him. Ravnik lowered his head, hoping the blood flow would rinse the last vestige of the image from his brain. When it vanished, Ravnik thought about his teenage years, a time when his father's abuse had stripped him of self-esteem. By then, young Ravnik had a death wish no psychologist could resolve. It was during these years he began to enjoy watching others suffer and developed his need to hurt people. The pain of others eased his own suffering and fortified him for his next battle with his father. He also remembered it was just before his eighteenth birthday when he planned to kill his father. It had been the only thing that gave him reason to live!

Ravnik slid off his bed and walked to the cracked mirror on the wall and looked into it. At first, he saw himself, then his father's face appeared. This time his father wasn't peering at him in a drunken stupor. His bloodshot eyes were wide with terror, circled by wrinkles as deep as walnut shells. He was staring into the double barrels of a shotgun that was only inches from his face.

Ravnik blinked his eyes. When he looked into the mirror again, his father's face had erupted into a red mist with flying pieces of flesh. His father's head had disappeared, then pieces of it splashed against the wall. Ravnik had dispatched his father in a fraction of a second. The moment Verton Ravnik died, Ravnik's fear of him shot from his body like a rocket. Ravnik wondered why he had waited so long. The relief was so great.

Stepping from the mirror, Ravnik slipped on a jacket and pulled on his gloves. He wanted to go out for some fresh air. Maybe that would dull his latest headache.

Ravnik opened his door but suddenly froze in his steps. His eyes took on a penetrating glare then spun up in his head. Stumbling, he leaned against the wall for support. His cheek rippled, an eyebrow arched, and a corner of his mouth lifted. After a few more flutters of flesh, the seizure passed. Ravnik's eyes dropped down in their sockets and his breathing eased back into a normal rhythm. He knew the pain in his head and the seizure announced the impending arrival of the voice.

Walking unsteadily down the stairs outside his room, Ravnik moved into the cool Baltimore night. Thoughts of murder were circulating in his mind. The urge to kill was coming again.

As Ravnik strode down the dirty sidewalk, his headache intensified. He knew the voice was about to occupy his mind. Except for the pain, his association with the voice had not bothered him so far. It was comforting to have someone to talk to. The voice was becoming like a friend, someone he could confide in, someone who understood his murderous feelings. He had never shared that with anyone.

"*Good evening, Leonard,*" the voice greeted. "*I must admit my spirit of recklessness has taken possession of me tonight.*"

"What do you mean?" Ravnik asked.

"*I am here because I require your assistance,*" the voice said. "*I am eager to commence my work.*"

"Your mission, right?" Ravnik asked.

"*Yes, it is time to begin,*" the voice replied.

"Will you give me the same strength you gave me at the graveyard?"

"*Quite probably more. As long as we work for the furtherance of my goal.*"

"I loved the rush it gave me when I threw the tombstone," Ravnik said, reliving that moment for a fraction of a second. "It was better than drugs or sex."

"*Yes, I am quite aware of your inner thoughts,*" the voice said. "*And you, like I, will always succumb to the forces that impel us. So, we will create a night that will appall the fine citizens of Baltimore.*"

Crossing the street now, Ravnik's eyes began to twitch and yaw. He could feel himself losing some control of his mind and body as the voice took command.

Even though his consciousness dimmed and his mental state was dream-like, Ravnik could still feel the experience of what he did when the voice controlled his mind and body. He looked forward to inflicting pain on others and watching their agony. Ravnik's face slowly twisted into a hostile mask. His eyes widened, his nostrils pumped with each breath and his mouth parted, baring his thick, yellow teeth.

When streetwalkers and panhandlers saw Ravnik approaching, an icy chill ran through them, causing them to wisely step out of his way.

EIGHT

• • •

The crickets stopped chirping as Ravnik crept cautiously down the rocky hill, threading his way through a stand of thin saplings. He halted in the shadows near an eight-foot chain link fence and looked down at the Patapsco River. The full moon reflected a dancing kaleidoscope image in the river's choppy waters. Looking down the slope in another direction, Ravnik could see the gray buildings and dry docks of United Shipworks, the Sparrow's Point shipyard built at the edge of the river.

Ravnik watched the yard's graveyard shift at work. Dozens of workers wearing hard-hats scurried about, plying their skills on two dry-docked ocean vessels. One group sand-blasted the hull of a ship, blowing a fog of pulverized paint into a breeze that swept it away. Other workers riveted, making the sounds of small caliber machine guns. Some drilled, filling the air with shrill noises. More men welded on various decks and compartments, spraying the area with showers of sparks and a few workers operated gantry and tower cranes, lifting and lowering equipment and supplies from the dock to the decks of the ships.

Rubbing his temples with his gloved hands, Ravnik

tried to rub away the last twinge of his headache—but he was unsuccessful. He attempted to control the unnatural twitching of his eyes, but with the voice in control, he could not stop it. Ravnik had asked many questions of the strange entity that dwelled in his head, like who it was or who it used to be? But it only replied that in time Ravnik would learn everything.

Ravnik's eyes steadied slightly, and he saw the coils of razor wire stretched across the crown of the chain link fence. Glistening in the moonlight, the razors were a deterrent to most trespassers but not to him. Ravnik felt impervious to pain tonight because the voice was with him.

Ravnik backed up a few paces from the fence, then charged forward and pushed himself from the ground with his powerful legs. He landed high on the fence, planting his fingers and shoes in the links. Climbing swiftly, Ravnik reached the razor wire at the top. Clutching the fence post near him, he pushed off the links with his legs and swung his body over the razor coils. He dropped inside the shipyard, landing gracefully on his feet. Glancing downward, he noticed the fence had ripped open the toe of his right shoe and blood was seeping through the torn leather. Choosing to ignore his cut, Ravnik trotted to the bottom of the slope and stopped at the shipyard's paved perimeter.

Intense light from several high-powered work lamps nearly blinded Ravnik. The yard was as bright as day in some areas, but between the lights were deep shadows. Ravnik rushed forward and crouched behind a stack of pipes.

Ravnik saw two workers standing near the hull of a ship. One of the men unfurled a blueprint and held it out for the other to study. Ravnik tried to listen to the men but their words were distant and undecipherable under the din of shipyard machinery.

"*These men are the purpose of our visit,*" the voice explained.

The words caused Ravnik's eyes to flutter again.

"*You will be their bane of death, and thus we will begin the destiny and legacy of our partnership.*"

Ravnik, without responding, moved to a tall crane near him. He studied its boom cable and cargo hook, then climbed aboard the crane and put the gear linkage in neutral. He twisted the key in the ignition and the engine fired up. None of the workers heard the large engine revving. Its decibels were well below the sounds of other equipment in operation.

Ravnik looked over the crane's hydraulic controls. As a youth, he had run farm machinery with similar controls. He manipulated the crane's pedals and levers until the tall boom moved. Ravnik guided the boom and its cargo hook toward a large pallet of crates on the dock. These crates were packed with heavy ship parts. He lowered the hook and slipped it under a rope securing the crates, then lifted the load from the dock. Working the crane's controls, Ravnik rocked the boom from side to side, causing the load to sway. It gained momentum and soon, it moved in long, sweeping arcs, high above the unwitting working crews. In a few more seconds, the load soared through the air like a runaway freight train.

Following the voice's orders, Ravnik shifted the boom, lowered the swinging cargo, and aimed it at the two workers who were still studying their blueprint. Now the load was only a few feet above ground at the bottom of its arc. Ravnik knew the moving cargo would have the force of a speeding bus when it hit the men.

As the workers rolled up their blueprint, they saw the cargo sweeping toward them. The men started to bolt across the dock. The fright in their faces excited Ravnik. It was what he liked, to see men terror-stricken in the last seconds of their lives. He shifted the controls, quickly lengthening the cable that held the load. His aim was precise.

The workers, sprinting toward the dock's edge to dive into the river, were too slow. The load slammed into them. The men's bones snapped like twigs and their limbs were ripped from their bodies. They fell to the dock in pieces.

Ravnik could only imagine the screams that would have come from the men's throats. But he knew they were dead before they could utter a sound. When he looked at the broken bodies, it reminded him of a plane crash he once looted, stealing valuables from mangled bodies.

A welder was the first to see his downed comrades. Throwing his welding mask to the ground, he shouted to other workers near him. The men dropped their tools and rushed to the fallen men, stopping and gaping at the carnage before them.

A thin smile pursed Ravnik' lips. It gave him great pleasure to see the workers' horrified expressions. Ravnik's moment of pleasure, however, abruptly ended. His eyes danced, and he felt the strong presence of the voice.

"*Leonard, you must remove yourself from the premises at once!*" the voice barked. "We have much work to accomplish. It cannot end here where it began."

Without argument, Ravnik leaped from the crane and began to run from the scene. But when he looked over his shoulder, he saw several workmen chasing him. Two of the workers, younger and in better shape than the others, broke from the group and charged ahead. In a dead heat, they pushed their legs to the limit and gained on Ravnik.

Ravnik, though sprinting with great speed, heard the pounding footsteps drawing closer. For a moment, he thought he would be caught. However, he felt a sudden surge of strength shoot through his flesh. His muscles flexed in a steady tempo, causing his legs to pump harder. His lungs felt like giant bellows, rhythmically sucking in extra oxygen for more speed. Ravnik knew the voice had given him the extra strength he wanted. Ravnik's legs became Olympian and he pushed ahead with renewed vigor, widening the gap between himself and the pursuing workers.

As Ravnik reached the shipyard fence, he knew his pursuers would assume he was trapped. But that was part of the fun. Following the voice's instructions and still running, Ravnik leaped on the hood of a truck parked near the fence. Using his momentum, he pushed off the hood high into the air and sailed over the fence and razor coils, landing on the other side without breaking stride. He charged up the hill, weaving through the trees until he reached the top.

Ravnik stopped and turned back toward the shipyard. The two young workers were gasping heavily, hunched over and hanging onto the fence for support. Ravnik saw their weary eyes darting at the darkness that had swallowed him. Not only were they exhausted, Ravnik realized, but they were astounded by his escape. Ravnik grinned, knowing he would be remembered for a long time, just like the voice had foretold.

NINE

● ● ●

Renee felt the warmth of the sun as its light filtered
through her bedroom curtains. When she opened her eyes,
however, the glow stung her senses. She felt nauseous and dizzy.
Her head throbbed, and she felt weak. Renee had a night of restless
sleep, but to feel this exhausted and sick from lack of sleep did not
seem normal. She closed her eyes, hoping the queasiness would
pass. Finally, she pulled back the covers and slid slowly from her
bed, wavering for a moment.

Downstairs, Alex walked into the kitchen, holding the
morning newspaper. He sat at the kitchen table; his eyes locked
on the bold headlines—*Multiple Murders at United Shipworks!*
He turned from the newspaper to a small stack of printed pages
near his bowl of cereal. He thumbed through the pages, alternating
curious glances between them and the newspaper headline.

Tightening the belt on her robe, Renee entered the
kitchen. She reached for an automatic coffee maker she had set
the night before. She poured herself a cup of steaming coffee.
"Morning, honey," she greeted with a weary voice, though trying
to sound cheerful.

"What's going on, Mom?" Alex asked, looking up.

"What do you mean?"

Alex pointed at the newspaper headline. "Did you write that?"

Renee glanced at the paper. "You know I don't work for the *Baltimore Sun*."

"But you wrote these pages last night, right?" Alex asked, pointing at the stack of pages.

Renee heard the confusion in her son's voice but didn't understand it. "No, honey. I didn't write anything last night."

"But I found these on your desk this morning."

"You couldn't have," Renee countered. "I had another one of those awful headaches. I couldn't write a word."

Alex pushed the pages across the table toward his mother. "Well, somebody in the house wrote them or they wouldn't have been on your desk. Take a look, Mom. The story in those pages is the same as what's in this morning's newspaper."

Renee sat at the table and looked at the first page. /
The opening paragraph was a jam of letters and punctuation that made no sense. It reminded her of what she had written during her blackout a few nights ago. Did she lose consciousness again? Renee wondered. Looking farther down the page, she found the letters finally formed words and coherent sentences detailing a grisly multiple murder at United Shipworks. Renee's vision shifted to the stark newspaper headline and the fine print below it. The words were different, but as Alex had said, the pages and the newspaper told the same story.

"I didn't know you were writing a murder mystery?" Alex said, moving to his mother's side. "It's really gross. How'd you know the murders really happened?"

"I didn't," Renee replied, bewildered, her eyes locked on the pages.

"C'mon, Mom. Somebody at the newspaper gave you a tip, right?"

Shaking her head again, Renee rose from the chair, temporarily tangled in her thoughts. She moved to a window carrying her coffee and looked out. She recalled her first blackout. She had no recollection of writing during it either. Did it happen again? she asked herself. If so, how could she write about real murders she knew nothing about?

Alex's persistence broke through Renee's thoughts. "Did you go to Sparrow's Point last night?" he asked.

Renee swallowed a taste of coffee, turned to her son and gave him an earnest look. "Of course not. You know I wouldn't leave you alone."

Alex shrugged. "Then how do you explain this?"

"I can't," Renee replied, still greatly perplexed. She walked back to the table, picked up one of the pages and studied it. "This isn't my style of writing. The words and punctuation seem old fashioned," she said, although she realized the pages did fit her sudden and inexplicable compulsions to write about murder. Were the pages a result of those impulses? Even so, how could they reflect a true event she had no knowledge of?

"Are you sure you've never been to that shipyard, Mom?"

"I've been to Sparrow's Point but never to United Shipworks."

"Well, why don't we go there and look around?" Alex suggested. "Let's see if your descriptions match what's really there."

Renee nodded. It seemed like a good idea, but part of her was afraid to go. If the trip added further proof to this coincidence, then she feared something bad was happening to her.

Renee managed a smile, balancing her teetering emotions. "I suppose we could go and take a quick look. Go get dressed."

"Great!" Alex exclaimed, scurrying from the kitchen.

Renee plopped down on a chair and studied another page, noting the vocabulary was more comprehensive than hers. She didn't know the meaning of several words. And the paragraphs were three times the size of any paragraph she'd ever written. Renee contemplated the question that still nagged her. Even if she wrote the pages during a second blackout, how could they reflect a true incident?

Renee rose from the chair and started for her bedroom, hoping the trip to the shipyard would produce a practical and believable explanation. She needed that for her peace of mind.

Renee pulled up and parked her sleek red sports car at the eight-foot high chain-link fence that surrounded United Shipworks. Following Alex's lead, she climbed from the vehicle and moved to the fence and caught a glimpse of the razor-wire that topped it. Peering in at the buildings now, Renee's spirits began a sickening spiral. The description of the shipyard in the mystery pages was very accurate. Two ships were in dry dock, tower and gantry cranes were in place and the drab gray buildings matched the descriptions in the pages. Thirty feet away, close to the fence on the shipyard's property, was a parked truck with a shoe-sized dent in its hood. That was also in the pages.

Alex's face wrinkled. "Mom, how could you write all that stuff without ever being here?"

"I don't know," Renee uttered weakly, noticing a couple of Baltimore police cars in the distance. Two suited detectives milled about on the dock near the Patapsco River's edge. Three uniformed officers were nearby taking down their yellow crime scene tape. A few shipyard workers somberly watched a man with a bucket of soapy water and stiff-bristled broom scrub an area of the dock. The suds were pink.

Renee was aware the men were cleaning up the blood of the murdered workers. "My, God. Those poor men," she mumbled, wondering how she could write about this and not remember. Was she developing a split personality—one half not knowing what the other half was doing?! The more Renee explored the possibilities, the more her mind thickened with apprehension.

The sleepless night and shock of what she had just seen made Renee feel faint. Gripping the fence for support, she closed her eyes and took in several deep breaths, wondering what was happening to her.

TEN

• • •

Homicide Lieutenant Kent Elinger's blue eyes peered through the windshield of his unmarked, 4-door black sedan. He watched as two uniformed Baltimore policemen opened the chain-link gates of United Shipworks, giving him a clear path to drive from the shipyard. As his tires crunched over the road's packed gravel, he contemplated the murder scene he had just spent the night investigating. After twenty years in the Baltimore Police Department's Criminal Investigation Division (C.I.D.), he had never seen a murder this grisly. The haunting mental images of the mangled bodies lingered in his mind. What kind of madman kills people like this? Elinger wondered.

Breaking from his thoughts, Elinger turned to his new partner, twenty-seven-year-old Rafael Torres. "I know this is your first day in Homicide, but what's your take on this?"

Torres, sitting on the passenger seat, pulled his dark, piercing stare from the harbor ships and gave a troubled look to Elinger. "When I see bodies in that condition and witnesses say the killer jumped an eight-foot fence without much effort, I don't know what to make of it. It's too weird, man."

Elinger shifted his trim, muscled body in the seat and ran his hand through his thick, sandy hair. He silently agreed with his new partner. The M.O. of the murders was indeed bizarre and so was the murder weapon. Not a gun, not a knife but a crane swinging a heavy load of cargo.

Elinger drew in a deep breath, still contemplating the scene. "Nothing on the security cameras either. Too dark and grainy."

Torres removed a handkerchief from his tailored suit pocket and wiped his handsome, genetically tanned features. "Well, thanks to the witnesses, we at least know our perp's missin' an ear," he said. "I don't think he can hide from us very long."

Elinger nodded, steering his auto from Sparrow's Point onto State Highway 695. "We'll check hospitals and emergency clinics to see if anyone's treated a one-eared patient recently. And we can talk to the victims' friends and relatives to find out if they had any enemies."

"Yeah, maybe we can turn-up a motive?" Torres replied with a nod.

Elinger looked at Torres for a moment then eyed the road in front of him again. He wondered how his young partner perceived him. Elinger glanced into the rear-view mirror and looked at his forty-three-year-old face. He was thankful his hair was not thinning and his hairline was still rooted firmly below the top of his forehead. His teeth were straight and white and only a deep smile could wrinkle his cheeks.

Torres shifted his vision from the road and glanced at Elinger again. "Detective Sanders told me you're the best homicide man in the department."

Elinger expression turned into one of mild surprise as he focused his eyes on Torres for a moment.

"Sanders said that?"

Torres nodded.

"Well, that's nice of him, but there's a few cases I didn't wrap-up. At least not yet. Until then, I'm not the best."

"He said you solved more cases than any other detective."

"Maybe so, but I've had a lot of help," Elinger replied modestly. "Good lab work, dedicated blue suits. And great prosecutors. Nobody does this job alone."

"He also told me you're the most educated detective at Headquarters. Summa cum laude in Criminology," Torres said.

Elinger's tossed a curious look at Torres. "Why are you so interested in my education?"

"I was just wonderin' why a smart guy like you can't stay off city hall's shit list."

Elinger turned the steering wheel to change lanes before he spoke. "Sometimes they don't like the way I do things."

"I can relate to that. Rules are for fools," Torres said with a cocky grin.

"You're no stranger to shit lists either," Elinger said. "You were kicked out of Robbery."

Elinger noticed Torres' face flush with anger.

"I wasn't kicked out!" Torres argued sharply. "I was transferred to Homicide. That's all. What'd the guys in Robbery say about me?"

"That you had some hot blood that needed cooling," Elinger replied, eyes steadfast on the road.

The statement ignited a sudden grin in Torres. "Respect

and admiration follow me wherever I go." Torres' face suddenly soured, and he gave Elinger an agitated look. "You've obviously read my file. But let me tell you something, nobody in Robbery has any *huevos*."

"I heard they just wanted to keep theirs," Elinger said.

"And what would that have to do with me?" Torres asked with an edge of anger in his voice.

"They said you put their lives in jeopardy by playing hero during a couple of bank robbery calls."

"They got mad 'cause I was showin' 'em up," Torres retorted testily. "When their asses were on the line, I came through! Two of 'em owe me their lives," he added indignantly.

Elinger watched the front end of his auto devour more highway as he considered Torres' attitude. He heard the shades of anger and defiance in Torres' voice. That was good. Torres was his own man, not one to be pushed around easily. And Elinger realized his young partner reminded him of another policeman he once knew years ago—a rookie named Kent Elinger.

Something outside the car suddenly caught Elinger's attention. He pointed out the window at Carroll Park. "Babe Ruth used to play ball there when he was a kid."

Torres looked at the park and the baseball diamond. It was bordered by rows of tall trees. "No heroes like that in my neighborhood. Just gangs and ex-cons."

Elinger nodded. "Yeah, your file says you were once a gang-banger. What was the name of your hood?"

"Why do you want to know that?" Torres asked after giving Elinger a guarded glance.

"I'm just curious about who I'm working with," Elinger

replied coolly.

Instead of responding, Torres looked out the passenger window. It was obvious to Elinger that Torres didn't want to talk about his past personal life.

Torres trained his eyes on Elinger again. "Okay, fair enough. You and I do need to know about each other. I need to know who's watching my back and so do you. We were called the *Los Latin Destripadors*. The Latin Rippers. We got our name because we carried blades. Nobody in East L.A. messed with a Ripper."

Elinger noticed the shadowy pride of Torres' words, but he was surprised by his statement. "So, the Rippers brought knives to gunfights?"

"We always had guys that packed," Torres said. "The Rippers weren't stupid."

"Did you ever carry a gun?"

"Sometimes," Torres reluctantly acknowledged. "But I never shot anybody like some of my homies. Most of the Rippers got killed or were sentenced to prison. There's no future in gang-bangin'. Only prison or the graveyard is in front of you."

"You seem too independent to be involved in a gang," Elinger said as he flipped on the turn signal and made a lane change.

"Not back then. I liked to chill with the *vatos* in my neighborhood and kick ass with 'em. They were my *familia*."
"I read that you worked for a power company before you became a cop," Elinger said.

Torres slid his eyes toward Elinger. "That was my first real job. Why do you want to know about that?"

"Just curious about what you did before you joined the force," Elinger replied simply.

Torres exhaled a long breath before he spoke. "Well, that career didn't go too well. I had a real piece of shit as a supervisor. He made me do crappy jobs. When I complained, the union protected him. So, I quit. Then I started driftin' back to my gang ways."

Elinger listened, impressed by the major life changes Torres had made. "Well, it's a big step from gang-banger to cop. That's something to be proud of."

"I had help," Torres said. "After I quit the power company, my Mom started dating a cop. He talked to me about how I would ruin my life if I got back into gang bangin'. We connected somehow. He became the father I never had. He helped me expunge my juvenile record when I went back to school and starting getting' good grades when he knew I was serious about changin' my life."

"Are you still in touch with him?"

"I wish," Torres answered in a sad tone. "He moved to Texas and was killed on-duty by some methed-out scumbag."

Elinger could see the pain in Torres' expression. "So, I'm hearing you grew up without a father?"

"Yeah, he ran off when I was a kid," Torres said in an unforgiving tone. "He left my brother Manuel and me with my mother. She worked in a factory and took in ironin' and sewin' at night to make ends meet. She died of cancer a few years ago."

Elinger steered the auto onto an off ramp and started applying the brakes.

"The best thing I ever did for her was to leave the

Rippers," Torres said. "The night my brother was killed," he added quietly, looking distantly out the window.

It was clear to Elinger that Torres was fighting a tide of emotions. Elinger recalled what he had read in Torres' file about the death of Torres' brother. It was a gang killing and Torres was the first one to reach his mortally wounded brother, but there was no further explanation. "Do you want to talk about it?" Elinger asked.

"No," Torres replied, shaking his head. "My brother's death is nobody's business but mine."

Elinger decided not to push Torres any further. This subject was obviously very painful to him.

As Elinger drove from the end of the ramp onto a busy downtown street, he knew that in time he would learn more about the death of Torres' brother. Partners always learned everything about each other eventually—the good and the bad.

ELEVEN

• • •

On the sixth floor of Headquarters' ten-story building, Elinger sat behind his cluttered desk in the detective's room. A dozen other detectives were sitting at their stations also, some where studying mug shot books on their computer screens while others were on their phones. Elinger peered into his computer monitor, reading the final pages of the shipyard murders investigation report and frowned. He had read nothing new that could help him with the case.

Elinger clicked his keyboard and mouse a few times and printed out an 8x10 photo from the printer near him. He then glanced up at the large cork bulletin board on the wall. It was crowded with photos of murder victims, crime scenes, and missing persons. He moved to the board and pinned the photo on the board. It was a gory color shot of the remains of the shipyard workers. Elinger would use it as a grim and daily reminder that this case was top priority.

Elinger walked to a nearby white Dry Erase board. All of the detective's names were written there with their current case assignments. Elinger picked up the marker from the tray and wrote

Sparrow's Point next to his name.

Elinger looked at the large grid map of Baltimore at the other end of the room. He could see the small red flag he had pinned at Sparrow's Point. It was another reminder of the heinous crime committed and added fuel to Elinger's duty-bound desire to solve the case quickly. The first 48-hours had already passed, however. And Elinger knew, as all other investigators, that with the passing of time, the odds of solving a homicide case became more difficult very quickly.

Elinger's phone rang, interrupting his thoughts. He moved back to his desk and picked up the receiver. "Elinger here..." He waited a moment for the caller to announce themselves. "Tell me you've got something, Sam."

Elinger listened for a moment. "Shit!" he mumbled into the phone. "Go over everything again and see if your men missed anything."

Torres sat at his desk nearby, looking through a photo array of felons on his computer. He, like the others, was searching for a one-eared man. He looked up at Elinger who had just hung up his phone. "Doesn't sound good," Torres commented.

Elinger nodded. "Sam and his CSI guys combed the crime scene and the suspect's escape route. The only fingerprints they found belonged to the hired crane operators, and they've already been cleared."

"Maybe the killer was wearin' gloves?" Torres offered.

"Yeah, no shoe prints on the hill either."

"What's our next move?"

"We're waiting on a call from downstairs," Elinger replied, then turned and moved to a desk occupied by thirty-five-year-old Detective Jay Sanders. Sanders glanced up at Elinger from beneath bushy eyebrows and thick glasses.

"How're you doing with the mug files?" Elinger asked.

Sanders pointed at other detectives who were still looking at photos on their computers. "Everybody I own is on it," Sanders reported. "We've got photos from Property Crimes, Robbery, Auto Theft, Vice, and Drugs. If there's a one-eared man in our database, we'll find him."

"What about the shipyard workers?" Elinger asked.

Sanders shook his head. "All of their crane operators have both ears. We're still interviewing witnesses."

"Keep me informed," Elinger said, moving back to his desk to answer his ringing phone. He listened for a moment, then said, "We'll be right down."

Elinger pivoted toward Torres who now rubbed a damp paper towel on the toes of his black dress shoes, trying to boost a shine through a layer of dust.

Elinger studied the fresh luster on Torres' shoes. He knew Torres' work on them would be futile within an hour. "Now that you've got them nice and shiny, let's get them dirty," Elinger said. "Marge has all the names and addresses of victims' friends and family," he added, snatching his coat off the back of his chair.

Torres wadded up the paper towel, tossed it into a waste basket and quickly followed Elinger out of the room.

Outside a nineteenth century Bolton Hill townhouse, Torres leaned against the fender of his gray unmarked police sedan. His fatigued eyes searched the street in both directions, reflecting his long day of interviewing families and friends of the victims without lunch. Torres' face lightened when he saw Elinger turn into the neighborhood and drive toward him.

Elinger parked behind Torres' car and rolled down the driver's window as Torres approached. "I need good news, Torres."

"Then you don't wanna talk to me," Torres replied. "According to this guy's friends and neighbors, he was a solid dude. Lovin' family. Active at church. He left two little kids behind. Damn!"

"Welcome to Homicide," Elinger said flatly.

Torres gave Elinger a look of surprise. "How can you be so cold about it?"

Elinger withdrew a piece of gum from his pocket and popped it into his mouth. "I'm not cold about it. Just used to it."

Torres stared pensively at Elinger. "I don't think I'll ever get used to it."

"You will in time. It's the only way you'll ever sleep again, Ralph."

"Ralph?" Torres repeated.

"Short for Rafael. You don't mind, do you?" Elinger asked.

Torres shrugged. "I've been called worse. Besides, if someone gives you a nickname, that means they respect you," he said with a small grin. "Did you come up with anything?"

Elinger could only shake his head when he answered. "We covered just about everyone and everything. The shipyard worker's families, their friends, business associates give all them a clean bill of health. No priors, no shady business dealings, no debts to the wrong people, or anything else that invites murder."

Torres allowed a frustrated breath to pass between his lips

before he spoke. "Maybe our guy is a vet? Maybe he got his ear shot off? Why don't we check veteran's records for soldiers who got purple hearts in Afghanistan, Iraq or even Desert Storm in case our guy's been missin' an ear for a long time."

Elinger nodded. "Good idea. Run with it. I'm going to talk to plastic surgeons in the area and find out if anyone around here has inquired about ear reconstruction lately."
Torres nodded, then turned from Elinger and headed toward his car.

As he walked, Torres reflected on his conversation with Elinger. He hoped his new boss had noticed his good ideas for the investigation. He knew Elinger could use an extra brain on this case. Maybe his suggestion for a veteran's search would turn up something viable. Torres promised himself to make his performance on this case stellar. He has a few smudges in his personnel file from his time in Robbery that needed cleaning. Maybe solving this investigation would accomplish that. Torres was going to do whatever was necessary to help Elinger crack this thing wide open.

TWELVE

• • •

"Good night, Alex," Renee said, pulling the bed covers up to Alex's chin.

Alex gave his mother a quizzical look. "Mom, are you all right?"

"I feel okay. Why?"

"Because it's been a long time since you tucked me in."

Renee smiled tenderly. "And because of that, you think your mother's losing it?"

"No, I'm just too old for this now," Alex said drowsily, settling his head on the pillow.

Renee knew her son was secretly enjoying the princely treatment. "Of course, you are, honey. But once in a while I like to pretend you're still my little boy. So, indulge me, okay?"

"It would be embarrassing if my friends ever found out."

"I won't tell," Renee promised, leaning forward and kissing Alex on the forehead. She noticed a worried look on his face.

"Mom, are you really doin' okay with what's been going on?"

"I think I'm handling it all right. What do you think?"

"On a scale of one to ten, you're a definite five."

"I don't know what to do about it," Renee said wearily, sitting on the edge of her son's bed. "I hope it's just a crazy coincidence."

"I hope so too, Mom. But—"

"No buts," Renee interrupted. "We agreed to put this behind us. Remember?"

"Yeah, but I still don't think it's a coincidence."

Renee rose from the bed, ignoring Alex's final comment. She didn't want to think about it anymore. "Sweet dreams, honey."

"Night, Mom," Alex said, rolling on his side and closing his eyes.

As Renee walked toward her den, she considered her good fortune to have such an open and honest relationship with her son. With her world topsy-turvy right now, nothing soothed her more than her rapport with Alex.

Renee entered her den and moved toward her desk. For the past few nights, she had not tried to write. Her mind was drained from her attempts to figure out her connection to the shipyard murders. Tonight, however, she was in the mood to write. Renee sat in the chair in front of her computer just as her cell phone rang. "Hello," she greeted.

"This is your conscience calling." Marty Zeller's gruff voice was on the other end of the line.

"What're you doing up so late, Marty?" Renee asked brightly, masking her uneasiness. She knew what Zeller would be asking.

"Well, it's about the time you usually start writing so I wanted to inspire you."

"You know I don't believe you," Renee said in a friendly tone. "You've never called to inspire me."

"Okay, so I called to push you. How's it going?"

"I'm just getting ready to start," Renee replied, knowing Zeller would sense a problem.

"For the night, or page one of the book?" Zeller asked.

Renee recognized the suspicion in Zeller's voice. "Both."

"You haven't done anything yet, have you?" Zeller said quickly.

"I've had more headaches, but I'm really going to concentrate tonight," Renee pledged, knowing if Zeller were in the room, she would feel the heat of his irritation.

"We're on the verge of losing the deal, Renee."

Renee had pondered this before and it never put her in a good mood. "I have no control over what's happening to me!" she replied harshly. "You know I want to live up to my contract!" Renee hoped her irate words would bite Zeller and make him realize he was treating her ungraciously.

There was a pause on the other end of the line. Then, "I should know you're doing all you can, but a deal is still a deal."

"I know, Marty. I think about it all the time."

"Guess I made my point. Why don't we talk later in the week?" Marty suggested.

Renee hesitated before she replied. She didn't want to end the conversation. She wanted to talk to someone about the shipyard incident other than her son. She needed a reality check from an adult. It was one thing to have her therapist hear her worries, what she needed was a friend to talk some sense into her frazzled mind. She wondered, however, if Zeller was the right person. His brusque personality didn't always lend itself to personal discussions. "Marty," Renee finally began. "I need to tell you something. Something very strange has happened," she reported, speaking softly.

"You've got my attention."

Zeller listened as Renee recounted the shipyard murders, her mysterious pages, and her futile struggle to believe their connection was merely a coincidence.

"It can only be one thing, Renee," Zeller replied. "In your own words, a coincidence."

"I'm afraid it's more than that."

"Like what? That you're the killer? Or you're snooping around shipyards at night watching people get murdered? Get a hold of yourself for Christ's sake!"

Renee shook her head. It was obvious Zeller wouldn't give her any sympathy or understanding. "But don't you understand. I'm afraid if I write again, someone else will die!"

"How can you believe that? It's just a quirk. Stranger things have happened in this world!" Zeller returned quickly.

Renee paused, started to say something, and then changed her mind. "Maybe you're right," she feigned her agreement, wanting to close the dead-end conversation.

"Of course, I'm right," Zeller said.

"I'll give it my best tonight," Renee promised. "I'm going to get started now, Marty. Thanks for calling."

"Just let me know when you've got something. Ciao," Zeller said just before he hung up.

Leaning back in her chair, Renee promised herself she would never tell anyone about the shipyard killings and her pages that described the murders again. It made her sound insane.

Feeling a sudden stab of pain in her head, Renee rubbed her temples. Another migraine, she realized angrily. Though the pain sliced deep through her brain, she was still determined to write. She turned to her computer and poised her fingers over the keyboard. Renee remained motionless, however, trying to collect her creative thoughts. The unwelcome and uncontrollable desire to write about murder was filling her head again.

Knowing it would be another wasted night, Renee turned away from her computer. Emotionally, she felt like something was invading her mind. Intellectually, however, that seemed preposterous.

Slightly anxious, Renee rose from her chair and turned off her computer. She flicked off the room lights and exited, disappearing down the darkened hallway.

The den was quiet for a moment, then the computer suddenly clicked on and hummed with power. Its light glowed in the room's muddy atmosphere.

Renee suddenly reentered the den. This time, however, her body wasn't fluid and natural—it was rigid. Renee walked stiffly toward her computer. Her half-open eyes twitched as she dropped into her chair. Her hands were drawn to the keyboard by an unseen force and her fingers began to tap the keys. Words appeared on the page giving way to clumps of sentences.

● ● ●

Twisting fitfully beneath the stained covers of his bed, Leonard Ravnik felt his brain being bulldozed by the voice's powerful presence. His eyes quivered beneath their half-closed lids. After a final spasm, the seizure stopped. He recalled the earlier conversation he had with the voice. It had explained what Ravnik would accomplish tonight. If he followed the voice's plan, he would be very proud of the results.

Ravnik slid from his bed and could still feel the voice's presence in his mind and body. He respected its strength. It was too powerful, too hypnotic to resist. The overwhelming control convinced him to obey its wishes. Besides, Ravnik rationalized, he was curious to know more about the voice's secretive mission—its *unfinished business...*

Ravnik's eyes shimmied in their sockets as he retrieved a heavy jacket from his closet, pulled on the gloves he kept in its pockets and stepped into the cool night.

Ravnik walked down the sidewalk, passing many of The Block's garishly lighted porno shops and strip joints. It was late and few people were on the streets.

Two middle-aged, chunky prostitutes stood in the doorway of a closed shop. They became frightened and withdrew deeper into the doorway when they saw Ravnik's dingy appearance and dancing eyes.

Crossing the street, Ravnik smiled when he spotted a lone prostitute standing on the corner. The voice echoed in his head, telling him she was perfect for both of their needs.

Ravnik stopped at the curb and studied the hooker. She was a striking, shapely African-American woman in a mini skirt and high heels. Her skin-tight blouse revealed the cleavage of immense breasts.

"Your women are scandalously under clad," the voice said. *"A woman should look like a beautiful garden—not dressed in violation of the laws of humanity. She would shock the social world where I once lived."*

Ravnik smiled, ignoring the disgust in the voice's tone. "I like my women under-clad," he mumbled, as he stepped onto the sidewalk and moved toward the woman.

"You lookin' for a between-the-sheets party?" the prostitute asked when Ravnik reached her side.

Ravnik nodded, his smile widened as his eyes locked on her.

"You'll have to clean up first," the hooker said after a closer appraisal of Ravnik's clothes and a whiff of his body odor.

Ravnik shook his head and reached into his pocket. He withdrew a wad of cash.

The prostitute glanced at the bills. "I guess you don't need to take a bath if you're a big tipper."

Ravnik nodded again.

The hooker smiled. "You must be the strong and silent type? How much you wanna spend?"

Ravnik shrugged as if money was of no consequence.

"If you've got fifty plus a tip, I've got the time. I've gotta place just down the street."

Ravnik shook his head and pointed toward a nearby alley.

The whore looked down the alleyway. "Oh, you want it down and dirty? Okay, but I get my money first!"

The hooker held out her hand. Ravnik peeled two fifties

from the roll and handed it to her.

"Oh, you are a big tipper!" The streetwalker said, pushing the bills into her purse. "Well, let's get to it," she said as she led the way to the alley.

As they entered the alley, Ravnik took the prostitute by the arm and steered her behind a large dumpster. He backed her against the wall of a building. The hooker began to unbutton her blouse. "Okay, come to Mama," she purred in a deep throated tone as she lifted her dress and revealed a thin strip of pubic hair.

Ravnik reached down and snatched an empty whiskey bottle from the pavement.

"That's really not my style," the hooker said. "Maybe you'd like some head instead?"

Ravnik looked into her eyes and nodded.

Kneeling, the whore began to unhook Ravnik's belt. Ravnik raised the bottle and whipped it downward. The bottle exploded on the back of the hooker's head, spraying the area with glass.

The woman groaned and sank to the pavement. Blood dripped from her split scalp. Ravnik pulled her to her feet by the hair and pushed her against the wall. He ripped off her skirt and blouse, unzipped his pants and penetrated the unconscious woman, thrusting wildly. Choking her with one hand, he continued to pump himself into the hooker's body.

When he finished, he used the jagged edges of the liquor bottle's neck to slice through the prostitute's cheeks from ear to ear. Ravnik stopped to admire his work. The hooker's teeth and gums showed through the gaping wound, giving her a jack-o-lantern smile.

Ravnik stepped back and released the woman. She slumped to the ground again. Sprawled on her back, she stared sightlessly at the night sky. Ravnik was pleased when he realized the grotesque smile he had cut on her face reminded him of his own grin of satisfaction.

"*Remember my request, Leonard,*" the voice interrupted quietly. "*I want to leave a clue to test the authorities' intellect. I do not want them to perceive this as a random murder.*"

Ravnik remembered. Earlier, the voice had asked him to leave a clue with a specific meaning. Ravnik had a good way to convey the message, and the voice had approved his idea.

"*A witty clue will make a game of this,*" the voice said. "*It will be fun, don't you agree?*"

Ravnik smiled, enjoying the sardonic timbre of the words he heard in his head. He nodded when he knew just what to do. He reached into his pocket and removed a small, dark object. He bent over and pushed the object into the wide, gapping mouth of the prostitute.

THIRTEEN

● ● ●

Renee tossed and turned with restless sleep. Under the covers, she felt like she was in a furnace. On top of the covers, her body shivered. During those moments, Renee painfully contemplated her inability to write anything for the past week. Whatever stopped her creative flow was far more serious than writer's block. She was sure something sinister was festering in her mind, giving her urges to write about murder. A prisoner of her own body, Renee realized she was desperate for relief.

Renee's heart jumped when she heard a knock on her door.

"Mom, are you awake?" Alex's voice filtered through the door.

"Not really," Renee replied groggily, her eyes blinking uncomfortably at a split of sunlight streaking through a small opening in her bedroom curtains. She sat up in bed, remembering she needed to take Alex to school. "But come in anyway," she said, sliding from beneath the covers and slipping on a thick terry cloth robe.

Alex bounded into the room.

Renee could see the excitement in her son's face. "You're really cool, Mom. You did it again!" Alex announced.

"Did what again?" Renee yawned.

"You wrote about another murder! It's just as gross as the first one!"

Renee tightened the sash on her robe, choosing to ignore the ramifications of Alex's words. "Wrong, Alex. I haven't written anything for days," she said, moving toward the door. "I need some coffee."

"But Mom, you did write something," Alex insisted, following his mother into the hallway. "I found more pages in your office like the ones from the other night."

Renee stopped. A feeling of dread enveloped her. She turned to Alex. "I don't remember writing anything."
Alex shrugged. "But you did. I put the pages on the kitchen table."

Renee clenched her fists. "No, this can't be happening!" she said, anger mixing with panic. Her mind twisted in protest as she tried to mentally answer a host of perplexing questions. Were the pages really coming from her? Was she possessed? Renee could only shake her head in frustration.

"Chill, Mom," Alex recommended. "There is good news. The murder's not in the morning paper."
Renee felt a sudden calm. If the murder's not in the newspaper then maybe it didn't happen?

Moving into the kitchen, Renee poured herself a cup of hot coffee from her pre-set coffee maker. The rich aroma filled her nostrils. It was one of her few remaining pleasures.
Renee sat at the breakfast table and leafed through the pages.
Her son was right. The brutal killing of a black prostitute in The

Block was described in gruesome detail. Renee's stomach churned as she read about the strangulation rape and the slicing of the woman's face with the broken bottle. The body had not yet been found, Renee learned as she continued to read. This darkened her thoughts. Maybe that's why the murder is not in the morning paper?

Renee pushed the pages across the table after she read where the killer had disposed of the prostitute's body. The corpse had been so cleverly interned she wondered if it would ever be found—unless she tried to find it herself by using information from the pages. Renee knew the dark side if she found the woman's body—it would prove this was a real murder like the shipyard killings, and she was somehow connected to both of them. On the other hand, if she couldn't find a body then maybe there wasn't a killing. Either way, Renee wanted to find out so she could try to straighten out her life.

After driving Alex to school, Renee sped across city streets in her sports car, following descriptions of landmarks and streets in the pages. She turned off the main highway and bounced down a dirt road. A hundred feet farther and she found herself beneath a closed section of freeway and surrounded by stacks of lumber and other construction materials.

Renee stopped her car near a parked bulldozer and several pieces of heavy equipment. According to the pages, this is where the prostitute was buried—at this freeway construction site. Looking through her windshield, Renee noticed several towering wooden forms that were braced by steel girders. These forty-foot columns and everything else near Renee were described accurately in the pages. The tall forms in particular, she noted. These would be the future support beams for the new freeway overpass.

Renee watched a small group of construction workers wearing hard-hats climb a ladder and mount a scaffold near the top of one of the high columns. Holding heavy power saws, they began to cut through the plywood, two-by-sixes and the she-bolts that held the column's mold together. Piece by piece, the materials fell away.

Renee's attention lingered on the men, her bright eyes dimming. She feared what they were about to discover. The pages had told her so. And the sight of several parked police cars and the police officers standing near the bottom of the column pushed her even closer to what she feared would be a severe anxiety attack. More police cars arrived as Renee opened her car door.

The workers suddenly turned off their saws and stepped back, staring at the dead woman embedded in the concrete of the column. Her body was twisted and frozen in a crucifixion position. Her breasts projected through the edge of the concrete as well as her face, hands, feet, knees and pubic mound. Her face was cut wide into an ear-to-ear ragged smile.

Feeling faint, Renee slid out of the car for a breath of fresh air. Her legs nearly buckled under her. She reached out and gripped her auto's front fender for support. She couldn't deny it any longer. The pages were as real as the dead woman—no uncanny coincidences, no simple explanations, this was a real murder and she had written about it without any knowledge that it really happened. Renee's mind screamed in silent agony, demanding to know how this was possible!

● ● ●

Walking toward his auto in a hospital parking lot, Elinger could feel the sag in his expression. His lack of success with the shipyard murder investigation was becoming a heavy burden. He wondered if he had been making the right investigative decisions. The past few days, he and Torres had scoured Baltimore's hospitals, interviewing dozens of plastic surgeons and emergency room doctors. Living on coffee and sandwiches with little sleep, they had learned nothing that would lead them to the one-eared man. The frustration was cutting into Elinger's nerves. He knew his suspect was lurking somewhere, probably seeking another victim. But without a clue or a break in the case, Elinger wondered if he would ever find this killer.

Elinger pulled into the construction sight first, then Torres behind him. They parked side by side and walked through the plume of dust their cars had created. The area was bustling with plainclothes and uniformed police officers. Elinger and Torres stooped under the yellow crime scene police tape that cordoned off the area and walked past six radio cars, the coroner's van and several unmarked police sedans. Elinger knew Sanders' urgent call was no exaggeration. Something really bad had happened to bring so many cops to the scene of a crime.

"Over here, Kent," Sanders called out, approaching. "You're not gonna believe this!" he added, motioning with his hand for Elinger and Torres to follow him.

Sanders led Elinger and Torres to one of the freeway's columns. Below the tall pillar was a knot of officers. They stood motionless, looking upward. Elinger glanced up and saw the prostitute's body in the uncured concrete.

"When the night crew started pouring concrete into the mold, they noticed a body wedged down in the rebar just as the concrete covered it," Sanders said. "They called us right away, but we had to wait about four hours until the concrete hardened enough for them to cut away the mold."

"Thanks, Jay," Kent said as he moved closer to the column. He watched the construction workers push the whirring blades of diamond tipped saws against the green, uncured concrete, cutting deep grooves around the corpse. Other scaffold workers squeezed the triggers of jackhammers, chipping the sawed paths into deep, wide grooves.

Elinger turned to Torres. "It'll be awhile before they get her down. Let's go see what Sam's got."

Elinger led Torres a short distance from the body where they stopped near three men wearing dark blue windbreakers with CSI printed on the back. Two were kneeling on the ground. One had a camera and was taking close up photos of a shoeprint in the dirt. As soon as he finished, the second man poured a soupy plaster mix from a small bucket into the print. The third man, Sam Evans, was Elinger's lead CSI lab man.

Evans, a small, slight man, approached Elinger. He looked at Elinger through his glasses and heavily creased features that made him look older than his fifty-five years. He pulled at his thick, gray beard before he spoke. "As I've already told you, Kent, the shipyard murder scene was the worst I've seen since I started my career in '85—but this is a close second."

Elinger took Evans' words to heart. Evans had been the police department's top lab man for over three decades. He had seen the worst humanity had to offer. Murdered children, decapitated bodies, close range shotgun wounds, brains dripping from open skulls like mushroom soup, arms and legs without bodies, bloated corpses in the bay and bodies half-eaten by animals and maggots.

Elinger looked at the plaster filled prints. "How many did you find?"

"Only four that don't match the shoes of the construction crews," Evans replied. "We're lucky the killer stepped in the soft dirt."

"How do you know those are the killer's footprints?" Torres asked, bending over for a closer look.

Evans placed his right foot next to one of the prints and leaned his full weight into the pliable soil. When he lifted his foot, his print was shallow in comparison to the others. "It took the weight of two people to make a print that deep," Evans said. "The woman was probably murdered somewhere else and carried here, then put inside the column mold knowing it would be filled with concrete."

Torres straightened and looked up at the top of the forty-foot-tall column nearby. "Was that scaffold there before the body was discovered?"

"No, it was brought in to cut away the mold," Evans replied.

"Then how did the killer put the body in the mold?"

"He must've climbed up the side of the mold. There's two-by-sixes and rebar sticking out that he could've used for steps," Elinger guessed.

"But there was a night crew working here. Why didn't they see him?" Torres asked.

"This is a twenty-four-seven project," Evans explained. "Three construction crews on eight-hour shifts. The third crew starts at midnight."

"So, at midnight, one crew is getting ready to go home while the new crew is getting ready to start work," Elinger said, thinking aloud. "Which could provide enough distractions for the killer not to be noticed if he wasn't here very long."

Torres glanced up at the tall column again. "He carried a body, dead weight, all the way to the top," Torres commented in awe. "I mean, what kind of perp are we dealin' with here?"

"One strong sonovabitch!" Elinger answered curtly.

●　●　●

Still leaning on her auto's fender, Renee studied the uniformed police officers and plainclothes officers who were fanned out over the area. Regardless of Renee's personal dilemma, she knew she had to tell the police what she knew. It was her moral obligation as a human being to help the police find out who killed this woman. But she wouldn't talk about the pages. She knew that would only make her sound crazy.

Gathering her nerve, Renee pushed herself from her car and walked toward the scene. She stepped under the police tape, moving toward the officers who were clustered below the tall column. The men's attention was transfixed on the construction crew above them so they did not notice Renee approaching them. They watched silently as the workmen continued to saw and hammer at the green concrete surrounding the dead woman's body. Renee halted near the officers and looked up, paying little attention to the concrete bits raining down near her. She noticed the hook shaped rebar sticking out of the concrete and the crane cables that were attached to it. She heard the deep grinding sound as the concrete chunk containing the body began to slip free of the column. The crew turned off their equipment and hastily climbed down from the scaffold.

Renee watched as the crane operator worked the crane's tower, pulling on the cables attached to the rebar in the concrete chunk that held the body. The tower strained and the cables tightened under the load, pulling the block from the column with a crunching sound. The concrete chunk swung out into the air, then dangled from the cables. The crane operator shifted levers again and he began to lower the block toward the ground.

Renee's eyes fixated on the dead woman. The wide slash across the prostitute's face seem to underline her stiffened expression of terror. Watching the block come down another five feet, Renee considered how the woman had suffered at the hands of her vicious attacker. Suddenly, a cable snapped, sending the concrete tumbling toward the ground. It pocked a deep impression in the earth and then rolled toward Renee. Renee stepped back quickly until the concrete stopped moving. With the corpse's face only a few feet from Renee now, Renee's stomach turned. The prostitute's hazel eyes, no longer shinning with life, had faded to a dull amber. They stared coldly, almost accusingly at Renee, urging her to tell what she knew. Renee involuntarily arched forward and vomited. Only when she had completely emptied her stomach could she stop retching. When Renee straightened up to recompose herself, she was staring into the handsome face of Lieutenant Elinger.

"I'm Lieutenant Elinger from Baltimore P.D. Are you okay?"

"Just give me a minute," Renee muttered, taking two deep breaths and composing herself the best she could under the circumstances.

"Did you know her?" Elinger asked after a moment. Renee pulled a handkerchief from her purse and wiped her mouth, feeling her embarrassment warming her face. "Not personally," Renee replied, trying to calm herself. "But I'm pretty sure she was a prostitute from The Block."

Elinger and Torres exchanged a look askance.

"How would you determine that if you didn't know her?" Torres asked. "Are you a physic?"

Renee recognized the cynicism in Torres' voice. "No," Renee replied, pushing the handkerchief against her mouth again, fighting another flutter of nausea. "I really can't explain it," she said, her words muffled slightly by her handkerchief. "I just know."

Renee was aware that Elinger was looking her over with curious interest. She was sure he noticed she was wearing an expensive pants and sweater outfit. She definitely looked out of place at the construction site. Renee knew the lieutenant was probably wondering why a woman like her would know a prostitute from The Block. And by studying Elinger's quizzical expression, Renee knew he didn't believe her. "Look, I can't really explain why I know she was a prostitute," Renee offered, putting her handkerchief back into her purse. "But she was. And I'm also sure she wasn't killed here."

Renee's statement snagged Elinger's attention. "Perhaps you could tell us where she was murdered?"

"In an alley behind Baltimore Street, I think."

Renee noticed Elinger and Torres exchanging puzzled and surprised looks.

"How would you know that unless you were there?" Torres asked.

Renee searched carefully for a plausible answer but couldn't find one. "I just have this weird feeling she was murdered there," she finally said, angry her desire to find the dead woman's killer had loosened her tongue. "I could be wrong," Renee recanted slightly, becoming nervous. "Look, I don't feel well. I should be going."

Renee turned from the officers and started to walk away, heading toward her auto in the distance. She hoped the lieutenant wouldn't stop her although she would clearly understand if he did. Renee knew she did the right thing. It was her duty as a human being to help the police find the murderer of this unfortunate woman.

"Hey, wait a minute," Elinger called out to Renee. "Where do you think you're going?"

Renee stopped and turned around to face Elinger and Torres who approached her. Now she was having second thoughts about telling the police what she knew. "Home," she replied simply.

"When someone makes a statement like you did, we need to know who we're talking to," Elinger said. "I need to see some ID."

Renee nodded, unhappy about the position she had put herself in. She reached into her purse and produced her driver's license.

Torres took the license and pulled a small notepad out of his shirt pocket. He wrote down her license number, her name and address.

Elinger asked for Renee's phone number and Torres jotted that down also.

"May I go now?" Renee asked. "I'm still feeling sick."

"Yes, but I hope you don't have any plans to leave town. If I find a murder scene on Baltimore Street, we'll need to talk again, right away," Elinger informed Renee as Torres handed Renee her license.

"I'm not going anywhere," Rene told Elinger as she placed her license back in her purse.

Without a word, Elinger and Torres watched Renee move off, then slip into her auto.

"Follow her," Elinger told Torres. "See if her address checks out and keep an eye on her. Call me with what you find out and I'll do a background check."

Torres nodded and hustled toward his auto as Renee drove from the scene, kicking up a trail of dust. A moment later, Torres gunned the engine of his auto and pulled out after her.

Elinger moved back to the column and looked up at the scaffold. Two policemen were up there now, inspecting the hole in the column.

Evans approached Elinger. Wearing latex gloves, he held a small dark object. He handed it to Elinger.

"What do you make of this?" Evans asked.

Elinger studied the object. It was a small 9-volt battery. The black cat on the logo is jumping through the hole in the number nine that symbolizes the nine lives of the battery. "What does this have to do with the victim?" Elinger asked.

"We found it tucked under her tongue," Evans reported. "No prints on it."

Elinger looked more closely at the battery, wondering why it was in the woman's mouth. Was it a calling card of the murderer? Did the black cat in the logo signify a racially motivated homicide? Elinger handed the battery back to Evans. "Bag it and photograph it. I don't know what it means."

Evans took the battery from Elinger and walked off toward his men.

Elinger shifted his vision back to the prostitute's corpse. His mind filled with a sudden flashback of the dead shipyard workers. In the last few days, two very bizarre murders, perhaps the strangest in Baltimore's history, had been committed and both had been dumped unceremoniously onto his lap. Elinger hoped he had the ability to solve them quickly.

FOURTEEN

● ● ●

    Sitting on a living room chair, Renee sipped Chardonnay from a gleaming crystal glass. It was her third drink of the evening, and she didn't care if she had three more. The day's events had warranted a few glasses of vino, she had convinced herself. It was now quite evident her unconscious writings are connected to real life. But Renee couldn't figure out how this was possible. How did she have the knowledge to write about reality as it happened? What was her connection to the victims or the killer? These questions hounded her relentlessly.

    Eventually, Renee's mind began to relax, and she let go of her internal struggle. Renee never felt the wine glass slip from her hand or heard it hit the floor. She had dozed off. When she awoke, she looked at her watch and discovered it was midnight. Renee yawned and stretched, feeling unusually refreshed. A fertile idea suddenly pranced through her mind, an opening to her new book. She would use a love poem by Emily Dickinson. It seemed so appropriate. Surprised to be in the mood to write, Renee wanted to seize this moment.

    Renee trotted up the stairs and headed down the hallway

toward her den. Just outside the door, however, she halted abruptly. She could hear the quiet hum of her computer penetrating the quiet of the room—but she had not turned it on! Someone was in the den, Renee realized. And she knew it wasn't Alex. He had gone to bed hours earlier. Who could it be? A scary concept suddenly shook her mind. It seemed preposterous, but what if the killer was sneaking into her house and writing the grisly pages after he killed someone? The idea horrified Renee.

Although gripped with inner terror, the prospect of catching her tormentor overruled Renee's sense of safety. When she noticed Alex's baseball bat lying on the hallway floor, she declared war on whoever was in the den. She grabbed the bat and crept cautiously into her office space.

Renee moved toward her computer, surprised to see that no one was sitting at her desk. Renee's vision tracked the room carefully but saw no one. Cocking the bat over her shoulder, Renee opened the door of a large darkened closet. Suddenly, a swirling mist of darkness filled her mind.

Renee's eyes snapped open and she found herself behind her computer with her hands shaking over the keyboard. Bewildered, she looked at her watch. It was a quarter past midnight. But that didn't seem possible. She had left the living room at exactly midnight and that was only a minute or so ago. Yet fifteen minutes had passed and she couldn't account for one second! Renee found the answer to the mystery on her computer screen.

My Dear Madam Holland:
I offer you my most humble bromides of gratitude. Because of

*you, I can now achieve a long overdue personal goal. I shan't be
a nuisance if I can help it; but indeed it is most difficult for me not
to interrupt your life with my murderous work. You will have to
overlook what you cannot control. Although I have assistance, my
task is still formidable so you must endure the necessary sacrifices
you will have to make. It will insure my success. There is much to
be done, and you can be sure we will meet again...*

Renee stared at the screen in disbelief. Who wrote this?
A ghost? A demon? Renee's lips trembled as she contemplated
something ominous had invaded her mind! "Damn you!" Renee
suddenly screamed. "Leave me alone whoever or whatever you
are!"

Renee snatched her computer monitor from the desk and
stepped backwards, yanking its cables loose. She ran to the nearest
window and threw the monitor through the glass. As the window
exploded, Renee dropped to her knees and sobbed.

● ● ●

Torres, who sat in his darkened auto outside the Holland
home, heard the bursting glass. His eyes jumped to the shattering
second story window as the monitor plummeted toward the ground
and crashed through a bed of roses before hitting the ground.
Torres studied the scene for a moment, remembering what
Elinger had said about Renee Holland when he reported in earlier,
something like *—this lady seemed too straight to be a nut case.*
Torres grinned. He liked to see his superiors wrong from time to
time. It made them more human.

FIFTEEN

• • •

With his coat draped over his shoulder, Torres stepped from the elevator. His shirt sleeves were rolled up and his tie was loosened. His face was drawn from a long night of coffee-fueled surveillance.

Elinger walked toward Torres. His expression was deeply troubled.

As Elinger and Torres met in the corridor, Elinger handed Torres a filled disposable coffee cup. "Black, just the way you like it."

Torres took the cup. "Thanks. I can use it. Coffee's the only thing that replaces sleep."

"Anything strange happen besides the flying computer monitor?" Elinger asked.

Torres sipped his coffee before he replied. "No, it was a long quiet night after that. What'd you find out about her?"

Elinger spoke as he led Torres toward the detective's room. "She's divorced, late thirties, no police record. Has a twelve-year-old son named Alex," Elinger said. "And she's highly respected in her profession."

"Which is?" Torres asked, stepping into the elevator with Elinger.

"She's a writer. Has a few best sellers and a couple of movie deals on the table."

"What does she write?" Torres asked.

"Historical romances."

Torres sipped from his cup again, absorbing the information. "What about the alley?" he asked, lowering his cup. "A waste of time, right?"

"Nope. The puking lady knew exactly what she was talking about."

Elinger could see the surprise in Torres' face.

"The woman in the concrete was really murdered in the alley behind Baltimore Street!" Torres exclaimed.

"It looks that way," Elinger replied. "We found a broken whiskey bottle with blood on it. Sam thinks it might be the murder weapon. He'll know for sure soon."

"And I suppose you're gonna tell me next that the dead woman was a hooker?"

"Another three-pointer for this Renee Holland."

"What about the battery in the woman's mouth?" Torres asked.

"It's still a question mark."

"Do we have a name for the hooker?"

"Mona Lewis. New in town. From Philly."

"Guess this means this Holland lady is our prime suspect?" Torres surmised.

"It would appear that way, but you and I both know that she didn't do it, couldn't have done it," Elinger said as he and Torres moved closer to their offices. "At least not alone," he continued. "She's not strong enough to carry dead weight up that overpass column mold, and she doesn't wear a size thirteen-D shoe. That's what the shoe print casts tell us. They also tell us the killer's shoes are pretty much worn out."

"You think he could be a transient?" Torres asked.

"Possibly. I've got undercover people on the street now," Elinger revealed as he and Torres walked into the detective's room. Elinger approached his desk to answer his ringing phone.

Torres finished the last of his coffee and tossed his cup into Elinger's wastebasket.

Sam Evans was on Elinger's line. Elinger grunted a few times, then thanked Evans for his prompt work.

"No prints on the bottle, Ralph," Elinger said, hanging up the phone.

"Guess the killer is always wearin' gloves?" Torres speculated.

"That's my guess," Elinger replied. "The DNA from the body and the blood on the bottle match. So, we've got the murder weapon, and we can assume the prostitute was killed in the alley. We also have a semen sample."

"Guess that's another reason the Holland lady didn't do it?" Torres said.

"Yeah. Sam's already working up the killer's DNA. Once he has that, he'll run it through CODIS for a match. Hopefully, we've got a repeat offender and we already have his DNA on file. Meanwhile, I want to know how this Renee Holland knew Mona Lewis was a prostitute. And how did she know Miss Lewis was murdered in an alley behind Baltimore Street?"

"Maybe she saw the murder?" Torres replied. "Or she knew the killer? Or maybe she was an accomplice?"

"This happened in The Block. I don't think this Ms. Holland is the type who hangs out there," Elinger countered.

"Unless she was researching?" Torres said. "Writers like to experience things first hand to be more realistic about what they write."

"I'd buy that, Ralph, but she writes historical romances. Not much romance in The Block. It's all cash and carry."

"What if someone told her about the killing, and she's protecting them?" Torres speculated.

Elinger was appreciative his young partner was trying to open a viable vein of investigation . "Whatever it is, I need to talk to Ms. Holland right away."

● ● ●

In Renee's upstairs den, Renee and Alex stood in front of a new computer monitor. Renee studied it through regretful features. "I don't want to do that again, no matter how freaked out I get."

"Yeah, it could become an expensive habit, Mom," Alex said quietly.

Renee nodded and started to sit down in front of her computer when her door chimes rang.

When Renee pulled open the front door, she found herself looking directly into the eyes of Lieutenant Elinger. The sight of his serious expression caused unpleasant images of the prostitute's corpse to flash before her eyes. A swell of nausea plumed in her throat. She turned quickly from her unexpected visitor and cupped a hand over her mouth.

"Women have reacted to me in many ways, Miss Holland, but never quite like this," Elinger said, trying to lighten the mood.

After a deep breath, Renee turned back to Elinger. "I'm sorry, but seeing you made me think of that poor woman in the concrete."

"I can't get her out of my mind either. That's why I'm here."

"I'm sorry, but I forgot your name," Renee said as she regained her composure.

"Elinger. Lieutenant Kent Elinger," Elinger replied, producing his I.D. and badge. "I'd like to ask you a few questions."

Renee quietly panicked, wondering what she could tell the lieutenant without appearing insane or being guilty of murder. She had been an imbecile at the construction site for telling what she knew. Renee covered her fears with a bright smile. "Please, come in," she offered, stepping back and allowing Elinger to enter her home.

Renee led Elinger into the living room, mentally reviewing her situation, planning answers for the questions she was sure the lieutenant would ask. But her dilemma was paradoxical— the truth was unbelievable and lies would make her appear just as guilty. Renee wasn't sure what to do. "We can sit here," Renee said, pointing at the nearest couch.

After Elinger and Renee seated themselves, Elinger cleared his throat before he spoke. "Ms. Holland, I'd like to get right to the point."

"I like people who don't waste words," Renee replied honestly

Elinger withdrew a pen and small notebook from his pocket. "Why were you at the construction site?" he asked.

"I saw the police cars," Renee answered. "I'm a writer, I'm curious about everything."

"How did you know where the woman was murdered?"

"When I saw her body, I just felt I knew where she was killed. I can't explain it."

Elinger raised his eyebrows.

Renee knew the lieutenant did not believe her. And why should he? Her statement sounded ludicrous.

"I don't want to be rude, Ms. Holland, but I find that hard to believe. You know things only the murderer, an accomplice, or a witness could know."

Renee felt uneasy. Lieutenant Elinger was right. She wondered if she should talk about the pages—but they were too incredible and she knew the lieutenant would never understand. "It amazes me as much as it does you," Renee finally said. She could think of nothing else to offer.

"I'm not amazed at all, Ms. Holland," Elinger replied. "I think you're hiding something."

"I'm not hiding anything," Renee replied defensively.

"Ms. Holland," Elinger began in a sharp tone, "it's obvious that you are. I can cause you a lot of grief if you don't cooperate. Just tell me what the hell's going on?"

"I can't tell you what I don't know," Renee lied stubbornly, feeling her facade crumbling.

Alex suddenly marched into the room and moved toward

Elinger. "Leave my mother alone!" he ordered. "I heard everything you said!"

"Alex!" Renee blurted in a scolding tone. "He's a policeman. He's trying to find out who killed that poor woman."

"I don't like the way he's talkin' to you!" Alex shot back.

"The last thing I want to do is upset your mother, son," Elinger said calmly.

"Then why don't you leave?"

Renee glared at her son. "I can handle this, Alex!"

"No, you can't, Mom," Alex returned quickly. "You don't sleep anymore. You're cranky all the time. Those pages are makin' you crazy! Why don't you just give them to him so he'll leave?"

The mention of the pages caused Renee's thoughts to jam. She wanted to ground her son for a year for bringing them up in front of the lieutenant. She had no idea how to explain them and still make herself sound sane.

"What pages?" Elinger asked.

Renee's look at Alex was piercing. "Go to your room Alex. Now!" she ordered as she rose from the couch.

"Tell me about the pages, Alex," Elinger asked as he also stood. "I want to help your mother as much as you do."
Alex stopped his retreat to the room and stared back at his mother.

Renee realized Alex's desire to help her was stronger than his fear of punishment.

Alex now turned to Elinger. "All the information about the murder is in the pages my Mom wrote," he explained. "That's how she knows what's going on." Alex glanced at his mother again. "Sorry, Mom, but I want to help you, and I think this is the best way to do it," Alex said, then moved out of the room as if he was going to bed. However, he stopped in the next room and pressed himself against the wall out of sight to listen in on the conversation between his mother and Elinger.

"What he's talking about, Miss Holland?" Elinger asked.

Renee felt her inner turmoil surface in her expression. Needing a moment to think, she turned her eyes from Elinger's. Maybe Alex was right, she reasoned. Perhaps she should give the pages to the lieutenant. Maybe he could figure them out. Renee looked at Elinger again. With an expression of uncertainty, she said, "I don't think you're going to believe me, Lieutenant. What I'm about to tell you will make you think I'm a lunatic."

As soon as the words left her mouth, Renee understood her emotions had overruled her better instincts. She knew better than to show the lieutenant the pages, but it was too late now.

Renee handed Elinger a cup of coffee, and they both sat on the couch. Alex reclined in a nearby chair, sipping a soda. The pages were spread out on the coffee table in front of Elinger.

Elinger felt numb as he read the passages. "Incredible! Everything I found in the alley is here. Even the body wounds are correct. How could you know this unless you were there?" Elinger asked, addressing what seemed to be obvious. "And you claim you did all this while you were unconscious?"

Renee nodded. "Believe me, I'm as confused about this as you are, Lieutenant."

"If you weren't there and have no connection with the murderer, what's your explanation?"

"I have no explanation. Why don't you tell me what you think?" Renee implored.

112

Elinger detected the quiet plea for help in Renee's voice. He wanted to believe her, but he had a job to do. "On the down side, you could've been an accomplice to the murder. But I don't picture you hanging out with killers and prostitutes in The Block. So, then I think maybe you're a reluctant witness? You see a murder and run—too frightened to tell anyone. But your guilt overcomes you and you write these pages in an effort to clear your conscience."

Renee shook her head. "You've got to come up with a better one than that, Lieutenant."

"I've known cases where people witness horrible things and their minds block all conscious memory of it," Elinger said. "Maybe your subconscious is pumping out this information as a subconscious catharsis to ease feelings of guilt?"

Renee shook her head. "I was home that night. I didn't see anyone get killed."

Elinger's strong gaze remain locked on Renee. "Then maybe someone gave you information about the killing, and you're an opportunist who's in the middle of a ghoulish publicity stunt for a new book—or a television series," Elinger suggested without tact, expecting an angry response.

Elinger watched Renee's expression closely. He was trying to fluster her, hoping he could shake loose an incriminating statement.

"If you know I'm an author, then I'm assuming you've checked into my personal background," Renee said. "And if you have, then you already know I'm incapable of doing anything like that. I had nothing to do with the murder, either conscious or subconscious."

"I'm thinking maybe the killer is a friend of yours and you're trying to protect him," Elinger countered, staying on track.

No sooner than the words left his mouth, Elinger realized he had taxed Renee's patience. He knew she was weary of his ploy, and certainly did not fit the profile of a murderer or someone who would consort with killers.

Renee rose to her feet. "I've heard enough, Lieutenant. I think it's time for you to leave."

Elinger lifted himself from the couch and riveted his look on Renee. "Okay, I'll leave now, but I might be back real soon. The last time I saw you, you lied to me. And I think you could still be lying."

Alex suddenly rushed into the living room and stepped toward Elinger with a scowl on his face. "Don't call my mother a liar! She's telling you the truth!"

Elinger glanced down at Renee's son. "I just want the truth, son," he told Alex then shifted his attention back to Renee. "May I keep these?" he asked, pointing at the pages on the table.

"If it'll make you leave, yes," Renee said in a nettled tone.

For a fleeting moment, Elinger noticed the beauty of Renee's features through her hostile expression. He nodded coolly. "Thanks for your time and the coffee, Ms. Holland. I'll be in touch."

Without another word, Elinger began to walk toward the front door. He had gone only a few steps when Renee's eyes suddenly twitched, then rolled upward, exposing full white orbs beneath half-closed lids. She began to cross the room with stilted movements.

"Now you can see it for yourself, Mr. Lieutenant!" Alex

shouted at Elinger.

Elinger stopped short, watching Renee's robotic behavior.

"She's havin' a blackout!" Alex yelled again, running to his mother and walking protectively alongside her as she began to climb the stairs.

Scarcely believing what he was seeing, Elinger followed. This was one for the books, he thought.

Renee entered her den and sat down in front of her computer. With a vacant look, she turned on the system and entered her word processing program. Renee began to rhythmically tap the keyboard with facile hands. Words and sentences began to form on the screen.

Alex, with his arm on his mother's shoulder, watched quietly while Elinger stood behind them and observed with a stone-like expression.

The spell passed quickly. When Renee blinked back to reality, she was surprised to be sitting at her desk.

"You had another blackout, Mom," Alex said. "Are you okay?"

Renee nodded slowly with a feeling of light headedness, then glanced at Elinger. You could see his eyes glinting with amazement. "You must think I'm really crazy now."

"Please print that out," Elinger asked.

Renee used the mouse to click the printer icon, and a page rolled out of the printer.

Renee held the page in a manner that allowed her and Elinger to read it at the same time:

My dear Madam Holland:

It struck my fancy to contact you again. I wanted you to realise that my notion is to be the undisputed centre of your life. Our relationship will remain permanent unless I personally decide to terminate it. But do not despair or fill your heart with wo. I will help you remain strong for the work that is yet to be done...

Renee began to sob. "I don't know what's happening to me! My life has become a marathon of misery."

Renee glanced at Elinger, sensing he couldn't determine if her trance was fact or fiction.

"What does this mean?" Elinger asked, looking at the page.

"I think it's a message from the murderer. He's obviously invaded my mind," Renee choked out the words, her eyes pleading for answers. Still, she knew Elinger was not totally convinced. "There's something else you might like to know," Renee added cautiously. "I have other pages. And according to them, the man who killed the prostitute also killed the workers at the shipyard."

Renee saw the look of incredulity in Elinger's face. "I know you haven't connected the shipyard murders to the prostitute's murder. You have no reason to because the killings were so different. But they are connected."

Renee opened a desk drawer and handed Elinger another stack of pages. "It's all here about the shipyard. And the killer only has one ear, but I'm sure you already know that."

Renee watched Elinger's expression as he read the accurate descriptions of the shipyard murders. She knew Elinger was trying to hide the shock that was evident on his face.

Elinger slowly emerged from his self-imposed silence and shot a look at Renee. "If you have any out-of-town plans," he began, "you need to cancel them. I will be calling you just as soon as I can study these pages and compare them to our detailed field reports about these murders."

Totally drained by the latest events, Renee could only nod her agreement.

Once Elinger was gone, Alex stood in the center of the living room, looking at his mother.

Renee knew her son expected to be punished for revealing the pages to the lieutenant.

"You're going to ground me for a month, right?" Alex asked.

"No, honey," Renee replied, moving to her son and placing a loving hand on his shoulder. "You were right. Hiding the pages won't do me any good. So why shouldn't I let the police have them? If they can find the cause, then maybe they can find the cure."

"I hope so, Mom."

Renee hugged her son, genuinely relieved the police had possession of the pages. Lieutenant Elinger had struck her as a man who was intelligent and fair minded. Maybe now, she had someone who could help her—someone who could destroy the madness that had overturned her life. But Renee also cautioned herself that Elinger could very well become her worst enemy.

SIXTEEN

• • •

Leonard Ravnik walked down a Baltimore sidewalk, brushing past briefcase-carrying businessmen and scurrying lunch time shoppers. His long, matted hair covered the hole in his head where he once had an ear. His eyes were clear and steady as he glanced ahead, noticing an old, two-story brick building. Faded blue lettering above its large door read Spartan Gym.

Ravnik was close to the entrance when he saw twenty-seven-year-old, Müeller the Masher push open the door of the gym and walk toward a gleaming purple Mercedes parked at the curb. Müeller's butch-cut, raven-black hair was streaked with green bolts, and his tall, muscle-bound frame was covered by a silken, scarlet robe. His neck was thick, supporting a head that carried the expression of an angry bulldog.

Two powerfully-built bodyguards, Cowan and Wicker, flanked Müeller. Cowan opened a rear door of the Mercedes for Müeller about the time he and Wicker noticed the shabbily dressed man approaching them.

Ravnik stopped in front of the men and glowered at the Masher, exposing his stained, crooked teeth. "Give me your money!" Ravnik ordered with cold, precise words.

Müeller gave his centurions a sidelong glance, then studied the stranger in front of him. "I am Müeller the Masher," he began in his thick German accent. "You do not vant to rob me. I am champion vrestler from Berlin."

Ravnik didn't answer. His glare remained pinned on Müeller. He stuck out his hand. "I want your money! Now!"

Müeller chuckled. "I vill not give you anyting! In da Deutschland, I vas trained to be de best. No American has beaten me. Now get out of my face or ve vill break your neck," he hissed.

Ravnik didn't budge. His expression remained iron-like.

Müeller returned the gaze. He was ready to fight. Cowan and Wicker curled their hands into hard fists.

"Give me your money!" Ravnik demanded again.

"I do not see a gun or knife?" Müeller replied. "How you take my money? Beat me up?" he asked with a laugh.

Cowan and Wicker chuckled at Müeller's question.

Without warning, Ravnik lunged at Müeller, closing the distance between them. He grabbed the Masher around the waist, and then Ravnik rammed his head into the wrestler's stomach. Ravnik spun the gasping Müeller around and pushed him toward the gym's brick wall.

The Masher hammered Ravnik's kidneys with stone-hard fists as he stumbled backward, but he was unable to break from the powerful grip. Crashing into the gym's wall, the back of Müeller's head struck the brick. Knocked senseless, the wrestler pitched to the sidewalk in a flaccid heap.

Crouching over him, Ravnik turned the Masher's robe pockets inside out, coming up with a clip stuffed with bills.

Cowan and Wicker, caught off guard by the sudden attack, rushed Ravnik and pounced on him, flattening him on the sidewalk. But Ravnik rolled from beneath them and sprang to his feet.

Ravnik jumped on Cowan first, straddling him by locking his legs around his waist. He pushed his thumb deep into one of Cowan's eyes, deeply penetrating the jelly-like vitreous. Cowan screamed and clawed at Ravnik's hand.

When Ravnik withdrew his bloody thumb, he jumped back to the sidewalk, ready for Wicker. But Wicker hesitated when he saw what had happened to his comrade.

Cowan staggered toward the street. Cupping his oozing eye with one hand, he waved the other at passing motorists. He was suddenly surrounded by a chorus of blaring horns and screeching tires as he stepped onto the street. A careening auto slammed into Cowan and knocked him down on the pavement— his body a network of broken bones.

Ravnik could tell that with one bodyguard twisted on the street and the Masher unconscious—the other bodyguard's bravado had buckled. Ravnik grabbed him by the ears, jerked his face forward, clamped his teeth on Wicker's nose and bit off its tip. Blood rushed from the bodyguard's ripped nostrils as Ravnik spit the piece of nose back into Wicker's face. Stunned, Wicker dropped to the sidewalk on his knees and picked up the tip of his nose. Ravnik jumped behind him, and snatched Wicker's wallet from a pocket.

Müeller regained consciousness and lifted his throbbing, bleeding head from the sidewalk. He saw Ravnik turn from Wicker and bolt away. Ravnik's hair jostled just enough for Müeller to notice the shabbily dressed man was missing an ear. He watched Ravnik run, shouldering his way through several horrified pedestrians who had seen the assault.

Mūeller was on his feet now, stepping toward the street to help Cowan who was still spread-eagled in the pavement. The Masher glanced at Wicker who was still kneeling on the sidewalk, painting the concrete with his blood. The Masher took another look in the direction where Ravnik had run off, vowing to himself he would find this one-eared man and repay him ten-fold for what he had done.

● ● ●

It was a late night. Elinger was alone in the detective's room, sitting at his desk, sipping cold coffee from a cup. He was thinking about the mysterious pages, Renee Holland and the conundrum they presented.

Torres entered the space, carrying a notebook under his arm.

"What'd you find out?" Elinger asked.

Torres sat on the edge of Elinger's desk. "Not much that can help us. All of Renee Holland's friends say she's not loco. But they did say she's had insomnia and headaches lately."

"Sounds like me."

"She only told one of her friends about the pages but didn't mention their real-life connection," Torres added.

"Who was the friend?"

"An awesome babe named Rebecca. We're talkin'

perfection," Torres replied as he slid from Elinger's desk and plopped down on his nearby desk chair. "The way she walked, the way she talked, her lips. Man, she was perfect all over."

Elinger listened, recalling his days of youthful non-stop sexual thoughts. "And what did this babe tell you?"

"She told me, probably because of my expert interrogation tactics and charm," Torres began in a joking tone, "that Renee Holland has recently gone to a shrink."
Elinger's face brightened.

Torres noticed Elinger's look. "Yeah, that's what I'm thinkin'. Maybe the shrink can tell us somethin' worthwhile?"

Elinger's expression dulled quickly, however. "We'll have to overcome doctor-patient confidentiality. He won't divulge anything unless he has her permission."

"Can you get it?" Torres asked.

"Only if I have as much charm as you," Elinger said lightly. "Where can I find the Holland woman in the morning?"

Torres reached into his coat pocket and retrieved a small notebook. He opened it and thumbed through the pages, finally stopping at one. "On Tuesdays at eight o'clock in the morning, she's usually jogging on the track at U.M."

Sam Evans, the CSI lab chief, entered the detectives' room and moved to Elinger and Torres. His face carried a look of mild amazement. "This case gets wilder by the minute," he said.

"I'm listening, Sam," Elinger said, hoping for good news.

"I went to the shipyard like you wanted," Evans started. "The killer cut himself on the fence when he climbed it. I got a blood sample so we have DNA." Evans handed Elinger a small white card. "Here's the analysis."

Elinger studied a series of numbers and blue dots on the card.

Evans handed Elinger another card.

"Now take a look at this one—DNA analysis of the semen samples taken from the prostitute. And guess what?"

"They match?" Elinger said, looking up at Evans.

Evans nodded. "You know what that means?"

"Yeah, the same guy was at both murder scenes—the shipyard and the alley," Elinger replied, looking at Torres through a contemplative expression. "Just like this Renee Holland wrote in her pages!"

"Yes, but the problem is—our killer is not in the CODIS database," Evans reported, dampening Elinger's enthusiasm.

"Sam, run it through every few days. New records are added every day."

"I already planned on it," Evans replied. "But there's something else. Something I've never seen before."

"What?" Elinger asked.

"There were extremely high levels of adrenaline compounds in your suspect's blood," Evans reported. "Maybe three to four times the levels you would find in a normal person under stress."

"What does that mean?" Torres asked.

"Think of the hundred- and twenty-pound panicked mother who can suddenly lift a car off of her child," Evans replied. "It looks like your guy can do that twenty-four-seven!"

● ● ●

The next morning on a College Park campus road, Elinger coasted into a parking spot in his unmarked auto. Emerging, he walked past a stand of pine trees, then entered the open gate of a tall, chain-link fence. In front of him was the home of the Maryland Terrapins, the college football team. He moved into the expansive stadium that was constructed in a cavity of the earth.

Elinger trotted down fifty-two steps to the stands and stepped onto the running track that ringed the playing field. True to Torres' notes, Renee, wearing sweats that clung to her shapely body, jogged on the red-clay track.

Renee was not pleased when she spotted the lieutenant. She suddenly regretted giving him the pages. Maybe instead of helping her, the lieutenant would start harassing her? She was angry with herself now that she realized the pages had made her the subject of police surveillance.

Trotting in place while she spoke, Renee paused near Elinger. "Why are you following me, Lieutenant?" Her tone was sharp.

"That's what we do when we think someone is withholding information. You'll find that we're very tenacious."

"I don't like being under a microscope," Renee responded tartly. "It makes a bitch out of me! So, you'll have to overlook my lack of manners."

With that, Renee pivoted from Elinger and began to run again.

Shaking his head, Elinger removed his suit jacket, slung it over his shoulder and began to jog after Renee.

By the time he was in step with her, Elinger was slightly winded. "You can't blame us, Ms. Holland. You're our best lead in this case."

Renee noticed Elinger was crowding his words with each breath he took. "Either arrest me or get out of my life, Lieutenant! I already told you all I know. You've got the pages, why don't you figure them out?"

"We're working on it," Elinger replied. "But right now, there's something else bothering us. You were right about the shipyard murderer being connected to the prostitute killing. Baffles the hell out of us how you would know that without being on the murder scenes or having privy knowledge about the killer."

"My pages say the murders are connected. That's all I know," Renee replied, pumping a steady rhythm with her legs.

"We've learned the killer is a male, Ms. Holland," Elinger puffed. "That's good for you," he added in a gentler tone.

"Gee, what a surprise," Renee said smartly. "I know you didn't come here to arrest me or I'd be handcuffed by now. So, what do you really want?"

"Just the answer to one question."

Renee began to realize her lack of cooperation and attitude would only make the police more persistent. "What?" she finally asked.

Elinger's breathing was more labored now. "I want permission to speak to your psychologist Dr. Lantz."
Renee stopped jogging in an instant. She could see in Elinger's face that this was a welcome relief. "How'd you know I was seeing a shrink?" she asked a bit surprised.

"I told you we were tenacious."

"Who told you?" Renee questioned, annoyed.

"A friend."

"A friend of mine?"

"Yeah. One who cares," was Elinger's reply.

The answer put Renee in a reflective mood, and she relaxed her guard. Even her friends were aiding the police. She must be worse off than she realized. Noticing Elinger's heavy breathing, she decided to give him some advice. "You really need to start exercising regularly."

"I used to run, but the last couple of years I've been too busy to stick with it."

"You think that's smart?" Renee reprimanded mildly. "You look like you're going to faint."

"That bad, huh?"

"It's never too late to rejuvenate yourself."

"I've heard that," Elinger agreed. "Now, what about your psychologist?"

"I'll call him," Renee replied. "I want to clear this up as quickly as you do, Lieutenant."

"We're going to be spending considerable time together until this is solved—so it's okay for you to call me Kent," Elinger told Renee. "Keeps things more casual, more friendly. I find it's easier to get to the truth that way."

"If it makes you feel any better, I'll think about it." Renee noticed Elinger's breathing was still slightly labored. "You really should get into shape. It'll keep you looking young."

"I don't mind if I don't look young," Elinger admitted. "As long as I look my age. I'm proud of the few wrinkles around my eyes. Each one represents a lesson I've learned."

Renee studied Elinger's face. "I wouldn't learn any more

lessons for a while," she quipped. "At least not until you start an exercise program."

With that, Renee turned and jogged away.

SEVENTEEN

• • •

Elinger sat on a chair in front of Dr. Edwin Lantz's desk. He had Renee's file in his lap, thumbing through its pages. His eyes stopped now and then to focus on something he felt was important.

Sitting behind his neat and tidy desk, Dr. Lantz looked at Elinger through a stern expression. "Normally, Lieutenant, I don't allow anyone to review my patient's files," he said from beneath a furrowed brow and lofty tone. "But Miss Holland insisted."

"We appreciate your cooperation, Dr. Lantz," Elinger replied, glancing up. "Miss Holland is involved in a bizarre homicide case, and we can use all the help we can get."

Elinger studied the doctor, guessing him to be in his early sixties because of the bags under his eyes and his thinning silver hair. Elinger closed the file. "There are terms in here I'm not familiar with. In plain English, what is Ms. Holland's state of mind?"

"There's no evidence of mental illness, personality disorders, or manifestations of schizophrenia," Dr Lantz explained. "Of course, she has her share of garden variety neuroses like most people, but nonetheless her mental health is excellent."

"What do you make of what she calls her unconscious writings about the murders?"

"That's a question with many answers, Lieutenant," Lantz replied.

"I'll take all you've got."

Dr. Lantz leaned back in his chair, organizing in his mind what he was going to say. "Well, at first I considered that her pages were related to traumatic amnesia—that Renee had witnessed the murders, and they were so horrible she blocked them from her mind. Then, later, she'd lapse into an altered state of consciousness with total recall and the ability to write about the killings from a somnambular state. But that's not what's happening. I believe she's never been at the scene of the murders during the murders."

"How did you come to that conclusion?"

Dr. Lantz arched forward in his chair. "Hypnotic regression."

"You hypnotized Ms. Holland?"

"She insisted. It's not unusual therapy when aberrant behavior presents itself," Lantz said as he rose from his desk chair, temporarily framing himself with his many academic diplomas and certificates of accomplishments framed on the wall behind him. He began to circle the office as he spoke, his face drawn with concentration. "While Renee was hypnotized, I took her back to the dates of the crimes. I wanted to know if she remembered the killings while under hypnosis. She had total recall of the day's normal events, but nothing about the murders. So, I'm fairly confident she didn't see them being committed."

Elinger stood and moved to Lantz. An important question

had floated to the top of his mind. "Doctor, if you took this beyond the field of psychotherapy—what would you make of the writings?"

"If I answer that, I would be speaking off the record," Dr. Lantz said in a low tone.

Elinger noticed Dr. Lantz's attitude was losing a bit of its lordly edge.

"Not that my answer is earth shattering, but it is outside the confines of my profession," Dr. Lantz said. "I wouldn't want my personal belief on this matter to be known to my colleagues."

"I'll respect that. You are off the record."

"Have you considered that extrasensory perception could be involved?"

"ESP has crossed my mind," Elinger acknowledged quickly.

"You'll have to seek the advice of someone other than myself, of course, but I think it's worth pursuing."

"Can you recommend anyone?"

"I'll inquire at the University. There's always someone working in the parapsychology field there."

After leaving Dr. Lantz's office, Elinger stepped into the sunlight at Charles Center. He paused to take in the successful urban redevelopment project that was a unique blend of office buildings, apartment complexes, retail and commercial spaces, and transit depots. It was a city within a city, years in the making, and continuing to grow and change.

Elinger had walked only a short distance when he discovered Renee Holland standing on the sidewalk next to his parked sedan.

Renee smiled. "Now you're being tailed."

Surprised, Elinger halted.

"I wanted to apologize. I was a real bitch yesterday," Renee said, extending her hand.

Elinger quietly recovered from Renee's unexpected appearance and completed the handshake. "Apology accepted."

"You really don't have many wrinkles," Renee said. "I really feel bad I said that."

"Yeah, you had me looking in the mirror," Elinger admitted. "What can I do for you?"

Renee focused her tired eyes on Elinger. "I need your help. I'm really lost with this thing."

"And so are we," Elinger said quietly.

Renee pointed across the street. "By the way, Lieutenant, you can get rid of your back-up man. Unless it takes two big strong men to watch me."

With his head buried in a newspaper, Torres sat in his unmarked auto. Occasionally, he peeked out from behind the paper.

"That's my partner, Rafael Torres. He's still learning," Elinger said.

"It's the newspaper. Right out of an old Bogart movie," Renee chided.

Elinger stuck two fingers in his mouth and whistled loudly.

Torres looked up and noticed Elinger waving for him to leave. He shrugged, started his auto and drove off.

"He'll be good in a few years. Meantime, I'll have to brush him up on his surveillance techniques."

"It's the car, too," Renee added. "A dead giveaway."

Elinger grinned. "He wanted a Mercedes."

Elinger and Renee began to walk, joining the tourists, shoppers, and businessmen who filled the sidewalk.

Renee asked, "What did Dr. Lantz have to say?"

"That you're the epitome of good mental health."

"Doesn't say much for Dr. Lantz, does it?"

Elinger could see in Renee's face she was disappointed that nothing more had resulted from the meeting. "Well, he did suggest something I think has merit."

"What?"

Elinger stopped and turned to Renee. "My stomach tells me it's lunch time. Why don't we grab a bite while I explain," he suggested, then gave Renee a smile. "You can pick the place."

"If I recommend something, that would mean I'm accepting your invitation."

Elinger nodded, knowing Renee was considering the offer but wondering if she thought the invitation was more personal than professional. "Strictly business, of course," he added quickly.

"I guess I can't refuse then," Renee grinned slightly. "I wouldn't want you to arrest me on an empty stomach."

"We'll just call it one hour of protective custody," Elinger replied off-handedly.

"Well, by the way you were jogging at the track, I think you should eat something healthy," Renee said. "Fish. You need to eat more fish—and I know just the place."

Elinger and Renee walked into a restaurant decorated in a turn-of-the-century seafaring ambience. As a young waitress led them to a table, they passed old fishing nets, anchors, copper lanterns and polished rails of brass mounted on the wooden plank walls.

When they reached an old weathered helm mounted on the wall by a wide window, Elinger and Renee were seated. Elinger looked out the window that revealed a panoramic view of Baltimore's famous Inner Harbor. Since the day was warm and bright, many sailing enthusiasts had launched their craft and filled the Harbor's waters with white, fluttering sails.

Elinger turned back to Renee and started the conversation on the paramount subject of his mind. "You still can't find a logical explanation for your writings?"

Renee shook her head. "Believe me, I've tried."

"Then allow me to be illogical for a minute."

"Why not? This whole thing's illogical."

"Let's assume you have a psychic power you're not aware of."

Renee wrinkled her forehead.

"Like ESP. I'm wondering if something like that could be causing you to write about the murders."

"I don't think so, Kent," Renee replied.

Elinger was pleasantly surprised Renee had called him by his first name.

"Is it still okay to call you Kent?" Renee asked.

Elinger nodded with a smile, content this was the first step toward a better working friendship that could lead to the truth. "Have you ever had any premonitions?"

"Not that I know of," Renee answered. "It seems strange hearing that from a detective. You guys are supposed to be practical?"

"Yeah," Elinger grinned. "I used to scoff at psychics, but something happened a couple of years ago that changed my mind."

Elaborating to satisfy Renee's curiosity, Elinger explained an old murder case. A middle-aged man had mysteriously disappeared. Although a body was not found, his friends and neighbors feared he was dead. A woman across town began to dream about a dead man sitting in an auto in a wooded area. The vision was reoccurring and filled with detail. The woman sensed her dream was a window to reality. She told her family. They believed her and convinced her to go to the police. The woman did and regretted it, however. The police scorned her. Elinger, though polite, was among a core of skeptics. So, this woman, with her son and daughter, searched for and discovered the mountain area in her dream. True to her vision, she found an abandoned auto, and rotting behind the steering wheel was a corpse. A positive identification was made—it was the missing man. The discovery instigated a murder investigation that lead to the arrest and conviction of the killer.

"This case opened my mind to psychic phenomenon," Elinger said.

"The subject has always fascinated me," Renee said. "But I don't think that's what I have."

"This woman didn't think she had ESP either."

"I've never had a dream like hers. And I can't remember writing the pages. So how could I have ESP?"

"I don't know, but I'd like to find out. You can be tested here at the University."

"And they can determine if I'm psychic?"

"That's what I'm told."

"I'd feel foolish."

"No more than me," Elinger replied. "But if it would provide an explanation for your writings, it'd be worth it. It might even help me track down the killer."

"I think we'd be wasting our time, Kent," Renee sighed restively. "Maybe I just need a trip out of town. Maybe the pages would stop then?" She lifted her filled water glass and sipped. She looked wistfully at Elinger. "Who am I kidding?" Renee said suddenly. "Something very weird is happening to me, and I want to know what the hell it is! Of course, I'll go for the test."

Elinger stared across the table at Renee, noting the strain in this lovely woman's face. He realized his attraction to her was growing. He was beginning to feel desires stirring in him as he studied Renee's delicate smile, her emerging charm and the soft feminine aura of her face. He liked the way she smelled, too, and how she did her hair and the soft creamy look of her skin. Elinger had to remind himself this was a business lunch and not a romantic date. He sensed he would need to remind himself every time he saw Renee that this was business or he would fall for her. It had been a long time since he had been so captivated by a woman.

He forced himself to think of the dead workers on the pier and the poor woman in the concrete column. It was his reality check—and for the moment it worked. His mind drifted back to the task at hand—to solve the murders and figure out Renee's unwitting involvement.

EIGHTEEN

• • •

Renee, sitting at the center of a long conference table in the ESP lab of Maryland University's Psychical Research Department, studied her surroundings. A few tables and chairs were scattered about the room and on the tabletops were digital book readers, digital tape recorders, a DVD player with two monitors, several laptop computers and half a dozen notepads with pencils. Most of the equipment, Renee noted, was a few generations older than current models. She figured the school's ESP unit didn't warrant much respect from other school departments and therefore forced to operate on a bargain basement budget. There were several small cubicles along the wall. Inside the cubicles, Renee could see more computer systems and in one cubicle she saw the blinking lights of a server. Her vision finally rested on the laptop computer within her reach. It reminded her of the last frightening note she had received.

Renee turned toward Elinger as he entered the room. "Are you sure you want me to go through with this?" she asked, her uneasiness evident in her tone.

Elinger nodded, sitting in the chair next to her. "Let's

keep an open mind. If things get too weird, we'll leave."

Renee shrugged, feeling comfortable with that. "Did you find out who's going to test me?"

"Yes, Dr. Lantz recommended him, but warned me that no one in Dr. Lantz's field respects this kind of research and testing or the researchers who pursue it. But this guy is a shaker and mover from the University's paranormal research team," Elinger replied. "I heard he favors New Age philosophies."

Renee rolled her eyes slightly. "I thought the New Age movement had faded away."

"There's still serious followers and hold-outs in Arizona and in some countries overseas," Elinger replied. "Academic scholars have added it to their courses of religious studies."

"Maybe we'll all harmonically converge during the tests?" Renee joked then became serious. "I guess I shouldn't pass judgment like that—but I don't believe in karma, reincarnation or Buddhism," she added. "And I'm not superstitious. Are you?"

Elinger shook his head.

"Does this guy have some real-world credentials?" Renee asked.

"Yeah, oddly enough, they're very impressive," Elinger began. "Nice thing about being a cop, it's easy to get a bio on someone." Elinger reached into his pocket and retrieved a piece of paper. He unfolded it and glanced at it. "His name is Dr. Derek Burris—he has a Masters in Psychology."

"From where?" Renee asked.

Elinger looked up from the paper. "Princeton."

"Oh," Renee said, clearly impressed.

Elinger focused on the paper again. "He's considered a

wunderkind in the parapsychology field, but there's little fanfare for him in the straight Psychology and Mental Health arena. He's studied this field for many years beyond college," Elinger continued. "He's thoroughly researched every modern physic event. He's only twenty-eight." Elinger folded the paper and put it back in his pocket. "Like I said, just keep an open mind and be prepared for some off-the-wall stuff."

Before Elinger could say more, Dr. Derek Burris walked into the room.

Renee gave Burris the once over. He was clean shaven. His features were wrinkle-free and his short-cropped hair was fiery red. Burris' wiry frame was partially hidden beneath a freshly pressed white lab coat, but the coat didn't conceal his confident enthusiastic stride and smile. He looked like a nerdy teenager who landed a prom date with the homecoming queen.

Burris smiled courteously at Elinger and Renee as he stopped at Renee's side. Renee looked uncomfortably at him. Burris noticed. "Please relax, Ms. Holland. These tests can be fun."

"But I feel a little silly about being here," Renee said. "I really don't think I'm physic."

"We'll find out soon enough," Burris said, extending his hand. "I'm Dr. Derek Burris as I'm sure you've already gathered."

Renee nodded and shook his hand.

Burris turned toward Elinger. "You must be Lieutenant Elinger."

Elinger stood and he and Burris traded a firm handshake.

"Just what are we going to do?" Renee asked Burris as Elinger sat down again.

"We're going to focus on the three most important

elements of ESP," Burris replied. "Telepathy, clairvoyance, and precognition. Your case will be a challenge. It's highly unusual."

"I keep hearing that. Why am I so *unusual*?"

"At least three reasons come to mind," Burris revealed. "First, there's usually a bond between the sender and receiver of telepathic broadcasts."

"A bond?" Renee muttered.

"Yes, a friend or relative usually," Burris answered. "But the Lieutenant says you don't know his suspect, and as far as anyone knows, he's not a relative of yours. Secondly, ESP usually happens during heightened states of consciousness."

"And I'm always unconscious," Renee offered.

"Exactly. You are in an altered state of mind when you have an episode," Burris explained, stretching out his arms and locking his fingers. He twisted his hands inward, then pushed them outward, cracking the knuckles of both hands.

Renee grit her teeth at the sound. "What's the third reason?" she asked.

"It's the most obvious. ESP insights are normally fragmentary, not in an orderly sequence like your pages."

Dr. Burris began wandering around to the other side of the long table as he continued. "ESP usually occurs under great duress. Like during grief over the death of a loved one, the trauma of a severe accident, that sort of thing. And from what I know, please correct me if I'm wrong, you haven't experienced anything like that recently. Is that true?"

Renee nodded.

"Well, if we can establish ESP, we'll try to find its source," Burris said. "But it's not always easy. ESP sometimes destroys our values of physics. Time and space particularly."

Elinger leaned forward in his chair and politely interjected. "You're referring to the concept that ESP doesn't depend on time and space because there's no loss of power between sender and receiver with an increase of distance."

"Very good, Lieutenant," Burris stopped and focused on Elinger. "Where'd you learn that?"

"College. My psychology professor dabbled in this kind of thing."

"Well, telepathy does contradict the inverse square law regarding distance," Burris added. "When it comes to precognition, time has little meaning. Test results are just as high if the subject identifies an event in the future or contemporaneously."

Elinger leaned back in his chair and folded one leg over the other.

Renee studied Burris. She was impressed with the young man's knowledge. It was refreshing to see an impassioned mind at work.

"And consider this," Burris continued. "Most ESP is triggered by the dead. At least death as we know it."

"Are you saying a ghost is causing all this?" Renee questioned incredulously.

"A troubled soul from the astral plane perhaps, waiting for its next placement on the physical plane."
Renee shifted her vision to Elinger and rolled her eyes.

"Don't mock what you don't understand, Ms. Holland," Burris cautioned, obviously irritated by Renee's reaction.

"Sorry," Renee said. "But I'm a Christian. I don't believe in ghosts."

"But as a Christian you do believe everyone has a spirit and there is life after death, right?"

Renee nodded.

"Then you do believe in ghosts. It's just a matter of semantics," Burris said on a final note as he sat in a chair across the table from Renee. He was separated from her by an eighteen-inch high board that divided the table lengthwise. Burris reached into his pocket and withdrew a deck of cards. "Let's begin," he said. "We're going to use Zener cards for the first group of tests. They're a simple way to test for ESP, but they're very accurate. Twenty-five cards, five different images," Burris said, reaching over the table divider and spreading the cards on the table in front of Renee.

Renee studied the cards as Dr. Burris singled out five different symbols from the deck: a square, a circle, three wavy lines, a plus sign, and a star were marked in thick, black lines.

"I'm going to shuffle and draw cards," Burris said. "You'll try to name the symbol that I concentrate on. If you see it in your mind, write it down." Dr. Burris pointed at the note pad and pencil near Renee. "I can't tell how happy I am you agreed to participate, Ms. Holland. You see, if I can prove ESP causes your episodes, you could be the case of the century!"

Renee folded her arms over her abdomen. She realized Burris noticed her negative body language. It was unmistakable.

"Just go with the flow, Ms. Holland," Burris offered gently. "It's no big deal."

"I'll try," Renee muttered.

Burris pointed to a video camera mounted on the wall near the ceiling. "You don't mind, do you? I video all of my experiments."

"Do you really need to?" Renee asked unhappily.

"Yes. I want everything documented. As I mentioned, if I can prove ESP causes your episodes, it could be a milestone in our research. Lieutenant Elinger said taping wouldn't be a problem for you."

"He did, did he?" Renee said as she shot an annoyed look at Elinger.

Elinger just shrugged.

Renee looked back at Burris and nodded in resignation. "Okay, but Lieutenant Elinger doesn't always speak for me."

Burris winked. "I understand."

The eighteen-inch table divider prevented Renee from seeing the cards in Burris' hands. Burris shuffled the deck and cut the cards.

"Anybody can get five out of twenty-five just guessing," Burris told Renee. "So, give it your best. We've got all night if that's what it takes."

"Great," Renee said with a lack of enthusiasm. "I forgot to bring my favorite pillow."

Renee noticed the look of reprimand Burris gave her. "I know you don't give this much credence, Ms. Holland," Burris said. "But keep in mind even the government conducted ESP experiments during the Apollo fourteen flight. And whether you want to admit it or not, you are mentally connected to a killer. Don't you want to know why?'

With her best manners, Renee nodded and smiled. She wanted to solve the mystery as much as Dr. Burris did.

Dr. Burris began the Zener card Forced Choice test. He drew a card from the deck, looked at it and then closed his eyes to concentrate.

Renee studied the five different cards face up in front of her. She waited patiently, but didn't receive any mental images from Dr. Burris' mind. After an awkward period of silence, Renee guessed and recorded her answer on the pad of paper.

When the exam was completed, Renee had only six of twenty-five correct. She wasn't surprised she failed. She had guessed at each time.

Dr. Burris proceeded with several other tests. During the Free Response exercise, Burris locked his mind on an object in the room, but Renee was unable to "see it" in her mind. For another experiment, Burris put Renee behind a computer. Using a REG (random event generator) and radioactive decay (strontium 90), Burris created points of light on the computer screen. Renee was supposed to "influence" the lights with concentration, making them blink more often than expected by chance. Again, Renee received a low ESP rating. Then came the Uniform Field experiment. Wearing headphones that hissed static, Renee reclined on a couch with halved ping pong balls over her eyes. Her face was flooded with a bright pink floodlight. The purpose this test was to use sound and light to block all stimuli interference, hypothetically creating an easier avenue for psychic phenomena to occur. But when Burris "sent" mental images to Renee, she could not respond correctly.

As the tests progressed through the night, Elinger occasionally wandered from the room. He had discovered a vending machine in a nearby corridor. Elinger chuckled to himself. Maybe he had ESP? No matter where he went, he had a knack for discovering food and drink vending machines. And on this long evening, he welcomed the eye-widening kick from a caffeine-loaded soft drink.

Elinger looked at his watch, hoping the long night would end soon.

For the final test, Burris directed Renee back to the long table in the main room. This test, invented by Dr. Burris' himself, utilized piezoelectric crystals and tourmaline stones that distorted molecularly under the influence of electrical energy. This was a PK (psychokinetic) exam, Burris explained ardently. The crystals will take mentally generated electrical discharges that alter the stone's electrical field and direct them into an electronic oscillator. The resulting impulses are converted into melodic tones. If Renee could create a pattern of musical notes, she would be controlling the equipment with the power of her mind.

Renee narrowed her concentration on the small bluish-black rocks wired into an odd-looking piece of electronic audio gear connected to the oscillator, hoping to create musical tones. After several attempts, however, it was evident Renee could not do it. Instead, the equipment droned. But Renee knew Dr. Burris was tenacious and would want to give the test another try.

Renee focused obediently, attempting to send mental impulses to the crystals. For a moment there was no response, then her head suddenly jerked back and her eyes shot upward, hiding her pupils beneath her upper lids. The audio equipment screeched with an ear piercing sound, then the glassy crystals exploded in a belch of sparks and acrid smoke.

"Holy shit!" Dr. Burris shouted.

Elinger grabbed Renee's shoulders just as she was about to wilt to the floor.

Renee opened her dulled eyes. "What're you doing, Kent?" she asked lethargically, feeling his strong hands on her shoulders.

"You passed out."

"Another trance?" Renee asked.

Elinger nodded and turned to Dr. Burris. "What the hell happened?"

"She destroyed the crystals!" The tone of Burris' voice was one of genuine delight. "I've never seen anything like it!"

Renee's mind was still clearing. "What're you talking about?"

Elinger's gaze was still fixated on the sparkling crumbs littering the table. "Your trance obliterated the crystals. Look!"

Renee gazed at the stone chips. Some no bigger than grains of salt. She was astonished. Then she noticed something that filled her with grave concern.

Elinger's and Dr. Burris' eyes were also locked on the screen of a computer near Renee. A message shined brightly.

"My God, Ms. Holland," Burris mumbled. "It's from the killer, isn't it?"

"He likes to send me messages," Renee murmured grimly, studying the words, weary of their foreboding meaning.

Elinger's eyes roamed the message, as he read the note aloud:

My dear Madam Holland:

Let me beg your notice that only fools waste their time. Whilst you pittle about, your physical life becomes preciously short. Do not dally and reek with the stink of death. Play your role and spank along as you go, for the inevitable, as gruesome as you might think it to be, cannot be stopped!

Elinger, Renee, and Burris exchanged a long look of astonishment. Renee could see the apprehension in her body expressed in their faces.

NINETEEN

• • •

Elinger, Burris, and Renee emerged from the parapsychology building and huddled near the door while they buttoned their coats. Renee looked up at the sky. With the rising sun behind them, the gray clouds glowed like a bed of half-spent coals. Though they appeared warm, Renee also noticed a thick coat of frost had stiffened the Maryland University lawns. It looked like a light snow had fallen on the campus during the night.

As Elinger, Renee, and Burris began to move down a brick walkway, Burris shook his head, his breath casting drafts of white condensation as he spoke. "I don't understand it, Ms. Holland. You failed every test. Then, boom! You blow up the crystals and make ESP history!"

"I still feel like you're talking about somebody else," Renee said. "I don't remember it happening."

Dr. Burris glanced at the flash drive in his hand. "Well, let's thank all of our Gods that it's on video," he said, leading Elinger and Renee through a stand of willowy trees. "And you know what's really amazing?" he added, giving Renee a quick but penetrating look. "I don't think you're the source of this power.

You appear to be a conduit for this killer's physic forces!"

"I always knew it wasn't me," Renee said with a breath of relief.

"The message said it all. He's in control," Burris added, then tossed Elinger an uncomfortable glance. "Lieutenant, I know a creep with karma like this needs to be taken from this plane as quickly as possible by any means necessary, but I hope you bring him in alive so he can be studied. We could break new ground with him. I mean, just think of it—he's in such a heightened state when he kills that his mental force is received by another human being!"

Renee listened, not feeling any of Burris' passion. She just wanted all of this to end.

As the group passed another stand of trees, birds began to chirp the first melodies of the day.

"I don't want to change the subject, Dr. Burris," Renee began, her mind roaming. "But couldn't my writings be classified as automatic writing?"

"Auto-writing was something I considered, too. But I ruled it out."

"Why? From what I've read, the writer doesn't remember the actual writing—like me?"

"But auto-writing is usually inspired by a previous life or a disincarnate," Burris argued. "And obviously this killer is not dead."

Elinger's expression became reflective. "Do you think Renee writes the murders before they happen, as they happen, or after they happen?"

"I've been curious about that myself," Burris replied. "I think she writes about them as they occur."

"Why?" Elinger asked.

"Well, within seconds of the crystals exploding, the message appeared on the computer. It fit in the time frame we exist in."

"But you agreed that ESP broke the rules of physics," Elinger debated. "That time has no meaning."

"There are instances when paranormal laws are broken," Burris said. "I think our time frame is what we should go by. Both Renee and the killer live in it."

Renee looked at Elinger, realizing the answer had satisfied Elinger as she and the men cut across the grounds, crunching icy grass beneath their shoes. Burris abruptly halted. Elinger and Renee also stopped.

"Something just occurred to me," Burris said, running his fingers through his crimson hair. "This could be more than just you receiving a burst of mental energy, Ms. Holland. Your brain wave patterns could very well be the same as the killer's—for brief periods of time. That might explain how you can write with so much detail!"

Renee hear the excitement in Burris' voice.

"But from what I've read that's not possible," Elinger interjected. "Everybody's brain frequency is different, just like everybody's fingerprints are different."

"I know, I know," Burris agreed quickly. "I'm still trying to figure this thing out. There's something missing. An unknown factor, and I don't know what it is. But I do know one brain can intercept another brain's thoughts and Ms. Holland's situation goes well beyond that." Burris turned to Renee; his voice carried a tone of wonderment. "Your brain hooks up with the murderer's for long periods of time. Otherwise, you couldn't write complete drafts about the murders."

Renee snagged and dragged a few thoughts through her mind. "Maybe our brain waves are jamming temporarily like radio frequencies?"

Burris nodded and smiled as though he anticipated Renee's statement. "The mental radio theory is a standard concept of telepathy—that brains broadcast thoughts like radio stations transmit signals over the air."

"So, could I be receiving the killer's thoughts as though I'm a radio antenna?" Renee asked, ready to accept the theory.

"It's more than that, Ms. Holland," Burris replied. "It's like he's inside your head. Look at the detail of your writings. You're hearing what he thinks and seeing what he does!"

The idea of having interwoven brain patterns with a killer sickened Renee. Her expression cast a shadow of exhaustion.

Renee glanced at Elinger, hoping the look on her face would let him know the night had been long and tedious, and it was time to end it.

Elinger got the message. He stopped and extended a caffeine trembling hand toward Burris and shook his hand. "Thanks for your time, Doctor," Elinger said, giving Dr. Burris his card. "If you can think of anything that might help us, please call."

"Count on it," Burris answered. "I want to be part of this. Lab experiments serve their purpose, but to observe paranormal events outside the lab is the best way to isolate conclusive proof of the experience."

"One other thing, Doctor," Elinger said. "Do you know anyone who's an expert in this brain wave area? You know, a thoughts-are-things type philosopher?"

"Good idea, Lieutenant," Burris said. "Somebody like that might be able to help you. And I know just the guy. I haven't seen him in a few years. He used to be a professor in the US, then he went to India for advanced metaphysical studies. I heard he was back in the states. I'll see if I can track him down."

"We'd appreciate it," Elinger said.

"You know, the more I think about this brain wave theory, the more it makes sense," Burris said just before he turned and headed back to his building.

Elinger and Renee approached Elinger's auto in the University parking lot. Renee's face reflected the uncertainty of her dilemma. She stopped and turned to Elinger. "What do you make of all this, Kent?"

"I think what Dr. Burris said about the brain waves could be true."

"I was hoping you'd say he was wrong. I hate to think my mind is connected to the brain of a monster!"

Elinger placed a reassuring hand on Renee's shoulder. "Remember, we're really not sure of anything yet. That's why we came here. We're just checking out all the possible explanations. Something will break soon."

Renee found courage in his words and managed a smile. "I just hope it isn't me that breaks."

Elinger withdrew his hand from Renee's shoulder and reached for the car door. But Renee wanted his touch to remain. She savored the strong masculine warmth that lingered on her body.

Elinger looked back at Renee as he swung open the door.

Renee shifted her vision to Elinger's eyes. She felt a magnet tugging at her. She felt safe and glad when Elinger reached out and slowly pulled her to his chest. It felt so natural. Renee closed her eyes and buried her head in his shoulder.

"It's going to be okay, Renee. We'll find out what's happening to you and end it," Elinger promised.

Renee felt like a child in surrender, wanting to believe everything would be all right—but also knowing her predicament was well beyond anything normal. Right now, though, at least for these precious moments while she was in Elinger's arms, everything was good and she felt protected. She didn't want to let go.

TWENTY

• • •

Leaning over his stove, Elinger stirred a large pot of simmering chili. He drew the ladle toward his nose, inhaling the spicy aroma that feathered upward. He opened his mouth and savored a spoonful. It was damn good. With its full rich Texan flavor, it was the best he had ever made.

As Elinger minced onions on a chopping board, he considered how preparing a meal relaxed him. Cooking cleared his mind of trivial matters allowing him to think more clearly about his cases. The more complex the recipe, the more Elinger could dissect his work. And chili, Elinger had learned, was the best mind food for him. He chuckled quietly to himself, realizing he was probably the only Baltimore citizen who had a penchant for Texas style chili.

Elinger crossed his living room, moving to his writing desk. The desk, with its tambour front and *églomisé* panel, was Elinger's one and only piece of antique furniture. When he bought it at an estate sale, he figured he needed something in his home that matched the ambience of his neighborhood. The Otterbein area, where he lived, was once a half-vacant, down-trodden enclave of Federal Period homes. But when city leaders offered the houses for one dollar to anyone willing to invest money to restore them, Elinger joined the rush to restore part of Baltimore's history. In a short time, Elinger had turned his home into a wise investment.

Elinger turned on his expensive stereo system that rested on the desk top. Tall speakers sat on the floor near him. He punched a button on the receiver and within seconds a Mendelssohn concerto flowed through the house.

Back in the kitchen again, Elinger stirred his chili and listened to the graceful Mendelssohn melody. It freed his mind to think about his case. His process of analysis was compulsive, perhaps obsessive, but Elinger wanted to find out what was happening to Renee Holland. He believed she didn't fake the trances and couldn't have staged the exploding crystals. As fantastic as it seemed, a strange force had taken over her mind, and he had seen it himself. Other aspects of the case puzzled him, too. Why were the M.O.'s of the killings so different and bizarre? A swinging crane as a murder weapon? A prostitute buried in concrete with a 9-volt battery in her mouth? Neither made sense, but Elinger knew they had meaning for the killer. If only the pages revealed more about the murderer, there would be better clues. But so far, nothing significant had been revealed about the killer's identity.

Elinger tasted his chili again as he contemplated his investigation's more practical side. He was using every available resource to track the killer. Downtown CI's (Confidential Informants) were alert for a one-eared man who might be living amongst them. Other police officers were undercover, giving up their personal lives to spend their days and nights in alleys and mingle with those whose only home was a piece of sidewalk. And still nothing turned in Elinger's favor.

The phone rang, breaking into Elinger's thoughts.

"You better come down to Headquarters right away, Kent," Torres' voice sounded strained through the connection. "The captain is really blowin' some smoke about you!"

"What is it this time?" Elinger asked, shaking his head regrettably.

"You really think he'd tell me?" Torres said with a dark chuckle. "I'm just a second-class citizen around here 'til I prove myself. Whatever it is though, he'll send out a SWAT team for you if you don't get your ass down here pronto."

"Okay, tell Ozzie to keep his hemorrhoids tucked in until I get there."

"He said to meet him out in front of Headquarters," Torres added.

Elinger shook his head. "He must be smoking again," Elinger surmised, hanging up the phone. He wondered what had inflamed Osborne? But it really didn't matter, he figured. He needed to see the captain and tell him what had developed in the Holland case. Elinger only hoped it wouldn't give Captain Osborne a stroke.

● ● ●

"What the hell's this all about, Kent?!" Captain Osborne spewed anger past the smoldering cigarette that dangled from his mouth. The fifty-seven-year-old Captain and Chief of Detectives paced stiffly in front of the Headquarter's building, his short, husky body as rigid as his mood. Above his bushy, gray eyebrows was a shiny patch of skin surrounded by thin, over-combed hair. His half-glasses had slid down his oily nose and perched at the loop of his nostrils.

Elinger approached Osborne, eyeing the sheet of paper the captain had just pushed into his hands.

"Do you know what this is?" Osborne asked, stopping at Elinger's side.

"Looks like the results of a psychic test," Elinger replied bluntly after a closer examination of it. "And it's addressed to me. Isn't it a federal crime to open other people's mail," Elinger asked Osborne directly.

"It came to me like this from the mail room," Osborne replied in a non-apologetic tone, locking his alert, red-rimmed eyes on Elinger. "I guess someone else here thinks you're losin' it besides me. Why are you testing our prime murder suspect for ESP, for Christ's sake?" Osborne fired, his tongue licking his upper lip without disturbing his cigarette. "Are you out of your fucking mind?"

"I thought you would be in a bad mood, Ozzie," Elinger said calmly. "It happens every time you start smoking again. I guess I shouldn't have come."

Osborne's eyes suddenly flamed. "Stop with that goddamn name! You can call me anything but Ozzie!" Clamping his nicotine stained teeth, Captain Osborne severed the cigarette in his mouth. The glowing end dropped into the sidewalk near a few other butts. Osborne turned from Elinger momentarily and spat the filter into a nearby trash can, then lit another cigarette. "Kent, from day one you've been my shining star. That's why I listen to you when you do something crazy—but this? How could ESP be important to this case?"

Elinger hesitated before he spoke.

Osborne realized Elinger would rather not answer the question.

"I think there's something paranormal about the killings, and they affect Renee Holland," Elinger finally admitted.

"Oh, really? And how did you come to that conclusion?"

"You read Ms. Holland's pages, didn't you?"

"Yeah, it's real simple. The killer confessed to her or she's the killer!"

"You're wrong, Cap," Elinger said.

"It doesn't matter if I am," Osborne replied, snatching the paper from Elinger's hand. "I can't let the Deputy Mayor know about this. Christ, he'd tell the Mayor!"

Osborne took in a deep breath, paced a few steps before returning to Elinger's side. He was trying to dismiss his temper. "Kent, talk to me. What's with this ESP shit?"

"Remember the Watkins case a few years back?" Elinger asked.

"She was the woman who had the weird dreams about a body in the woods, right?"

Elinger nodded. "We all laughed at her until she led us to the corpse and made fools of us. After that, we all agreed there was something to psychic phenomena. Remember?"

"So, what are you trying to tell me?" Osborne asked. "That this Holland woman is a psychic?"

"Something like that."

The captain took a long drag on his cigarette and frowned.

"Now that you've officially certified her, maybe you'd like for her to open a palmistry shop in our lobby? Or conduct a séance at our next briefing? And if she can talk to the dead, I still have a few things I'd like to say to my dearly departed ex-wife!"

"Just let me do the work I need to do, Cap," Elinger implored. "Like you did when I worked the Harbor Strangler case."

Elinger's words stirred Osborne's memory as Osborne was sure that was Elinger's intention. After a long, cheek puckering inhalation of his cigarette, Osborne's expression lost its hard edges. "Yes, the Strangler case. You really had me on that one. God, how long has it been, Kent?"

"Fifteen years, maybe?"

A rare smile crossed Osborne's lips. He reflected on the years that had caused him to develop great respect and admiration for Elinger. Elinger's nearly flawless crime solving abilities had placed him at the top of Osborne's great cop list. Elinger had been instrumental in solving many of Baltimore's most heinous crimes—the Harbor Strangler, the East Baltimore Rapist, and the Sterling Street Stalker. Elinger had been just a green cop when Osborne first met him. When Osborne, then a sergeant, found himself short of officers during a severe flu epidemic, he had no choice but to assign Elinger to the Harbor Strangler Case. Ten young women were murdered. The older pros had come up empty handed so Headquarters was desperate.

Osborne recalled how the case held many peculiarities for Elinger. Elinger had wondered why did the victims' bodies show little signs of a struggle. Why were there no shrieks of terror heard by others? How could the women be lured from the heavily populated Harbor area and later found dead in secluded environs? From the onset, Elinger realized the victims had trusted their killer. Were they killed by a friend? A relative? Or by a figure of authority?

Upon close examination of the victim's personal lives, Osborne remembered how Elinger had pieced together the clues like an architect builds a house and soon discovered the strangler was a cop. In uniform, the rogue cop lured young women from the Harbor to secluded areas on the pretext they were helping with a crime investigation that offered a large reward. The women were unsuspecting until it was too late. The case had been unsolved for over a year. When Elinger cracked it, he earned the instant respect of his peers and Robert Osborne. Osborne rationalized that was why he allowed Elinger to occasionally employ inventive methods of investigation that don't always square up with police procedure.

"Fifteen years, huh?" Osborne muttered, finishing the march of years through his mind. "Where does the time go? I've backed you nine out of ten times ever since the Strangler case, but it's not the same anymore. The mayor and his brown-nosing deputy mayor watch everything we do like we're a bunch of kids who fuck up all the time."

Osborne moved closer to Elinger and placed an arm on his shoulder. "Let's face it, Kent. The Watkins case was a fluke. We've never encountered ESP since then."

"Until now," Elinger countered. "I have no other explanation for Renee Holland's pages or her trances."

Osborne lapsed into silence, losing his will to fight for control of the conversation any longer. He pushed his cigarette into a nearby planter. "Goddammit, Kent! We go through this ritual every time, don't we? And *every* time you prove me wrong!"

"I think you're burning yourself," Elinger said, pointing at the planter.

Osborne looked down. He hadn't removed his thumb from the burning cigarette. "Shit!" he exclaimed, withdrawing his hand from the hot ember.

Osborne rubbed his thumb and growled with resignation. "Okay, Kent. Prove me wrong. Just keep it quiet. I can't have anything like this floating around Headquarters," Osborne warned, tearing the ESP report into shreds and tossing it in his wastebasket. "I'll make sure nobody opens your mail from now on."

"Okay, Cap."

Osborne reorganized his frown. "If the deputy mayor finds out what you're doing, I'll need a bulldozer to cover my ass, but it would only take a teaspoon to bury you! Do you understand?"

"Perfectly."

"And if he does finds out, I'm going to pretend it's one helluva surprise to me," Osborne added regretfully.

"I knew I could count on you," Elinger said dryly.

Osborne shook his head. "Just get the hell out of here and bring me back a murderer! Personally, I don't give a damn how you do it. Just do it!"

"Okay, Ozzie," Elinger said.

"And don't call me that anymore! I hate that fuckin' name!" Osborne shouted as he moved toward the entrance of Headquarters.

TWENTY-ONE

• • •

Sitting at a table in the George Peabody Library, Renee was studying the half-dozen books she had spread out in front of her. She read from one of them for a moment, then blinked her tired eyes, and glanced at the neo-Renaissance grandeur surrounding her. The black and white ceramic floor beneath her feet, the open, interior five-story courtyard where she sat, the grooved columns rising to the high ceiling, the tiered floors housing over 250,000 books and the massive, paned skylight were familiar sights to Renee. She happily recalled her many visits to the Peabody to research bygone eras to enrich her novels. Renee regretted thather visits to the library had become less frequent with the wealth of research available online.

Across the courtyard from Renee, Elinger leaned over the second floor's gold-leaf handrail, his eyes quickly searching every face that occupied the levels above and below him. After a moment, he found what he was looking for—Renee.

Elinger moved down a flight of stairs to the first floor and approached a nearby table. Renee glanced up from a book and was surprised to see Elinger. Watching his self-assured, masculine strides caused her to forget what she was   reading.

Elinger slid into a chair next to Renee and greeted her with a broad smile.

"What're you doing here?" Renee asked in a whisper, secretly glad to see him.

"I have an overdue book," Elinger joked quietly. Renee grinned. "I don't recall asking for a guardian angel."

"Did it ever occur to you that you could be in danger?" Elinger asked.

Renee noticed Elinger's light mood had suddenly evaporated. He was being protective of her. She liked that.

"If the killer can find your mind, he can probably find you," Elinger added.

"You're following me to protect me?" she asked, touched by Elinger's concern.

Elinger confirmed it with a nod.

Renee's mood softened. "I guess I won't mind a little baby-sitting," she said, studying Elinger's strong features, wondering if he was experiencing the same attraction she did. His presence made her feel safe. She already had too many anxiety-filled days and nights alone—and the resulting vulnerability worried her. She didn't want to become entangled in an improbable romance. She thought she might surrender to Elinger under the right conditions. Renee wasn't sure of his feelings, however, and for the moment she hoped nature would either draw them together or keep them apart.

Elinger glanced at the books on the table and read aloud from the bindings: "Doyle, Collins, Sue, Hume. They wrote detective mysteries in the eighteen-hundreds, didn't they?"

Renee grinned at Elinger. "I guess I shouldn't be too amazed you knew that. You did take some American Lit classes in college, right?"

Elinger cocked his head. "How'd you know that?"

"Research," Renee answered, happily smug. "You've been checking me out so I thought I'd do the same to you."

"What else did you learn?" Elinger asked.

Renee smiled confidently, knowing she would surprise Elinger with what she knew. "You're a graduate from the University of Maryland with a Masters in Criminal Justice and Criminology. But you went to law school first, and you dropped out. Why?"

"A law career was my father's idea," Elinger answered. "I wanted to please him. What else do you know?"

"After college you joined the Baltimore P.D.," Renee continued. "Then you solved the Harbor Strangler case. That made you a prince among detectives."

"You've put royalty in my veins. I'm flattered."

"What made you decide to become a cop?" Renee asked.

Elinger reflected for a moment and gave Renee a brief, whimsical smile. "When I was younger, I was sure I could make the world a safer place—that I could make a difference by being a cop."

"Have you?"

"Not exactly. The most we can do is keep the balance. We can confuse and defuse the bad guys, but most of the time we're just postponing their next crime."

"So, you don't like being a policeman either?"

"Actually, I love it."

"But you sound so grim about it."

"Only when I think of the big picture. Day by day, it's great. When I get up in the morning, I don't know what my day's going to bring. Anything can happen. I like that. I hate routine."

"One more question, okay?"

"Sure."

"County records say you're married. I wondered about that because you don't wear a ring."

A shadow crossed Elinger's face. "I'm a widower."

"I'm sorry," Renee said, regretful she had pried.

"It's okay, really." Elinger said. "I've worked through it, I think. It's been five years now. A drunk crossed the center line. It happened so fast my wife didn't know what hit her. Thank God, she didn't suffer."

Elinger glanced down at another of Renee's books. "Francois Eugene Vidocq?" he abruptly said. "If I remember correctly, Vidocq was a French detective who wrote mysteries based on his experiences as a policeman."

"Yes," Renee answered.

"Do you like to read old detective stories?" Elinger asked, studying the books with obvious interest. "Or are you researching?"

"You're probably going to think I'm crazy, but I'm comparing my blackout writings to the works of last century authors."

Renee saw Elinger's mouth tighten with surprise. "Why?" he asked.

"Some of the words in my pages are anachronisms," Renee explained. "And many of the passages read like they were written last century. I wanted to find out if I was right."

"You think someone who knows nineteenth century literature is the killer?"

"My trance writings are not contemporary," Renee said, slapping a hand on one of the books. "It's from this era. And I can't find much of this era online, but this place has it all."

"Have you found anything to prove your theory?"

"I think so. In the first note, the killer used the word *prolixity*. It's not common today, but it was in the eighteen-hundreds."

"What does it mean?"

"Verbosity of writing or speaking," Renee replied. "Just like my writings. An excess of words to express ideas. It's the way most authors wrote back then."

"What else did you find out?"

"In the second note, the word *woe* is spelled *w-o*. That's an archaic spelling," Renee explained. "I'm trying to find it spelled that way in one of these books."

"Have you?"

"Not yet, but there's hundreds more to go through,' Renee answered, briefly despairing about the amount of work that would entail.

Elinger leaned forward in his chair. "Did you notice the word cattymount in your pages?"

"Yes, but I haven't looked it up yet."

"You won't find it spelled with a *y*," Elinger reported. "Unless you have a very old dictionary. Today it's spelled with an *a* instead of a *y*."

Renee tilted her head with confusion. "You've been

researching the writing?"

"The old words and phrases caught my eye, too," Elinger admitted with a grin.

Looking at Elinger's expression, Renee realized he had enjoyed his brief charade of ignorance.

Faintly amused, Renee shook her head. "So, why'd you ask me all these questions?"

"I wanted to see how resourceful you are. I could use you at Headquarters."

"Thanks anyway, but I happen to like routine. Now tell me what you found out," Renee asked impatiently.

"Nothing that'll help us."

Renee closed the book she was studying. "I still think the killer likes nineteenth century literature. Maybe he's a literature professor or something?"

"Or a literate actor," Elinger added. "Or a librarian? Or a literature student? Maybe a publisher? Or someone who simply loves to read nineteenth century books."

Renee sighed. "You're saying I'm wasting my time?"

"Not at all. I think you should keep at it, and I'm going to help you."

Elinger's arms were filled with a dozen books when he and Renee emerged from the Peabody's Greek-Revival building. Walking against a skyline plumed with the bonnets of stately trees, Elinger allowed a relentless, puzzling thought to turn into words. "I can't figure out why the killer's M.O. is so strange," he said through his gravely composed face. "Why did he use a crane to kill those men at the shipyard? Why not a gun or a knife?"

"And why did he bury a battery with the prostitute?" Renee added, further fanning the mystery. "Makes your job more difficult, doesn't it? When there's no pattern to the murders?"

"Yeah, but I think I know how to get to him."

"How?"

Elinger's reply was short and to the point. "By using you."

Renee stopped walking and turned to Elinger. "Using me? How?"

Elinger halted and faced Renee. He had already given his answer much credence. "When you're in a trance, you write where the murder is taking place. If you're writing reality as it happens like Dr. Burris thinks, maybe I could get to the location and catch this guy in the act."

Elinger watched Renee as she considered it.

"It's worth a try," Renee agreed. "Obviously, I don't want anyone else to get killed."

"I'll need to spend a lot of time with you," Elinger said, attempting to conceal his personal enthusiasm for the assignment.

Renee smiled at Elinger. "That's better than being followed like a criminal."

"And much easier to do," Elinger said.

As Elinger and Renee continued walking from the library's grounds, Renee slipped her arm though the crook of his elbow to test his reaction. She didn't have to wait long. Elinger pulled his arm close to his side, snugly tucking Renee's arm there. This made Renee feel more comfortable with Elinger than ever before—and safer.

As they approached the cobblestone street where
Renee had parked her sports car, Renee contemplated Elinger's
willingness to help her. He didn't have to put in the extra hours
that he did. She knew he was a good man who cared about people.
He was compassionate, handsome and cerebral. She liked those
qualities. But what woman didn't? Renee couldn't remember the
last time she had met someone like him. And, she admitted to
herself, there was another, more primal attraction. She wanted
Elinger. She pictured him as an imaginative and athletic lover. She
could only hope he wanted her, too.

Elinger sat on Renee's couch, admiring her staircase's
Victorian handiwork. He had missed it on his first visit. Glancing
at other items, he silently praised Renee's taste for antiques.

Renee entered the room holding two snifters half-filled
with brandy. She handed one to Elinger, then raised the other. "To
the evil that lives in my head and fingertips," she toasted in a half-
serious, half-jest tone. "May we cancel its lease on my life."

"Amen," Elinger said as he and Renee clinked glasses,
then sipped their brandy.

After savoring the brandy's flavor, Elinger asked,
"Where's Alex?"

"With his father for the weekend."

"That's great they spend time together."

"I only wish it was quality time," Renee said.

"They don't get along?"

"Considering that my ex is a dour, cynical, self-centered,
image-conscious, full-time jerk, they do okay."

"How did you get mixed up with someone like him?"

Elinger asked with a deep note of curiosity.

"He was charming when he wanted to be. As smooth as this brandy," Renee said, rotating her glass and watching the fingers of the liquor cling to its sides. "I was young and dumb, but it didn't take me long to find out how cold and uncaring he really was. Toward me, I could understand. But to his son is unforgivable. I could go on and on about that, but I don't want to bore you."

Elinger grinned. "I believe the word is *prolixity*."

Renee smiled. "Yes, and I don't want to bring it back into the twenty-first century."

"You're very candid," Elinger complimented. "I like people who are honest."

"That's what dear ol' mom taught me," Renee said. "Always be honest. I was honest to everyone but myself when I fell in love with William. Nothing makes a young woman more stupid than love. But I should've known our marriage was doomed from the beginning anyway."

"Why?"

"Because William and I met in a traffic jam," Renee said. "And that best describes our marriage. Our tempers were short, we never yielded, we overheated whenever we discussed anything, and we went nowhere in a hurry." Renee hesitated before she spoke again. "I must feel comfortable around you," she said. "It's obvious I don't mind baring my soul to you."

"It's okay," Elinger said. "I won't call the tabloids."

"Thank you for that," Renee smiled at the remark and sipped the last of her brandy.

"I wanted to ask you about your book," Elinger said. "Have you been able to make any progress?"

"Not a word," Renee replied. "My agent Marty called me and said the publisher had cancelled our contract. So, I gave them back their advance and told Marty I would call him when I felt like I could get back in the game."

"Sorry to hear that."

"It's just one more kink in my life right now," Renee said as she yawned. "I'm going to bed, Kent," she said, drowsily. "If anything's going to happen, it won't matter if I'm asleep or awake."

"I'll listen for you."

Renee turned and padded across the room toward the staircase.

Elinger watched Renee, wishing he could follow her. Her round, firm buttocks seemed to sway to the cadence of a poem as she moved up the stairs and disappeared into her room.

Kicking off his shoes, Elinger leaned back on the couch. His mind boiled over with thoughts about the case. He needed a break in his investigation and he hoped Renee would provide it with her next trance.

Later that night, Renee tossed and turned fitfully. A piercing headache had awakened her, pounding her skull with the force of a sledgehammer. Sitting up in bed, she realized fearfully she was only minutes from another trance and possibly another killing. As the black cloud began to engulf her, her last conscious thought was a prayer that Elinger could prevent another innocent person from being murdered.

TWENTY-TWO

• • •

Faint and rhythmic clicking sounds slowly pulled Elinger from a deep sleep. He rose from Renee's couch, realizing they were coming from the upstairs den. Renee was working on her computer, and she was probably in a trance, Elinger concluded quickly as he bolted up the stairs. He entered the room and stopped abruptly when he saw Renee.

Renee sat in front of her computer. Her eyes were sightless agates, rolled up and locked in a dead stare at the ceiling. Her fingers tap-danced across the keyboard, adding the soft tapping sounds to the quiet of the night.

Elinger rushed to Renee and waved a hand in front of her zombie-like stare. There was no reaction. Elinger glanced at the monitor, reading a few of the sentences as they streaked across the screen. The words detailed a colorful sunrise behind a small 2-story home. Elinger turned toward Renee's window and saw the same fiery sun in the distance. Dr. Burris was correct, Elinger realized. Renee wrote reality as it happened—murder in real time. A rush of adrenaline shot through him when he became aware he had a chance to stop the next killing.

Elinger read more of the passages. Renee described a small, imported hybrid sedan rolling to a stop in front of a home. A bald-headed man in his forties emerged. The man's face tightened with pain as he closed the car door with bent and curled fingers. His shoes were clotted with fresh blood.

• • •

Across town, Ravnik was crouched in curbside bushes, watching the bald man that was the focus of Renee's latest trance-writing episode. He saw the man retrieve a jacket from the small hybrid sedan and walk toward the house.

Ravnik's twitching, blood lined eyes trailed the man entering the house. Ravnik blinked away the quivering movements of his eyelids. As he stood, he recalled how he had arrived at this address. Before dawn, the voice had entered his head and directed him to the Hampden community. It had been a long walk, Ravnik remembered, ending here where row houses were made of clapboard, shingle, stone and brick shell. During the trek, the voice explained Ravnik's task—the killing of a bald-headed man with blood caked shoes.

Ravnik stepped from the curb and began to cross the street toward the house.

"*Stop*," the voice suddenly ordered in Ravnik's head. "*There are policemen in the immediate vicinity! We must terminate our plans!*"

Ravnik stopped, noticing approaching headlights that beamed through the day's first gray light. He quickly stepped back and crouched behind the curbside shrubbery again. A blue and white patrol car cruised past him. Ravnik was impressed the voice knew there were cops in the neighborhood.

"*We cannot eliminate this man with police in our proximity, Leonard,*" the voice warned. "*Your escape would be compromised.*"

"But they're gone now," Ravnik argued. "Just a routine patrol."

"*You are involuntarily compulsive, Mr. Ravnik. We have many future acts to commit, and we cannot chance their failure on this one man,*" the voice stated matter-of-factly. "*It would be foolish for us to think so paltry.*"

"But you sent me here to kill him before, and I failed," Ravnik reminded the voice angrily. "I want to finish the job tonight!"

"*There is no great difficulty in waiting for the right time,*" the voice said. "*We will kill him on another day. Do not contest this point with me!*" the voice warned.

Ravnik did not reply. He considered what the voice said as he studied the house across the street. He still wanted to kill the bald man.

"*The unexpected appearance of the police has bestowed a grand idea upon me,*" the voice revealed. "*We will take the life from this man in a different manner than we planned. This would confuse the police and make their search for us a fantastic conundrum!*"

"A what?" Ravnik asked.

"*An intricate and difficult problem,*" the voice replied. "*I must congratulate myself! The killing will be as spectacular as your shipyard mayhem. Suffocating this man would only make our game mundane and easy to solve.*"

Ravnik contemplated the voice's words. If the voice has new plans for a special killing, he knew it would satisfy his lust for blood. So far, the voice had lived up to its promises of grim grandeur. The more bizarre and gruesome the murder, the more Ravnik would be pleased.

● ● ●

Back in Renee's den, Renee's fingers tapped the keyboard a few more times, then she stopped with a sudden, stroke-like tremor. A guttural moan parted Renee's lips and her pupils dropped into their proper place. She glanced weakly at Elinger, looking like a drunk surfacing from a blackout.

Elinger regretted he could not offer Renee comforting words. He knew they were both powerless against their adversary, whoever or whatever it was.

Renee inhaled deeply, clearing the final fog from her head. "What did I write?"

"I couldn't keep up with all of it," Elinger replied. "Print it out."

Renee clicked the print icon on the screen and paper began to emerge from the printer.

Elinger grabbed a few pages and began to read. "You've described a man," he began. "He's bald, in his forties and probably the next victim. He lives in the Baltimore area, in a two-story, clapboard house and drives a small import car."

"Was he murdered?" Renee asked in a concerned tone.

Elinger did not reply immediately. He extracted more

pages from the printer and scanned them quickly. "Not according to this," he answered. "It says this bald guy is coming home from a graveyard shift." Elinger lifted his eyes from the pages and looked abruptly at Renee. "You wrote his name!"

Renee's expression became one of surprise. "His name?"

"Yes, Richard Smith. Maybe we can get to him before the murderer does?" Elinger said hopefully, then his tone of optimism faded. "But let's not break out the champagne yet. There's probably fifty Richard Smith's in Baltimore."

Renee nodded, taking a couple of pages from Elinger's hand. She read a few lines. Her expression clouded. "That foul-looking, one-eared man was there."

Elinger bobbed his head. "Yeah, same guy at the shipyard, same guy who killed the prostitute," he said, still browsing the pages.

Elinger began to pace the room as he read. "It says here that although this Richard Smith was not killed today, he will be killed soon." Elinger stopped and looked at Renee. "So, I don't have much time to find him. I'll send someone over to watch you," he added, suddenly moving toward the door. "I'll call you every hour," Elinger promised, pitching his words over his shoulder. He didn't want to leave Renee, but he felt he had no other choice. Time was running out. A second attempt to murder the bald-headed man could occur at any time.

"I'll look forward to your calls," Renee said.

But her words were not heard by Elinger. He had already disappeared from the room.

● ● ●

An hour later, Elinger and Torres exited Headquarters and headed for their autos in the parking lot. They discussed their search for Richard Smith. Elinger had been correct. Over fifty Richard Smith's were listed in the telephone directory. The ones he and Torres had already reached by phone did not work night shifts or match the sketchy description in Renee's pages. Several of the Smiths were not at home. Elinger put their homes, especially the two-story clapboards, under surveillance so he could talk to them as soon as they returned.

Elinger wondered how many unlisted Richard Smiths existed. Because of Maryland law, Elinger gave a subpoena to the local phone company for those records. He was told he would have them by dusk, including all cell numbers. Elinger had also asked the DMV database for all the addresses of Richard Smiths who have driver's licenses. And finally, because of the blood on Smith's shoes, Elinger ordered his men to check-out hospitals, medical labs, mortuaries, University test labs, veterinary hospitals, butcher shops, and meat packing plants for employees named Richard Smith who worked a graveyard shift. But all of this, Elinger knew, could take up a lot of time. He wondered how much time he really had to save Richard Smith.

TWENTY-THREE

• • •

Richard Smith's alarm rang at six p.m., waking him for his graveyard shift. He slid from beneath the covers and sat on a corner of his bed, wearing a loose-fitting T-shirt and boxer shorts. Wincing painfully, he rubbed his stiff hands on his thighs, trying to splay his curled fingers. He hoped the warmth would ease the ache and loosen the tendons.

Smith's eyes roamed his dim bedroom. The sparse decor of second-rate pine furniture reminded him of his mediocre existence. More failures than successes made his life what it was. Although he worked hard and saved, Smith regretted he had never become financially comfortable—the good life was always just out of his reach. Looking at his hands again, Smith saw that his fingers had retracted into their painful fetal positions again.

Smith moved into his kitchen and stopped at a sink full of dirty dishes. He wrapped a gnarled finger around the faucet handle and turned on the hot water. He let his hands absorb the heat, uncurling one finger at a time under the water. This was his daily ritual. Without it, he would not be able to do his job. If only his hands would hold out a few more years, he hoped. He would retire and use his pension to start another life.

Back in his bedroom, Smith opened his closet door to remove the clothes he was going to wear. He somberly remembered the day his doctor diagnosed him with arthritis and how this degeneration of his fingers would be aggravated by his job. Smith worked at the most hand-straining job in the meat processing industry—boning meat. His hands, in near freezing temperatures, made the same cutting motion at least fifteen thousand times a day. The doctor had told Smith to quit, but he couldn't. Being a butcher was his only skill.

●   ●   ●

"Lieutenant Elinger is having a detective come over tonight, honey," Renee said, standing in the doorway of Alex's bedroom. "If I space out again, Kent will be notified immediately. He's hoping my writing will help him catch the killer."

Alex stood next to his bed, unpacking his suitcase from a weekend visit to his father's. He stopped and looked up at his mother. "What's with this Kent stuff?" he asked.

"He said I could call him by his first name."

"Do you like him?"

"Maybe? Does that bother you?"

"I don't like him!" Alex said honestly.

Renee could hear the anger in Alex's voice. She stepped into Alex's room and began to help him pull his clothes from the suitcase. "I admit he was a little brash at first, but he's really a nice man. Just give him a chance, okay?"

Alex shook his head. "You can like him, but I don't have

to."

"Just try, okay?" Renee urged, irritated by Alex's attitude. "He really cares about what happens to us. And believe me, we need all the help we can get."

Alex fell silent and said no more.

Renee looked at her son, realizing she had made her point. Alex knew it was useless to try to change his mother's mind.

When the Holland doorbell rang, Alex bolted down the stairs and opened the front door. Standing on the porch was Detective Jay Sanders. His hands were buried deep in the pockets of a long tan overcoat. Alex could easily read into Sanders diffident expression. It was clear the detective wanted to be somewhere else.

Sanders looked past Alex when Renee approached the door. "Ms. Holland?" he said, extending his hand.
Renee shook Sanders' hand. "Yes."

"I'm Lieutenant Sanders. You were expecting me," Sanders said.

"Yes" Renee greeted. "Please come in."

Sanders stepped into the living room, slid out of his jacket and handed it to Alex as though Alex was a butler.
Sanders scanned the interior of the house. "So, where's the big event usually take place?" he asked.

Renee could not hide her aggravation of Sander's sarcastic remark. "Excuse me?"

"You know, when the bogeyman takes over your body."

"Drop the attitude, Mister!" Alex exclaimed, turning to his mother. "You don't have to take this crap, Mom!"

"Alex! Watch your language!" Renee ordered.

Alex shook his head and moved toward the stairs, tossing Sanders' jacket on the couch in a rumpled heap. "If this Kent dude is so cool, why'd he send over such a jerk?"

After Alex climbed the stairs out of earshot, Renee hooked eyes with Detective Sanders. "Let's get one thing straight, Mr. Detective," she bristled her words. "My son is right. I don't have to take any crap from you. What's happening to me is very real. Treat it that way or get the hell of my home! Do you understand?"

Sanders appeared caught off-guard by Renee's fiery directness. "Hey, don't panic, Ms. Holland. I just don't believe in this stuff. There's always a logical explanation."

Renee slowly let an off-beat smile blossom on her lips. "Well, Mr. Sanders, maybe I can give you a new perspective on the bogeyman," she said, suddenly feeling the first twangs of another monster headache.

A crescent moon was embedded in the black fabric of the night sky. A single light shined from the den window of Renee's otherwise darkened house.

Renee sat in front of her computer, staring blankly through hazed eyes. A new trance was at work. Although Renee's fingers tapped the keyboard, she was oblivious to the description she was writing. She detailed how Richard Smith drove his small hybrid car into a large parking lot and parked it in a neatly lined space. A moment later, Smith emerged from his auto carrying a lunch pail. Renee continued typing, writing that Smith walked across the lot toward a block-long brick building and entered it.

Renee's fingertips continued to drum the keys, sending

more information zinging across the screen. She described Smith moving from a locker room into the plant's main working area. He was now wearing a hard hat and long white apron.

In the living room, Renee's television broadcasted a late night talk show. Detective Sanders was slumped on the couch in a deep snore.

Alex, wearing pajamas, dashed into the living room, grabbed Sanders' arm and shook it urgently. "Wake up! Wake up!" he yelled.

Sander's eyes suddenly popped open. "What's the matter?" he asked with a start.

"It's my mom! She's whacked-out again! C'mon!" Alex shouted as he bolted from Sanders and sprinted up the stairs toward the den. Sanders jumped to his feet and followed quickly.

Alex rushed to his mother's side and stood there. He watched her through an expression tensed by fear.

Sanders hesitated in the doorway, perplexed when he saw Renee. She sat stiff, like she was frozen, hammering the keyboard, sending sentences shooting across the computer screen. Her eyes were locked with the stare of a dead person.

Sanders stepped farther into the room, his reaction softening. He suddenly spoke with a humorless grin. "Great performance, Ms. Holland. Had me fooled for a minute."

Renee didn't respond. Her granite expression remained as she continued to strike the keyboard.

Sanders moved behind her, placing his hands on her shoulders and shook her. "Great fun, Ms. Holland. But spook time is over. Now snap out of it!"

Renee spun toward Sanders and elbowed him mid-chest with a powerful sweep of her arm.

Sanders was thrown backward with his feet lifting from the floor for a moment. He stumbled across the room, crashing into a wall and sagging to the floor.

Hardly missing a keystroke, Renee redirected her energies on the computer's keyboard.

Alex rushed to Sanders who was trying to corral his senses. "Are you okay?"

Sanders clutched his side. "I think she broke a couple of ribs."

"Do you believe us now?" Alex asked in a smug voice.

Sanders nodded quietly. "I've got to call Lieutenant Elinger. Go see if your mother wrote anything that can help us. I'm not getting near her again."

Alex hurried back to the computer and studied the screen for a few seconds. "The guy named Smith works in a slaughterhouse! He's there now!" Alex called out to Sanders.

"Does it give a name of the place?" Sanders asked as he stood, sucking air carefully. He raised an arm and gingerly braced his throbbing side with his other hand.

"I don't see any."

"Shit!" Sanders uttered, pulling his cell phone from his pocket.

● ● ●

Driving down a Baltimore street, Elinger and Torres were

headed for the next address on their Richard Smith list. Elinger's cell phone rang. He pulled it from its belt clip and heard Sanders' voice squawking loudly. "She's in a trance, Kent, and going crazy on her computer!"

"What's she writing?" Elinger asked anxiously.

"This Smith guy works in a meat processing plant," Sanders reported. "He's on his shift now. But the pages don't name the place."

"Is there anything that'll help us? Like is it big, small, old, new?"

"It says here, it's a big place where they do everything— kill, bone, and grind."

Urgency crept into Elinger's voice. "Anything about a one-eared man or a homeless type person being there?"

"Yeah! There's a description of a guy with one ear and shitty looking clothes. He's in a field near the plant."

"Thanks, Jay." Elinger said, then clicked a button on the police radio microphone. "Dispatch, this is Elinger."

"Yes, Lieutenant," the dispatcher's voice crackled.

"Tell my guys to drop everything and get me a list of the largest meat processing plants in the city!"

TWENTY-FOUR

• • •

Wearing his gloves, Ravnik stood on a grassy knoll that overlooked the slaughter-house. He had seen Richard Smith enter the building earlier. Ravnik's eyes tremored slightly as the voice entered his head.

"*Mr. Smith will be engaged in his work now. The hour has arrived,*" the voice said.

Ravnik nodded in agreement to the smooth yet forceful tone. He, too, was ready to carry out the mission.

Ravnik trotted down the hill, feeling the Spartan strength that filled his body whenever the voice was in his head. His muscles swelled with energy. He felt invincible.

At the bottom of the slope, Ravnik sprinted forward and leaped over an eight-foot fence crowned with razor-wire. He landed on the slaughterhouse's property as sure footed as a cat and trotted toward the slaughterhouse. He lowered his head so the outside security cameras could not record his face.

• • •

Back in the Holland home, Renee continued to write. Her body trembled, her eyes pitched and rolled like a ship in high seas, but her hands remained steady and accurate as she wrote about the one-eared man entering the slaughterhouse through a side door.

Unable to help his mother, Alex did the only thing he could. He stood beside her, ready to catch her if she pitched off the chair when the trance ended. Alex looked from his mother's death-like expression to the dangerous words tumbling across the computer screen. He feared someone would die tonight.

Clutching his bruised ribs, Sanders approached Renee and Alex cautiously. Alex could tell Sanders was still marveling over Renee's strength.

"Shit! The killer's in the building!" Sanders reported in a panicked voice as he read from the screen.

Sanders snatched his cell phone out of his pocket and dialed Elinger.

● ● ●

In the slaughterhouse, Ravnik walked into a locker room, listening to the voice.

"*Clothe yourself as one of the workers,*" the voice advised. "*You must remain discreet until the last possible moment.*"

Ravnik dutifully grabbed an apron from a wall hook and a hard hat from a bench. Ravnik agreed in his mind with the voice. Blending in with the workers would give him the ability to move about the plant freely while he searched for Richard Smith.

Ravnik walked across the sawdust and blood-spattered floor into the main processing room. He glanced around, surprised by its gymnasium size. He walked alongside hundreds of skinned beef carcasses hanging from metal hooks. Pulled by rattling conveyor chains, these carcasses moved in a long train-like line. Ravnik followed them deep into the slaughterhouse, studying his surroundings with a sleepy fluttering of his eyes.

Ravnik's head turned from side to side as he probed the worker's faces looking for Richard Smith. He noticed one group of men cutting into the parade of beef with pneumatically powered saws. They buzzed through the bovine bodies in less than twenty seconds. The screeching noise was deafening when the jagged-toothed metal ripped through the thick, hard bones. Ravnik smelled the manure and urine that rode the air. Sucking in a deep breath, he felt comfortable in this warehouse of carnage.

Ravnik walked into another room, passing apron-clad men and women who flanked long stainless-steel tables. Slicing meat with razor-sharp knives, these workers tossed large beef chunks on conveyer belts near them. The conveyors, Ravnik noticed, dropped the beef pieces into box-like machines that diced the meat into stew-sized pieces. Ravnik scanned more faces then grunted angrily. Smith was not in this room either.

Ravnik wandered into the grinder room, where workers used chopping machines that cleaved hunks of beef. Wide metal mouths of oversized grinders swallowed the chunks like hungry sharks, pushing the meat through powerful augers to make one of the world's most popular foods—hamburger. Ravnik soon unhappily realized Richard Smith was not in this area.

● ● ●

Elinger was speeding down a city street, talking into his cell phone, giving Torres directions to a slaughterhouse. Elinger's men had obtained the addresses and phone numbers of all meat processing plants that operated a graveyard shift and only found two. And, as expected, those slaughterhouse personnel departments were closed until morning. Elinger knew he had only one chance to find Smith before the killer. He and Torres would have to cover both slaughterhouses simultaneously. And because Renee's pages indicated the one-eared man was in one of those plants already, Elinger knew he might only have minutes to save Smith.

"You got the address, Ralph?" Elinger asked.

"Got it," Torres replied, his voice coming through Elinger's cell phone.

"If Smith isn't at your plant, get your ass over to the one I'm covering. And I'll do the same."

"You got it," Torres replied.

Elinger could hear the excited edge to Torres' voice. "And Ralph, no hero shit like in Robbery," Elinger warned. "We take him together! Understood?"

"Yeah, understood," Torres repeated.

Elinger glanced at his cell phone, hoping his partner would truly heed his words.

Elinger punched the gas pedal and blue smoke trailed from the rear of his fishtailing auto as it sped down the street.

●　●　●

Still moving among the plant's workers in the grinder room, Ravnik continued his search for Richard Smith. As he passed a chopping table, he noticed a collection of boning knives. He picked up two with the longest blades.

●　●　●

At a slaughterhouse across town, Torres wheeled into its parking lot and rushed into the building. Brushing past dozens of apron clad workers and questioning others on the way, Torres located the night foreman. When he asked if Richard Smith was employed there, the foreman shook his head.

Running from the plant toward his auto, Torres hoped he would be able to help Elinger. He jumped into his vehicle and stood on the throttle, speeding out of the parking lot for the other slaughterhouse.

●　●　●

Outside the slaughterhouse where Richard Smith worked, Elinger screeched to a halt and rushed inside the plant building. Once he located the night foreman, Elinger received the answer he wanted. Richard Smith did work there and was on the clock at this very moment.

In the slaughterhouse's grinder room, Ravnik tightened his grip on the knives in his hands.

"I see him," Ravnik muttered for the benefit of the voice. Smith was standing on a metal boning platform several feet above the floor not far from Ravnik. Smith sliced meat and fat from leg bones with a long-bladed knife. His scraps dropped onto a chute that sloped downward like a playground slide. The meat slid into the two-foot wide mouth of a large grinder. An auger bit twisted through the meat, crushing and squeezing the beef into the machine.

"*I know you are governed by the influence of habit in these matters,*" the voice stated. "*But on this occasion, you must utilize the element of surprise. Be quick and decisive, then escape from the premises before the police can be summoned.*"

Ravnik nodded. He had no problem with that.

Smith, unaware he was being watched, continued to cut meat. More pieces of beef slid down the greasy chute into the grinder's mouth. The machine made sucking sounds as it swallowed the meat and pushed it through the auger. At the other end of the machine, the beef writhed outward, like earthworms, through small holes and dropped into a large stainless-steel vat.

Smith stopped slicing meat from the bones for a moment to massage his aching fingers.

Ravnik glanced at the steel blades he gripped in his gloved hands. A look of sadistic pleasure smoothed the hard lines of his face. With that, Ravnik began to walk toward Smith, moving in for the kill.

TWENTY-FIVE

• • •

Richard Smith continued to work at his station on the boning platform. He sliced and hacked at leg bones, pruning the excess meat and fat. Every few seconds Smith pushed the freshly cut meat onto the chute in front of him. The pieces slid down the metal surface into the wide mouth of the churning grinder below him. Piece by piece, the beef was swallowed and minced by the powerful auger, writhing out the opposite side of the grinder as hamburger.

Ravnik's attention was on Smith as he walked purposely toward the boning platform and climbed its stairs. His eyes shifted in and out of focus, then, suddenly, he lunged forward, thrusting both knives into Smith's lower back, burying them to their hilts. Ravnik held on to the knives, waiting excitedly for the first spurts of blood, then released his grip and stepped back.

Ravnik could see Smith was stunned and confused by the abrupt burning feeling that arched through his back.
Richard Smith dropped the boning knife in his hand. He reached behind himself and discovered the deeply imbedded knives. He turned and saw the menacing face of the one-eared man.

Ravnik grinned when he saw that Smith's expression was a portrait of agony.

Smith reached for his back again and felt the blood slickened knife handles. Raising his hands in front of his face, Smith stared in shock at the rich shade of claret dripping from his fingers.

Feeling weak, Smith clutched his work table for support. His grip faltered, and he slipped to the grated floor. The sudden and heavy loss of blood took its toll quickly. Smith's eyelids grew heavy, then closed as his brain began to shut down.

● ● ●

Within seconds, when there were panicked shouts from workers, Elinger and the night foreman ran into the room. When Elinger saw Smith on the grating and the one-eared man standing over him, he realized he was finally face to face with the killer who has been terrorizing Renee Holland. Trying to ignore his thoughts of vengeance, Elinger reminded himself he was a cop and couldn't let personal feelings interfere with his sworn duties.

Elinger yanked his revolver from beneath his coat and aimed it toward the boning platform. "Everybody out of here!" he barked at the foreman and workers.

Everyone scurried toward the exit doors.

Ravnik, ignoring Elinger, hooked his hands under Smith's armpits. He yanked the unconscious meat-cutter from the grating and lifted him above his head like a barbell.

"*Are you mad?*" the voice shouted in Ravnik's head. "*The policeman has a weapon! You must flee!*"

"Not until I'm done," Ravnik argued unflinchingly.

"*I am thunderstruck by your insolence,*" the voice said. "*You must not be captured tonight!*"

"I know. We have much work to do, right?" Ravnik mimicked what the voice had told him many times before. "Just give me a couple of minutes. I wanna let the police know not to fuck with me!"

"*As you wish,*" the voice finally agreed in a reluctant tone. "*I admire your boldness. But remember, there is a close parallel between a brave man and a fool.*"

Elinger, having seen Ravnik talking to himself, rushed toward the boning platform now. He cocked his pistol. "Put him down!" he shouted, fighting an urge to shoot Smith's assailant without further warning.

Exposing his rust-colored teeth in a half-cocked grin, Ravnik ignored Elinger and pitched Smith on the steel chute above the grinding machine. Head-first, Smith slid down the greasy metal toward the spinning auger blades. His apron, however, snagged the chute's edge. The cloth held him above the grinder's mouth, his hands and arms were only inches from the spinning blades. Smith's blood from the knife wounds streamed down the chute into the twisting auger blades and spattered back onto his unconscious face.

Elinger climbed the platform stairs, his weapon still trained on the attacker. "Step back! Put your hands on your head!" he shouted again, his finger tightening on the trigger.
Ravnik responded by shooting a wild-eyed look of defiance at Elinger.

Elinger moved quickly to Smith who still hanged upside down on the chute. When Elinger saw the knives in Smith's back, he placed a finger on the Smith's carotid artery and felt the weak but steady pulse. It was a miracle considering the amount of blood running down the chute. Elinger moved toward the grinder's controls to shut off the equipment before Smith slid into the grinder's jaws.

"*My patience has escaped me, Leonard. Exert yourself to the utmost and kill the policeman now!*" The voice's order abruptly pounded into Ravnik's head.

"That's the plan," Ravnik muttered, grabbing a power knife from the boning table and blocked Elinger's path to the grinder's on-off switch.

Ravnik studied the knife in the one-eared man's hand. Its round jagged-toothed blade was a lethal weapon. Elinger stepped back a few paces when the one-eared man pointed the shiny blade at him.

Elinger looked down the barrel of his revolver and sighted it on the killer's head. "Put it down!" he ordered. "Or you're going to the morgue!" he added, feeling the urge for vengeance again.

Ravnik answered by thumbing the saw's power button. The blade erupted with an explosive shrill.

"*Adios*, scumbag," Elinger uttered, squeezing off a round. Gray smoke shot from the barrel of his revolver, mushrooming toward Ravnik.

Elinger expected the one-eared man to drop, but Ravnik whipped the saw upward and deflected the bullet with the saw's thick metal housing.

Elinger reacted with disbelief. He'd never seen anyone move that fast. He aimed at the one-eared man and began to pull the trigger again.

In a blurring move, Ravnik whipped his leg upward and kicked the pistol from Elinger's hand as it spit fire. The bullet plowed harmlessly into the ceiling. The revolver sailed through the air and dropped into the grinder's jaws. The machine stalled for a moment, then crunched the gun, spitting out bits of blue steel into the red hamburger.

Again, Elinger was taken aback by this man's agility. But Ravnik moved even more deftly now. He threw a fist into Elinger's abdomen.

Elinger stumbled backwards, fell off the platform and crumpled on the sawdust floor below. That punch was like the kick of a mule! Elinger thought.

Pleased with his easy dominance over the policeman, Ravnik jumped from the platform, feeling the voice's strength flow through his veins and empower him. Holding the power knife like a sword, Ravnik moved toward Elinger.

Elinger struggled to his feet quickly to avoid the high-pitched blade. Common sense warned him to run, but Elinger knew he couldn't leave Richard Smith to die.
Lunging with the screaming knife, Ravnik fenced Elinger into a corner of the room.

Elinger stopped retreating and faced his attacker. He had an idea. With his hands, he motioned for his attacker to come forward and fight. "C'mon, let's see what you've got!" Elinger challenged bravely, lacing his insult with a tone of contempt. "You can stab a man in the back, but let's see what you can do face to face, you piece of shit!"

"*He is cunning, Leonard,*" the voice warned. "*Do not be fooled by his ploy. Other policeman will arrive ere long and take advantage of your delay. You must extract yourself from this circumstance at this instant!"*

Ravnik ignored the voice. He lunged toward Elinger but, as Elinger had planned, Ravnik overran the length of the knife's pneumatic air cable. The hose popped free from its connection, causing the shiny blade to lose power.

Ravnik's face reddened with anger. He tossed the weapon aside, grabbed Elinger's throat with one hand and lifted Elinger from the floor. He began to choke Elinger with his uncanny strength.

Unable to breathe, Elinger punched Ravnik's face, hoping to break free. But Ravnik's flesh was like leather and his head seemed as hard as stone. Elinger felt the vise-like grip tightening around his neck. He grabbed the one-eared man's fingers and tried to pry them free, but their grip remained firm.

When the voice empowered Ravnik with another surge of strength, Ravnik carried Elinger toward a large band saw and slammed him face-down down on its cutting table.
Elinger realized this saw could cut through bone like it was butter. He twisted violently and broke free from his attacker's choking hold. He rolled off the equipment and swung up his leg, kicking Ravnik in the groin. Elinger felt the hard toe of his shoe hitting soft flesh.

Ravnik, doubled over, holding the knot of agony between his legs. Coughing and rasping, he looked up and glared murderously at Elinger.

Elinger was also bent over. His chest heaved as he sucked in air. He needed a lot of oxygen. He had been on the verge of blacking out.

The voice hammered Ravnik's brain, telling him to point his fingers at the band saw control panel. When Ravnik obeyed, blue sparks streaked from his fingers and shot into the saw's control box. The cross-cut blade, in the center of the saw's table, suddenly whined with power.

Elinger had seen the tiny bolts shooting from Ravnik's fingers, then saw the spinning teeth of the saw blade.

Ravnik quickly straightened up and grabbed one of Elinger's arms and locked it behind Elinger's back. He pushed Elinger face-down on the saw table again and planted his free hand on Elinger's back. He began to push Elinger's head and neck toward the rotating blade.

Elinger tried to roll off the saw table again, but the hand on his back was as heavy as an anvil. Elinger could only twist his head slightly. When he did, he saw Smith still hanging upside down on the grinder's metal chute. The meat-cutter's apron was beginning to rip. With every thread that tore, Elinger could see Smith's body slip closer to the grinder's open, hungry mouth.

As Ravnik shoved Elinger's head closer to the saw's blade, Elinger expected his life to flash before his eyes. Instead, he saw the sunny face of Rafael Torres and his devil-may-care smile. The sight infuriated Elinger. He wondered what was delaying his partner! Surely Torres had plenty of time to check out the other slaughterhouse and know to come to this one!

Ravnik lowered his ugly, sweating face inches from Elinger's and taunted him with a humorless, rotten-toothed grin.

Elinger noticed his assailant's zoned-out expression—the same as Renee's whenever she was in a trance. Elinger was sure this man, like Renee, was not in full control of his actions at all times. The fathomless cold stare in his eyes seemed to come from hell.

Helpless, Elinger glanced in Smith's direction again and saw Smith's bloody apron tearing more, lowering the meat-cutter closer to the grinder's auger.

●　●　●

Although Renee's body trembled and her eyes were hazed-over, she tapped smoothly on the computer keys, writing about the slaughterhouse fight between Elinger and the one-eared man.

Reading from the monitor, Sanders was on his cell phone again, summoning back-ups for Elinger.

Sanders shifted his vision toward the monitor again, catching Renee's next batch of sentences. He read that the one-eared man had pushed Elinger only inches from the whirling, cross-cut saw blade. Sanders' jaw tightened, an involuntary reaction of his fear Elinger would be decapitated in a matter of seconds.

TWENTY-SIX

• • •

With a look of urgency, Torres jammed his foot on the brake pedal. His sedan skidded in the slaughterhouse parking lot, stopping near Elinger's parked car. Torres wisely figured his partner could be in trouble. Throwing open his door, he jumped from his car and ran toward the building. He drew his service revolver and plowed into the door.

Making his way to the grinder room, Torres found Elinger in Ravnik's deadly hold. Only an inch separated Elinger's neck from the spinning saw.

"Call for backups!" Elinger shouted when he saw Torres.

"No, I got this!" Torres yelled back as he wrapped both hands around his revolver's grip and aimed. Without a word, he yanked the trigger. The explosive flash sent a bullet ripping through a loose-fitting apron strap on Ravnik's left shoulder.

The gunshot was barely audible over the shrilling sound of the saw but enough to alert Ravnik to the danger. He released Elinger and turned toward Torres as another shot erupted from Torres' pistol. This bullet punched a hole in the apron tail between Ravnik's legs.

Elinger gasped for air as he slid from the saw's platform. Without hesitation, Elinger slammed his foot into Ravnik's balls.

The spikes of pain in Ravnik's groin caused him to bend over and dry-heave. He cupped his throbbing testicles as if they were about to explode from his scrotum.

Torres was amazed as Ravnik's face suddenly lost its hard lines of pain and his body seemed to have renewed energy flowing through it.

Ravnik turned quickly toward Torres who still had his firearm aimed at him. Ravnik grabbed a small boning table and threw it at Torres. Torres fired again. This bullet punched a hole in the table near Ravnik's hip and slammed harmlessly into a wall. Before Torres could pull the trigger again, the table hit him in the knees. Pain rippled up Torres' legs. He wavered, trying to steady himself to shoot again. But Ravnik had followed the flight of the table and jumped on Torres, snatching the revolver from his hand. Ravnik threw the gun across the room.

Torres realized the one-eared man wanted to fight him hand-to-hand, *mano-a-mano*.

Torres saw a tenderizing mallet on a table near him. He grabbed the mallet and cracked Ravnik on the forehead, driving the sharp points of the mallet into Ravnik's flesh.

Ravnik's head flew back. He staggered, raising his hands to his head. The spike marks on his forehead welled with blood, sending a red flow down his face.

Charging from behind, Elinger hooked an arm around Ravnik's neck and put a choke-hold on him. Torres moved in and struck Ravnik's head and face with the mallet again, splitting tissue and denting bone.

Ravnik's features began to disappear beneath the blood and torn flesh, but Ravnik reached up and wiped the blood from his eyes to clear his vision. And in a second, the pain vanished from his face and his limbs were charged with energy again.

Ravnik broke Elinger's hold with a violent twist of his body, wind-milling Elinger over his shoulder. As Elinger sprawled on the sawdust, Torres raised the mallet and rushed Ravnik again. But Ravnik threw his head forward and head-butted Torres. Stunned, Torres fell back, and the mallet slipped from his grip.

Rising groggily from the sawdust, Elinger wished he had brought a shotgun. He pulled his cell phone from his pocket to call Headquarters, but the phone was cracked and would not work. Elinger looked at Smith and realized the meat-cutter was in more danger now. Smith's apron had ripped again. A few more inches of torn material and Smith would slide head first into the grinder.

Ravnik grabbed a knife from a boning table and took advantage of Elinger's distraction. He jumped forward and shoved the blade deep into Elinger's forearm. Pulling the knife downward, he made a long, deep slice. Blood erupted beneath Elinger's coat sleeve and flowed over his hand and fingers. Elinger tried to pull back, but Ravnik pressed down on the knife, imbedding the tip in the bone of Elinger's arm. The more Elinger moved, the more tissue damage Ravnik inflicted by pressing down on the knife. Back on his feet now, Torres rushed forward and drove his shoulder into Ravnik's side, knocking him away from Elinger. The knife, still held tightly by Ravnik, slipped out of Elinger's arm, glistening with blood.

Elinger clamped his hand over his coat sleeve above the wound and pressed down to stop the bleeding.

Ravnik hesitated, wiping the blood from his eyes again. As he did, Torres scooped up the tenderizing mallet from the grating, cocked it over his shoulder and hit Ravnik's face again. Ravnik's head bobbed violently and he staggered drunkenly. His nose was the only feature visible beneath the fresh sheet of blood.

"We've got him now, man!" Torres shouted to Elinger, raising the mallet and charging Ravnik again.

But Ravnik was ready for Torres. Lifting the knife he used on Elinger, he pushed it into Torres' upper left chest. Torres own momentum buried the blade deeply, cutting through muscle.

Torres pulled back from Ravnik and looked down and saw the blood oozing from his chest. He stumbled backwards, slipping on the greasy floor and hitting the back of his head on a boning table. By the time he hit the floor, Torres was out cold and blood pooled beneath him.

Enraged by Torres' injury, Elinger yanked a meat hook from a nearby conveyor chain. When Ravnik tried to wipe his vision again, Elinger lunged forward and buried the hook deep in Ravnik's right bicep. This wound caused Ravnik great agony. His body jerked into a rigid posture and he dropped the knife.

Elinger leaned on the hook, forcing it deeper into Ravnik's flesh, pulling it the length of Ravnik's upper arm. The tip scored bone and stopped only when it snagged the inside of Ravnik's elbow socket.

Releasing the hook, Elinger stepped back. No matter how strong this guy was, he can be injured and killed just like anyone else. *Bleed and die, you sonovabitch!* Elinger's mind screamed. But Elinger knew his wish wasn't going to happen when he saw Ravnik's suffering frown suddenly twist into a sadistic grin. His attacker's pain had mysteriously vanished again.

Ravnik pulled the hook from his arm as if it was an annoying splinter. He paid little attention to the blood erupting from his arm, but he couldn't ignore the words that shot through his mind.

"*Escape! Flee!*" the voice commanded.

Perplexed, Elinger watched Ravnik as Ravnik clamped his hands over his ears. It was as though he were trying to shut out a loud noise.

"*Tonight's mission has been accomplished!*" the voice shouted clearly in Ravnik's head. "*Other important work awaits us. Work destined for a grander purpose!*"
Ravnik glared at Elinger with animosity filling his expression.

Elinger stared back, sensing Ravnik was not finished with the fight.

"*There is no more time!*" the voice snapped in Ravnik's brain.

Elinger watched as Ravnik seemed to lose control of his own body. Ravnik's eyes snapped upward and his body quivered in a violent spasm. Ravnik's legs began to move and then he unexpectedly bolted toward the nearest exit. In an instant, Ravnik was out of the building.

● ● ●

"Call an ambulance!" Elinger shouted to a sprinkle of employees who began to return to the room.

Elinger studied the blood streaming from Torres' deep stab wound. Since Torres was unresponsive, Elinger removed his jacket and placed it over him, worried there wasn't much time to save his partner. There was not much else he could do until paramedics arrived.

Concerned for Smith, Elinger trotted up the platform stairs and moved toward the chute above the grinder. As he did, Smith's apron ripped again and the meat-cutter slid toward the machine's churning mouth. Lurching forward, Elinger grabbed Smith by the belt with his uninjured arm, yanked him from the chute and pulled him down to the grating.

Elinger cradled Smith's head in his lap. The meat cutter was limp. When Elinger probed Smith's neck for a pulse, he found none. Elinger closed his eyes and lowered his head. If only he had arrived at the slaughterhouse sooner. Perhaps he could have saved Smith.

Elinger laid Smith's head gently on the grating and moved off the platform. He ripped open his shirt sleeve and glanced at his own wound—an ugly inch-wide rip, brimming with a mixture of fresh and coagulating blood. Figuring it would take no less than 60 stitches to close it, Elinger knew he was lucky the knife missed the artery.

● ● ●

As Ravnik sprinted across the slaughterhouse parking lot, his eyes softened and became normal again, peering through the layers of blood on his face. Ravnik was angry to find himself running from a fight. He didn't like being forced to flee like a coward and loathed being helpless against the voice when it decided to exert full power over him. No one ever gave him orders, Ravnik angrily reminded himself. But then he'd never had the great strength the voice could give him. It was something to respect and appreciate, Ravnik decided. He was also curious about the voice's grand *purpose*. He wanted to know what the murders really meant and what was the voice's real goal? In time, Ravnik knew he'd have the answers. He was sure it would be worth the wait.

As Ravnik neared the border of the slaughterhouse's property, he looked at the wound in his arm. The blood was coagulating now, but it still bled. Ravnik wiped a hand across his face, smearing congealed blood. There was no fresh blood there. He knew he would survive his injuries if he stopped the bleeding in his arm. He hoped the voice would return to put some energy back into his weakened body and make him strong again.

Ravnik climbed onto the hood of a company truck and leaped over the razor-wire fence. He disappeared into the cloak of darkness—his trail as cold and dark as the shadows that engulfed him.

● ● ●

Renee's word processor abruptly shut down. Sagging over her keyboard, Renee looked through glazed eyes at her son's worried face. "Hi, honey," she mumbled with great effort.

"You okay, Mom?" Alex asked.

"I think so," Renee said, trying to reclaim her mind. She slowly sat up in her chair, regaining a little of her strength. "What did I write?"

"I couldn't keep up with it, Mom."

Renee lifted a flaccid hand and punched a command on the keyboard. "I'll print it out."

Renee looked at Sanders who stood near her. "You still think this is hoax?" she asked.

Sanders was bracing his side with one of his hands. He shook his head and pulled up his shirt, revealing his reddened and bruised ribs. "You've got a funny way of getting new fans, Ms. Holland. But you made a believer out of me."

After the printout, Renee studied the pages. A grave look crossed her face when she read about Elinger's and Torres' injuries. She was thankful the name of the hospital where they were was included, but a passage on the last page drilled a well of fear in her heart. She pulled the page from the rest of the sheets.

"Please take me to University hospital," Renee asked Sanders as she stood, folding the paper neatly and stuffing it into her blouse.

Part Two
Shadow Man

• • •

The boundaries which divide Life from Death are at best shadowy and vague.

Edgar Allan Poe

TWENTY-SEVEN

• • •

After Ravnik's escape, an ambulance arrived at the
slaughterhouse and dispatched three paramedics. The paramedics
covered Torres' chest wound with a sterile, pressure-dressing to
stem the blood flow. Torres remained unconscious as the men
checked his pulse, his pupillary response and monitored his vital
signs. They radioed the closest hospital for emergency surgery
preparation.

After stopping the blood loss in Elinger's arm with a
compression bandage, one of the paramedics told Elinger he was
lucky—the knife had missed Elinger's Axis artery by a quarter
inch. As it was, Elinger only required a stitch job.
Climbing into the ambulance's rear compartment, Elinger sat next
to Torres. He wanted to stay close to his partner until they reached
the hospital, and Torres was in the hands of a competent surgical
team. Elinger was concerned about Torres' short, shallow gasps.

Elinger glanced through the ambulance's rear window and
saw the Coroner's van roll to a stop in the slaughterhouse parking
lot. The coroner's men stepped out under the moonlight. One was
carrying a body bag for Richard Smith.

Elinger closed his eyes, grieving that he couldn't save the meat cutter's life. One more reason he was determined to catch the savage murderer who dispensed death so freely.

At the University of Maryland's Shock Trauma Center, Torres was quickly given a CT scan of his brain. Once doctors established there was no subdural hematoma in progress, they wheeled Torres into surgery to repair the damage of his chest wound. The small group of surgeons discovered Torres was lucky. The knife had missed his heart and vital arteries. It had cut through the muscle wall and scored a couple of ribs. The doctors gave Torres fresh blood and stitched up the internal and external injuries. The surgery went well but they had to wait for him to regain consciousness to determine the severity of his concussion.

With his arm stitched, and in a sling, Elinger went to the hospital lobby where he was greeted by Renee and Sanders. Renee rushed toward Elinger while Sanders veered off toward the elevator, quickly explaining to Elinger that he was going to have his ribs X-rayed.

Renee flung her arms around Elinger. "Thank God, you're all right!" she exclaimed.

Elinger reciprocated with a one-armed squeeze. "I wish I could say the same for Ralph. He's in serious condition, and I don't know the results of his brain scan. I was told when he regains consciousness, the docs will know more about his condition."

Renee closed her eyes, trying to block the tears. "I know. It's in the pages."

"Is that how you knew to come here?" Elinger asked.

Renee nodded, releasing her embrace, but staying toe

to toe with Elinger. "Yes, and there's more," she informed him, reaching into her blouse for the page she had taken with her. She handed it to Elinger. "He isn't finished, Kent—with you or me!"

Elinger's vision bored into the paper:

My dear Madam Holland:

May I extend my sincerest gratitude to you for bringing Lieutenant Elinger to my attention. He is an extraordinary man of stalwart character—a man of fine honed intelligence—the perfect complement to our marvellous game, would you not agree? I can understand the tendresse betwixt you and him. But beyond matters of love, you have created, perhaps unwittingly, a most perfect example of good against evil. The policeman and I are indefatigable and formidable adversaries. Thenceforward, I will treat Mr. Elinger with the utmost respect. Madam Holland, you have no idea how enjoyable you're making my task. Good luck with your hunt for me...

"The archaic words again," Renee said.

"Yeah, look at *thenceforward*."

"It's in the old books, from the same era you'd find *marvelous* spelled with two *ll's*," Renee explained. "Mostly nineteenth century."

"How's that search coming along?" Elinger asked.

"Nothing yet, but I'm not giving up."

Elinger pointed at the note. "May I keep this?"

Renee nodded. "It's certainly not going in my scrapbook."

Elinger folded the paper and pushed it into his pocket.

"I'm really sorry about this, Kent," Renee apologized unexpectedly. "Now, whoever or whatever this thing is, knows who you are, and he's thanking me for getting you involved. All because you tried to help me!"

Reaching out with his uninjured arm, Elinger took Renee's hand and held it tenderly. "Renee, it's not your fault. I've been involved since I watched the coroner's men put those innocent shipyard workers in body bags."

Renee looked off distantly before she spoke again. The internal tide of guilt, justified or not, had not subsided. "Maybe I should just move away? Like out to the boonies."

"The killer would probably follow you. Would you want to be alone in the woods with him?" Elinger asked.
Elinger's words clearly made their point with Renee. "Bad idea," she admitted, turning back to Elinger.

"I got a good look at him tonight," Elinger revealed, releasing Renee's hand. "And I saw something strange."
Renee slipped her arm through Elinger's arm. "Like what?"

"His eyes. Sometimes they looked normal, other times they looked like yours when you're in a trance," Elinger said as he and Renee left the hospital.

"What does it mean?" Renee asked.

"I can only guess, but I think there's—" Elinger stopped himself.

Renee realized Elinger was worried that what he wanted to say would alarm her.

"What?" Renee asked.

"Never mind. Until I'm sure, I don't want to speculate."

"I want to hear it anyway," Renee said in a quiet,

imploring voice. "If anybody deserves to know what you're thinking, it's me."

Renee could see Elinger considering her statement, then he nodded.

"Okay. I think the killer is being controlled, just like you," Elinger revealed.

Renee weighed Elinger's statement for a moment. "You mean, you think something is controlling both of us?"
Elinger nodded.

Renee could clearly see in Elinger's expression that he was convinced of what he just told her.

Captain Robert Osborne's older-model, unmarked sedan coasted to a stop near Elinger and Renee as they walked down the sidewalk. Its engine idled roughly, rumbling through a cracked muffler. The noise interrupted Elinger and Renee's conversation.

Osborne stepped from the vehicle and parked his elbows on the roof. He peered at Elinger through lethargic eyes. "We need to talk, Kent."

"Be right there, Cap."

"Go back in the hospital and have Sanders take you home," Elinger told Renee. "I'll check in on you later."

"I'd rather you took me home," Renee said.

"I wish I could, Renee, but I can't run the investigation from your house."

"Do you think I'm being selfish?" Renee asked.

"You're being human."

"You're the only who makes me feel safe," Renee said. "I'm afraid you won't be there the next time something happens."

"I'll do everything I can to be with you," Elinger

promised, knowing he could not guarantee that.

Renee nodded reluctantly.

As Renee approached the doors of the hospital, she juggled her feelings about Elinger. She had respect and admiration for him, but she also felt fear. Never before had she known such a benevolent fear. Her romantic interest in Elinger was the root of that feeling—the apprehension of her emotional vulnerability if she gave in to her feelings. She felt so at ease with him, and she didn't want to fight her feelings for him.

Renee's ardent thoughts faded quickly, however, when she stepped into the hospital. The antiseptic smells reminded her of Torres' injury and her predicament. The cloud of gloom settled over her again.

Renee's mind raced as she recalled what Elinger told her—that possibly she and the killer were controlled by something else. Could it be a demonic force? The murderer's heinous actions certainly could prove that. Was it possible an evil possession was the cause of this madness?

● ● ●

"Hop in," Osborne ordered as Elinger approached his car. "Let's go for a ride around the block."

After Elinger climbed inside the auto, the Captain cast a look at Renee as she walked toward the hospital entrance. "So that's the famous Renee Holland. What a shame. She's too pretty to be crazy."

"She's as sane as you or me. What's happening to her

would make anyone nuts," Elinger said with a tone of annoyance.

Elinger's attitude surprised Osborne, but he chose not to challenge it as he weaved his vehicle into traffic—more important matters were on his mind.

"Great job, Kent," Osborne congratulated as he turned the steering wheel, changing into the fast lane. "I'll see that you get a Citation of Merit."

Elinger cocked his head toward Osborne. "Great job? For what?"

"Bravery, of course."

"I wasn't brave. I was fighting for my life."

"The public doesn't know that," Osborne advised. "It's great press for us. And believe me, we need it right now."

"I'm only interested in what really happened. My suspect got away! I don't want an award for that," Elinger fired back.

"You're the only person I know that's as bullheaded as I am," Osborne growled.

Elinger looked suspiciously at Osborne. "What'd you really want to talk about, Ozzie? I mean, Cap," Elinger suddenly added when Osborne's glare drilled a hole in him. Nothing incurred Osborne's wrath more than his unofficial nickname.

Osborne began dryly, "Well, I've heard more wild stories about this case since you pulled that physic shit on me."

"You won't call it *shit* after you talk to Sanders."

"That's what I'm talking about. He called me on his way to the hospital."

"Well?"

"Well, okay," Osborne shrugged. "There are some strange wrinkles to this case. I guess you won't need to see our shrink."

"You're losing your step, Cap. I've already been in to see him." Elinger cracked a grin, glad to be one up on Osborne.

"What'd he say?"

"That you were pig-headed and I should ignore you," Elinger quipped.

Osborne's face slowly smoothed out. "Okay, I deserved that. What'd he really say?"

"What he tells everybody. That I need some time off."

"He might be right. You haven't had a vacation in what—three years?"

"Yeah, you must be overworking me," Elinger smiled. "Maybe I should report you to the Labor Board?"

"You wouldn't know what to do with yourself if you had some time off," Osborne said as he flicked on his signal and steered the auto into a curve. A moment of silence passed before Osborne spoke again. "You've got free rein now," he said unexpectedly. "Use any method you want. I don't care if it's voodoo, just get this bastard off our streets!"

Elinger was surprised. "You're serious?"

"Yeah."

"Why the change of heart?"

"Because you work best when there's nobody on your back."

"That's not the only reason," Elinger said sagely, searching for Osborne's hidden agenda. "What else?" Elinger noticed his question had made Osborne fidget uncomfortably in his seat.

"I'm catching a lot of heat from the mayor and his dickhead assistant Montagna," Osborne said. "Most days, you can

214

fry eggs on the back of my ass when they're done with me. They want this piece of shit dead or alive. And they want him now!"

Elinger grinned. "That's the Ozzie Osborne I know and love. Always tangled up in city politics."

"Stop with that name goddammit!" Osborne snapped. "Just remember one thing, Kent. As long as I have a job, you have a job! If you make me happy, they're happy, and we both can continue our careers. That's not hard to understand, is it?' he asked, piloting the auto back toward the front of the hospital.

Elinger shook his head.

"And one other thing," Osborne continued. "Keep the bogeyman side of this thing quiet. Don't make a circus out of this, or you'll lose me."

Before Elinger could reply, Osborne noticed something on the sidewalk that caused him to grimace. "Oh, shit," he grumbled.

Glancing out the window, Elinger's face also soured.

A knot of trendily dressed men and women rushed toward the auto from the hospital parking lot, carrying cameras, lights, microphones, and tape and digital audio recorders. Every pretty face and orthodontic smile from the six o'clock news crowded the car as it rolled to a stop at the curb.

"First thing you can do for me is hold a press conference," Osborne grumbled again.

Elinger knew this was more of an order than a request. "You know I'm not good at that."

"You're better at it than I am."

Elinger knew it was futile to argue. He opened the door and stepped into the knot of journalists. Osborne's auto screeched back into traffic as the reporters jammed microphones and cameras toward Elinger, hurling dozens of overlapping questions.

Elinger raised his uninjured arm to settle the flutter. Choosing his words judiciously, he recalled the confrontation at the slaughterhouse and the evening's events, omitting Renee's trance writing. The police had reacted on a tip, Elinger explained, and that's how he found the suspect.

The reporters recorded every word with video and audio. Only one reporter questioned the story. "I have a source that says you're holding back information, Lieutenant."

Recognizing the voice, Elinger's expression drew tight. He focused on the news people one by one, finally singling out a face. It belonged to Mervyn Amos, a dogged reporter who often betrayed truth in his rush to be first with a story. Amos had interfered with Elinger and other officers before, earning the enmity of Headquarters personnel. The puffy face, rubbery jowls, and dark, pin-point eyes were unmistakable on the thirty-four-year-old man. And his pants and shirt, always a tad large and wrinkled like a pair of pajamas. The hair hadn't changed either—a dark and dull wave at the crest of the forehead.

"Is that really you, Anus?" Elinger asked, calling Amos by the moniker bestowed upon him by the entire police department. He had earned it because of his inaccurate reporting, and irritating, abrasive behavior.

"Yeah, it's me, Lieutenant," Amos replied.

"Who you working for now?" Elinger asked, genuinely curious. "The *Gossiper* isn't interested in a real story."

"I'm with the *Sun* now."

Elinger heard the pride in Amos' answer. His face creased with mild surprise. "I can't believe they'd stoop that low."

"They need hustlers like me. Now what about my question? What're you holding back?" Amos asked again. "I have sources that say you're not telling everything you know."

Elinger wondered if the reporter really knew something. Though Amos was the king of schlock, at times he did produce facts.

"Be more specific," Elinger said, deciding to find out if Amos was bluffing. "What am I supposed to be withholding?"

"Well, you haven't said anything about the link between the shipyard murders and this thing at the slaughterhouse. I've already talked to some of the witnesses at the slaughterhouse, and they described a man that's a dead ringer for the guy who killed those shipyard people."

The words caused a ripple of excitement to pass through the reporters. They crowded Elinger, pressing for his answer.

Elinger flushed with anger. The last thing he wanted was the case's bizarre facts to become public. He hated to admit it, but this was one of those rare times Amos was on target.

Elinger covered with a forced chuckle. "That's ridiculous! The M.O.'s are totally different."

"But the description is the same. Mated hair, filthy clothes, bulky physique," Amos argued.

"Witnesses are not always accurate. As a reporter, you should know that," Elinger reminded. "But I'm not surprised you fell for it."

The group chuckled, but Amos paid no attention.

"Just level with us," Amos said. "What's really going on?"

Elinger ignored the question and looked past Amos now.

He directed his attention on the other news people. He knew what he had to do. "For those of you who don't know Mervyn Amos," he began, "this is a good time for an official introduction. Mr. Amos used to work for the *Gossiper*, the rag that hangs from supermarket racks. He's written such memorable stories like—*Woman Gives Birth to a 3-Eyed Lizard Boy*, or *Werewolf Discovered Living in Cleveland as Mild-mannered School Teacher*."

The journalists chuckled again.

Elinger hoped his ploy to discredit Amos would work. "And I can't figure out why he's no longer at the *Gossiper*, unless someone finally flushed their toilet."

Laughter swept through the reporters now, leaving Amos' jowls as red as a rooster's comb.

"The only important thing I can tell you about the case right now," Elinger began, now off the subject of Amos, "is that I got a good look at the suspect tonight. And I'll have a facial composite of him. It'll be posted on our website in the morning."

"There's something else you're not telling us, Lieutenant," Amos interjected.

Elinger sensed Amos was quietly seething. "What is it now?" Elinger asked impatiently.

"The witnesses at the meat plant gave your suspect a nickname—*Shadow Man*." Amos said it slowly for dramatic effect. "They said he was like a shadow because no one noticed him until it was too late. Like the guy at the shipyard."

Now the creep's going to give the killer a nickname, Elinger bemoaned in his mind, hoping the media wouldn't promote it. He needed to discredit Amos again. "They were under duress,

Amos. People say a lot of off-the-wall things when they're stressed out. I'd think you'd know that by now."

Amos continued, ignoring Elinger. "Some of them said this Shadow Man was as strong as five men."

Caught off guard by the accuracy, Elinger hesitated momentarily, planning his response. "He's only one man, Amos. No stronger than most men his size."

"So why is Richard Smith dead and your partner in critical condition? And why do you have an arm full of stitches?" Amos stepped aggressively toward Elinger as he spoke. "I mean, you and your partner had guns, and this guy brings a knife to a gunfight and he wins. How did he do that, Lieutenant? How did he get away?"

Amos is still as tenacious as a cockroach, Elinger thought. "He got lucky," Elinger replied. "This time he won, next time we'll win. That's the way it goes sometimes." Elinger decided to end the meeting before Amos could say anything else. "That's it for now. Don't forget to check our website in the morning for the composite."

Elinger turned from the group and walked off, fielding any straggling questions with silence. Moving toward the hospital, he thought about Amos, hoping the reporter hadn't created a stir in the media.

"Lieutenant!" The voice came from behind Elinger. Turning, Elinger looked directly into Mervyn Amos' face. "I didn't appreciate what you did back there," Amos stated simply.

"I didn't hurt your feelings, did I?" Elinger replied sarcastically. "I've seen enough of you to last me a lifetime. Just stay out of my way, or I'm going to throw you in jail."

"Still a fascist, I see."

Elinger took a step toward Amos, clenching the fist of his uninjured arm.

Amos smiled from the corner of his mouth. "Go ahead, Lieutenant. Give me some credibility."

Elinger realized Amos was right. If he punched the troublesome reporter, other reporters might believe what Amos had said was true. He opened his fist.

"What do you want from me, Amos?" Elinger asked.

"I just wanted you to know that you really pissed me off."

"Am I supposed to feel bad about that?"

"Actually, I wanted to make you nervous, and I can see I did that very well tonight," Amos said. "I'm going to find out what you're withholding and print it. I'm going to prove you're a liar. I have a big forum out there. About a million people read the *Sun*," Amos smiled. "Have a pleasant evening, Lieutenant."

Amos turned and moved away. Elinger watched him strut off into the night, agitated he has another obstacle to overcome in an investigation already overly complicated.

● ● ●

With his face covered with dried blood, Ravnik crawled dizzily out of the broken window of a small, darkened grocery store. He pushed a small package and bottle of rubbing alcohol into his coat pocket as he leaned against the building for support. Ravnik ignored the shrilling burglar alarm and kept his head down so the security camera could not video his face while he waited for his head to clear. He touched his face, feeling the swollen bruises and split tissue, all resulting from Torres' mallet blows. Ravnik's fight with Elinger and Torres had been costly, he knew. Blood still oozed from the deep split in his bicep, enough blood lost to kill most humans.

Once his equilibrium settled, Ravnik pushed off the building and moved down the darkened alley in his weakened condition. He hoped the voice would help him find his way home without being spotted by the police.

Ravnik stepped into his small apartment. The room was like a kaleidoscope, spinning before his eyes. Sitting on his bed, he lowered his head between his knees, hoping to fill his brain with what little blood remained in his body. When he raised his head a few minutes later, the room had settled slightly, but he knew he had to work fast.

Ravnik removed his ripped and blood-soaked coat and his gloves, wincing briefly from the jabbing pains in his arm. He tore open his shirt and peeled it from his torso, exposing his well-muscled chest. Next, he pulled the small bottle of rubbing alcohol from his coat pocket and uncapped it.

Stretching his injured arm, Ravnik purposely opened the gaping bicep wound and poured the full bottle of alcohol onto the red, oozing flesh. The pain would've caused most men to faint, but Ravnik only flinched.

Next, he retrieved the package from his coat pocket and withdrew a long, curved sewing needle. He ripped a long strand of thread from his bed cover and threaded the needle with it. He began to sew up the wound, pushing the needle through his flesh at the wound's edges and yanking the string taut, pinching his bicep together in small knots. Ravnik was aware the work was Frankenstein-esque, but nonetheless efficient.

As Ravnik closed the wound, he became elated. His self-doctoring would put him back on the streets within a few days. The thought manufactured a smile on the man who was devoid of heart and soul. He would soon be ready for the voice's next murder.

TWENTY-EIGHT

• • •

Wearing a sweat suit and nestled beneath a thick blanket, Renee reclined on an over-stuffed chair in her living room. The fatigue of her ordeal was wearing her down. Dark crescents had formed under her eyes and the deep green of her irises seemed faded.

With his suit hopelessly wrinkled, Sanders sat on a couch across the room from Renee. His shoeless feet were propped on a coffee table, and he was reading a magazine. His eyelids were heavy. He was nodding off.

As opening credits of a late-night religious talk show rolled across the TV screen, Renee nervously recalled Elinger's depressing speculation—that she and the killer were probably being controlled by a third force of some kind. Obviously, it is evil, Renee bleakly reasoned. If it was true, Renee wanted to know. She felt her sanity was at stake.

Renee suddenly focused on the talk show when two middle-aged Catholic priests revealed their backgrounds to a wavy haired, religious host. They explained their special calling for the Catholic Church. Exorcism. During the last two decades they had freed dozens of people from demonic possession. When the oldest priest described possession manifestations such as sleeplessness, trance-like states and irrational behavior, Renee became frightened. She had experienced those symptoms and others the priests described.

Renee reached for her cell phone on a small table near her.

●　●　●

Feeling disoriented and weak, Torres regained consciousness early the next morning. The doctors informed him his vital signs had stabilized, that his chest injury would heal, and his CT scan did not show any sign of brain bleeding. However, he needed to stay in the hospital a few days for observation to make sure there was no swelling of his brain. He also needed some time for his chest to start healing. Torres was surprisingly alert, the doctors explained, considering he had a concussion.

A few minutes after sunrise, Elinger arrived and took a seat next to Torres' bed. "I didn't expect you to look so perky this morning."

Torres peered out at Elinger from beneath his rumpled sheets. He managed a glimmer of a smile, then his look turned quite serious. "Did we get 'im?" he asked.
Elinger shook his head.

"And I had a chance to waste 'im," Torres lamented. "I'm just no good with a short-barreled pistol."

Elinger nodded. "I don't think you could hit Headquarters if you were sitting at your desk," Elinger said jokingly to lighten

Torres' mood.

Torres grinned slightly.

Elinger pointed at Torres' chest. "I thought for sure he got your heart. You had us all worried for awhile."

"Don't remind me," Torres replied, noticing Elinger's sling. "Looks like he got you too, man. How bad?"

"Forty-seven stitches."

Torres blanched suddenly, feeling pain in his head. "Man, I've got a really bad headache. They said it might last a few days even with the meds they're givin' me."

"Pain is the least of your worries," Elinger advised quietly. "You're lucky to be alive."

"Yeah, what's with this guy?" Torres began, sharing Elinger's unspoken thoughts. "He's like a gorilla. What're we gonna do to stop him?"

"First thing—you're going to knock off your hero shit," Elinger replied bluntly. "I told you to call for backup."

"I know," Torres said, regretfully.

Elinger spoke in a cautionary tone. "You looked like you were trying to prove something—by saving somebody single-handedly like you did in Robbery. This is all about your dead brother, isn't it?"

"What?" Torres blurted, annoyed and surprised by the question.

Elinger's expression bore down on Torres. "I think you do these heroic things because of the loss of your brother. And you might even have a death wish, too."

"What are you now, a psychiatrist?" Torres asked, sarcastically.

Elinger ignored the comment. "If I'm wrong, why then? Why do you play hero when you don't need to?"

"Hey, I was just tryin' to save you!"

"Believe me, I appreciate it. But you should have called for backup instead of trying to handle it by yourself. You've got to be honest without yourself, Ralph. Why are you always trying to be a hero?"

Torres absorbed Elinger's words, knowing there was something important to what he said. He retracted his combative edge from the conversation and looked at Elinger somberly. "I don't know why. It's something in me that gets the best of me sometimes."

"Have you ever considered it might be some kind of self-punishment because your brother died while he was with you? Or is it to prove to yourself that you are brave?"

Torres turned away from Elinger and gazed out the window at the city's hazy skyline for a long time. Elinger had hit a soft spot. Torres admitted to himself that he was harboring a secret about the death of his brother Manuel. Over the years it had caused him deep personal loathing. He knew he needed to talk to someone about it. Someone he could trust. Someone who wouldn't judge him and make him feel ashamed. Maybe Elinger was that person. Torres rolled back toward Elinger. "Do you think it would really help if you knew everything?"

"I think it would help you," Elinger replied.

"I guess you're right. I do need to talk about it," Torres admitted. "And right now, while I'm on these pain meds, is probably a good time. But it stays in this room, okay?" Torres added.

"You've got my word," Elinger promised.

Torres gave Elinger a downcast look then mumbled softly, "I ran."

"What?" Elinger asked, not sure what he heard.

"I fucking ran!" Torres repeated, biting into his trembling lip. "I really fucked up." Tears filled his eyes as he spoke. "I ran when my brother got killed."

Elinger looked hard at Torres. "I don't picture you running from a fight. You were very brave in the slaughterhouse."

Elinger's words bounced off Torres. Torres was still mentally back in the past. "It was night when me and my homies were out on the streets. We crossed paths with another set," Torres said, wiping his eyes on the sheet. "Those *vatos* started shooting at us. One of 'em had an A-K. I wasn't strapped that night. We couldn't match the firepower so we ran. Manuel was slow. I heard a shot… I looked back and Manuel was down… This *vato* was standin' over him, pointin' a nine mill at him. Manuel pleaded for his life. Then he called for me," Torres added, sucking in a breath before he resumed. "But I couldn't move. It was like I was standin' in concrete. And while I'm playin' statue, my *mijo* got shot in the head. Then that son-of-a-puta points his niner at me and fires. So, I took off," Torres choked out the final words. "I left my little brother to die in the street! I should've tried to help him. Maybe I could've saved him."

"You were unarmed. You would've been killed, too," Elinger reasoned. "Anybody else would've done the same." Torres understood Elinger's point intellectually, but his emotions didn't. "I promised myself I'd never run from anybody again."

"But you can't always do that when you're wearing the

badge," Elinger warned.

Torres knew Elinger was right, and he despised what he was about to say. "I guess you probably want to take me off the streets and make me take some chill time?"

"Maybe that would be good for you," Elinger replied mindfully. "Maybe you've got a lot to think about."
Torres did not respond. Instead, he cast a sad, regretful look at Elinger.

"Do you think you need time to cool off, to get a handle on your personal demons?" Elinger asked.

Torres' response was instant. "No, I want to get that bastard. We can do it without me tryin' to be a hero. Look at what he did to us!"

"Do you think you'll have enough time to work things out while you're healing in here?" Elinger asked.

Torres nodded. "Yeah, I'm gettin' the message."

"You let me know how you feel when they're ready to release you," Elinger said. "At your word, you can go back on duty with me if that's what you want."

Torres' face shined. "Hey thanks for cuttin' me some slack. What did I do to deserve that?"

"You saved my life. So, I know I can count on you when I need to," Elinger said simply, then leaned toward the bed and riveted his eyes on Torres. "But I don't want to bury you, Ralph. So, I'm hoping you can get your head on straight."

Torres nodded, quietly understanding. "I know it's now or never, man."

Elinger rose from the chair and moved across the room. He paused at the doorway and looked back at Torres. "Just keep the promise you never made to your mother."

"What do you mean?" Torres asked in a surprised tone.

"You never promised her she'd have two dead sons before their time!" With that, Elinger exited the room.

Elinger's words bulls-eyed Torres. Torres didn't promise his mother two dead sons. If she were alive, she would want Torres to live and succeed at whatever he did, and live for both himself and Manuel. But his brother's death was difficult to forget. Every suspect Torres confronted seemed to resemble the gang banger who killed Manuel. That *vato* was everywhere yet nowhere, always lurking in Torres' mind. Torres realized that every chance he took with a dangerous suspect was his way of trying to prevent his *mijo* from being murdered again and to prove to himself that he was brave—that he really didn't run that night! Torres knew he would have to work hard to temper his heroics. Strong emotions didn't always follow logic, Torres knew. Graveyards were full of young men like him.

Returning his gaze to the window, Torres observed the distant city now fully lighted by the morning sun. He wondered how he would react in his next encounter with danger. But more important, how would he handle his next confrontation with the man who had tried to stab him in through the heart?

TWENTY-NINE

● ● ●

To create an accurate facial composite of Richard Smith's murderer, Elinger hurried back to Headquarters from the hospital. He had already summoned a computer specialist from the Maryland State Police. He watched the middle-aged female officer as she used Faces—a software package that generates thousands of different ears, noses, chins, eyes, mouths, and hairstyles to create millions of photo-quality faces. Elinger was glad his years as a trained witness would help this fellow officer produce a striking portrait of his suspect in less than an hour. The finished image was as though the one-eared man had posed for a photograph. Elinger would turn the composite into a BOLO and send it electronically through Headquarter's computer systems for every officer in the BPD to see; every officer in the city would be on the look out for this monster. He would also post it on the BPD website as he had promised the reporters.

As soon as Elinger returned to his desk, Detective Brown called him. In his records search for crimes that involved a one-eared man, Brown had found one—an unsolved, vicious mugging that happened in the middle of his serial killer's timeline. Detective

Brown had summoned the victim to Headquarters, and Elinger was all to eager to meet with him.

The hulking figure of Müeller the Masher straddled a chair in front of a table in an interrogation room. Detective Brown, a portly officer in his late thirties, sat near Müeller.
The Masher told Brown he was determined to find the man who made a fool of him and mercilessly beat his bodyguards. Müeller vowed to personally search the streets for him. The Masher wanted to deliver swift justice without burdening the American court system.

When Elinger entered the room, he was holding a photo spread of six men for Müeller to review. One of the images, mixed in with the standard booking shots, was the new composite of the one-eared man. Müeller rose from the chair to shake hands with Elinger. He sized him up as he squeezed the detective's hand with a crushing handshake.

Detective Brown briefed Elinger on the Spartan Gym mugging. Müeller's bodyguard Wicker remained hospitalized and the Masher's other muscle man, Cowan, was blind in one eye because of the brutal attack.

"Do you see your attacker in these photos?" Elinger asked, handing the wrestler the six-man photo spread.
Müeller's expression was instantly aglow when his eyes set on the composite image. "*Ja*, dat's zee *schweinehund* I vant! Is he here, in the building?" the Masher asked quickly, clenching his fists with such force his knuckles cracked and turned white like bone.

"No, but with this we hope to pick him up soon," Elinger replied, indicating the composite of the one-eared man on the photo spread.

"May I have dis?" Müeller asked.

Elinger nodded.

"Tanks," the Masher said, folding the photo spread and tucking it into his shirt pocket. "I vant to break dat *drecksau's* back with my bare hands!" Lifting his bulging arms, the Masher curled his palms and fingers. He pulled his arms down as he raised a knee as though he was snapping the mugger's back over his leg like a twig.

"We understand how you feel, Mr. Müeller," Elinger said. "And I'm sure you could do just that. But the pleasure will be all ours. Believe me," he added, raising his injured arm still in a sling. "I owe him, too."

It was scant satisfaction for Müeller. He galvanized his face in an expression of hatred. "Lieutenant, I have not been in your country long, but I've learned one ting very fast. Americans are always in a footrace. They vant to be first at everything! I'm no different now! I vant to be first to catch dis schweinehund! Do not trouble yourself. The Masher vill get him for you!"

"If you know Americans that well, then you know that vigilantism is against the law," Elinger stated firmly. "And if you take the law into your own hands, I would have to treat you just like I would treat him."

Müeller stared brazenly at Elinger, then grinned sardonically. "I vould thank you for dat. I vould like nothing better than to be in jail vith him."

"Then take this as a warning, Mr. Müeller," Elinger said simply. "Stay out of this."

"You are not much different den your judges or your

courts," Müeller commented. "Americans have forgotten how to punish criminals. But I have not. So, I'll see you in de footrace, *ja?*"

"If you interfere with us in any way, I'll arrest you." Müeller considered Elinger's sharp and direct statement. "Your badge does not protect you from all men, Mr. Lieutenant," he warned. With that, Müeller moved across the room, the floor creaking beneath his feet. He exited, slamming the door behind him.

"You think he's gonna give us a problem?" Brown asked.

"I don't think he'll ask us to join him for a plate of *sauerbraten* if that's what you mean," Elinger answered.

After Brown had left the room, Elinger was concerned how Müeller could screw-up his investigation. He didn't need any more obstacles in the case. First Amos the reporter, now Müeller the wrestler.

Elinger became introspective, aware a part of him sided with Müeller—he, too, wanted a personal rematch with the one-eared man away from the eyes and ears of the law. American justice was too good for this killer, but Elinger was sure he'd never cross that line.

Right now, Elinger could only hope that when all BPD officers saw the composite, they would spot the one-eared man on the street and apprehend him quickly. And when the reporters printed the composite photo in their newspapers, the suspect would be indentified by someone in the public.

THIRTY

• • •

Father Andrew Blair stood quietly in a dark room of the tall, century-old Gibbons Hall. He peered out the dormer window across the campus grounds of the Norte Dame of Maryland University's all girl college. He focused on the timberland that surrounded the school, then bent his delicate frame forward and buried his face in the eyepiece of a powerful telescope. The scope was pointed at the star-freckled sky through the open window.

As Blair observed the stars, he heard the elevator creep upward from the ground floor. When it stopped on the floor below him, he could only hear the steps of the visitor climbing the shadowy staircase.

When the visitor stepped into the room, the lunar glow from the window illuminated the soft features of Renee Holland. Renee looked at the priest and recognized him to be the same clergyman she had seen on the religious talk show the previous night.

"Father Blair?" Renee greeted, approaching Blair. "Security told me I would find you here. I'm Renee Holland. We talked on the phone."

"Oh, Yes," Father Blair said, extending his hand. "But I

thought we were meeting for lunch tomorrow."

"Please forgive my impatience," Renee said, feeling guilty for imposing. "But my situation is getting desperate. I was afraid to wait any longer."

"It's all right, my dear," Blair comforted. "It was late last night when you called. It was thoughtless of me not to agree to meet with you sooner. I sometimes forget how urgent these matters can be to the victim," Father Blair added as he pulled a lens cap from his pocket and covered the telescope eyepiece. "I was looking at Saturn. It's one of the Lord's most beautiful landscapes."

"Do you do this every night?" Renee asked, glancing at the telescope.

Father Blair chuckled. "Yes, you might say my main interest has always been in the heavens. It's my way of seeing God, or at least God's work."

Renee smiled graciously, then the humor slowly faded from her face.

"How can I help?" Father Blair asked.

Renee drew in a deep breath. Breaching the subject always made her feel weak. "I want to know if I'm possessed," she said. "But I'm not so sure I believe in the devil."

"He and his minions are very real, my dear," Father Blair said with divine assurance. "As real as you and I. I was a young priest when I first encountered him."

"Really? What happened, Father?" Renee asked, hoping she would gain some insight from his experience.

"It's not pleasant," Father Blair frowned. "I'll tell you about it, but would you care for a cup of hot tea first?"

"Yes, I'd love one."

"Gets rather cold in this room," Father Blair commented, moving to a small table and chairs where there was a large thermos and one tea cup.

Blair opened the thermos and poured Renee a cupful in the thermos cap and handed it to her. "Sorry I don't have any extra cups up here. I wasn't expecting company." He lifted the thermos to his nose, sniffing the berried aroma with an affable smile. "Warms the body as well as the soul," he said as he poured some tea into his cup on the table.

Renee nodded, then sipped the tea.

Blair took a drink from his cup then settled into a chair by the table. Renee sat beside him.

"I first met the devil at an Inter-Denominational meeting in England," Father Blair began. "During our first day, Satan worshipers picketed the church. They harassed us with profanities and defiled God's teachings with blasphemies. But they also taunted us with personal things they had no way of knowing!"

Renee's curiosity was aroused. "Like what?"

The priest glanced warily at her. "They knew where I grew up—and how poor my family was. They knew my father was an alcoholic. They knew he killed himself. They used this to try to humiliate me in front of my colleagues," Blair added. "They did the same to everyone else."

"You're saying they learned about your father through the devil?"

"Exactly," Father Blair said with a sigh. "These people didn't know me. I'd never been to England before. So how else could they know? I knew my calling that day, to spend the rest of my life keeping the devil in hell!" The priest drank more tea before he continued. "Once I became involved in exorcisms, I saw the vilest things. Children speaking in the coarse tongue of the devil, living bodies decaying before my eyes, murders committed by the devil's will, souls lost forever."

"Nothing like that is happening to me," Renee said, suddenly feeling silly for taking up the priest's time. "It doesn't sound like I'm possessed."

"Before we decide that, I'd like to ask you a few questions?"

"Okay."

"Does your mind ever feel controlled?"

"Only briefly, just before I go into one of the trances I told you about."

"Do you have any ancestors who were involved in witchcraft or belonged to the occult?"

"Not that I know of. Why is that important?"

"A verse from Exodus explains it," Father Blair replied. "*You shall not bow down to them or serve them; for I the Lord your God am a jealous God, visiting the iniquity of the fathers upon the children to the third and fourth generation of those who hate me,*" Blair recited from memory. "The Bible is saying a child can be cursed by what his or her ancestors have done."

"That can bring on possession?"

Father Blair nodded. "They're the most difficult to exorcise because it's part of God's law. I thank Him for His forgiveness though."

Renee shifted uneasily in her chair as goose bumps peppered her neck.

"When you were young, did you ever see spirits?" Blair

asked.

"No."

"Have you ever dabbled in the occult?"

"No."

"Do you have trouble sleeping?"

"Yes, the worst of my life," Renee replied.

"Do you eat properly?"

"Yes."

"Can you think clearly when you're not in a trance?"

"Yes. Is that a good sign?" Renee asked.

"Absolutely. The devil was an archangel, Miss Holland. And with an intelligence far superior to ours, his strongest weapon is his ability to control our will."

Father Blair drained the last of his tea then looked directly into Renee's eyes. "Most important, Miss Holland, do you believe in Jesus Christ?"

"Yes."

Blair smiled. "Good. That keeps the devil on a leash. You don't have the classic signs of possession. Perhaps it's a medical or mental issue that triggers your writing trances?"

"I've already been to both kinds of those doctors," Renee said bleakly. "I was hoping there was something you could do, Father."

"Perhaps," Blair replied curtly. "I could bless your home."

Apprehension shrouded Renee's words. "You think my house might be possessed?"

Father Blair nodded. "It's possible."

"Can we do it now?"

"Now?" Blair repeated, glancing at his watch.

"Please, Father," Renee implored. "It's only seven o'clock."

Blair lifted his eyes from his watch. "Of course, Miss Holland. I planned to watch Venus until the early morning hours anyway. Some believe it is the very star that guided the wise men. Perhaps it will give me some wisdom about your troubles."

● ● ●

A couple of hours later, Elinger drove over darkened Baltimore streets, heading for Renee's home. He had called Renee earlier, but she didn't answer. And Sanders hadn't reported they would be away from the house. Elinger tried to ease his worry by thinking about his visit with Torres earlier in the day. Torres was improving. He was walking now, eating his first cheeseburger since the injury. The nurses said he was feeling his oats because he had asked for their phone numbers and wanted to date all of them. Torres' only regret about improving, he had told Elinger, was that he'd no longer receive sponge baths from the pretty nurses.

Renee opened her front door and greeted Elinger with a hug. Elinger gave Renee his best one-armed squeeze.
Alex, wearing stripped pajamas, poked his head over the second story rail near the stairs. "What're you doing here? It's almost time for bed," he called down to Elinger as Elinger entered the house.

"I came to give you something."

"Huh? It's not my birthday."

Elinger reached into his coat pocket and pulled out a baseball. He tossed it up to Alex who snatched it out of the air. Alex studied it, his face suddenly flashed an appreciative smile.

"Wow! Autographed by Cal Ripken, Jr.! How'd you know he was my favorite player?"

"Your Mom told me."

"How'd you get it? I mean, he's retired now."

"And in the Hall of Fame," Elinger added. "I helped him out once. He owed me a favor."

Alex read aloud the words on the rawhide.

Best Wishes, Alex

Cal Ripken, Jr.

Alex shot another bright look at Elinger. "Wow, this is awesome!"

"Time to go to bed, Alex," Renee said. "You need your sleep if you're going to play ball like Mr. Ripken did."

"Aw, Mom. Let me stay up awhile."

"School night."

"Yeah," Alex grumbled. "Okay. Thanks, Mr. Elinger."

"You can call me Kent."

"Okay, thanks, Kent." Alex said, watching his mother and Elinger. They always stood close together, almost touching whenever they talked to each other. Alex knew his mother liked Elinger—and he was beginning to approve. Alex smiled down at the baseball in his hands, then turned and withdrew into his bedroom.

Renee turned to Elinger with a smile. "You've got a friend for life."

"He's a good kid," Elinger said. "And all good kids should have a baseball autographed by their favorite player."

"Why'd you really come over, Kent?" Renee asked.

"Surely not to deliver a baseball?"

"I called earlier but your phone went straight to voice mail."

"I forgot it when I left," Renee replied. "That's not like me, but nothing's like me anymore."

"And Sanders didn't call in. Where is he?" Elinger asked.

"In the living room. I told him he could take a nap while Alex was still up. I heard you're working that poor man on a double-shift just to watch me."

"Yeah, but don't worry about him. He likes the overtime," Elinger said. "Why didn't you answer your phone?"

"I was out."

"Without Sanders?"

Renee nodded sheepishly. "I snuck out the back door. I went to see a priest."

Elinger frowned. "You're not supposed to go out alone. And why a priest?"

"I thought I might be possessed," Renee said, slightly embarrassed. "He blessed the house and me."

"Your will is too strong to be possessed."

"Is that a compliment or an insult?" Renee asked.

Elinger smiled dryly. "A compliment, of course. But I don't want you going out alone again. Okay?"

"I promise," Renee replied, appreciating Elinger's desire to protect her. It made her feel safe if only for a moment. "Would you like to come in for a cup of coffee?" she asked.

"We don't have time."

"Sounds like we're going somewhere."

"Yeah, to the mountains, up to the Patapsco River,"

Elinger said. "Sanders will take care of Alex."

"Okay, but why are we going?"

"Derek Burris located the *thoughts are things* guru he talked about," Elinger said. "This guy is an ex-professor who used to teach Moral Philosophy. He's been at a mountain commune for a few years, still preaching *New Age* ideas. He's agreed to talk to us. Derek thinks he can help."

THIRTY-ONE

● ● ●

Glancing out the driver's window, Elinger admired the wooded countryside as he steered his auto west on Highway 70 toward the Patapsco River. He inhaled the crisp, clear air as it flowed in through his half-open window.

Renee, sitting on the passenger seat, gazed at the vast spread of oak trees and wild flowers and then glanced at Elinger's strong hands on the wheel and his alert eyes probing the highway and mountainous surroundings. He looked more handsome now. His features seemed more distinguished. He had lost a few pounds, too, making him look a bit trimmer and more virile. Every time she was near him, Renee became aware of her physical attraction to him.

When Elinger looked at Renee with a tender smile, Renee sensed he felt the same about her and hoped he would tell her soon.

A few minutes later, Elinger pulled off the highway and parked at a scenic lookout point above the waters of the Patapsco River.

While he and Renee stood at the rocky parapet taking in the beauty of the countryside, Elinger put his hand on Renee's waist and pulled her close. Renee felt her pulse quicken and a warmth spread throughout her body. She nuzzled closer to Elinger waiting for his kiss.

Elinger removed his injured arm from the sling and gently embraced Renee. "I'm sorry for what's happening to you. I wish I could've stopped it by now."

"I know, Kent," Renee said, resting her head on Elinger's shoulder.

Elinger cupped Renee's chin in his hand and gently pulled her head toward his. He pressed his mouth against her lips. Welcoming the kiss with an eager embrace, Renee's moist lips parted with passion. In moments, Elinger's and Renee's tongues were caressing, deepening the fervor of their growing affection.

After the embrace, Renee nestled her head on Elinger's shoulder again and breathed deeply. "That was nice," she purred. "What took you so long?"

"I think I've wanted to do that since the first day I met you," Elinger confessed.

"That's hard to believe," Renee chuckled quietly. "I made a horrible first impression—leaning over a car vomiting?"

Elinger laughed. "I guess it was the second time I saw you, then."

Renee smiled good-naturedly. "I was your prime murder suspect."

"Not really," Elinger said, kissing Renee long and ardently. They stood there holding one another for a few minutes longer before they returned to Elinger's car.

Back on the road, Elinger continued to drive higher into

the mountains and Renee was asleep in the passenger seat. The sun beamed through her window, keeping her warm and comfortable as she dozed.

"Elinger here," Elinger greeted as he answered his cell phone prompt on his auto's Bluetooth connection.

"Kent, it's Evans," Sam Evans' voice filtered through the FM band of the car's radio. "I found something interesting."

The call had awakened Renee.

"I'm listening, Sam."

"I analyzed some of the killer's blood from the slaughterhouse. Remember the high levels of adrenaline we found before?"

"Yeah," Elinger recalled. "I'm sure you found more."

"But this time there were very high levels of endorphins as well," Evans reported.

"That's a chemical the body produces to kill pain, right?" Elinger asked.

"Yes, and from what I saw under the microscope, I think your perp could be impervious to pain at times."

"Yeah, Torres beat his face to a pulp with a mallet, and I almost tore his bicep out of his arm, yet he recovered quickly and fought us like those injuries were nothing more than a skin rash."

"I just wanted to give you a heads up," Evans said. "You got yourself some kind of superman. I've never seen anything like it."

"Thanks, Sam," Elinger said as he punched the phone icon on his steering wheel, ending the call.

Elinger glanced at Renee's concerned expression. He was sorry she heard the conversation. She already had enough worries to last her a lifetime.

●　●　●

Ravnik slowly opened his eyes and squinted. Rays of light filtered through a torn window shade and lit his beaten face. Climbing from his bed, Ravnik moved to his dresser. He could barely recognize himself when he looked into the mirror. His eyes, nose, cheeks, and forehead were swollen and bruised. His injuries were well worth it though. At least he had stabbed the policeman who beat him with the mallet. As far as Ravnik knew, that cop was dead and that made him happy.

Ravnik sat on his sagging bed and pulled off his blood-stained T-shirt. His eyes drifted to his injured bicep. Pus oozed from the flesh beneath his ragged stitch job—and the edges of the wound were crowded with writhing maggots. This was the voice's idea, Ravnik recalled. When the infection began, the voice warned him he could lose his arm if the infection didn't stop. Since it was too risky to seek medical help, the voice led Ravnik to a grocery market dumpster where dozens of flies ate rotting foods. There, in the afternoon heat, Ravnik exposed his wound above the garbage to attract flies to his infected flesh. The flies gorged themselves on Ravnik's wound and laid their eggs. Maggots would be born and would clean the wound, the voice had explained. Maggots were used in surgery long ago to kill bacteria by eating necrotic tissue. Although the practice wasn't common anymore, the voice had assured Ravnik it was still effective.

Ravnik moved from his dresser to his only window. He

yanked open the shade, allowing the sun to flood his room. The warmth felt good, he thought. He studied the maggots in his bicep. The hotter the day, the faster they worked, and the quicker they would put him back on the street, according to the voice.

● ● ●

Elinger noticed the high-altitude morning was still crisp when he and Renee arrived at the mountain retreat. Parking his auto on a dirt lot carved from a hill of volcanic rock, he realized the forest view was spoiled by the retreat's row of rusting Quonset huts.

Emerging from the car, Elinger and Renee saw a few young men and women entering and exiting various huts. Most were wearing pumpkin colored saffron robes resembling Krishna dhotis. Others stood motionless with their hands extended toward the sky, meditating or droning their mantras. Many of the youths had shaved heads, while others had long, braided ponytails.

"The guy who runs this place is supposed to help us?" Renee asked Elinger.

Elinger noticed Renee's tone of disbelief. "We're desperate, remember?" he reminded as he joined her at the side of his car. "Burris said this guy was a brilliant professor before he dropped out."

"I just don't understand what philosophy has to do with me."

"I hope we're about to find out," Elinger replied optimistically.

After entering the first Quonset hut, Elinger and Renee walked across an old faded carpet to a group of young female disciples who were wearing wrinkled *dhotis*. They were sitting in a circle on the floor, chanting unintelligible words.

When Elinger asked the women where he could find Kirk Dennington, he drew puzzled looks from them. They didn't know anyone by that name. But when Elinger explained Dennington was the retreat's guru, the women understood he really wanted to see *Akbar Jahan*. They directed Elinger and Renee to an old, pitted asphalt driveway behind the huts. At the end of the drive was a dilapidated garage with a basketball hoop mounted above its door. Elinger and Renee expected the retreat's guru to be wearing a robe and have flowing hair. Instead, Dennington wore a T-shirt, baggy shorts and running shoes as he bounded down the driveway dribbling a basketball. He stopped suddenly near Elinger and Renee and swished a jump shot fifteen feet from the hoop.

Elinger was surprised by Dennington's physical appearance. It was certainly untrue to Burris' description. He guessed Dennington was in his late thirties, and Dennington certainly looked too hip to be an eccentric recluse.

"*Akbar Jahan*? Kirk Dennington?" Elinger asked, not sure what name to use.

Dennington reached out and shook Elinger's hand. "Kirk or Dennington will do," he greeted enthusiastically, flashing a flawless set of gleaming teeth. "You must be Lieutenant Elinger?"

Elinger nodded. "And this is Renee Holland."

"My pleasure." Dennington pumped Renee's hand, smiling through his handsome features. "Your career is very impressive."

"Thank you."

Dennington pulled a large handkerchief from his pocket and wiped the sweat from his forehead. "Sorry you had to drive up here, Lieutenant, but I couldn't get away. I had pressing matters here."

Elinger glanced at the basketball rolling toward Dennington's feet.

"Besides this, of course," Dennington grinned, picking up the ball and stuffing the handkerchief back into his pocket.

"We appreciate you taking the time to see us," Elinger said.

"It's partly selfish, you know," Dennington said. "The conversation I had with Derek Burris was most interesting. He told me about your problem, Ms. Holland. I thought nothing could surprise me anymore."

Dennington suddenly pivoted and swung an arm over his shoulder, releasing the basketball. The ball swished through the basket. He turned back to Elinger and Renee. "I don't care what they say about baseball, I think basketball is America's greatest sport. I was a varsity man. Class of ninety-nine." Dennington pointed toward a nearby wooded area. "Why don't we go for a walk? My mind is freer when I'm close to nature."

"Sure," Elinger said as he and Renee followed Dennington into the forest, hiking down a winding dirt trail.

"May I ask you a personal question, Kirk?" Renee said in a polite voice.

"Sure, I'm not a private person anymore."

"We heard you were an honored academic. Why did you give that up?"

"You mean, why did I drop out?"

Dennington noticed Renee's sudden expression of embarrassment. After all, her question sounded a bit disparaging. "It's okay, Ms. Holland. You didn't hurt my feelings. I don't carry emotional baggage anymore," he said. "I'm here because I concluded being a college professor was intellectually stifling. I wanted to solve the mysteries of life. On campus, everyone thought I was a throwback from the hippie era even though that was before my time. Coming up here where minds are more open allowed me to find the answers to human and spiritual existence that I was looking for."

"Do you think any of those answers can help me?" Renee asked.

"I hate to think you drove all the way up here for nothing," Dennington grinned before a more serious look altered his expression. "It's obvious you're involved in a metaphysical phenomenon of some kind, Ms. Holland. And that's my specialty. Do either of you know much about metaphysics?"

"We're not experts," Elinger said.

"Then I'll give you a little background to help you understand what you're dealing with."

Elinger nodded, indicating his appreciation.

"It was Aristotle who started it all," Dennington began, leading Elinger and Renee deeper into a maze of trees and ideas. "He intellectualized ultimate truth and reality to systematize knowledge for all existence whether it was physical, astral, or ethereal. He believed the universe was a warehouse of knowledge that held the answers to the perplexing questions of our existence. If any of this was ever *all Greek* to you, now you know why,"

Dennington joked.

"How does this relate to my predicament?" Renee asked.

"You're recording, in written form, physical reality as it happens, in real time, although you are not there when it occurs," Dennington began. "That's what makes your situation unique. As Lieutenant Elinger explained on the phone, you're mentally linked to a flesh-and-blood killer—a link well beyond simple mental telepathy. If we subscribe to the Derek Burris' theory—that your brain wave frequency sometimes connects with the killer's brain frequency—it gets very intriguing. According to the Laws of Physics, that's impossible."

"Why is that?" Renee asked.

"Because everything is supposed to occupy its own time and space," Dennington said as he stopped and picked up a pine cone. He lifted it to his nose and savored its aroma before he turned back to Elinger and Renee. "So, if individuals share the same brain wave length, it should be for only a fraction of second. The thoughts should find their own time and space on their electromagnetic plane in an instant. But your writing trances last much longer, don't they?"

"Ten, fifteen minutes sometimes."

Dennington chuckled. "Sure blows a hole in the Laws of Physics, doesn't it?"

"But it is happening," Elinger added. "How do you explain it?"

"I'm guessing only a freak of nature with incredible force could cause an aberration in physics," Dennington theorized. "At first, I told myself no natural force could create supernatural phenomena!" Dennington shook his head and tossed the pine cone aside. "So, I assumed this was a hoax, but when Burris told me about the exploding crystals, I was hooked. I tried to postulate it, but I think your phone call, Lieutenant, holds the key. You said you thought a third party might be involved, something that's controlling both the murderer and Ms. Holland."

"When I was close to the killer, just inches from his face, he looked like he was being controlled by something," Elinger began. "It was the same look in Renee's face when she is trance-writing. And for a moment, the killer was talking to someone—but no one was there but me."

"Or talking to himself? Schizophrenia, perhaps?" Dennington interjected.

"It crossed my mind, but I come across schizophrenics in jail and this was different," Elinger explained haltingly, trying to believe his own words. "I'm a cop. I believe in facts, but what I've seen happening to Renee, the trances, the messages, my encounters with the killer, especially at the slaughterhouse, are beyond explanation from my normal frame of reference. That's why I'm here. Whatever was talking to the killer was telling him what to do, I think, and somehow it filters down to Renee."

"You're sure about that?" Dennington asked.

"Well, it's what I keep coming up with when I try to make sense of this," Elinger replied. "And then there were the sparks."

"Sparks?" Dennington repeated.

"Coming out of the killer's hand at the slaughterhouse," Elinger said, hardly believing what he had seen. "He pointed his fingers at the control box of a band saw and turned it on with an electrical charge from his body!"

"Did this happen when he appeared to be in a trance?"

Dennington asked.

Elinger nodded.

"Incredible!" Dennington exclaimed. "You may have seen an actual physical manifestation of thoughts outside the human brain. What a powerful force is at work here! It could only come from the other side, probably the astral plan since these events are too evil to be ethereal."

"What exactly are you saying?" Renee asked.

"I'm afraid Lieutenant Elinger is probably right," Dennington mused aloud. "That a third party is involved. A disincarnate would make the most sense," he added without pause. "And obviously a very evil one."

"Disincarnate? You're saying a dead person is the impetus for my trances?" Renee asked in a non-believing tone.

"Only dead as far as physical life is concerned," Dennington replied.

"Sorry, Kirk, but I don't believe in ghosts," Renee argued.

"Derek Burris told me you are a religious person who believes in life after death, right?" Dennington asked, planting his eyes on Renee's.

"Yes, I'm a Christian," Renee said. "But I don't believe God allows our spirits to roam the earth after death. I believe we go to heaven or hell immediately."

"Ghost is merely one of many descriptions of a spirit, Ms. Holland," Dennington said casually. "They're also called disincarnates, souls, disembodied spirits, entities, monads, a consciousness and atman's. But no matter what term we use, we shouldn't forget they used to be one of us."

"If ghosts exist, how is it that I'm connected to one

through the one-eared killer?" Renee asked.

"The dead have always channeled through the living," Dennington stated. "But in your case this spirit is broadcasting its thoughts to the killer, and then your brain picks them up like a radio. You couldn't write the killer's thoughts if your mind wasn't linked to his."

Elinger could tell Renee was uncomfortable with Dennington's postulations. He sensed she was afraid to learn more about what had invaded her life. But he did not end the conversation. Instead, he allowed Dennington to lead them down a fork in the trail to the shady side of the mountain where a cool breeze rustled through the trees. When Renee became chilled by the dropping temperature, Elinger gladly welcomed Renee when she moved closer to him and slid her arm though his.

Dennington continued his thought as the three of them moved down the trail. "Look at it this way, Ms. Holland. We all know there's a spiritual world. Descartes maintained the mind and body are two radically different entities. And the esoteric English author—C.E.M. Joad—wrote that the principle of life expresses itself at *the level of what is called mind, that this mind is distinct from both body and brain*," Dennington recited from memory. "You could say our brain waves are the frequency of our souls."

Dennington led Elinger and Renee into a lush meadow dotted with blooming purple and yellow wild flowers. The sun again brightened the forest and warmed them slightly. Dennington stopped near a log by a churning stream. "Why don't we take a breather?" he suggested. "I forgot you two aren't used to the thin air up here."

Elinger and Renee settled on the log with Dennington.

Elinger took a moment to assemble his thoughts. He had a few questions for Dennington. "Kirk, let's say this is an entity—why would it be interested in interacting with us? Don't they have their own world?"

Dennington pulled a violet from the ground and opened its petals as he spoke. "Yes and no. Most are dormant when their physical life ends. They're waiting for acceptance into the spiritual world. The Mormons and Catholics call it Purgatory. Islamic souls wait for their Day of Judgment. Christians wait for the return of Jesus. Buddhist and Hindu spirits wait for their next earthly life. But some disincarnates go into a karmic limbo. They cross over to our plane of existence and interfere with our lives."

"But how can a spirit project thoughts into this world?" Renee asked.

"A consciousness has emotions, and emotions magnetize thoughts," Dennington explained. "These thoughts have enough power to cross over. They have physical properties on the subatomic level. But what's happening to you is far more powerful, Ms. Holland. That's why you can be sure we're dealing with an entity."

"Back up a minute. You're saying thoughts have physical properties?" Renee asked. "Just exactly what do you mean?"

"Yes, all thoughts have electromagnetic energy, electricity, vibration, sound, light, and temperature whether they're from a disincarnate or a human. And what do those properties remind you of?" Dennington suddenly asked.
Elinger and Renee exchanged a blank look.

"Lightning!" Dennington answered himself. "Our thoughts are like lightning. Our brain creates a miniature electrical storm whenever it manufactures a thought."

Dennington suddenly stood and moved toward the trail. Without a word, Elinger and Renee rose from the log and followed him.

"Kirk, could this entity have a purpose or goal?" Elinger asked. "These murder scenes seem weirdly staged and the clues are odd—like we found a battery stuffed in the second victim's mouth. I don't think this thing is doing random killings. It has a goal of some kind."

"I would agree," Dennington answered. "Perhaps it's seeking karmic justice from a past life? If we could learn its identity, perhaps we could discover something we could use to stop it."

"And how in the hell would I find out the identity of a ghost?" Elinger asked with a tone of incredulity.

Dennington took a few more steps down the path before he spoke. "I understand your frustration, Lieutenant."

"Look, I know what you're saying," Elinger said. "Treat it as though it's a flesh and blood suspect. Find out who it is to gain insight on how it thinks, what it likes, what is doesn't like, and maybe find a weakness to use to stop it."

"Precisely," Dennington replied.

Elinger glanced at Renee askance. "Maybe the Pratt Library has a copy of *Who's Who in Ghostland*?"

"No one said this would be easy," Dennington commented.

Elinger had another thought surface. "Kirk, the killer is extremely strong and doesn't react to pain very much. Could that be caused by an entity?"

"Most definitely. When a consciousness controls a human, I've seen cases where it can manipulate the body's functions, including adrenaline flow and the body's endorphins. Why do you ask?"

"We found high levels of both chemicals in the killer's blood samples," Elinger said. "He is so powerful. I have to stop him anyway I can. Next time, I'm going to call in S.W.A.T."

Dennington's face suddenly showed alarm. "I wouldn't advise that, Lieutenant. Killing the murderer would require precise timing."

"What do you mean?"

"You've got to destroy the entity as well—at the same moment you kill the murderer."

"Why?" Renee asked.

Dennington continued to walk his steady pace through the woods. "Because the killer is the only thing that separates Renee from the entity. The killer uses up some of the entity's energy because his brain is the host. So, if the killer dies, the entity might jump ahead in this three-way connection and focus all of its power on Renee. Maybe even force her to become a murderer."

Renee's face tightened with fear when she heard this.

"Okay, if we're dealing with a bona fide entity, how can we get rid of it?" Elinger asked Dennington.

Dennington hiked farther down the trail before he replied. "You've got to disrupt its electromagnetic plane of existence. In this case, it lives in the electrical system of the killer's brain." Dennington stopped and pivoted toward Elinger and Renee. "If you destroy the killer while he is trancing under the control of the entity, you would obviously terminate the electrical system of the killer's brain and therefore disrupt the entity's plane of existence at the same time."

"I want to make sure I understand this, Kirk," Elinger began in a facetious tone. "The next time I corner the killer, if he's not trancing and even if he's trying to kill me, I still need to take him alive and jail him until he trances out again. Then, when he's trancing again and no one's looking, I sneak into his cell and kill him in cold blood, right?"

"I know this is not easy," Dennington said, his words echoed Elinger's mood. "But it is what it is. Besides learning the identity of this consciousness, we also need to find out how it's connected to Renee and the killer in the beginning. There is always an event involved to trigger this sort of thing. If you learn what that is, that would also be helpful."

"What if we can't find out who it is—or was? Or what started the connection?" Renee asked. "That sounds impossible."

"Don't worry, you can do it," Dennington said in a confident tone.

"Why are you so sure of that?" Elinger asked.

"Because truth always manifests itself."

"What do you think, Kent?" Renee asked as she and Elinger walked toward Elinger's sedan on the retreat's parking lot. "Do you believe him?"

Elinger evaluated his reply before he spoke. "I don't really know how to answer that. I have a good job, a good pension and my peers respect me. Now I have a chance to flush it all away by admitting I believe in ghosts."

"Definitely a bad career move," Renee said.

"Do you still have those old books?"

"They're all overdue."

"I'll pick up the tab," Elinger promised. "Just keep analyzing the writing styles."

"You think I'm right, that this entity was once a writer?"

"That's your expertise so I'm going to follow your instincts," Elinger replied, stopping at his auto's passenger side. "I hope you'll find something that'll help us."

"Like matching the writing style of the killer's notes to some literature from the past?"

"Yeah, if it's there, I'm sure you'll find it."

"Because truth always manifests itself, right?" Renee mocked Dennington.

"Yeah, something like that," Elinger replied.

"Well, I've got the time. My career is on the skids right now anyway," Renee said. "And my agent thinks I'm a whack job."

Elinger swung open the car door. "Well, let's try to change his mind."

"How?"

"Maybe your friend Professor Winfield can help us with the old writing styles? He must have some literature experts in his department."

THIRTY-TWO

• • •

A week had passed since Renee met Kirk Dennington. She considered his theories often, searching for insight but finding none. Instead of eliminating the writing spells and bloody headlines, she felt Dennington's dark projections were the fodder of nightmares. Evil specters with narrow, fiery eyes appeared in Renee's mind whenever she slept. She could see their gnashing, rotting teeth and smell their sulfuric breath.

As the days wore on, Renee waited with dread for the next trance. She knew the hammering headache, the catatonic eyes, and the obsession to write about murder could start at any time.

Renee could temporarily overcome her murky frame of mind whenever she hit Alex ground balls in the backyard. It was such a joy to see her son develop his physical coordination and catch a fast-moving baseball. He had the moves of a natural athlete, she noted.

Many times, when Elinger stopped at the Holland house, he would join Renee and Alex for a few minutes in the backyard. He was the catcher, taking Alex's fast throws after he scooped up a grounder hit by his mother. Elinger enjoyed this, realizing these baseball sessions with Alex were bonding him to Renee's son.

● ● ●

Bare-chested, Ravnik stood in front of his mirror and studied his face. The swelling was almost gone now. The whites of his eyes were jaggedly traced with thin red veins that were much larger yesterday. His nose was straight again although still peppered with the small holes left by the spiked mallet. The purple bruises on his forehead and cheeks had turned yellow. The deep cuts on his lips had healed with thick scar tissue.

Ravnik looked at the large wound in his bicep. The maggots had done their work well, he observed. The swelling was gone and the wound was clean and free of infection. Only the crude stitch job remained.

Ravnik sat on his bed and retrieved scissors from his old bed stand. He snipped the threads that sealed his wound and clamped his teeth on the cut ends. He yanked the stitches from his bicep, one by one. The wound had healed grotesquely, leaving a wide welder's seam of flesh and tattooed X marks left by the ink in the dark thread. Another battle wound, Ravnik contemplated proudly.

Ravnik pressed and kneaded the scar. He flexed his arm, bringing his fist to his shoulder and down again. The movement was stiff at first but became more fluid as he repeated it. Ravnik grinned with delight. He was going to be one hundred percent again. Now, with the voice encouraging him, it was time for more people to die.

THIRTY-THREE

• • •

With his arm healed, Elinger turned the helm of his sailboat with both hands, steering through Chesapeake Bay's deep blue water. The boat's thirty-foot fin keel cut the bay, its jib and mainsail ballooned in the morning winds and carried the craft toward open waters. The cool spray on his face reminded Elinger that he was glad to leave a foamy trail between himself and the city. Sailing his boat, *Just Cruisin'*, was the only time he could completely relax. He felt better now that his arm had healed even though the Holland case continued to drain him. Elinger hoped a day of boating and scuba diving would give him the sharper mind he needed to solve his case. Besides, Renee had not had a trance for nearly a week. If there was ever a time to grab a few hours of personal time, it was now.

As Elinger guided his craft, he recalled why Chesapeake Bay was a great place to scuba dive. The alewives, squeteague, croaker, and shad were always worth a grand meal. But the blue crab had made the Chesapeake legend. Nothing like cooked crab and a cold beer, Elinger thought.

Renee, sitting on a deck chair near Elinger, leaned forward, rubbing a Brasso pad on a sparkling stretch of brass railing. "Is this your idea of a date?" she asked in a flippant tone. "I thought you were going to pamper me?"

"Bright work is part of being a good sailor," Elinger grinned. "You wanted to know more about sailing. It's tradition."

Renee stroked the rail a final time. "Then let me be the first to break tradition," she said, tossing the pad aside. After frowning at her blackened fingers, she suddenly smiled at Elinger. "Now I know why Popeye has such big forearms. It had nothing to do with spinach."

Renee wiped her hands on a rag, then reached into a small ice chest and handed Elinger a cold beer. "It's so peaceful out here," she said. "Just what I needed."

Elinger sipped his beer as he steered the craft. "I used to come out here with my uncle when I was a kid. You could fish just by dipping a skillet in the water. This is where I learned to sail. It's the only place you can work with wind, currents, and tides at the same time. Can't do that on a lake."

Renee spoke while she gazed at distant boat profiles on the horizon. "Too bad Alex had to visit his father."

"I don't know about that," Elinger replied honestly. "I think we were ready for some more alone time," he added, kissing Renee's neck, then playfully nipping at her ear.

Renee closed her eyes.

Elinger sensed Renee was feeling a rush of arousal. "Are you trying to make me forget about the dinner you promised?" Renee asked.

"Absolutely not. I promised you a fine seafood meal and that's what you'll have," Elinger reminded, withdrawing from

Renee,

Renee opened her eyes. "A shipboard barbecue if I recall."

"That's right."

"But when I was below in the kitchen, I—"

"The galley," Elinger corrected.

"The galley. I didn't see any food in the fridge."

"That's because we have to catch our meal. Nothing like fresh seafood."

"Oh? Where are the fishing poles?" Renee asked, scanning the deck.

"Fishing poles? We're going to dive."

"Dive?" Renee asked.

"When I checked into your background, I found out you did some diving when you were in college and became qualified."

Renee nodded. "Yes, but it's been awhile."

"The basics of diving haven't changed," Elinger said. "I brought some gear that should fit you, and I'll stay close to you."

Renee thought about it for a moment before she spoke. "Okay, let's do it," Renee said playfully, ready for a little adventure.

Elinger locked his vision on something behind Renee. "This looks like a great spot for fish. We'll drop anchor here."

"How do you know this is a good spot?"

"Fisherman's intuition."

Renee noticed the focus of Elinger's attention. She saw a gadget attached to a rail above the deck. Its screen displayed dark shadows moving across it.

"A fisherman's intuition, huh?" Renee said.

"Okay, it's a sonar transducer, a fish finder. Those black things on the screen are edible."

"It doesn't seem very fair."

"Never underestimate a fish," Elinger warned with a half smile. "Finding a good spot by trial and error could take us all day, and I don't want you to go hungry."

Elinger tossed *Just Cruisin's* anchor over the side. The boat began to sway gently in the rhythm of two-foot swells. Elinger had already tied its main and jib sails to their masts. He noticed the golden horizon was clear of ships and land, and the eerie quiet was only interrupted by an occasional splash against the boat's hull.

Wearing wet suits, fins and weight belts, Elinger and Renee moved to the helm. Scuba tanks were strapped on their backs with air tubes, regulators and face masks hanging over their shoulders. Elinger had a large, sheathed knife strapped to his calf.

"Keep in mind we can breathe with one tank if there's an emergency," Elinger instructed, taking in two breaths from his regulator, then holding it to Renee's lips. "Put it in your mouth and let it mold to your lips like a kiss. Then draw in two breaths."

Renee placed the mouthpiece in her mouth. After inhaling twice, she handed the regulator back to Elinger who repeated the process. The third time, however, Elinger placed his mouth on Renee's and allowed the air to flow gently from his lungs into hers. In a moment, the couple's lips began to move together, and Elinger wrapped his arms around Renee and kissed her more passionately.

When the embrace ended, Renee spoke in a thick voice. "You have such a personal touch when you teach safety," she grinned.

Elinger smiled back and reached for the mesh game bag that lay on the deck and clipped it to his belt. He then opened a cabinet near the helm and withdrew a three and a half-foot long case. He opened it, revealing a long, sleek, double-barreled aluminum spear gun. Also, inside were two reels of metal line, two spears, and two large CO_2 canisters. "I call it my *Shark Buster*." Elinger said, pulling the weapon, an extra reel of metal line and two spears from the case. "It's a very powerful European spear gun."

"You think we'll see some sharks?" Renee asked. Elinger noticed the slight nervousness in Renee's voice. "It would be unusual if we saw one," Elinger assured Renee while he attached a reel to the spear gun in front of the trigger guard, then a CO_2 canister behind the rear grip. He pushed a spear into each barrel.

Elinger and Renee slid on their masks. Elinger grabbed Renee's hand and led her to the starboard side of the vessel. Without uttering a word, they jumped over the side of the boat and splashed into the water.

Flippering alongside Elinger, Renee kept pace with him. She was amazed by the beauty of the colorful flora that swayed with the currents and the myriad of fish darting past her. It was like being in an aquarium.

Elinger led Renee to deeper waters where they discovered larger fish and hundreds of blue crab on the sandy floor. Elinger plucked a few crabs from the rocks and dropped them into his game bag. Swimming to the bottom, he raked his fingers through the sand, freeing dozens of oysters. He snatched them as they floated upward, placing them in his bag.

When Elinger found a bottle buried in the sand, he placed it on a boulder and swam several yards away. He aimed the spear gun at the bottle.

After a muffled explosive sound, Renee watched as the spear streaked through the water and shattered the bottle. She was impressed by the power of the weapon and Elinger's good aim.

Elinger swam to the spear and retrieved it. He pushed the spear back into its barrel. He turned and swam toward a school of yellow fish, motioning for Renee to follow him. Renee followed, enjoying her colorful surroundings. She was distracted, however, by Elinger's body. His muscles looked hard and well defined. He certainly wasn't the winded guy she talked to on the running track a few weeks ago. His strong muscular legs pumped and propelled him through the water with ease. She wanted to reach out and touch him.

Elinger glanced occasionally at Renee, and Renee could see that he was appraising her body and its underwater movements. She knew her curves were accentuated by the pressure of her wet suit showing off her firm thighs and buttocks—the full roundness of her breasts with her nipples feeling as hard as marbles.

Elinger pointed up toward the water's surface, letting Renee know it was time to surface.
Elinger and Renee began stroking and flippering toward the hull of *Just Cruisin'* about sixty feet above them. Elinger held Renee's arm as they ascended slowly to avoid the bends. Elinger and Renee's bodies drifted together. When their hips touched, Elinger pulled Renee closer, intertwining his arms and legs with hers. He

removed his regulator and Renee's, then kissed her on the lips as he grabbed the anchor rope to stop their ascent for a moment.

Renee moved her lips in unison with Elinger's. And, as they floated upward, Renee let Elinger caress her nipples through her wet suit, spreading tingles of pleasure throughout her body. Soon her lungs were ready to burst, but still Renee didn't want the moment to end. After the kiss, Elinger gently slid Renee's mouthpiece into her mouth and bit down on his.

Splashing into the daylight, Elinger climbed the boat's ladder, grabbed Renee's wrists and drew her aboard.
Removing their equipment quickly, they peeled off their wet suits and lay on the foredeck, bonding hastily with the demand of first-time lovemaking. They pumped toward ecstasy, thrusting with an animalistic appetite.

Renee felt Elinger's warm eruption inside her as she reached her own summit, more intense than anything she had ever experienced.

She was in love.

Later that afternoon, Elinger and Renee, wrapped in towels, sat at a deck table finishing a delicious seafood barbecue. The sun was a distant orange ball on the horizon, cooling the calm Chesapeake waters. *Just Cruisin'* was drifting freely.

Elinger opened the second bottle of champagne and asked, "How do you feel?"

"If I have to answer that, I'm going to give you an I.Q. test," Renee chided.

Elinger grinned. "Just making sure you weren't bored."

"If this is boredom, any excitement would kill me."

Elinger and Renee sipped their champagne as the sun dimmed further. What little light remained, illuminated Renee's pleasantly relaxed face.

Elinger savored the image. "I think you know I really care about you," he admitted openly.

Renee nodded. "Any regrets?"

Elinger shook his head. "But it is a breach of professional ethics."

"Since when do you go by the book, Kent?" Renee asked, brushing her hand tenderly across Elinger's cheek.

"Never," Elinger smiled wryly, placing his glass on the table and reaching for the towel that covered Renee. He pulled it from Renee's naked body.

Renee reached forward and quickly yanked the towel from Elinger, exposing his nude frame.

Elinger rose from the table and lifted Renee from her chair. He carried her below deck to the berthing compartment and laid her on the bed. They plunged into each other's arms, intoxicated with passion.

● ● ●

Wearing his sleeve-ripped, blood-caked coat and gloves, Ravnik moved down a night-darkened, grimy sidewalk in The Block. His eyes darted about, probing passers-by, looking for a purse to snatch or someone he could drag into an alley and mug.

Ravnik stopped when he recognized the two men who had just stepped into an adult bookstore a few doors away. He moved to the shop and peered through its front window. One of the men was the big wrestler he had beat up outside the Spartan Gym. The other man was one of the wrestler's bodyguards. Ravnik recalled how he had beat the bodyguard mercilessly, making jelly out of one of his eyes. Now the empty socket was covered with a black patch. Ravnik watched as Müeller the Masher held up the photo spread with Ravnik's police composite likeness on it for the young man behind the counter to study.

Ravnik was concerned about the accuracy of his software-generated likeness. It had been ten years since his last mug shot was taken. With no current photos, it would be difficult for the police to recognize him as long as he concealed the side of his head where he was missing an ear. But with this facial composite in circulation, Ravnik knew his chances of being captured had just increased dramatically.

Ravnik watched as Müeller grilled the shop clerk impatiently, demanding to know if the young man had ever seen the face before.

Intimidated by Müeller's manner and size, the youth nervously stroked his spiked haircut. Though he admitted the face was familiar, he couldn't come up with a name.

Standing in the shadows of a nearby alley, Ravnik watched Müeller and Cowan exit the store and move down the sidewalk. The two men mingled with pimps and hookers and showed Ravnik's computer generated likeness to anyone who would look. Ravnik wanted to kill the wrestler and his bodyguard right then to get the photo out of circulation. But there were too many people on the street. Besides, the composite was produced by the police so that meant others were in circulation. Too many to hide from. Ravnik realized what he really needed to do was change his appearance.

Müeller and Cowan approached an adult movie theater. Most of the neon tubes on the marquee were broken. Others flickered garish hues, faintly illuminating a decade of candy and gum embedded in the graying sidewalk near the ticket booth of this old, run-down movie theater. A half-dozen college students, two mini-skirted hookers with their "dates," and several middle-aged men formed a line on the dirty sidewalk, waiting to buy a ticket from a pale-skinned young woman. Showing the police photo spread, the Masher moved down the line and asked each patron if they'd ever seen the man. Cowan followed Müeller, offering a hundred-dollar bill to anyone whom could produce the fugitive's name and address. The patrons studied Ravnik's hardened features, but no one recognized him.

The owner of the theater, a wizened old man named Byron, was on a ladder in the lobby mounting a movie poster of two nude women. His wrinkled clothes, thin graying hair and scraggly, hillbilly beard made him look homeless. When Byron swept back the wisp of hair that covered his dark eyes, he suddenly recognized Müeller. A wide grin transformed his serious expression. He hurriedly climbed down the ladder and moved eagerly toward the wrestler and his bodyguard who were still questioning his customers.

"Hey, ain't you Müeller the Masher?" Byron asked.

Müeller glanced distantly at the theater owner and nodded. Byron stuck out his hand. "Glad ta meet 'cha. I'm Byron Tanner. I'd rather lose my dick than miss one of yer fights. What can I do for ya?"

The Masher gave Byron a meager smile and pumped his hand. "If you're a fan, you can do me a favor."

"Sure thing. Whaddaya need? Good pussy. I know where ya can get the best."

"I only vant to know who dis guy is and vhere he lives," Müeller pointed at the Faces composite in the photo spread, speaking with a hate-filled voice. "I vill pay anyone who finds him for me."

Byron studied the computer sketch for a moment. "I can't say I ever seen 'im. What's yer beef with 'im?"

"Beef? Vhy are you talking about cows?" Müeller asked, confused. "Are you making fun of me?"

"Oh, hell no! Sorry!" Byron apologized quickly. "I forgot you was new to this country. Sometimes the words here don't mean what they're supposed to. What I meant was, why are ya mad at 'im?"

The Masher's face tensed. "*Ja*, I'm mad at him. Can you help me find him?"

"Don't ya worry none, Mr. Masher," Byron replied, twisting his head to toss his hair out of his face. "I know this part of town inside out. I'll look for 'im. And ya wanna know why I'll do it? 'Cause yer the best goddamn wrestler that ever lived!" Byron blurted, then added, "but besides some money, I'll need a favor, too."

"The Masher doesn't do favors," Cowan answered for Müeller.

Müeller lifted his hand, signaling for Cowan to withdraw. "Vhat can the Masher do for you, Mr. Tanner?" Müeller asked politely.

"If I can find this guy for ya, can I get a front row seat at yer next match?"

Müeller bent forward until his face was only inches from Byron's. "If you find him, I'll let you sit in my corner right next to me."

"Shit! Yeah! I'll hit the streets tonight!" exclaimed Byron. "I'll find that scum for ya!"

●   ●   ●

"How long are we gonna keep this up, Karl?" Cowan asked as he and Müeller walked from the theater, passing a chattering group of short-skirted prostitutes.

"Until I find dis *aschlock* and break his neck!" the Masher snarled.

"But nobody's seen him around," reminded Cowan. "Maybe he left town? And you've got matches comin' up. You've got to spend some time working out, man."

Müeller suddenly stopped and turned on Cowan. "Don't piss on your own belly like a *schweinehund*!' he snapped.

Cowan glared at the Masher with his good eye. "Don't call me a pig-dog!"

"Den act like a man! Tink of dat black hole in your head. Are you going to let that *aschlock* get away vith dat?"

Cowan's expression shifted into an angry scowl. "Okay, Karl. Fuck your matches. I want this motherfucker as bad as you."

"But now you'll have to prove it to me."

"Whaddaya mean?"

"I vant your word that you'll crush his balls vith your bare hands vhile I snap his neck. I vant him to hurt badly for vhat he did to us! Do you tink you can do dat?"

Cowan nodded. "Yeah, I can do that."

"Den after dat ve'll stuff him down zee gutter like zee piece of scheisse dat he is!"

The Masher and his bodyguard began to walk again. "I live for dat moment," Müeller's voice trailed off in a murderous, unshakeable tone.

● ● ●

Ravnik stood in front of his sink mirror, scissoring his stringy, shoulder-length hair. He snipped carefully, leaving enough hair to cover the thick scar on the side of his head. The police composite still worried him; the likeness was uncannily accurate.

As Ravnik continued to cut his hair, he thought about the big man in the adult book store. The one who couldn't defend himself outside Spartan Gym. Ravnik knew the wrestler and his buddy wanted revenge. That's why they wanted to track him down before the authorities did. Too bad. This was one rematch the wrestler should avoid. But that didn't matter now. Ravnik had already decided he wasn't going to let them flash his picture in the neighborhood anymore. It was way too close to home.

The voice suddenly jumped into Ravnik's thoughts. "*It is most pleasing when our minds agree. The wrestler does indeed present a problem and he should be dispatched immediately. He can do us great malice!*"

Ravnik was glad to hear the voice. It gave him such immense power. And that's what he respected the most—the raw, brute force. Together they were invincible, Ravnik had learned. The wrestler wouldn't stand a chance.

When Ravnik finished his haircut, he stared at the mirror again and carefully noted the scar, that had once been his ear, was still hidden beneath his hair.

"*Your countenance is too distinct to be concealed by a mere haircut,*" the voice warned. "*You must do more.*"

Ravnik had already considered that. He grabbed a bottle of peroxide from a sink drawer and poured the fluid on his head. He rubbed the peroxide deep into his matted hair, wondering if blondes did have more fun—even when they were on a killing spree.

THIRTY-FOUR

• • •

Elinger and Renee arrived at Renee's home by nine o'clock in the evening. No longer tranquil from her day on Chesapeake Bay, Renee had been struck by a stabbing headache after her final lovemaking session with Elinger. Elinger knew the pain signaled another writing episode. And even more frightening, it could mean another murder would take place.

Elinger had decided to spend the night at Renee's. If she went into a trance, he could study her writing and pinpoint the killer's location. Maybe he could capture him before he killed again? Prepared for anything, Elinger had alerted Sanders, Brown and the rest of his men. They were battle-ready and on the streets, waiting for Elinger's next command.

While Renee took a couple of painkillers, Elinger settled on the couch to begin his vigil. As he reached for a TV remote on the table near him, he heard a car pull up in front the house. After a moment, he could hear the auto drive away from Renee's home. The front door opened and Alex entered the house and moved toward Elinger.

"Did you have a good time with your father?" Elinger

asked.

Alex shrugged. "It was so-so, I guess. He was in a bad mood. He was having some problems at work. Where's Mom?"

"Upstairs. She has a really bad headache."

"Not again," Alex uttered regretfully.

Suddenly, the clicking sound of Renee's computer keyboard echoed down the staircase filling Elinger and Alex with alarm. They both knew Renee was trancing again. That meant another murder could happen.

THIRTY-FIVE

• • •

Elinger and Alex stood near Renee, watching her fingers dance on the keyboard like a pianist building to a crescendo. Renee sat at her desk in a coma-like state, writing another chapter in her real-life murder mystery. Her eyes were rolled back, the whites glistened like wet porcelain. Bright letters flashed across the computer screen, forming syllables, then words. Sentences began to flow, streaming from margin to margin. Elinger felt helpless, knowing he could not intervene. He would have to wait until the spell broke before Renee became herself again.

With the printer on line, Elinger read the first pages. When he saw the description of the next victim, his expression altered. He was amused then angry. Defense attorney Sidney J. Harrison, Elinger's long-time nemesis, was next on the death list. Elinger was surprised by the accurate description of Harrison. The lawyer was indeed arrogant, aloof, and obnoxious with his bellicose personality. He was a man who had no respect for law enforcement personnel or the law.

Renee's trance ended as quickly as it started. Her hands went limp on the keyboard and she sagged in her chair. After a moment, she sat up and opened her eyes. She reached for Elinger's arm and pulled him close, then stretched for Alex and held his hand.

"Are you okay, Mom?" Alex was the first to break the silence.

Renee nodded and squeezed her son's hand. She then looked at Elinger. "Well?"

Elinger pulled the last pages from the printer and handed them to Renee. "Well, no murder this time, but you've described the next victim. You've even got his name. And I know him."

Renee glanced up from the pages. "You know him?"

Elinger chuckled darkly. "Sidney Harrison. He's a defense attorney that's been an adversary of mine for years. Now it looks like I need to protect him when a part of me would like to let the killer do his work," Elinger added with his lips drawn tight. "I guess this thing that's controlling you wants to make my life miserable, too."

"Apparently it finds this amusing," Renee contemplated aloud. "You protecting your enemy. Why is this Harrison guy on your bad side?"

Elinger took in a deep breath and steadied his thoughts before he spoke. "Justice has little meaning for him. He's kept a lot of guilty scumbags out of prison."

"How can he do that?" Renee asked. "If they're tried and convicted, they're guilty no matter what an attorney does. Right?"

Elinger sat in a chair next to Renee. "That's the problem. Many of his clients never see the inside of a courtroom. And the ones who do watch Harrison make a mockery of our justice system. He uses legal maneuvers that should be illegal to manipulate the law and the court system."

"And now you need to save Harrison from the killer," Renee said.

Elinger reflected on the irony of the situation for a moment, then stood and moved toward a window and stared out at the darkened neighborhood. "I wonder why this thing is toying with me."

"The last note did say you'd be part of the next murder and that you were a great asset to a thrilling mystery," Renee reminded Elinger.

Later, after Alex went to bed, Renee and Elinger sat on the living room couch, drinking coffee.

"Kent, tell me how this Harrison beats the justice system so often?" Renee asked.

The idea of discussing Harrison soured Elinger's stomach. "Why do you want to know?"

"Writer's curiosity, of course," Renee replied with a grin.

Elinger took a sip of coffee before he spoke. "Well, he makes any cop want to quit his job," Elinger began, injecting his words with venom. "His pursuit of justice is an obstruction of truth. He uses the law to fight the law and to fight us. He's a self-appointed protector of evil."

Elinger placed his coffee cup back on the table and continued. "Harrison's most common ploy is to create mistrials so new court times are calendared. With crowded courts, it's months, sometimes years before a new trial begins. Harrison knows time erodes the prosecution's case. It gives suspects time to intimidate the witnesses. And witnesses move away—or their memories fade—or they die. This leaves the prosecution with a weaker case. When the new trial begins, Harrison uses more unethical tactics to try to get another mistrial declared. If he succeeds, there's a chance the judge will dismiss the charges, claiming the lengthy incarceration of the suspect is cruel and unusual punishment. Then another criminal who should be in prison is free to roam the streets."

"Has he ever got the best of you in one of your cases?" Renee asked.

"Once," Elinger said. "I was working a double-homicide, a retired husband and wife were killed over thirty dollars! The suspect was a real dirt-bag named Allard. We knew he was guilty and so did Harrison. We had motive, opportunity, and we placed Allard at the murder scene. It doesn't get any better than that."

"So, what went wrong?' Renee asked, sipping from her coffee cup.

Elinger's mouth dried as though the subject of Harrison stuck to his tongue. He swallowed another gulp of coffee, hoping to lubricate his words. "Harrison leaked false information to the D. A. about a witness who allegedly could help his case. When the D.A. called this guy to the stand, Harrison yanked the hook. He told the judge this witness had perjured himself in another trial. Harrison knew the D.A. wasn't aware of that so the D.A. had no defense against it."

"But how does that make a mistrial?" Renee asked.

"If a witness balks at any questions regarding a previous perjury conviction, the judge has only two choices: strike the witnesses' entire testimony or declare a mistrial."

"Why?"

"Because most judges believe the jury can't remove such damaging testimony from their minds."

"So, the judge doesn't think the suspect is getting a fair trial?" Renee asked, setting her cup on the table.

"Exactly. In this case, the judge called a mistrial and Allard was a free man while the prosecutors decided if they would retry him. A few days later he killed two bank clerks during a robbery. We got him on video, we got his prints, but he's still on the run because we can't find him," Elinger's words were mired with disgust and frustration.

"You make Harrison sound invincible. Has he ever screwed up?" Renee asked.

Elinger smiled, remembering. "Yeah, he outsmarted himself once." Elinger placed his coffee cup on the table. "This guy murdered his neighbor, and the neighbor's wife saw him do it. She became the state's prime witness. But while Harrison represented his client, he played Cupid."

Elinger saw the surprised look in Renee's face. "Cupid?" she repeated.

"Yeah, Harrison manipulated the witness and the suspect. He got them to date and fall in love!"

Renee cocked her head when she heard this. "You're kidding, right?"

Elinger shook his head. "He found out these two were once lovers and had concealed their neighborhood affair from their spouses. So, he got them to fall in love again. Then at Harrison's urging, they got married."

"So, he called *Spousal Privilege*—when a husband and wife can't testify against each other?" Renee surmised.

"That's how it usually works, but the judge ruled Spousal Privilege did not apply to someone already accused of murder before they got married. This guy got life without parole," Elinger reached for his coffee cup and turned it up for the last mouthful. "That's what I call justice."

Renee placed her empty cup on the table. "It seems like Harrison is overly protective of his criminal clients. Why?"

"I think he's fascinated by their lifestyles. I think there's an adrenaline rush in it for him," Elinger said.

Renee glanced down at the pages for a moment. "But according to this, Harrison is a rich man. He drives several luxury cars; wears silk suits and owns several expensive homes. How can he have all of that when his clients are criminals who usually don't have much money?"

"I've been asking myself the same questions for a long time," Elinger said. "Harrison has a few wealthy clients but not enough to sustain homes in the Easton area or Talbot County. I think he uses his low-life clients as connections."

"For what?"

"Guns, drugs? I'm not sure. But I do know he's dirty and someday I'll catch him."

"So, you've investigated him before?"

Elinger nodded. "But Headquarters stopped me."

"Why?"

Elinger frowned. "They think it's too speculative on my part—but he's on my list of things to do anyway. Maybe this is my chance—while I'm watching him?"

Renee leaned toward Elinger and hugged him. "Just be careful."

Elinger kissed Renee tenderly on the cheek and rose from the couch. "I've got to go and arrange for Harrison's baby-sitting. I'll have Sanders and his men come right over."

"Too bad you're not available," Renee teased. "I'd love for you to baby-sit me."

Elinger smiled. "You know I'll be here every chance I get. Count on it," Elinger pledged as he kissed Renee again.

The day on the Chesapeake Bay and his few hours at Renee's house had sapped Elinger's energy. He was tired when he climbed into his darkened auto. He backed his car from Renee's driveway and drove from the residence. As Elinger passed the prowl car parked in front, he nodded at the officer behind the wheel. The policeman waved back.

Through his open window, Elinger could feel the breeze that flowed down the street. The leaves in the treetops fluttered near the rays of the street lamps. The shimmering effect on the blacktop made the road look like a wide, bubbling creek. Elinger had driven only another fifty feet when a shadowy figure sat up in the back seat. The sudden image in the rear-view mirror caused Elinger to slam on the brakes. His vehicle screeched to a tire burning halt. Elinger shouldered his door, dove to the pavement and rolled. He sprang to his feet, aiming his pistol at the rear of his auto.

The car door swung open and the intruder stumbled out, obviously shaken by the sudden stop.

Staring down the barrel of Elinger's weapon was Ralph Torres. A surprised look was carved deep in his features. "Don't shoot! It's me!" Torres exclaimed. Torres was wearing a hospital gown. The bottom tie was loose, allowing the gown to flap in the breeze. His bare ass exposed to the cool night air.

Elinger holstered his pistol. "Christ, Ralph! You scared the shit out of me!"

"You! What about me?"

"Well, what the hell are you doing in the back of my car?"

"I was asleep."

Elinger studied the hospital gown for a moment. "Doing a little flashing now, are we?" he chuckled quietly.

"They hid my clothes," Torres grumbling under his breath as he tied the rear of the gown.

"I don't blame them. You had a few more days to go."

"Hey, I got tired of the few days of observation. I feel great, man! I could bench press a house! But what would really make me feel better is to catch this bastard."

"You and me both," Elinger replied. "How'd you get out?" he asked, moving back to his auto now.

Torres broke into one of his easy, calm smiles. "I told the nurses I couldn't sleep, and that I wanted to go for a little walk."

"Just a short stroll down the hall, right?"

"Yeah, but then the next thing I know, I'm out the door."

"C'mon, I'll give you a lift back to the hospital," Elinger offered as he slid back into his car. "I don't want you to get arrested for indecent exposure."

Torres moved to the passenger door and opened it. Elinger could see Torres grimace from the pain when he pulled on the door handle.

"Bench press a house, huh?" Elinger wisecracked, starting the engine.

"It's your drivin', man," Torres countered as he slowly lowered his butt onto the seat. "A little heavy on the brakes, don't you think?"

Elinger smiled, glad to see his partner's strength returning. He dropped the auto into gear and drove off, realizing how much he had missed Torres. "How'd you know where to find me?' Elinger asked.

Torres snapped his seat belt in its lock and gave Elinger an all-knowing smile. "Everybody knows where you spend most of your time now."

"You know something, Ralph? You're a real pain-in-the-ass," Elinger said, turning from the quiet residential neighborhood onto a busier four-lane highway.

Torres stared out the windshield and looked at a few houses as Elinger's car passed them. He then turned to Elinger. "Kent, I've done some thinkin' in the hospital—about the stupid chances I've taken with my life. You were right. It's been all about my brother. A part of me did want to die. Another part of me wanted to prove that I'm not a coward. I know that now. I mean, I really know it."

"That's good to hear," Elinger said. "Now when you put yourself at risk, maybe you won't be so impulsive. You might even give what you do some thought?"

"Yeah, but you know what? This dickhead we're after really fucked me up! I owe him. I want to get even!" Torres proclaimed.

"Yep, it's payback time all right," Elinger agreed quietly.

Torres' eyes hung on Elinger for a moment.

Elinger noticed Torres' was caught off-guard by his

vengeance laced remark. "You heard me right. I owe him, too."

Elinger moved his rock steady gaze back to the highway that was disappearing beneath the hood. "I might be taking some chances of my own. I'm going to get this guy, and I don't care what it takes," he added.

"Hey, that's cool with me," Torres said, allowing a grin to curve his lips.

THIRTY-SIX

● ● ●

Elinger peered through the window of a courtroom door in the Clarence M. Mitchell, Jr. Courthouse. Inside, Sidney Harrison was locked in a heated debate with a young, female deputy D.A.. The D.A. was red-faced, bursting with anger and tears. The judge hammered his gavel while the jury looked on wide-eyed. The judge finally received the silence he demanded, then he made a brief statement. The judge's words put a bemused smile on Harrison's face. The D.A. glowered at the judge and Harrison, then she moved back to the prosecution's table where she began stuffing her paperwork into her briefcase.

Still observing, Elinger correctly assumed Harrison had just won another case. Elinger mulled over the mixed feelings he had while he and his men tailed Harrison. As a cop whose duty is to keep the streets safe, he knew the world would not miss Sidney J. Harrison. But, as a potential victim, Elinger had to do whatever he could to protect Harrison.

Elinger backed from the door as Harrison turned to exit the courtroom. As soon as Harrison exited, he was surrounded by several newspaper people, a TV crew and a knot of spectators.

Elinger mingled with the crowd, hoping Harrison wouldn't notice him.

Harrison focused on the reporters with a proud smile. Cameras flashed and video cameras hummed when Harrison bragged about the excellent defense he had provided for his client, and complained how the authorities had mistreated that client. As Elinger watched, he was reminded of Renee's accurate description of Harrison in her most recent trance writing session. Harrison was flamboyant and flashy, almost burlesque. At forty-four, he was still a vain man with his hair dyed black to cover the indefatigable gray of middle age. Harrison sported a waxed handlebar mustache and a finely crafted, double-breasted, pinstriped suit reminiscent of the 1920s. Although he had never been on a horse, he wore eight-hun-dred-dollar cowboy boots. Elinger always considered Harrison as a cross between Andrew Carnegie and Wyatt Earp.

When Harrison finished his self-congratulatory spiel, the reporters turned off their cameras, closed their laptops and began to disperse. Harrison headed for the staircase at the end of the cor-ridor.

Elinger waited for Harrison to disappear down the stairs, then turned to move toward another exit—but a voice stopped him.

"Hey, Lieutenant!"

Elinger suddenly found himself looking at Mervyn Amos.

"Well, Lieutenant, what brings you to the courthouse today?" Amos inquired.

"Anus, what are you doing here?" Elinger asked guarded-ly, ignoring Amos' question. Hoping the insult would drive Amos in another direction. "I thought rodents stayed in their holes during the day."

Amos did not respond to Elinger's insult. He glanced down the corridor at the staircase where Harrison had departed. "What's your interest in Harrison?" Amos asked. "Is he involved in the murders?"

"I have no interest in him," Elinger lied. "Now get out of my way before I yank a knot in your tail!" he added as he brushed past the reporter.

Elinger looked back and noticed Amos' inward grin, realizing Amos was suspicious that Harrison was somehow involved in the bizarre string of murders. Elinger was also aware Amos enjoyed irritating him.

After Elinger faded down the hall, Amos moved to a nearby window and peered down at the front of the courthouse. The wide stairs and large rounded columns made the entrance of the courthouse look like the Acropolis.

A moment passed as Amos watched Harrison trot down the stairs, cross to the curb at St. Paul Street and climb into his rare luxury car. After Harrison pulled into traffic, Elinger appeared, hopped into his vehicle and tailed Harrison onto the busy street.

Amos smiled with confidence. He was right about Harrison being involved in Elinger's case. But how did the attorney fit in with the murders?

THIRTY-SEVEN

● ● ●

Elinger and Torres sat in Elinger's vehicle under a star-filled sky. They were parked in the expensive neighborhood of Guilford Estates across the street from Sidney Harrison's stone-masonry home. Elinger studied the large two-story mansion. It was shrouded by trees and lush foliage on two acres of prime real estate. Elinger couldn't help but think of the innocent blood that had been spilled so this man could live like a king.

Elinger felt numbness in his legs, reminding him that he and Torres had been sitting in the car for several hours. Elinger shifted in his seat and sipped coffee from a thermos.

Torres read a newspaper with a penlight clamped in his teeth.

"That sonovabitch!" Torres mumbled.

"What?" Elinger asked.

Torres pulled the light from his mouth and read aloud.

"Police still in the dark over Shadow Man! Only the Shadow Man knows where he will strike next!" Torres looked at Elinger. "I'm sure we can thank *Anus* for that!"

"You know where that paper belongs, don't you?"

"Yeah, under a German Shepherd puppy!" Torres replied,

wadding up the newspaper and tossing it on the back seat.

"Are you sure you feel up to being here, Ralph?" Elinger asked. "You didn't stay in the hospital as long as you were supposed to."

"I only left a day, maybe two days early. Besides, I signed an A-M-A form," Torres explained.

"Against Medical Advice?"

"Yep," Torres said. "My only regret now is that Headquarters still has me on medical leave. I'll have to sneak around for a little while longer."

Torres shifted his attention back to Harrison's estate. "If Harrison's dirty, do you think we'll be able to nail him? He's got all the legal loopholes figured out. Everything's so perfect with him. He probably blowdries the hair on his ass after he showers."

"He'll make a mistake some day, and when he does, we'll be there, Ralph," Elinger said, then drained the last drips of the coffee from the thermos. "Why don't you check in with Sanders? See what's going on at Renee's?"

Torres grinned. "We just checked in half an hour ago. You're really tight with her, aren't you, man? And you told me never to break house rules."

Elinger cracked a smile, amused by his own double standard. "It was an accident."

"And I suppose you're going to tell me you regret it?"

"Absolutely not."

Something in the darkness suddenly snagged Torres' attention. "Wait a minute! Looks like somebody's crawlin' around the North side of the house."

Elinger perked up quickly, a combination of caffeine and

raw nerves. He pushed open his door and jumped from the vehicle. He sprinted across the street with Torres following and moved onto the grounds of Harrison's residence. Drawing his firearm, Elinger's eyes inched across the terrain, dissecting every square foot. The one-eared man's strength was still vivid in his mind. He didn't want to give him the benefit of surprise.

Still probing the darkness, Elinger and Torres found nothing.

"Are you sure you saw something, Ralph?" Elinger asked, slightly irritated.

"Yeah, I'm sure," Torres replied, scanning the estate.

● ● ●

In an upstairs bedroom, Sidney Harrison awakened with a full bladder. He slid out of bed without disturbing the young, large-breasted woman who was sleeping nude next to him. Harrison took a moment to view the young lady's shapely body. She was his prize catch for the night. Harrison preferred young women who chased nice suits, expensive cars, and flush bank accounts. He knew they were an easy lay once they saw the money.

As Harrison walked toward the bathroom, he glanced out the bedroom window and saw two armed men creeping through his backyard. Stepping back into his bedroom, he moved to a bureau drawer and withdrew a 9mm semi-automatic handgun and a pair of binoculars. He slid a loaded clip into the pistol and racked a round into the chamber.

Staring through binoculars from his bedroom window,

Harrison watched Elinger and Torres under the light of the moon. He recognized Elinger, wondering why he was on his property. He smiled as he moved to the bedroom phone.

● ● ●

For several more minutes, Elinger and Torres searched the property. A whimper from a nearby bush brought them to a sudden halt. Closing in cautiously, Elinger pointed his handgun at the shrubbery while Torres pulled back the branches. What they saw unhappily surprised them. A Great Dane was lying on the ground, giving birth. Two glistening, squirming pups were already out, nosing their mother's belly in search of a nipple.

Elinger gave Torres a sidelong glance. "Somebody crawling, huh?"

"Well shit, it's as big as a man!" Torres argued in a weak tone.

Suddenly, the rumbling of heavy vehicles bouncing onto the property caught Elinger and Torres off guard. In seconds, the area was bleached by flood lights.

"Drop your weapons!" A voice commanded from behind the brilliance. "And get your hands in the air!"
Elinger and Torres dropped their pistols and raised their arms.

A small squad of uniformed police officers carrying riot guns emerged from behind the lights and approached Elinger and Torres. An officer recognized Elinger. "Shit, Lieutenant! What are you doing here?"

"Just call off the troops, Sergeant," Elinger ordered. "Detective Torres will be happy to tell you all about it."

Torres' face flushed red.

The sergeant pivoted back toward his men. "It's okay, guys. It's only Lieutenant Elinger and Detective Torres—out on a midnight stroll."

Elinger and Torres heard the chuckles from the officers as the men lowered their weapons.

Humiliated, Elinger retrieved his weapon from the ground. Torres did the same.

"Yes, why are you out for a midnight stroll on my property?" a deep, commanding voice asked.

Elinger immediately recognized the tone. It unmistakably belonged to Sidney J. Harrison.

Wearing a red silk robe with his initials monogrammed in gold above the breast pocket, Harrison strolled toward the men with a scowling expression. "What the hell are you doing in my backyard, Lieutenant? I can think of a half dozen laws you've broken."

"We heard you met a bitch and got her pregnant," Elinger quipped. "We just came to help with the delivery."

Everyone glanced at the Great Dane who had just given up two more pups. The uniformed officers chuckled again.

"And we were wondering how many in the litter would be bastards like you?" Elinger added.

The men laughed again.

Elinger could see Harrison's expression was suddenly aflame with anger.

"None of you will think this is funny when I see you in court!" Harrison barked. "You'll all be whining like those goddamn pups! Now what's going on?" he said.

Elinger knew he couldn't explain the complexities of the case to Harrison. If anyone could disrupt police work, it was this attorney. "There's been a threat on your life," Elinger answered simply.

The look on Harrison's face became one of amusement. "So, you're here to protect me? Well, that's a switch! It wasn't long ago you were swearing at me in a courtroom."

"You got a good D.A. fired."

"Reading the juror's notebooks was unethical," Harrison fired back.

"He was young and gullible. You set him up!"

"I was protecting my client."

"Yeah, nice client, counsel," Torres interjected. "Two days after he's out on bail, he killed somebody!"

"That didn't have anything to do with the case," Harrison argued.

"Even you don't have the balls to tell that to the victim's family," Elinger said.

"What could I say to the family?" Harrison asked. "A man is innocent until proven guilty in a court of law. Or haven't you read the constitution, Lieutenant?"

Elinger had the urge to punch Harrison. He stepped toward him, then stopped, barely managing to restrain himself.

Harrison rolled the tips of his handlebar mustache with his fingertips and aimed a fierce look at Elinger. "Let's cut the shit, Lieutenant. Who wants to kill me?"

"It's police business. That makes it none of your business."

"I'm sure I can get a judge to change your mind."

"I'm sure you could," Elinger agreed then broke into a shallow smile. "However, if a judge interferes, it could affect how well I protect you. Maybe that gets you killed?"

Harrison glared at Elinger. "If that's a threat, I'll add it to the list of charges I can bring against you."

Before Elinger could respond, a flash unexpectedly washed everyone in bright light. When it faded, Mervyn Amos walked toward the group, clutching a flash mounted camera.

"That was a great picture, gentlemen," Amos said nonchalantly. "Could someone tell me what's going on?"

Elinger cringed when he saw Amos. The reporter was proving to be more persistent than a New York cockroach. He was just one more obstacle to interfere with Elinger's investigation.

After a tirade of condemnation against Elinger and the police, Harrison repaired to his house. The police squad departed, leaving Elinger, Torres, and Amos alone in Harrison's backyard. They began to walk toward the front of the property.

"Mervyn, we need to talk," Elinger said.

"Oh, it's *Mervyn* now?" Mervyn said with a raised brow. "I thought you didn't like me."

"I don't. You earned your nickname all by yourself, Anus. I'm just trying to be polite."

"What do you want to talk about?" Amos asked through an expression of suspicion.

"I need a favor."

"And I want a story."

"Then we're both going to be very happy," Elinger promised.

"So, what's my story?"

"The biggest of your career, but you've got to put it on hold for now. That's the favor I need."

"You want to give me a story that I can't write!" Amos asked, halting in Harrison's front yard. "What should I write about meanwhile? The city's shortage of school crossing guards?"

"Just give me some time," Elinger said quietly, his patience fading.

"Asking me to wait on this is like asking the Heisman Trophy winner not to go into pro football for Christ's sake!" Amos countered.

"If you want an exclusive, this is the only way you're going to get it!"

Elinger studied Amos for a moment. He had the feeling he was making some headway with the reporter.

"But Lieutenant, you're really giving me nothing. Just a promise. How can I count on that?"

Elinger knew he would have to set the rules here and now on how Amos would get his story. He suddenly grabbed the reporter by the lapels and pulled him within inches of his face. "Because I'm giving you my word! I'm offering you something that'll keep you from going back to the tabloids. But it's going to be on my terms, not yours!" Elinger spit the words into Amos' face. "And you're right. You've got nothing right now."

Torres tapped Elinger on the shoulder and pointed toward Harrison's house. Elinger looked at where Torres was pointing. Harrison was watching the men from an upstairs window.

"Shit!" Elinger muttered, releasing Amos.

Amos tugged on his lapels, smoothing out the wrinkles.

He then shifted his vision to Elinger. "They say when a man becomes violent, he has run out of words."

Elinger whispered in a menacing tone. "You want more proof of that?"

"You made your point, Lieutenant," Amos said with reluctance in his tone. "I'll take the exclusive, even on your terms. Do you know when that might happen?"

"Just take your nose out of my ass, and you'll be the first to know when something breaks," Elinger replied as he headed toward the street with Torres trailing him.

Amos watched Elinger and Torres drive away. He admitted to himself that he had no intention of backing off. He would stay on Elinger's heels for the story that could change his life. Maybe even earn him a Pulitzer! He could hope.

Hearing a quiet whistle from above, Amos glanced up at Harrison who was still at the window. Harrison tossed a business card out the window. It fluttered down toward Amos.

"Police brutality is a specialty of mine," Harrison announced with a proud voice.

The business card dropped near Amos. He picked it up and tore it into small pieces in plain view of Harrison. "No thanks," Amos said. "I think you're an asshole, too!"

With that, Amos turned and moved off Harrison's yard, hustling toward his auto. He didn't want to lose sight of Elinger.

THIRTY-EIGHT

• • •

Captain Robert Osborne stood on the baseline between home plate and first base in Oriole Park at Camden Yards. He checked his watch through a pinched expression. He was obviously waiting for someone who was late.Osborne's eyes roamed the stadium grounds impatiently. The first light of day had pierced the muddy horizon. Osborne scanned his long shadow on the field then glanced over the outfield fence at the Baltimore and Ohio Railroad warehouse. That brick building, he recalled, could only be hit by a 460-foot home-run.

A door suddenly opened and shut in a darkened pocket near the grandstands and interrupted Osborne's thoughts.

Elinger emerged from the third base dugout and walked toward Osborne. Elinger admitted regretfully to himself that he felt hung-over. Not from liquor but from the long hours of tailing Harrison. The duty had left him little time to sleep. Today, he didn't bother with a change of clothes, tie, or a shave.

"You look like shit," Osborne commented with a lack of fanfare.

"What'd you expect, Cap? You called me at four-thirty in

the morning. Why'd you want to meet here?"

"It's a good place for a private conversation."

"Sounds like trouble."

"You've reached a new pinnacle in mind reading, Kent," Osborne said.

Elinger and Osborne began to walk the base line toward first base.

"I got an early call, too," Osborne began. "About four twenty-five, the deputy mayor himself called. Montagna must be on overtime like you."

The mention of Montagna's name sent a pain of aggravation through Elinger's brain. Elinger was aware the deputy mayor was an unscrupulous, power-seeker who led politically motivated witch-hunts for rogue cops. He had found a few, but along the way, he had destroyed the careers of a few innocent officers. Elinger had figured out Montagna's agenda long ago. If Montagna could convince the public he was creating a corrupt-free police department, he assumed he'd be a shoe-in as Baltimore's next mayor. But right now, as Elinger knew, Montagna was simply the mayor's lackey, bridling the city leader in directions he thought would groom his own political future.

"He called on the mayor's behalf, of course," Osborne added, pulling Elinger from his thoughts.

"Of course."

"It seems your friend Harrison wants to sue you and Headquarters for harassment," Osborne said. "The report said there'd been a threat on his life. What's that all about?"

"I've got information he might be the next victim in the killings."

"Really?" Osborne said in a tone ignited by curiosity. "What kind of information?"

"You said you didn't want to know the details of this case," Elinger reminded. "They get wilder all the time."

"Yeah, a few more could give me a heart attack," Osborne said. "You know that Harrison and Montagna are buddies. Old college pals."

"Yeah, that means they partied together, got drunk together, and got laid together," Elinger mumbled.

"Montagna is taking what happened in Harrison's backyard personally," Osborne reported. "He doesn't want us hassling an attorney with an anti-police agenda. Goes against his grain. He thinks we're all a bunch of Fascists anyway. You know I don't like Montagna, but he's got juice with the mayor."

Elinger and Osborne had rounded first and were now walking toward second.

"What'd you tell him?" Elinger asked.

"Just what the report said. That there'd been a death threat against Harrison. An anonymous phone call. Maybe from an unhappy client?"

"And then you probably told him you were pulling me off the stakeout, right?" Elinger asked.

"What the hell else could I do? But don't worry, you're still on it. I've got it all worked out," Osborne cracked a thin smile at Elinger.

"You're gloating," Elinger said upon seeing Osborne's expression.

"You're damn right I am," Osborne said. "And do you want to know why?"

Elinger nodded.

"Because I know exactly what to say when he asks me to make a gelding out of you."

"What?"

"I'm gonna tell him you're on vacation."

"Vacation?"

"You're way overdue. I don't want Harrison or Montagna putting shit stains on your record because of this," Osborne cautioned. "I don't need to yank your ass off the case if you're on vacation, right?"

Elinger nodded, grinning himself now. "I'll leave the politics to you, but Torres is with me, okay?"

Osborne nodded. "He's still on medical leave for a few more days as far as I'm concerned."

Elinger only nodded. He wasn't about to explain Torres left the hospital early.

Walking again, Elinger and Osborne passed second and were now walking on the hallowed ground once covered by Cal Ripken Jr.

"You know we could both get fired if Harrison catches you tailing his ass again," Osborne clarified.

"So, why're you risking your retirement with me?"

"I'm covered," Osborne replied confidently. "My brother has a fish farm in upstate New York. Wants me to work for him. No stress. Makes getting fired look good. I don't think I'll miss the grind."

"I don't want to piss on your dream, Cap, but Harrison won't see me. I've got an idea how to blend in with his world."

"Is that something you want to tell me about now or will

it be better as another unpleasant surprise?" Osborne asked.

"A surprise, definitely."

"But there's one more thing, Kent. Don't call me at the office anymore. Use my cell."

"Okay, Ozzie."

"Stop with that goddamn name! How many times do I have to tell you that?!"

"But you don't look like a Robert. More like an Ozzie."

"It's a great name for a possum!" Osborne barked.

Elinger concealed the smile generated by Osborne's annoyance. The men approached third base and rounded it, heading for home plate.

Osborne gave Elinger a personal, one-on-one look. "I hate that dirt-bag Harrison as much as you. Protecting him must be a real bitch."

"There is an up-side, Cap. I can use him as bait for the killer."

"You do have a point," Osborne agreed in a tone of better spirits. "Make him sweat if you get the chance."
Elinger nodded. "I plan on it."

When the men reached home plate, they stopped again.

"It's up to you, Kent," Osborne said, dropping his vision to Elinger's feet. "You're in the batter's box, really."

The corny remark made Elinger smile. "And now you're going to tell me not to strike out."

"You damn well better not!" Osborne ordered. "The whole city of Baltimore is counting on you."

THIRTY-NINE

• • •

Elinger and Torres sat in a black spit-shined luxury sedan, parked a short distance from Sidney Harrison's residence. Elinger turned his eyes from Harrison's house for a moment to take in the violent storm that had moved in over Baltimore. The dark rolling clouds filled the sky, blocking the stars and moon. The air was filled with rain, and peals of thunder followed the rips of lightning that splintered the sky. It was a bad time to be dressed like a Europhile, Elinger realized unhappily, glancing at the expensive silk suits he and Torres were wearing. Elinger figured the suits would be good camouflage if he and Torres had to leave their auto to follow Harrison.

"I still can't believe you pulled it off, Kent," Torres said. "These thousand-dollar suits and this awesome car!" Torres rubbed his hands across the soft, pliable upholstery. "Is this leather or kid?"

"Kid, I think."

"I bet Ozzie had a heart attack," Torres said with an impish chuckle.

"He doesn't know," Elinger said. "He won't know until I

turn in my expense report."

"Jesus!" Torres shook his head. "You want a simple Christian burial or should I just toss your ashes down a toilet?"

Despite Torres' ribbing, Elinger hoped his plan would work. The sleek luxury auto blended well with Harrison's neighborhood. That was proven earlier when Harrison drove by and didn't give the car a second glance. And, Elinger contemplated, Harrison had unwittingly helped with his own stakeout. When Harrison heard Osborne's story about the threat coming from an anonymous caller, Harrison insisted no policeman was to tail him to protect him. He's had plenty of phone call threats over the years and nothing ever came of any of them. Harrison told Osborne he would be able to take care of himself. Osborne agreed to Harrison's request, admitting he could not spare the extra man hours with the string of recent murders baffling his department anyway.

Studying the neighborhood through the water-streaked windshield, Elinger watched the high-class homes dance like drunken apparitions on the glass. He knew this was probably the only entertainment he would have for the night. Elinger checked his watch. It was a few minutes past midnight.

To pass the time, Elinger thought about Renee. She was his first serious relationship since his wife died. He felt lucky to be falling in love with her. With Renee, Elinger felt safe to express his emotions openly. He could be himself.

Elinger's mind slowly shifted to the murder case. He thought about Renee's search through the 1800s books for a writing style similar to her somnambulistic writings. Renee had reviewed dozens of volumes but found nothing helpful. At times, Renee become disenchanted with the search. But she stayed with it, feeling it could lead to an important revelation. Renee was positive the entity's strange notes and her trance writings clearly suggested they were the work of a nineteenth century writer or someone with expertise of that era's literature.

Elinger was glad Renee followed his advice and asked her friend Professor Winfield to help her. The pragmatic professor's brow had creased with incredulity when Renee admitted that the writer she was looking for was probably long dead, yet somehow connected to the modern day murders. Since Winfield believed his star pupil wasn't insane, he had agreed to help her. He promised to recruit scholars with consummate knowledge of nineteenth century mystery writers.

A wash of light suddenly bathed the interior of the auto, scattering Elinger's thoughts.

Torres looked through the rear water-streaked window and saw an SUV curbing a few houses behind them.

Elinger peered into the outside rear view mirror as the auto's lights blinked off. He studied the blurred image, waiting for someone to exit the auto. But no one emerged.

"You think Harrison's on to us?" Torres asked.

"It's *Anus*," Elinger replied, irritated.

"That bastard's gonna give you an ulcer!" Torres exclaimed.

"Don't worry about him," Elinger advised calmly. "We've got him where we want him."

Torres raised his eyebrows. "How do you figure?"

"I bet he doesn't screw with us anymore," Elinger

answered. "He can't get his story unless we put it together for him."

"But he's made a career of distortin' the truth," Torres reminded Elinger. "God only knows what he can do to our investigation if he follows us!"

Elinger understood Torres' pessimism. He had felt it often himself. "I think we're going to see a change in Amos," Elinger speculated, settling back in his seat. "The other night in Harrison's yard, I could tell Amos was serious about his career. He's been writing for the tabloids too long. None of his peers respect him. I found out he's on probation at the *Sun*. He knows he's headed for the unemployment line unless he comes up with an important story. And we're his ticket to success, Ralph."

"I think you're dreamin', man."

"He's already proving himself."

"How?"

"I didn't see you or me on the front page of this morning's paper. There could've been a photo of us standing next to the dog and pups in Harrison's backyard."

Elinger glanced at Torres and could tell in his expression he had already reconsidered his point of view.

"Yeah, I was sure we'd be headlined for that," Torres said.

Suddenly, something outside the auto caused Torres to point in the direction of Harrison's home.

Sidney Harrison, wearing faded jeans, a baggy sweatshirt, and a light waterproof windbreaker, darted from his house. He ran through the rain toward his expensive auto parked in the driveway.

"I think we're overdressed!" Torres said when he saw Harrison's clothes.

"He must be slumming tonight," Elinger replied.

Harrison climbed into his auto, backed it out of the driveway and drove down the street.

Elinger fired up his auto and eased onto the roadway, cranking up his windshield wipers as he followed Harrison. Elinger was now thankful for the rain. The poor visibility would make it almost impossible for Harrison to know he was being tailed.

Determined not to let weather or lack of sleep keep him from his story, Amos twisted the ignition key and fell in line behind Elinger and Torres. He would not be left behind.

With tires hissing on slick streets, Elinger and Torres trailed Harrison across Baltimore. The storm had reduced visibility to less than fifty feet, making their task more difficult. After several miles, Harrison finally led them to Fell's Point.

As the auto's wheels dribbled over the old London-esque cobblestone streets of the two-hundred and fifty-year-old neighborhood, Elinger kept a steady hand on the wheel and glanced at the area. Modern street lamps had become turn-of-the-century iron lamp posts. New businesses in various stages of restoration peppered the older structures to match the look of that bygone era.

Harrison parked his auto in front of a bar. He emerged and dashed through the rain, passing the pub's crudely painted sign of two battling Civil War ironclads. The neon-sign of the bar displayed the words, *The Merrimac 'n Monitor*. It cast a dirty yellow glow on the entrance door Harrison had just entered.

Torres wiped the condensation from the window for a clearer view of the bar and neighborhood. He knew this part of town attracted the rougher citizens of the area. "What's he doin' here?" Torres asked with surprise.

"You'll be the first to know," Elinger replied, parking in an alley a short distance from the bar.

"Why's that?"

"Because you're going in. He's only seen you once."

"I can handle that," Torres acknowledged, eager for adventure.

Elinger reached under the dash and pushed a button. The trunk lid sprung open.

Torres slid out from the car and was hit by the chilly rain as he trotted to the rear of the auto. He retrieved a small sports bag from the trunk and climbed into the back seat of the car. He removed his expensive suit jacket and recalled how he and Elinger thought the fancy clothes would help them blend in with Harrison's world. "*When in Rome*—who the hell ever made that up?" he mumbled.

"Probably a Carthaginian," Elinger joked.

"A who?" Torres asked as he removed his tie and dress shirt. He opened the sports bag and looked over the contents—a sweater, jeans, and deck shoes.

By the time Torres ran across the street, his change of clothes was nearly soaked. He entered the bar and suddenly breathed in a foul odor that almost gagged him—it was a mix of spilled liquor, sweat, and vomit.

Crossing the sawdust floor, Torres passed chipped tables and chairs that looked like they came from a skid row thrift shop. He maneuvered through the imposing patrons who were mostly warehouse and dock workers. Their bodies were muscled from long hours of loading and unloading ships. Torres sensed their temperament probably matched the appearance of their sun-tortured skin.

Torres reached the bar and planted his forearms on the bar-top that was sticky with finger grease and carved with initials. He scanned the room until his eyes settled on Sidney Harrison who was seated at a corner table. Harrison was engaged in a conversation with a thin black man who gesticulated wildly as he spoke. The man, Torres guessed, was in his late thirties. He wore expensive clothes that didn't fit in with the neighborhood. Thick gold chains hugged his scrawny neck and a Rolex banded his bony wrist. The man's eyes bulged from shallow sockets, darting from side to side as he talked.

Torres wanted to eavesdrop but there were no empty tables near Harrison and his friend. His only choice was to read lips from the bar. But the black man, who did most of the talking, spoke too rapidly for Torres to understand.

The owner of the pub, Mona Rowe, was behind the bar, wiping a glass with a towel. When Torres saw her, he figured her for the bartender. He thought she had an attractive face though wrinkled by what he guessed to be five decades of life.

Torres suddenly realized Mona was staring at him with an inviting smile. When he turned away to keep an eye on Harrison, Mona pulled back her mane of red hair, sucked in a deep breath and pushed her ample cleavage forward, parading it from her low-cut blouse. She approached Torres and leaned forward on the bar directly in front of him.

When Torres turned his gaze from Harrison and the man, his eyes automatically locked on Mona's cleavage. Mona's voluptuous breasts looked like they belonged to a twenty-year-old.

"What can I get for you, honey?" Mona asked through a dimpled smile.

Torres hesitated, lifting his vision from Mona's chest. "Uh, how about a beer?"

Mona noticed Torres' soaked clothes. "A beer? You're drenched to the bone. How 'bout a hot buttered rum? On the house."

"Okay, load me up," Torres said, then glanced over his shoulder at Harrison and the black man who were still jabbering in the corner.

Mona reached under the counter, retrieved a cup and filled it with a deep brown fluid from a steaming, stainless container. She handed the cup to Torres and extended her hand. "Name's Mona Rowe. I own this dump."

Torres shook her hand. "Rafael Torres. Glad to meet you."

"My first husband was a Latino like you," Mona said. "He was a great lay!" she added casually, wasting no time in revealing what was on her mind. "He knew all the right moves. Must be in your people's blood."

"All the way back to Cortez, I think," Torres replied, humoring Mona and sipping from his cup. "Does your husband run this place with you?" he asked, making small talk.

Mona smiled. "Nope. Poor soul died right on top of me. Our best night in bed, but his last," she said frankly.

"I'm sorry," Torres offered.

Mona chuckled. "Sorry? He still had a smile on his face when they embalmed him."

"Oh," Torres mumbled, sipping from his drink. He gave Mona a wink in appreciation of her humor. "I guess that's not a bad way to die."

Mona winked back.

Mona had been right, Torres realized. The hot rum was exactly what he needed on this cold, wet night. He looked over his shoulder again and found Harrison and the man still engrossed in their conversation.

"I haven't seen you in here before," Mona commented. "I know all of my regulars. You new in town?"

"Just got in yesterday," Torres lied. "How long have you owned this place?" he asked, continuing his small talk front.

"Too long," Mona said sadly as she sipped an amber colored drink in a half-filled, jumbo-sized glass. "I used to be a topless dancer at North Beach in Frisco," she recalled. "I used my money from those days to buy this place. Those sailor boys used to come in and drool all over themselves when I was on stage," Mona laughed heartily, cupping her hands under her breasts without reservation. "I've been lucky. I'm getting older but these can still point at the North Star when I need them to."

Torres shook his head and smiled. "I think I know where you got the name for this place."

"Yep, the *Merrimac and the Monitor*," Mona quipped, squeezing her breasts together. "They're as firm as those ironclads. Can you tell?" she asked, her scotch-laced breath wilting Torres' features.

"Shit!" Torres suddenly exclaimed when he looked over his shoulder and noticed Harrison and his friend were no longer at their table. After a quick scan of the room, he realized they were not in the bar. Torres jumped from his stool and bolted for the exit.

Mona watched Torres' departure through a souring

expression. "That's the first time anybody's called them shit, you bastard!" she shouted.

When Torres hustled out of The Merrimac 'n Monitor, he spotted Harrison and the black man. They were still talking, standing under the arched entrance of a nearby store.

Torres trotted across the street and into the alley where Elinger had parked their rented auto. He jumped into the car.

Elinger's vision remained anchored on Harrison and the man. "What'd you find out?" Elinger asked.

"He's been talking with that dude," Torres replied. "But I couldn't get close enough to hear what they were sayin'."

"Franklin Tyler," Elinger muttered. The name tripped over his vocal chords, bringing a foul taste to his mouth.

"You know him?"

"I've popped him a few times."

"For what?"

"Pandering and dealing. But I didn't know he and Harrison were pals."

"You think they're dealin'?"

"I would have assumed Harrison had more class and more sense. But we can get to Harrison by using Tyler."

"Tyler's an informant?"

"Not really, but I think we can make him turn," Elinger said.

"How?"

"Well, I know he already has at least two felony strikes against him," Elinger began. "I'll check his records back at Headquarters. If that's the case, drug dealing would be strike number three. I don't think he'd like a long spell in prison."

Elinger's cell phone rang. He pulled it from his coat pocket.

"Renee's under again!" Detective Sander's urgent voice reported from the phone. "She's writing about you and Ralph being at Fell's Point!"

"What else?" Elinger asked with urgency.

"It's weird. One minute she's writin' about Fell's Point then all of a sudden, she's writing about City Nights, a club for rock n' rollers over on Cathedral Street."

"Anything about the killer?" Elinger asked.

"He's in an alley near the club," Sanders said. "The pages say he's going to murder a young couple."

"At the club?" Elinger asked with more urgency this time.

"That's what I'm reading!"

"We're on our way," Elinger said, then turned to Torres. "You ever been to City Nights?"

"Yo," Torres nodded. "Great ladies prowl there, man."

Harrison and Tyler no longer occupied Elinger's mind. Elinger started the car and fishtailed from the alley. The auto's smoking tires spit a cascade of water.

FORTY

● ● ●

Todd Richards, a tall, sinewy twenty-five-year-old, was enjoying a night of dancing and drinking with his fiancée Laura Kimura. He held Laura's left hand tightly as they danced to the beat of a tattooed and body-pierced punk group inside the chic club, City Lights. Todd glanced at the wide bands of rainbow-colored lights that strobed from the ceiling, flashing on the couples who crowded the dance floor. Todd knew the club would be loud and packed on a Saturday night but he didn't care. This is where he wanted to bring Laura. This is where they had met and, Todd fondly recalled, this is where they fell in love.

One of the club's mini-skirted hostesses, balancing a tray of drinks, stopped next to Todd and Laura. Todd stopped dancing and dropped a twenty-dollar bill on her tray and retrieved a glass of champagne. As the waitress moved off toward more patrons, Todd handed the glass of bubbly to Laura.

"To you," Todd toasted.

"To us," Laura added, smiling. She sipped from the glass and handed it back to Todd who also took a drink.

Todd put his arms around Laura, kissed her and then looked into

Laura's face. He had always been struck by her beauty. She was twenty-four years old with refined and model-like features.

Todd whispered into Laura's ear, then watched as a look of caution swept her face only to quickly fade into a dreamy look.

Laura hooked her arm through Todd's as he led her toward the exit, suddenly oblivious to the music and dancers that surrounded them.

Exiting City Nights beneath its large red neon sign, Todd turned and kissed Laura again. In a second, he became lost in the moment of passion. He didn't care about the rain that peppered his clothes during their long and ardent clutch. And he knew Laura felt the same way.

Laura stared sleepily into Todd's pale green eyes. "I don't know if we should, Todd. I mean, we've waited a long time— what's a couple more weeks?"

"That's the point, Laura. We're both tired of waiting," Todd countered with a smile, his groin throbbing as steady as the rhythm inside the club. "The big white bells ring for us next month. After the wedding, we'll be doing it all the time anyway. My parents are out of town. It's perfect!"

Laura hesitated then smiled. "You promise not to tell anybody?" she asked, her voice was thick with desire.

"Of course, I won't, baby. You're going to be my wife. It'll be our secret," Todd whispered as the rain dampened the coils of his dark hair.

"Okay," Laura agreed, grinning in a playful manner. "Let's do it."

Intoxicated with the rush of hormones in their blood, Todd and Laura hurried down the sidewalk. After a few yards, they stopped and kissed again. Their tongues fenced with passion.

When Laura withdrew, she was short of breath. "You're right, Todd. We've waited way too long!"

Walking again, they were now a few feet from Todd's gleaming white Corvette at the curb.

"I love you," panted Todd.

"I love you, too," Laura panted back.

Leonard Ravnik lurked in the mouth of the alley near Todd and Laura. Pressed against a wall in shadows, he stared at the young couple. He hoped his raggedly cut, bleached hair and dark clothes gave him the appearance of a club rocker on break.

Todd opened the passenger door of the Corvette. Turning to Laura, he pulled her close for another kiss, pressing his torso against her firm breasts.

Ravnik stepped from the darkness and moved toward the embracing couple.

Todd noticed Ravnik first. He pulled from Laura with a start. "Hi," he greeted innocently. "What group you with?"

"The *Grave Diggers*," Ravnik replied, toying with Todd.

"Never heard of you guys?" Todd asked. "Are you going to play tonight?"

Ravnik did not respond. Instead, he leaped forward and grabbed Todd and Laura by their throats. With one in each gloved hand, he aborted any cry for help. The couple clawed at Ravnik's hands but his powerful grip was unyielding.

Ravnik began to drag the young couple toward the center of the street. Once there, he dropped them next to a manhole cover.

Todd and Laura, clutching their throats, sucked for air like fish on land.

Ravnik yanked the heavy manhole cover from the pavement, exposing the dark orifice leading to the city's underground drainage system. As Ravnik turned back to Todd and Laura, he was suddenly caught in the beams of approaching headlights.

"There he is!" Torres exclaimed to Elinger, looking through the windshield of their rented luxury auto. "With a bad hair job!" he added.

Elinger stepped on the accelerator and sped toward Ravnik, then slammed on the brakes, screeching on the rain-slicked street to a broadside stop near the manhole. Torres withdrew his pistol and started out of the car but Elinger grabbed his arm.

"No guns unless he's in a trance," Elinger ordered.

"Are you sure about that, man?" Torres argued. "This guy almost killed us once!"

"Dennington told us we can only kill him when he's in a trance so Renee can be free from all this," Elinger reminded Torres. "Otherwise, she gets a direct link-up with this thing, and it will control her."

"Shit," Torres muttered as he pushed his firearm back into its holster and glanced at Elinger. "So, what's your plan? I don't feel like dying tonight!"

Elinger pulled a Taser gun from his jacket pocket and held it up for Torres to see.

Torres grinned with a look of relief. "Guess we'll kick some ass tonight after all!"

Elinger and Torres jumped from their car and rushed Ravnik who was pulling the struggling Todd and Laura toward the edge of the manhole. Each one was in a chokehold. Their faces were swelling and turning blue now.

Elinger stopped behind Ravnik, aimed the Taser gun and fired two tethered darts into Ravnik's back. As the electricity crackled through the dart cables, Ravnik's head snapped backward, and he released his grip on Todd and Laura. The couple slumped to the pavement, heaving for air.

Ravnik's body quivered as he moaned, then he pulled his head forward, fighting the current in his body. He staggered, then slowly steadied himself and turned toward Elinger.

Elinger's expression turned into one of disbelief but then he recalled the results of the one-eared man's last blood sample— high levels of adrenaline and endorphins—extra strength and natural pain killers. It made sense to him now why Ravnik could recover quickly from the affects of a Taser gun.

Ravnik's eyes were riveted on Elinger as he yanked the Taser darts from his back.

Torres rushed the one-eared man, realizing this man recognized him as the guy he stabbed at the slaughterhouse. Before Ravnik could make a move, Torres gave him a field goal kick square in the balls. Ravnik gasped and dropped to his knees.

Elinger and Torres pulled handcuffs from their belts and grabbed Ravnik's gloved hands to double-cuff him.

But Ravnik jumped abruptly to his feet and slammed his fist into Torres' jaw. While Torres stumbled, trying to recover from the punch, Ravnik hit Elinger on the chin, knocking him down. Ravnik pinned Elinger to the street by dropping his knee on his chest.

Elinger knew he was running out of options. He wanted to call for backups but he couldn't take the chance an officer might kill Ravnik when he was not in a trance.

"Shoot him in the legs, Ralph!" Elinger shouted, his chest heaving against the brutal weight of Ravnik's knee. "Blow out his knees!"

Torres had regained most of his senses when he heard Elinger's order. He yanked his firearm from its holster.

Amos wheeled up and parked down the street from City Nights. He looked through his windshield and gladly saw Elinger and Torres had the infamous Shadow Man on his knees. Now he would get his story with the capture of Elinger's suspect. Amos pulled out his camera to take photos for a story he was sure would make him famous.

FORTY-ONE

• • •

Ravnik continued to press his knee on Elinger's torso. His weight and the strength of his arms pushing on Elinger kept the detective pinned to the watery pavement.

Elinger knew he couldn't fight the one-eared man one-on-one. If only Torres would hurry with his weapon. It was time to take this guy down.

Torres, holding his pistol, rushed up behind Ravnik. He aimed at the one-eared man's legs but he did not have a clear shot without the chance of hitting Elinger. Torres suddenly stepped forward and kicked Ravnik on the side of the head.

Ravnik's upper body jerked sideways. Falling to the pavement, Ravnik looked stunned. Blood streamed down from above his right temple as Torres shot at one of his legs. The bullet missed its mark by an inch and sparked off the wet pavement.

Ravnik sprang to his feet and kicked Torres, directly on the slaughterhouse wound site. The force of the blow, caused the pistol to slip from Torres' sweaty grip. It bounced on the pavement and dropped down the open manhole.

Torres' knees buckled from the pain coming from his healing

wound. He dropped face down on the street, and rolled on his side, dazed.

On his feet now, Elinger could see the killer's trance-like expression as Ravnik made a sudden move toward the open manhole.

Elinger drew his weapon and aimed it at Ravnik's head. With the spaced-out look in the killer's face, Elinger knew this was the time to kill him and take out the entity and free Renee from its control. Tonight, the one-eared man's actions had given Elinger the right to use any force necessary to end his life.

Elinger pulled the trigger. In that instant, however, Ravnik dropped down into the open manhole as Elinger's bullet whizzed over his head.

Elinger angrily lowered his pistol and rushed to the open manhole.

Torres moved to Elinger's side, gingerly rubbing the left side of his chest. Elinger and Torres stared down the dark hole, seeing nothing, only hearing the thunder of turbulent water below.

Elinger glanced toward the sidewalk and saw the young couple, Todd and Laura. They were sitting on the curb, wrapped in each other's arms. Their faces were pale with shock, but Elinger could tell they would recover from the attack.

Amos sat quietly is his car. His face and shirt were soaked with sweat. After what he saw tonight, he knew this case could be the story of lifetime for a reporter.

Amos removed a handkerchief from his pocket and wiped the moisture from his face. Looking through his windshield, he saw Elinger step down the manhole ladder and disappear under the street.

"What the hell are you doing', man?" Torres yelled down the manhole. "There's a river down there!" Torres waited for a reply but heard none. "Shit!" he muttered as he dutifully descended the ladder to join his partner.

Beneath the street, Torres stepped off the ladder and slid down a ribbed, 10-foot by 10-foot underground pipe. He splashed into a mainline of surging, muddy water and waded toward Elinger. Suddenly, Elinger and Torres were swept away by the strong current. Bobbing like corks, they were at the mercy of the white caps that pulled them down the tunnel.

Farther down the system, Ravnik was also weak against the strength of the violent eddies. Kicking his legs and wind milling his arms, he tried to keep his head above the rising water. But the water pounded his face and rushed into his mouth. Ravnik coughed and sputtered for breath he could not find.

`Elinger and Torres pitched and rolled down the mainline, struggling to stay afloat. The storm's heavy downpour had increased the water levels, giving the underground river a white-water force.

"Let the harbor have him!" Torres shouted in the dark, his voice competing with the din of the underground river. "He'll be dead by the time he gets there—like we're gonna be if we don't get out of here!"

"I've got to make sure he dies when he's in a trance," came Elinger's curt reply from the blackness.

Sinking in the choppy flow, Ravnik had heard Elinger and Torres in the darkness behind him—but he was sure death would arrest him before they could. He could feel his arm and leg muscles knotting with cramps. As the water flowed into his mouth and nose, Ravnik gagged. His thoughts became thick and slow as he started to lose consciousness.

Suddenly, Ravnik's pain and exhaustion began to dissipate. A feeling of strength filled his body, swelling his muscles with power. The voice had taken command of his flesh again and pumped more life preserving chemicals into his blood. He welcomed the relief and renewed energy.

"*Regulate your breathing, Leonard,*" the voice advised unexpectedly. The words seemed to come from behind Ravnik's eyes. "*Do not be tainted with fear. I am here to assist you!*"

Ravnik's eyes suddenly rolled up and hid beneath their lids. Under the influence of the voice, Ravnik paddled and kicked with the new energy. He spun into a back floating position. His head turned, his mouth opened, and he puked up the water he had swallowed.

In a moment, Ravnik was riding the current, feet first on his back, his nose free to breathe again. The oxygen rewarded him with even more strength.

Shooting out of an underground culvert like a cannonball, Ravnik tumbled through a heavy mist and splashed into the churning waters trapped in a large 50-foot by 50-foot concrete room. Although he was in a trance, Ravnik could hear the roar of the mainline channels spilling their turbulent waters toward him. He felt the circular motion of the water, realizing he was in the current of a large whirlpool. Confined in the watery sweeps of the room, Ravnik felt himself sliding down toward the vortex. He tried to swim out, but the elephantine force sucked him downward.

Elinger and Torres plunged into the thundering maelstrom also, but unlike Ravnik, they splashed down higher on the whirling bank. Spinning past a wall, Elinger reached out and grabbed the rung of a ladder that led to an overhead manhole. Elinger pulled himself from the dizzying ride, then extended an arm toward Torres who was circling back in a mountainous wave. Grasping Torres' arm, Elinger jerked him toward the ladder and out of the whirlpool.

After climbing the ladder a few feet, Elinger and Torres gazed down into the eye of the whirlpool and saw the one-eared man sinking into the swirling vortex. They noticed the one-eared man's eyes were rolled-up. He was obviously in a trance so if he died now, Renee would be free from him and the entity. The magnetic plane Dennington had mentioned would be broken. And that's exactly what Elinger wanted.

"*Adios*, motherfucker," Torres mumbled in an obvious tone of satisfaction. "Enjoy your ride to hell!"

At the culvert's ceiling, Elinger pushed aside the manhole, climbed upward, and stepped onto the city street.

Torres climbed topside and joined Elinger where they savored deep breaths of the dry night air. They glanced down the street and noticed their rented auto was a couple of blocks away. Flashing lights indicated that an ambulance was on the scene.

Elinger began to move purposely toward their car.

"Where are you going?" Torres asked.

"To the harbor."

"It's a big harbor," Torres said. "You think we can find him ourselves?"

Elinger didn't answer. He continued to walk toward the auto.

"Our guys can dredge him up at first light," Torres reasoned.

"I need to find him tonight," Elinger said, throwing his words over his shoulder. "Renee's life could be in danger if he died when he wasn't in a trance!"

Torres mentally agreed with Elinger. "Wait up!" he yelled, trotting toward his partner.

Elinger glanced back at Torres who was rushing toward their auto. He was glad Torres was becoming just as consumed by this case as he was.

FORTY-TWO

• • •

Knowing he had to race the underground river to the Inner Harbor, Elinger throttled the rented auto and sped down several city blocks. Torres grabbed the armrest on the passenger door panel as the tires screeched at every corner. After a two-mile run, Elinger veered into a vacant lot. The car skidded to a halt near a sagging chain-link fence fifty yards from the harbor's dark waters.

Elinger and Torres rushed from the vehicle and climbed over the fence. They slid down a small hill into mud that quickly covered their shoes. After wading through several yards of ankle-deep weeds and sludge, Elinger and Torres reached the bank of the harbor. Elinger looked ahead at the bay, mentally cursing the fog that shrouded the water and made visibility poor. At first, all he could see were the ghostly shapes of boats in the distance. Then, about forty yards away, his vision settled on a large, wide, ribbed pipe protruding from a wall of earth twenty-feet above the harbor. A torrent of water rushed from the pipe, carrying the dirt of the city into the bay.

"This is where he'll come out if he's not already in the bay," Elinger told Torres, pointing.

"I guess, in a way, we're hoping he's alive," Torres said in a tone filled with irony.

"Yeah, unless he drowned while he was in a trance," Elinger replied with mixed emotions. "That's what I've got to find out."

Elinger and Torres suddenly heard a splash beneath the run-off pipe. They focused on the darkened bay and saw what appeared to be a body sinking beneath the water.

Elinger tore off his coat, shirt and pants and kicked free of his shoes. Torres began to peel off his sweater.

"No, you stay here in case I need you to pull us in," Elinger ordered. "The water's real cold this time of year. I don't know how long I'll last."

"But I'm younger, stronger," Torres argued. "I should go and you standby."

"This is personal, Ralph. I want to bring him in," Elinger said, making it obvious there was no room for argument. "Besides, you're still not completely healed." With that, Elinger trotted forward, splashing into the bay.

Torres reluctantly pulled down his sweater. He folded his arms over his chest looking as though he was trying to hold back his own welling frustration.

Underwater, Elinger could see very little in the murky depths. He reached out with his hands, groping, hoping to find the one-eared man by touch. In less than two minutes, however, the near frigid temperature of the water had penetrated his flesh. Elinger's arms felt like lead. He realized hypothermia was setting in. In a few more seconds, his lungs demanded oxygen.

Elinger paddled toward the surface. As he moved upward,

something heavy brushed his shoulder. He reached out and grabbed what felt like an arm. When he tugged on it, he could feel the weight of a body. Elinger extended his other hand and felt the head of the body. One ear was missing.

Elinger kicked hard, trying to pull his trophy to the surface—but his arms and hands were weak and numbed by the cold bay. The more he squeezed, the more his hands cramped. Suddenly, the body slid from his weakening grip. Elinger lurched forward to grab it again but clutched only water.

Elinger broke through the water's surface and sucked in breaths of needed air, then dived back down in desperation to find the one-eared man again.

For two more minutes, Elinger swept the water with his hands but could not relocate the killer. His eyes were useless, too. The water was too dark and cloudy to see anything. When his lungs begged for air again, he knew his search was over. Elinger headed for the surface, figuring he would be lucky to muster enough strength to swim back to shore.

Thankful to reach the shore, Elinger looked wearily at his partner and then sat on the beach. He breathed deeply, staring fiercely at the bay from his weakened physical condition.

"*Personal* is going to get you killed," Torres said pointedly. "Nobody knows that better than me."

Elinger knew his partner was right, but at the moment his mind was a jumble of emotions, too mixed and contradicting to create a reasonable thought. He wrapped his arms around his torso to retain body heat, then shook his head with disbelief. "I found him," Elinger said. "Had him in my hands. I don't know if I lost my grip or he pulled away."

Torres panned the misty harbor, seeing nothing but calm water.

Elinger glared angrily at the bay. "Ralph, when I get my hands on that sonovabitch—I'm gonna bury him so deep you'll need a Chinese passport to piss on his grave!"

"I'd like to leave something a little more disgusting," Torres replied candidly.

Elinger and Torres trudged through the weeds, moving back to where they parked their car. Elinger was speaking to Renee on his cell phone. He learned her trance was over. She was resting and was waiting for Elinger to come to her house to read the new pages.

Amos pulled in near Elinger's auto. His headlights flooded the area, included Elinger and Torres who had just hopped over the sagging fence. Wanting to shoot advance photos for his story, Amos aimed his camera at the detectives.

Shifting his bloodshot eyes toward Amos, Elinger shouted, "I'm in no mood, *Anus*! Put it away!"

Amos lowered his camera, deciding it was in his best interest to follow Elinger's order if he were to get an exclusive story. "Okay, No photos. But what are you doing here, Lieutenant?"

Elinger stopped and pierced Amos with a hard stare. "The question is—what are you doing here?"

Amos' mind locked for a moment as he reminded himself to pretend he didn't know anything about tonight's events. "I had my scanner on. I heard you calling in for divers," Amos lied, hoping Elinger really had called for divers. He did not want

Elinger to know he saw the confrontation outside the nightclub. "It's just Reporting 101."

When Elinger didn't respond, Amos figured his answer had satisfied the lieutenant. "Guess it's all over then?" Amos' words sounded like a question. "Police divers usually fish for dead bodies. Means I should be getting my story soon, right?"

"It's not over until I see him in the morgue," Elinger replied in measured words. "Now get the hell out of here before I give your story to one of the interns at the *Sun*."

"Okay," Amos said, quietly retreating into his auto. He felt a great sense of relief knowing Elinger hadn't seen him at City Lights. He didn't want the images in his camera destroyed.

● ● ●

Spent from the trance, Renee was resting on her couch, trying to rub away the fading pain in her temples. When Elinger arrived, he dismissed Sanders for the night, then settled in next to Renee and embraced her.

Renee looked at Elinger through narrow, red-rimmed eyes. "I'm so tired, Kent," she murmured. "Did you get him?"

"He's in the bay, and I'm not sure if he's dead," Elinger answered regretfully. "Our divers are setting up now. They'll be looking for him at first light."

"There's another note," Renee reported in a drained tone. She sat up and retrieved a page from a nearby table and handed it to Elinger. "Please make him stop," Renee begged, tears welling in her eyes.

Renee's plea made Elinger feel even more ineffective. He

read the note quietly through troubled eyes:

My dear Madam Holland:

What a pitiful night this was! Fruitless for both of us, I'm afraid. And now I am overpowered with an intense sentiment of rage against your policeman friend who saved the young couple. In time I will make him my bounden slave. I do hope he will maintain his earnest endeavors although he is upset, and there was no tintinnabulation of victory for him tonight. But to solve a murder, one must know who the murderer is? He will surely need Providence on his side to accomplish that. My best to you, dear Madam. Please do not worry unnecessarily about all this...

Anger vibrated through Elinger's frame. He wadded up the note and tossed it back on the table.

"Am I going to be cursed for the rest of my life?" Renee implored as her eyes glittered with tears. "When does it stop, Kent? When does it stop?"

The question haunted Elinger because he didn't have the answer. "Soon, Renee," he finally replied, willing to say anything that would comfort her.

FORTY-THREE

• • •

Sitting at his desk, Elinger reflected unhappily on the conversation he just finished with Sanders. Sanders reported the harbor dredging operation had not produced the one-eared man's body. Elinger knew he had no choice but to assume the one-eared man was still alive. And he had mixed feelings about it. If the killer had survived, Elinger would have another chance to destroy him while he was under the influence of the entity. This, according to Dennington, would free Renee. On the down side, however, he realized more murders were likely to occur.

A look of futility contaminated Elinger's features as he glanced at his computer screen. He was reviewing the reports written by the officers who had investigated the incident at the nightclub and what he saw was a major disappointment. No fingerprints were found on the scene because the killer wore gloves. The blood samples taken from the pavement near the manhole were added to the DNA samples already collected from the earlier crime scenes. As before, high levels of adrenaline and endorphins were found in the samples. Elinger admitted to himself he and his men were still in the starting gate, and their one-eared suspect still remained the elusive Shadow Man.

Elinger leaned back in his chair and grimaced. Although he had survived another bout with the killer, every inch of his body was sore and ached. He could handle that, but what dogged him mercilessly was Renee's emotional torment and his inability to solve the case quickly to prevent more murders.

Elinger shifted in his chair again, lifting his weight off one sore spot only to find another. He contemplated the newest FACES police composite he had just helped create with the department's computer specialist. This life-like photo image featured the killer's new look—the rough-cut, bleached hair. It was as good as a real mug shot. Elinger would post the composite online and send it to the entire BPD department. His men would hit the streets with printed copies. If the one-eared man was still alive and in Baltimore, they would find him.

Elinger turned from his computer monitor, considering his next step in the investigation. It was time for him to vacate his office. Officially on vacation, he took a risk by being in the Headquarters' building. But he wasn't too worried. He could handle Captain Osborne, and his men were loyal to him. It was Deputy Mayor Willard Montagna who could make real trouble. Luckily, the deputy mayor had not graced the halls of Headquarters for several months. He only appeared for investigations of rogue cops or police brutality when his cause and his face could be promoted by television crews and newspaper reporters.

Elinger reflected on another change he made in his investigation. He assigned two detectives, Mellis and Ward, to tail Harrison should the attorney be the next intended victim. So far, this extra surveillance had produced nothing.

Elinger also assigned a couple of officers to surveil Franklin Tyler after he read Tyler's criminal record. He was hoping these men would find some kind of *probable cause* so Elinger could search Tyler's auto or his house to turn up something criminal he could use against Tyler. Elinger wanted to use Tyler to nab Harrison. But Elinger knew it would not be easy to gain Tyler's cooperation without some heavy leverage.

When Elinger reviewed Franklin Tyler's arrests for drug trafficking, he found just what he needed. Tyler was on parole for a drug violation. And he already had a third-strike against him, but the judge was lenient and only gave Tyler ten years. With a fourth strike, Elinger knew Tyler would go away for a very long time in the state penitentiary, no matter who the judge was.

Elinger was unable to hide his delight when he received a call from his men who discovered Tyler had a tail light out on his car. And when they pulled him over to ticket him, they smelled marijuana coming from the auto.

"We've got him in our unit in the four-hundred block of Lombard Street," the officer reported on Elinger's cell phone.

"Hold him until I get there," Elinger ordered. "And search his car. You've got the probable cause with the weed. Notify Torres to meet me there."

Elinger pocketed his cell phone and moved out of his office, hoping the officers would find something in Tyler's auto that he could turn into a fourth-strike.

As Elinger drove across the city streets, steering toward Lombard Street, he reviewed in his mind everything he read about Tyler's past. There were many arrests for dealing and pandering.

One aggravated assault bust, too. Franklin Tyler was a Pittsburgh bastard, born of a prostitute and raised in the crime-ridden Shady Side District. At twelve, he cut school regularly and roamed the streets with older boys who sold drugs and pimped. He quickly learned the street's lucrative ways. By sixteen, he was pulling in three thousand a week. During that time, however, he had incurred the wrath of the police and faced a long stretch in reform school. A generous social worker intervened and gave him the choice of military duty or jail. Suddenly becoming patriotic, Tyler joined the Navy and was assigned to the Small Craft Facility in Annapolis.

Elinger was amazed to learn that Tyler had used the U.S. Military to transport his drugs. Spending his weekends in Baltimore, Tyler migrated to the seedier sections of Fell's Point and Sparrow's Point and associated with hookers, pimps, and drug dealers. He was looking for a way to reinvent himself and found it. When he was caught using naval craft to transport his drugs, he was found guilty by court martial. Tyler was dishonorably discharged and sentenced to four years of hard labor at Leavenworth. After his sentence was served, he gravitated back to Baltimore where he whittled a deeper notch in the street crime hierarchy and was caught again, this time serving time in the Maryland State Penitentiary.

Elinger steered his auto to the curb and parked behind the BPD patrol car on Lombard Street. In front of the squad car was Franklin Tyler's rare, black 4-door sedan. It was a fully restored 1960s model with a body and rims that glistened like a glassy lake.

The uniformed officers, who pulled Tyler over, indicated to Elinger that Tyler was in the back seat of their vehicle. Torres was already there, sitting on the passenger seat.

Elinger slid into the back next to Tyler who had his hands handcuffed behind his back.

Tyler's face tightened when he saw Elinger—a cop who had arrested him before. "Oh, fuck, it's you!" he lamented.

"Sorry, we're all out of friendly scoutmasters today, Tyler," Elinger said, casting a penetrating look at Tyler.

Torres tossed Elinger a large plastic bag packed full of one-gram bundles of heroin. "We found this in the trunk of his car."

Elinger studied the bag. "This is obviously *possession with intent to sell*. You get hard time for that, Tyler."

"I wanna call my attorney!" Tyler whined.

"Why? I didn't say I was going to arrest you," Elinger said calmly.

Elinger's statement surprised Tyler. "What? What kinda game are you runnin' on me?"

"Well, if we're playing a game, you've already set the rules," Elinger said as he held the bag of heroin up to Tyler's face.

Tyler's expression stretched tight with worry. "That's not mine!"

"And I'm the Prince of Wales," Torres said.

"We're not stupid, Tyler," Elinger said. "We know you deal this shit, and we think you move a lot of weight sometimes."

Tyler looked at Elinger through a belligerent expression. "If you're not going to arrest me, what the fuck do you really want with me?"

"Cooperation."

"What kind of cooperation?"

"I want you to help us put Sidney Harrison away," Elinger replied.

Tyler cocked his ears, pretending he didn't hear correctly. "Sidney Harrison?"

"Yeah, your attorney," Torres added.

"Put him away for what?" Tyler asked, acting dumb.

"He has two careers. One in law, and we think the other is in drugs. And we're sure you help him with the drugs. You've been spending a lot of time with him lately," Elinger said.

Tyler chuckled dimly. "Even if he's doin' what you're sayin', I don't flip for nobody! Nobody can touch that cracker anyway."

"I can prove you wrong," Elinger said, leaning closer to Tyler's face.

Tyler shrugged. "I still ain't gonna help you."

"Do you really want to spend the rest of your life in prison?" Elinger asked, indicating the bag of heroin.

Tyler studied the bag nervously. Since it was in his possession, he knew he could be dead meat on this bust.

"This is just one bag, I know," Elinger began, "but it's enough for a search warrant to toss your house. Our Narcotics Division knows how to find all the best hiding places. What do you think they're going to find at your place?"

Elinger's words hit Tyler hard. His expression told Elinger that more drugs would be found.

"We're not talkin' trash time at a country club prison!" Torres warned Tyler. "We're talkin' hard time at Jessup."

A shock wave whipped through Tyler when he heard the name *Jessup*. He fidgeted in his seat.

"As you know, possession of heroin is a parole violation of your third-strike drug offense, and it will send you back to prison. It will also count as a fourth strike," Elinger explained.

Torres locked eyes on Tyler's. "If we send you to the Court Commission, you'll have to finish the ten-year term you were paroled on plus at least twenty-five to life for a fourth strike. If you're lucky, you'll be eighty-years-old when you get out."

Tyler's cocky demeanor was fading quickly. His heart was racing.

"In other words, Tyler, you're really screwed," Elinger said. "So, let's cut through all the bullshit. We can make all this go away if you help us."

Tyler exhaled a labored breath. Sweat began to pepper his forehead. "You say all I gotta do is set up Harrison?"

"Yeah, you're simply going to do what you normally do with him—peddle drugs," Elinger said, handing the heroin back to Torres.

"Well, I don't wanna go back in, that's for sure," Tyler said nervously. "But Harrison might have me whacked!"

"We'll protect you," Torres said.

"Yeah, sure. For a month. Then what?"

"We'll protect you until Harrison is behind bars," Elinger promised.

"I don't know, man," Tyler said. "I ain't never done nothin' like this before."

"There's nothing to think about, Tyler," Elinger said. "If we call your parole officer and the Court Commission, you're going to Jessup."

Tyler sucked in a deep breath, reviewing his options

mentally. He could find none. "How do you want me to set 'im up?" he asked, clearly thinking of his freedom.

"Real simple," Elinger said. "The next time you bring heroin to Harrison, just let us know. We want to catch him while he's holding."

"I ain't never set anybody up to go to jail," Tyler said, mustering a fraction of his earlier combative attitude.

"You just weren't motivated enough," Elinger said.

"There's a good chance you'll die in prison if you don't help us," Torres reminded. "And keep in mind that in prison there's no liquor, no drugs, fancy cars, and no pussy. All the things you love."

Torres' words weighed on Tyler's mind.

"If you help us, I'll cut you loose today, right now," Elinger said, adding icing to the deal.

"Right here and now?" Tyler asked, wanting to reaffirm what he just heard.

Elinger nodded and pulled a handcuff key from his pocket and held it up for Tyler to see.

"Okay, I'm in," Tyler nodded and pulled his handcuffed hands from behind his back to his side.

Elinger unlocked the cuffs and put them in his pocket.

Tyler rubbed his wrists and let out a breath of relief. "You and I got a deal. Harrison for my freedom."

"Yeah, but there's one more part to our deal, Tyler," Elinger said.

Tyler gave Elinger a perplexed look. "What?"

"Once we have Harrison in custody and you walk away, you need to retire from the drug business immediately and permanently," Elinger said. "You need to be squeaky clean from that day forward."

"And if I don't?"

"All of your records will be going to our Narcotics Division," Elinger explained. "Our narcs will watch you like a hawk. You make one wrong move, and you're going straight to prison as though you never made a deal with us. Do you understand?"

Tyler eyed the floor of the auto as a nervous tic caused him to bounce his right leg. "But I've always worked the streets, man. I don't know how to do anything else."

"I don't care if you have to get a job at a car wash," Elinger said. "You need to find honest work."

Tyler put his hand on his leg to stop the bouncing. His mind was fluttering with worry. "Why are you doin' this to me, man?"

"You did it to yourself," Elinger said. "So that's the deal. We're giving you an opportunity that most scumbags never get."

Tyler took a long pensive look out the window, taking in the busy city surrounding him. He was facing a big challenge and felt trapped. He turned back to Elinger and Torres. "I don't have much choice, do I?"

"You're right. You don't," Torres said.

With that, Torres exited the car and moved around to Tyler's side of the auto. He opened the door since squad car rear doors are locked from the outside. Tyler stepped out, and Torres handed him his car keys. "Don't screw this up, Tyler," he warned.

Tyler nodded. He knew what Torres said was the truth. He wiped his sweaty brow with his shirt sleeve and walked toward his auto. Tyler's once cocky, straight shouldered stride was now slower and stooped. The prospect of a dim future affected his whole body. He climbed into his car, started it and drove off into city traffic.

Elinger and Torres approached the two uniformed officers who watched Tyler disappear down the busy street. They gave the detectives a questioning look.

"It's okay, guys," Elinger said. "He's a C-I for us. We've got him from here."

"Yeah, he's goin' lead us to a bigger fish," Torres added.

This satisfied the officers. They shook hands with Elinger and Torres and climbed back into their squad car.

As Elinger and Torres walked back toward their autos, both were still digesting their conversation with Tyler.

"Do you think Tyler will come through?" Torres asked.

"Yeah," Elinger nodded. "He's got too much to lose if he doesn't."

"What's our next move?"

"I'm going to pull Mellis and Ward from their surveillance of Harrison," Elinger said, reaching for the door handle of his auto. "I want Harrison to be all mine when this goes down."

FORTY-FOUR

● ● ●

Renee moaned and writhed, responding to strong, primitive urges. Following a rhythm that pushed her toward her peak, her breaths became choppy, and her heart pumped rapidly. Renee's toes curled as she soared over the barrier and felt the gratifying spasms between her legs.

Later, while basking in the glow, Renee considered how glad she was that making love to Elinger helped her forget the turmoil in her life. She was grateful Alex had gone to dinner with his father giving her and Elinger intimate time together.

Renee looked at Elinger who was lying in bed with her. Elinger smiled at her as they touched hands, interlocking their fingers.

Renee slipped on her nightgown and lay back down next to Elinger. Suddenly, she sat up in bed and pushed the palms of her hands against her temples. Struck by a piercing pain, she tried to scream but no sound emerged from her throat. Renee slid off the bed and walked toward the door. A pale zombie-like stare governed her expression.

Having seen Renee's dulled eyes, Elinger rose from the

bed. He slipped on his pants quickly and trailed Renee into the den.

Elinger watched Renee at her computer as she began another session of trance writing. Words and sentences flowed from her possessed mind through her fingers and onto the computer's keyboard.

Elinger read the passages as they emerged from the printer. He learned the one-eared man was in a dingy, one-room apartment. He was nude, sitting on the edge of a bathtub, pouring rubbing alcohol on the wounds caused by his fight with Elinger and Torres. There were many cuts, large and small on his head. The larger ones were crudely sewn shut with threads of various colors. As Elinger read more, the one-eared man's plans were revealed. He was preparing to kill again.

Elinger pulled his cell phone from his pocket and called Torres, instructing Sanders and Torres to come to Renee's house immediately.

● ● ●

Wearing incandescent green workout shorts, a wide leather weight belt, and a tight tank top, Müeller the Masher was lying on a weight bench inside Spartan Gym. As he rapidly pressed a 350-pound barbell, sweat glistened on his bulging muscles and the thick worm-like veins swelling beneath his skin.

Cowan's eye scanned the gym as Müeller continued his workout. Two wrestlers, rehearsing for a television bout, were locked in a body hold in a wrestling ring. Other wrestlers stood ringside, watching the men and chatting casually. Cowan knew that although these men were bitter adversaries during their televised bouts, most were good friends off screen. A few men in suits, the agents and managers, stood near the ring talking to their clients. Other grapplers, wearing Speedos, pumped weights and worked the weight equipment mounted on the walls. A few more were in the locker area, removing their workout clothes and heading for the showers.

Cowan looked down at the Masher. He was Müeller's safety man today to ensure the Masher did not drop the weights on his windpipe. Cowan knew the Masher took great pride in driving his body to the limit, attacking his workouts with total commitment. Cowan missed his days when he was a champion like Müeller. He was a star in the ring, as mean and tough as the best of them. But when steroids became the norm to build bodies, he opted out. Cowan thought of steroids as body poison. He'd rather be healthy than have a contaminated system. Cowan knew that even though Müeller used weights to build his strength, he still relied on testosterone cypionate to give him the edge.

The Masher was a closet steroid abuser, injecting himself regularly. When the Masher's huge arms rose, lifting the weights again, Cowan caught a glimpse of the purple acne on the back of Müeller's shoulders—silent testimony to the Masher's excessive use of steroids. Cowan regretted he had slowly become Müeller's drug supplier—but since he was no longer in the spotlight and needed to make a living, he had weakened. He tried to justify this by telling himself it was the only way he could stay in the life he loved.

Thirty minutes later Müeller finished his workout. As Cowan stacked the weights on the wall, Byron, the porno theater owner, suddenly shuffled toward Müeller and Cowan. "'Cuse me, Mr. Masher," he said in his choppy, short-change English. "I look all over for you. Lucky you here. I find man with one ear. Police picture you give me was good help," he added in an enthusiastic tone.

The news hit the Masher like an electrical shock. "Vhere?" he asked.

"You said I get money?" Byron reminded.

"Vhatever you vant!"

"Right now, I could use a Benji Franklin?"

"Give it to him," Müeller ordered Cowan.

Cowan reached into a pocket of his tight-fitting sweat suit, and retrieved five twenties. He handed them to Byron. "Five Andrew Jackson's okay?"

Byron nodded, obviously pleased, then turned to the Masher. "I still get tickets?"

"*Ja*! Now vhere is he?!" Müeller's question was a loud demand.

"I see him—I follow," Byron reported in a low, humble tone now. "He go home to The Block, to a room on top of Huan's Massage Parlor. It's got big sign. Easy to find."

The Masher stepped toward Cowan impatiently. "Let's go!" he ordered Cowan. "Time to teach dat *scheisse* a lesson!"

Müeller brushed past Byron, moving toward the locker area with Cowan in tow. The publicity resulting from his confrontation with the one-eared man had made him appear weak to his colleagues and fans. The humiliation gnawed at Müeller constantly. He was going to break the one-eared man's neck with his bare hands and let the world know about it. Consequences be damned.

●　●　●

Ravnik, wearing underwear now, stood in front of his stained sink and gazed into the cracked mirror above it. He studied the stitched wounds that seeped blood. He was prideful of the stitch job that ran from his temple to an inch behind his left eye where Torres kicked him. It gave him the look of a horror film monster. His eyes dropped to his lower body's reflection in the mirror where a deep bruise ran from his groin area to the inside of his thigh. This, too, was caused by a solid kick from Torres. Ravnik had felt only a fleeting moment of pain. The voice had instantaneously pumped more endorphins into his blood to numb the injuries.

Ravnik splashed water on his face then ran his wet hands through his hair, pulling it tightly over his scalp. He carefully covered the scar tissue on the side of his head, the absence of his ear a mark of his power. A narrow smile bent his lips when he peered into the mirror and admired himself. As he studied his rough features, he recalled the voice had warned him that physical strength alone could no longer beat his adversaries. Ravnik needed something more powerful than the chemicals in his bloodstream. And tonight, the voice had promised to help him even the odds.

Ravnik moved to his stained and chipped dresser and pulled out a pair of pants and a sweater. Once he dressed, he slipped on his jacket and his gloves, then headed for the door. He stepped into the night, wondering what kind of murder the voice had planned for him. Whatever it was, he was sure he would enjoy it as much as the others.

• • •

Müeller marched down a sidewalk in The Block, passing several garishly lighted pornography shops. The Masher had dressed for war. Military camouflage pants hugged his bulky legs and an Army green tank top stretched over his muscular torso and a long-sleeve body shirt. It was the costume he wore in the ring—his marketing image. He wanted everyone to know what he was going to do on this night. He wanted to repair his injured macho image even if it meant spending a few years in jail.

Cowan was at the Masher's side, wearing a tight sweat suit that allowed his heavily muscled body to bulge from beneath and his thick neck to squeeze through the opening in the top. He and Müeller earned the instant respect of passersby who smartly stepped out of their path.

Nearing Huan's Massage Parlor, Müeller and Cowan stopped about a hundred feet from the building when they saw Ravnik descending the outside stairway. Müeller recognized the one-eared man despite the bleached hair. He was only inches from that ugly face during the attack outside Spartan Gym.

Ravnik stepped off the sidewalk and disappeared between two buildings, moving toward a vacant alley.
Müeller grinned at Cowan. "Good. He's going to make it easy for us!"

Although he was aware of the movement behind him,

Ravnik didn't look back. His eyes quivered and rolled occasionally as he kept his head straight and walked down the trash-strewn alley. He knew who was following him. The voice had already told him, promising not to interfere if Ravnik wanted to kill the two wrestlers. After all, they were the ones who exposed Ravnik's face to the neighborhood. For that, death was justified. Breaking into a warped smile, Ravnik never felt stronger. He was ready to take on the wrestler and his bodyguard.

● ● ●

Elinger and Torres sped across town, still using their rented luxury car. Elinger gripped the steering wheel with one white knuckled hand and the other held his cell phone to his ear. Torres sat tensely on the passenger side.

"What does it say, Jay?" Elinger asked Sanders who was at Renee's house monitoring Renee's writing.

"Down an alley… He's walking down an alley," Sander's voice filtered from the phone as he read from the pages Renee was writing.

"Where?" Elinger asked.

"Doesn't say exactly," Sanders replied, hesitating briefly before he spoke again. "But there's a lot of porno shops. He's gotta be in The Block. And there's two guys following him," he added quickly. "Big guys. One of them is a wrestler."

Elinger slowed the auto for a turn, then accelerated, realizing angrily that Müeller the Masher was following their suspect. He quickly recalled the wrestler's interference had already jeopardized their case—but more important, the Masher's life was in danger. He was no match for the one-eared man.

● ● ●

Ravnik approached the rear of a store and saw the two deadbolt locks in the door and the vertical spear-tipped security bars covering the windows. He looked up at the small shop sign above the door—Cooper's Gun Shop.

Ravnik backed from the door a few steps, then threw his shoulder into it. The door splintered off its hinges. Before the last piece of wood hit the floor, a shrill alarm sounded.

As Ravnik started to enter, a massive hand grabbed his shoulder and pulled him back into the alley.

"I owe you, schweinehund," Müeller growled in the one-eared man's face, spraying Ravnik's features with spittle.

The Masher drew back a clenched fist and drove a powerful blow into Ravnik's jaw. As Ravnik recoiled, Cowan counter punched, knocking Ravnik's head in another direction. The blows would have knocked most men cold, but Ravnik merely shook his head, almost grinning.

Ravnik suddenly punched Cowan and shattered his jaw with a heavy-weight class jab. As Cowan staggered, Ravnik kicked the bodyguard's legs out from under him, flipping him face down on the pavement. With much dispatch, Ravnik stepped on Cowan's back and yanked his legs upward. Cowan screamed when his spine snapped like a twig.

Ravnik released his hold and Cowan's legs flopped like rubber to the pavement. Cowan convulsed once, then his eyes closed, and he became still.

Mueller jumped on Ravnik's back and grabbed his hair. He yanked and twisted Ravnik's head violently trying to break his neck. But he found Ravnik's neck to be as rigid as a flagstaff.

Ravnik back-stepped quickly and slammed the Masher into the gun shop's brick wall. The air shot from the wrestler's lungs. He fell from Ravnik's back and doubled over, drawing for wind.

Ravnik grabbed the Masher around the torso and slammed him head first against the shop's wall.

A bright flash bleached the Masher's mind, then it began to darken. Müeller stumbled in circles, disorientated, and unable to focus.

With the voice pumping large amounts of epinephrine into his bloodstream, Ravnik shoved the Masher toward the window. Müeller grabbed one of Ravnik's arms and yanked it downward in an effort to pull Ravnik to his knees—but Müeller only managed to pull off one of Ravnik's gloves.

Ravnik grabbed the wrestler's left wrist, raised it skyward, then slammed it down on a window bar spike, impaling it there. He saw that the spearhead had torn through Müeller's radial artery and blood began to pour from the wound. Ravnik then snatched the Masher's other wrist and punctured it over another bar. More blood flowed.

The pain cleared the Masher's mind. He flamed with rage, struggling to free himself. The more he moved, however, the more the spear-tipped bars widened his wounds. Müeller glanced at his bleeding limbs, noticing his blood running down his arm like water. A large crimson puddle began to form on the dirty alley below him. Müeller knew years of steroid use had thinned his blood, making it slow to clot.

Ravnik moved toward the door of the shop. Paying no attention to the ear-piercing alarm, he entered the business.

Elinger rounded another corner and pushed the speaker button on the phone so Torres could hear.

"He's broken into a shop," Sanders reported then paused. "Shit! It's a gun shop! No name is coming up on the pages."

"Thanks, Jay," Elinger said, turning off his phone. "Only one gun shop in The Block," he told Torres.

"Cooper's?" Torres said. "Isn't that the place BPD has been investigating for selling automatic weapons?"
Elinger nodded, watching traffic as he accelerated into it, dodging a chorus of angry horns and near crashes.

Responding to the shop's alarm, a prowl car bounced to a halt at the rear of the gun shop. The officer, carrying a shotgun, leaped from his unit. His throat blanched when he saw Cowan's twisted body. And when he noticed Müeller skewered on the window bars, the mucus in his throat hardened.

The officer cautiously approached the shop and looked past the broken-down door. Suddenly, Ravnik sprang from the darkness with an AK-47 assault rifle strapped on one shoulder and an Uzi machine gun on the other. In his hand was a .9-millimeter semi-automatic handgun. It spat fire, pumping two bullets into the policeman's bulletproof vest. The officer staggered backward and raised his shotgun. But Ravnik fired again and hit the policeman in the head. The officer dropped his weapon and dropped to the pavement.

Elinger and Torres pulled up on their car and saw the one-eared man standing over the policeman's body. They jumped from the auto and yanked their pieces from their holsters.

"Aim for the legs!" Elinger shouted.

Ravnik jammed the pistol into his belt and jerked the Uzi from his shoulder. He aimed it at Elinger and Torres and fired.

A deafening spray of lead chipped the pavement surrounding Elinger and Torres, forcing them to dive for cover. A trail of bullets followed them, peppering dozens of holes in the car and shattering its windows.

Torres glanced at his puny service revolver through the showering glass. "We need at least a shotgun against an Uzi!"

"It's in the trunk," Elinger told Torres.

"You got the keys?" Torres shouted above the sound of the firing Uzi.

"Shit! In the ignition," Elinger shook his head ruefully. "My bad. I go."

Suddenly, dozens more slugs ripped into the auto, pinning Elinger and Torres to the asphalt. A bullet ripped through the rear fender and punctured the gas tank. In an instant, the auto mushroomed into a ball of fire with a thundering roar. Jagged pieces of metal shot through the air like the fragments of a 2,000-pound bomb. Much of the blast blew over Elinger and Torres, but the part that hit them threw them across the alley.

Sprawled and dazed on the pavement, Elinger glanced up and saw the rented luxury car was little more than a smoking scorch mark and a few twisted chunks of metal on the alley.

Thankful most of the explosive force had passed over them, Elinger and Torres watched more pieces of the auto rain down.

Attempting to steady his senses, Elinger moved his arms and legs and curled his toes and fingers, checking for broken bones. He found none but a loud ringing echoed in his ears and a dizzying, mind-numbing feeling filled his body.

Noticing the Uzi's fire had stopped, Elinger climbed slowly to his feet and peered through the smoke, fire, and debris for the one-eared man.

When Elinger noticed Torres stirring, he grabbed his arm and pulled him from the asphalt. Torres was also without broken bones or serious injury. Looking through the clearing smoke, Elinger and Torres both could see the one-eared man had vanished.

Elinger glanced at the remains of their car and said regretfully, "I just filled it up this afternoon."

"With high octane I bet," Torres said in a wry timbre.

Elinger and Torres moved toward the gun shop. The sight of Cowan's bent body and Müeller hanging dead from the bars by his wrists stopped them in their tracks. *It will take a fire hose to wash away all that blood*, Elinger thought.

Elinger stepped around the Masher's blood and studied the wrestler's pale face. The wrestler's expression was petrified in death. Not frozen in a look of immense pain as would be expected, Elinger noted, but one twisted with what looked like profound hate.

Elinger's thoughts scattered when three blue and whites arrived on the scene. The officers emerged, full of grief when they saw their fallen comrade.

Mervyn Amos drove up in his SUV and climbed out. He saw the dead bodies and moved toward the dead policeman whose skull leaked brain tissue on the pavement. Amos bent over the body, aimed his camera and snapped a picture.

The flash drew Elinger's attention. He saw Amos hunched ghoulishly over the officer's body. Elinger's animosity toward the reporter suddenly heated again. "This is a crime scene! Get the hell out of here you morbid bastard!"

"I need some photos for the exclusive you promised me," Amos replied, sounding like his old belligerent self.
Elinger moved to the reporter and leveled a deadly gaze. "This isn't the time."

Amos glanced at the destroyed car and the three corpses. "I'd say you've run out of time, Lieutenant."

Elinger mentally agreed with Amos. He was out of time. Frustrated, Elinger snatched Amos' camera from the reporter's hands, popped open the card slot and yanked out the memory card. He tossed the camera back to Amos, pocketed the memory card and turned to the officer nearest them. "Get him out of here!" Elinger snapped, shoving Amos toward the officer.

The officer grabbed the reporter's arm and ushered him to his car. Amos climbed into his vehicle and glared back at Elinger.

FORTY-FIVE

● ● ●

Still wearing his torn and dirty suit, Elinger sat at his kitchen table, reviewing the entity's notes. He was searching desperately for a clue—anything that would burn a productive path through his dry investigation. But it was late, and he regretted his mind was still glitching from the explosion. The words seemed to bounce off his eyes. He knew only sleep would correct his nagging grogginess.

Elinger was thinking about a hot shower and a soft bed when his cell phone rang. He glanced at his watch. Through the cracked crystal, he could see the hands were frozen at the exact time of the explosion. He looked at a clock on the wall and wondered who would be calling him at 3:00 a.m.

"It's Sam," a nasal voice said through the phone when Elinger answered.

"Sam? What the hell are you doing up so late?"

"Being thorough like you wanted."

"You've got something?"

"It's gonna make your night, Lieutenant. C'mon over, I'm in the lab."

Elinger looked at his ripped and dirty clothes that still smelled of gas from the explosion. "A quick shower and I'm there," he promised, hanging up the receiver and sliding out of his jacket. *And it would be a fast shower*, he told himself. When Evans had something, it was usually important.

Elinger stepped from the elevator wearing fresh clothes and entered Headquarters' 5th floor where the labs were located. Sam Evans moved into the corridor from his office and tossed a watch in a clear evidence bag at him. Snatching it from the air, Elinger gave Evans a quizzical look.

"That belonged to Müeller," Evans said. "And I almost missed it."

Looking curiously at the time piece in his hand, Elinger wasn't sure what Evans meant.

"It's a beauty isn't it?" Evans said, moving toward Elinger. "Probably worth a few grand."

Elinger nodded. The watch was gold and Swiss-made with diamonds on its face.

"But it's worth more than money to us, Kent," Evans reported, stepping closer to Elinger.

"Get to the point, Sam. My driver's license is expiring," Elinger joked, impatiently.

"The State Coroner gave it to me after he collected Müeller's effects," Evans said, taking the watch from Elinger's hand. "Just for the hell of it, I dusted it. And guess what I found on the crystal?"

Elinger was suddenly a man reborn. "A print?"

Evans smiled. "A thumbprint. As clean as a booking print!

And it doesn't belong to Müeller."

"Have you run it through AFIS yet?"

"Not yet. I knew you'd like to be here for that."

Elinger and Evans moved into a room and sat down in front of a sophisticated looking computer system—an AFIS: Automated Finger and Palm Print ID system. Elinger focused on the blue-green hardware and monitor in front of him.

"We just updated the database, Kent," Evans said. "Eighty million criminal fingerprints, and it's over ninety-nine percent accurate. If your perp has been arrested for anything, his prints should be in here," Evans added, holding a 5"x7" card with the thumbprint on it. He laid the card on a glass window beneath the AFIS processing unit and typed in a command on the keyboard.

Elinger watched the computer scan the thumbprint and then automatically search its database for a matching print.

Evans leaned forward slightly for a closer view of the ID case numbers that appeared on the screen. Evans then typed in another command, and the monitor presented two gray-scale prints on a split screen. Elinger studied the two thumbprints for similarities.

"The one on the left is from Müeller's watch, the other was selected by the machine," Evans explained, studying the circled numbers on the prints that indicated matching whorls, arches and loops. "What I like about his baby is that its image enhancement gives more resolution than can be appreciated by the human eye."

When Evans cocked his head, Elinger noticed his grin of victory through his tired features.

"We've got a hit!" Evans said. "The tented arch, the

pattern and core-delta distances match."

Weeks of sleeplessness vacated Elinger's face in an instant. He leaned forward and kissed the computer's screen. "I love computers, Sam! You have mug shots in this thing?"

"Sure do," Evans replied, fingering the keyboard. A mug shot of a glowering Leonard Ravnik popped-up on the screen. Below it was information concerning an arrest in Baltimore.

"That's him," Elinger confirmed, reading the information on the screen. "Shit! We had him on purse snatching a few months ago."

Evans squinted at the screen. "Looks like he met bail and never showed up for court."

"What else do we have on him?"

Evans pressed a keyboard button but the screen didn't change. "Guess that's it."

"Let's run him through NCIC and see what we get," Elinger suggested quickly. "I want to know everything about this bastard before the sun comes up."

The rising sun, just burning in over the city's high rises, caused Torres to squint as he wheeled his vehicle onto the parking lot at Headquarters. He moved briskly toward the building not minding that Elinger had awakened him from a deep sleep with an urgent phone call. When Elinger had explained he had the killer's identity, Torres had dressed in less than two minutes. The sense of relief from making headway in the case made him feel like he had slept for twelve hours.

Elinger was sitting at his desk reviewing a report on his computer screen when Torres arrived. He was glad it hadn't taken Evans long to connect with NCIC and receive a lengthy accounting of Leonard Ravnik's criminal history.

"What's his name?" Torres asked immediately, looking at the monitor.

"Leonard Ravnik," Elinger replied, looking up from the screen. "Born in Louisiana twenty-nine years ago."

Torres grabbed a chair and straddled it near Elinger's desk.

"He started as a teenage runaway," Elinger reported, gleaning bits of information from his computer screen, "because of alleged abuse at home. He ended that by blowing out his father's brains. He was convicted and sentenced to the electric chair. But he escaped from prison through an air vent and went down the side of a three-story building with a bunch of sheets tied together."

"You can't say he's not resourceful," Torres commented. "When did this happen?"

"Ten years ago, but that's only the beginning," Elinger replied, scrolling more pages of the report on his monitor. "Ravnik's wanted for murdering a sheriff and two deputies in Alabama. He's wanted for killing a rancher in North Carolina. He's the suspect in a half dozen hitchhiking murders in Georgia and Missouri. He's also on the hot sheets for a rape-killing in Illinois and a double rape murder in Kentucky."

"He makes Jack-the-Ripper look like an amateur," Torres said.

"We had him on a purse snatch, but he skipped after bail."

"Why didn't these other warrants show up in our computer when we had him?" Torres asked.

"Same question I had," Elinger said. "The day we booked

him, NCIC's computers were down. His wanted check was put on hold. By the time it went through, he was already out on bail."

Elinger glimpsed at Ravnik's report again. "A few years ago an FBI psychologist jotted down some notes about him." Elinger read from the pages: "*Leonard Ravnik harbors a loathing memory of his childhood. He was controlled by a cruel, alcoholic father and a submissive mother who stood by and allowed the psychological destruction of her own son. Leonard believes rules and laws were made for other people. He feels he has the right to take what he wants despite the rights of others. He lacks natural, positive emotions. He is cold, unforgiving and sadistic and carries an unbearable grudge against society. I'm sure Leonard Ravnik will someday commit a crime that will bring him the death penalty.*"

"No shit," Torres said in a bleak tone.

Elinger turned from the computer screen and looked at Torres. "I'm going over to Renee's to relieve Jay," he said. "Make sure Ravnik's photo is posted online and plastered all over Baltimore by breakfast."

Torres nodded. "You got it."

● ● ●

A short time later, Elinger and Renee were sitting on Renee's living room couch. Renee's eyes were red and slightly swollen from crying. Elinger was reading the latest note from the entity.

My Dear Madam Holland and Detective Elinger:
What a baroques night this has been! I tip my hat to you, Detective
Elinger. By now, I'm sure you've learned the identity of my earthly
counterpart. A careless oversight on his part, I'm afraid. But alas,
even if you capture that wretched creature, you still haven't found
me. And what a pity! You've worked so hard to solve only half a
crime! By now you must think I possess a fanciful mind. And I must
admit, as of late, there has been a sudden elevation in turpitude for
me. Of course that's no excuse to stop the game.

It is becoming more interesting all the time. Especially
since you, Detective Elinger, are a reflection of the first literary
detective, the great Chevalier C. Auguste Dupin. Perhaps not as
verbose, but much the same regardless. And Madam Holland, as
always it is a pleasure to work with you, or should I say through
you? I am growing quite fond of you. Please don't become overly
attached to Detective Elinger. Providence will be taking him
soon...

The frustration in Elinger's expression showed clearly to
Renee.

"I guess we have no choice but to stand by helplessly and
watch him destroy lives," Renee said grimly.

Elinger sensed that Renee was fighting tears. "At least we
know who the killer is now," he reminded her. "And we will find
him."

Renee's cell phone rang. She reached for the phone on the
table and hesitated.

Elinger watched Renee as she took a deep breath to
compose herself before she spoke.

"Hello," she greeted off-key. "Oh, Dr. Winfield, how are you?"

Elinger noticed Renee's expression was lifting as she listened to the professor.

"They did!" Renee exclaimed. "Yes, we'll be there right away."

Renee hung up the phone and turned to Elinger who noticed her face was radiating a softening look of hope. "Dr. Winfield says his people have figured out who writes like this," she pointed at the note in a timbre full of optimism. "They've been up all night. They're waiting for us at the University."

FORTY-SIX

● ● ●

At the University of Maryland, Elinger and Renee walked down a brick pathway lined with thick shrubbery and leafy trees. As they moved through the belt of fog that strapped the campus grounds, Elinger noticed how the stately buildings looked as though they were built on a cloud. It was like a metaphor, very fitting for his unearthly case.

Professor Winfield stepped into view from the mist and greeted Elinger and Renee outside his office. "I'm sorry you had to come out. I just couldn't get away."

"Don't be sorry, Scott," Renee said as Elinger and Winfield exchanged a cordial handshake. "You're doing us a big favor."

Elinger handed the latest note to the professor. "From the last trance, Dr. Winfield."

Winfield unfolded the note and read it carefully. His face seemed to lose a shade of color. "May I keep this?"
Elinger nodded.

"What did you find out?" Renee asked Winfield in an impatient tone.

Winfield took a moment before he answered. "Do you mind if we walk?" he asked, pushing the note into his jacket pocket. "I usually go for a stroll before my first class."

Renee and Elinger followed Winfield's lead, moving down the fog shrouded walkway, blending in with the morning's first trickle of students.

"Well, as they say, if you don't know where to start, try the beginning," Winfield began. "I had two literary experts evaluate your writings about the murders, Renee. And they couldn't believe their own findings. They said your work reads like the work of a very famous author who's been dead for over a hundred and sixty years. It was a shock when they told me his name," Winfield reported in a halting tone.

Elinger could tell Winfield was a bit rattled by what he was about to reveal.

"Edgar Allan Poe," Winfield finally muttered.

Elinger and Renee stopped quietly. Elinger's mind was fettered by the news. Winfield also halted.

"You're joking, right?" Renee asked.

"You know me better than that," Winfield said. "Since my colleagues didn't know you were writing in trances, and your manuscript takes place in modern day, their conclusion obviously didn't make sense to them. So, they settled on a more palatable theory."

"Let me guess—I've suddenly switched genres, from a romantic novelist to an Edgar Allan Poe copy cat," Renee finished what Winfield was about to say.

Winfield nodded.

"Why didn't you tell your people that I've been writing in

an unconscious state?"

"I think he did the right thing, Renee," Elinger interjected. "That would only bias their analysis."

"Yes, these gentlemen are not the types who would believe in ghosts or channeling or auto-writing or anything like that," Winfield stated in a voice of assurance. "They simply think you studied Poe very carefully for a very long time and copied his style. They are very impressed—but you and I know you were never a big fan of Edgar Allan Poe."

Renee nodded. "I only studied his works as required study assignments when I was a student," Renee said. "Do you think it's really Poe?"

Elinger watched as Winfield gave Renee what looked like his best grandfatherly smile.

"I am a religious man, Renee," Winfield said. "I believe in life after death. And because I know you and know you're unconscious during these writing trances, I think something evil has indeed invaded your life. It could very well be Poe. My colleagues are very accurate, the best in their field—so I'll give Poe a nine out of ten on this."

"But why would someone like Poe be involved in these awful murders?" Renee wondered aloud. "He wasn't like that in real life."

"But he was considered The Master of the Macabre and a little crazy at times," Winfield replied off-handedly as Elinger, Renee and Winfield began to walk again, joining a growing stream of chattering students.

"How did your experts determine Renee's work was exactly like Poe's?" Elinger asked Winfield.

"You're asking me to recall a two-hour meeting."

"Whatever you can remember."

"You have more faith in my memory than I do," Winfield smiled. "They found matches in word usage, vocabulary, grammar, sentence structure, elements of style, that sort of thing. They talked about the power of Poe's analysis—the way he mixed reality with fantasy. They noted how Poe dissected mental aberrations and followed their consequences. This kind of analysis is in Renee's manuscript. And there's a word in the note you just gave me that my colleagues talked about. It caught me by surprise."

Winfield withdrew the message from his pocket and found the word—*Baroques*. "It's an uncommon French word meaning odd or bizarre. It's in Renee's manuscript and Poe's writings. That brings to mind Poe's immense vocabulary. The esotulary words he used are also plentiful in Renee's writings. Many of them are considered archaic today," Winfield added.

"From my studies, I recall most people just assume Poe loved his Gothic horror tales, but he didn't," Renee commented. "He preferred puns, satires, and parodies."

"Yes, and all of this is quite evident in your work," Winfield agreed and turned to Elinger. "They bombarded me with a lot of information, Lieutenant. I couldn't tell you a fourth of what they said."

"Can you set up a meeting so we can talk to them?" Elinger asked. "I'd like to hear everything first hand if I could."

"I was about to suggest that," Winfield replied. "This is urgent so how about tonight?"

"Good."

"We could meet at my house," Renee offered. "Seven

o'clock okay?"

"That'd be fine, Renee," Winfield said as he stopped walking and turned to Renee and Elinger. "I've got an early class," he said. "Time for me to find another Renee Holland."

Renee smiled broadly. "Thanks for your help, Scott," she said, then kissed him on the cheek.
Elinger and Professor Winfield shook hands again.

"I'll see you tonight, Lieutenant," Winfield promised, then moved off toward a nearby building, fading into the student traffic.

Renee took in a deep breath as she and Elinger walked across the wet grass toward the parking lot. "Kent, this can't be true, can it? The horrors of Edgar Allan Poe unleashed on modern society."

"Let me answer that after I meet Professor Winfield's experts," Elinger replied.

"And then what?" Renee asked directly.

"I think we need to read up on Poe in case the experts are right," Elinger suggested. "Maybe we'll gain some insight that'll help us."

Suddenly, a movement nearby snared Elinger's attention. He moved to a tree with a wide-trunk, reached behind it, and pulled Mervyn Amos by the lapels into the open.

"*Anus*, why are you still following me?" Elinger asked in a threatening tone.

Amos made a bulldog face and responded with a sarcastic voice. "Lieutenant, my editor wants me to write a story about these killings. I told him I had an inside source, but he doesn't believe me anymore because you haven't given me shit to write about! You said you'd give me an exclusive, but you're giving me an ulcer instead!"

Elinger considered the reporter's point-of-view and admired his tenaciousness. He released his hold on Amos' lapels. "I didn't have much until a little while ago," Elinger said, figuring publicity might help the investigation. Elinger said his words slowly, "We have a suspect. Leonard Ravnik. Not only do I have his name but a photo, too."

Elinger watched as Amos suddenly became quiet. He knew Amos was dumbfounded, never expecting anything like this.

Amos snatched a small notebook and pen from his pocket. "How do you spell the last name?"

"R-A-V-N-I-K," Elinger pronounced the letters slowly and clearly. "Call Rafael Torres at Headquarters for this creep's photo and more details. And be damn sure you run it in your paper. It might help us catch him."

"You can count on that!" Amos acknowledged, stuffing the notebook back into his pocket. Without another word, he twisted on his heels and moved away.

Elinger and Renee reached for each other's hand and resumed their walk toward the parking lot. Elinger's expression was somber as his mind dissected and analyzed the latest information. He knew Winfield's report didn't make sense in the real world but it had a ring of truth when he considered the past events of horror.

FORTY-SEVEN

• • •

Elinger and Professor Winfield sat on one of Renee's sofas. Elinger felt the warmth of the small blaze crackling in Renee's fireplace. He looked past the flickering light on Renee's living room walls and glanced at the two tenured literature professors selected by Winfield to analyze Renee's writings. They were sitting on chairs across from the sofa. Each one had a laptop computer in their lap.

Elinger's gaze rested on the first scholar, forty-year-old Robert Biggs. He was a lauded expert of Gothic writers. Elinger watched Biggs teethe an unlit pipe that dangled from his thin-lipped mouth while he worked his laptop with his small, pale hands. Biggs studied his research from beneath bushy eyebrows and a drawn face. Elinger had a feeling this man rarely exercised or left the confines of his office.

Elinger looked at the second scholar Edward Schroen. He was a mystery writer specialist. Elinger noticed Schroen was not the bookworm type. When the forty-five-year old scholar leaned back in his chair, it was clear he was larger and more robust than Biggs. Schroen had a tight crew cut and his face shaved so close it shined. He wore a tight-fitting polo shirt inflated with oversized biceps and pecs. The only thing that gave away Schroen's desk bound profession, was the thick-rimmed reading glasses hanging from his neck on a cord.

"Well, it's everybody for themselves," Renee said as she entered the room, carrying a tray of assorted cookies, antique coffee cups, and a silver pot of steaming coffee. After she placed the serving tray on a table between the men, she settled on the sofa between Elinger and Winfield.

"Splendid, I could use a caffeine boost after my day," Biggs said as he leaned his slender body forward and reached for the pot. "My students are so demanding this year." Without offering the others, Biggs poured himself coffee. His large eyes roamed the cookie tray until they locked in on a thick chocolate chip cookie. Biggs withdrew it from the plate.

Once everyone held cups of coffee, Elinger directed his attention on Winfield's colleagues. "I'd like to ask a favor of both of you. While you explain your analysis, I'd like for you to suspend reality and pretend Edgar Allan Poe is actually writing Renee's pages."

"Any particular reason for that?" Biggs asked in a tone of surprise as he bit into the well-worn grooves of his pipe stem.

Elinger sensed Biggs was a natural born debater, someone who challenged everything and didn't mind being obnoxious about it. "I have my reasons," Elinger replied curtly.

"But that's ridiculous," Biggs returned.

Winfield frowned and locked eyes with Biggs. "Robert, I asked you here as a personal favor. As your Department Chair, you owe me a favor or two, and I want to collect tonight. So be polite."

Biggs gave Winfield a sour look with a mock salute.

"Please begin, Lieutenant," Winfield said. "You won't be interrupted again."

Appreciating Winfield's intervention, Elinger resumed. "I want to know in detail what is in the writing that makes you think Edgar Allan Poe wrote these pages."

"Why don't you begin this fairy tale, Edward," Biggs suggested, shifting in his chair. "I'll bring up the rear. That seems to be my position tonight."

Elinger and Renee listened attentively as the two professors detailed the similarities they found in Edgar Allen Poe's stories and Renee's manuscript. They learned *fancy* or *fanciful* were found in both works and were words Poe often used to describe an unbalanced mind. And sometimes Poe spelled it as *phantasy* which was also found in Renee's pages. The professors discovered another matching phrase in both works—*a sudden elevation in turpitude.*

"The word *turpitude* means inherent baseness or depravity," Biggs explained. "Poe used it in his story *William Wilson.*"

The professors made it clear that Poe's vocabulary was more extensive than most writers of his time and many of the words he used have become archaic—like *cattymount.* "It is now spelled as catamount to describe a mountain cat like a Cougar or a Lynx. It's not found in dictionaries today, but we discovered it in Renee's work. *Ere kind of* is another phrase Poe used, that we found in Renee's pages exactly as Poe used it," Schroen added.

There were other matches, too. *Eros* to describe lust,

spanked along, meaning to move quickly, *larboard* for port. Biggs and Schroen also found what they called the little things—like the spelling of *forever* and anything. In Poe's time, they were spelled as two words instead of one, just like they discovered in Renee's pages. Elinger and Renee also learned that the spelling of *woe* in Renee's manuscript is *w-o* just as Poe spelled it. It is considered the poetic spelling.

"Poe loved to write poetry," Schroen explained.

"Makes sense to me. His name is in the word poetry," Elinger added on a light note.

Schroen was pleasantly surprised. "Very observant, Lieutenant. Few people notice that, although it's so obvious. A book of Poe's poetry was published in 1827. It was called *Tamerlane and Other Poems.*"

"Back to the drama for a moment," Biggs interjected. "Poe's spelling of woe is also indicative of overly-dramatic passages we find in Poe's *The Premature Burial.*"

"Yes, Poe's heavy dramatics, what we would call melodrama today, in no sense ever diminished the power of his work," Schroen added. "It was his way of telling a story. Many passages in Ms. Holland's work are also overly dramatic, and she uses Poe-like monochromatic descriptions." Schroen searched through his papers, finding the one he wanted. "Here's an example. It describes the killer on the prowl, Lieutenant," Schroen said. "And I quote—*the shadowy man moved straight for his victim as steady and purposeful as a wild predator homes in on its unsuspecting prey.*" Schroen looked up from his paperwork. "This style of one dimensional visual is the same as Poe used often to project his powerful images."

Biggs returned his attention to Elinger. "We also used computer software to compare the basic mechanics of the writing. And again, we found similarities between Poe's works and Ms. Holland's," Biggs revealed, then looked down at the screen of his laptop. "The Fleshch Reading Ease Score gave them both scores in the low eighties. The Gunning Fog Index, which also determines reading ease, matched them at eight. There was an average of twelve and a half words per sentence, four letters per word, and one percent passive voice. There were one and a third syllables per word and the average paragraph contained nine and one third sentences," Schroen said, glancing up at Elinger. "It's pretty conclusive, Lieutenant. If Poe were alive, I'd say he did indeed write Ms. Holland's unfinished manuscript."

Biggs planted his eyes on Renee and leaned forward in his chair, removing the pipe from his mouth. "But we do know better, Ms. Holland. You're one helluva copycat. Why don't you admit it?"

Elinger noticed Bigg's comment caused Renee's face to contort with anger. If Biggs only knew the grief her manuscript had caused her.

When Biggs noticed Professor Winfield glaring at him again, he withdrew and leaned back in his chair.

"Now let's look at the basic concept," Schroen suggested. "Ms. Holland's pages are about the investigation of a series of murders, the same story line Poe used when he invented the detective genre in three of his stories including *The Murders in the Rue Morgue.*"

Elinger poured himself another cup of coffee. His curiosity was beyond just the writing style now. He didn't need more proof that Poe could be the author. Elinger wanted to know if Poe was capable of cold-blooded murder and could he have brought a killing spree to the modern world?

"What about Poe the man?" Elinger asked. "I understand his personal problems were severe enough to cause mental instabilities?"

"Most certainly," Biggs replied, after drawing on his empty pipe. "He was self-destructive, trapped in an emotional pressure cooker since he was a child."

"What else?" Renee asked. "It's been a long time since I've read about Poe's life."

Biggs began without hesitation. "Well, his parents were drifters— actors who followed the theater. His father deserted the family shortly after Poe was born, and his mother died when he was only two. He was adopted by a wealthy merchant named John Allan who was cold and impersonal and expressed little affection for Poe."

Schroen lowered his glasses before he jumped back into the conversation. "And this started an alienation between Allan and Poe that never ended. Poe was really hurt when he discovered he was excluded from Allan's will. He planned to use that money to fulfill his life's dream—to be the editor of his own magazine. Even Allan's illegitimate children were beneficiaries in the will. This rejection launched the final episode of Poe's dark, brooding adult life. A friend of Poe's once said Poe rarely smiled, and no one ever heard him laugh. What Poe had feared most was happening. He was doomed for a life of poverty, and he was correct. In his best year, he made only eight-hundred dollars."

"Yes, a sad figure, full of emotional conflicts," Biggs added. "He needed a full time shrink, and he proved that even more when he got married."

Schroen nodded. "The union with his thirteen-year-old cousin, Virginia, was quite interesting. Poe called his wife Sis and claimed to love her."

"He never loved her!" Biggs argued. "Few, if any, believed he ever consummated the marriage. This was Poe's conniving way to get close to Virginia's mother, Mrs. Clemm. Some say it was part of an Oedipal complex, that Poe was emotionally searching for his dead mother."

"I don't think his relationship with Mrs. Clemm was Oedipal," Schroen countered. "He was afraid of sex."

"But only with women," Biggs countered. "Oscar Wilde publicly said Poe was a homosexual."

Schroen nodded. "Yes, but never proven. And Poe did have his good times, like when he finally became the editor of a magazine." Schroen turned toward Elinger. "You see, Poe reached his dream with *The Broadway Journal*—but it had financial troubles the same year he started it. Poe became despondent and began to drink heavily."

"Most of the magazine or newspaper jobs he held didn't last long because of his alcohol abuse," Biggs said. "With Poe, even a small glass of wine distorted his thinking and actions. Liquor had a terrible influence on his life. He even wrote about his problem."

Biggs looked at his laptop, then read aloud from what he brought up on the screen. "*I have absolutely no pleasure in the stimulants in which I sometimes so madly indulge. It has not been in the pursuit of pleasure that I have periled life and reputation and reason. It has been in the desperate attempt to escape from torturing memories—memories of wrong and injustice and imputed dishonor—from a sense of some strange impending doom*." Biggs looked up at the others. "He wrote that within a year of his death. For Poe, there was always an impending doom. He tried to commit suicide with an overdose of laudanum once, that's opium dissolved in alcohol, but he failed."

Schroen nodded again. "He really wanted out of this life. I believe Poe had a death-wish. It's seems very clear in his writings. He dwelled on pain and death, man's inhumanity to man, premature burials, torture, dismemberment, suffocation, poisoning, cruelty to animals, disease, violence and myriad other morbid subjects. It was his subconscious talking. Subjects from a person with a solid death-wish."

"I read that no one really knows what happened to Poe during the last few days of his life," Elinger said.

"Yes," Biggs replied. "The last five days are still a complete mystery."

"There was some speculation during that time that he was a repeater, stuffing ballot boxes with multiple votes during an election in Baltimore," Schroen said.

"And that's exactly what it is, pure speculation," Biggs disputed. "No one knows for sure. He was probably in an alcoholic haze. Someone had seen him drink a glass of wine just before he disappeared."

Schroen picked up where Biggs ended. "But that's been disputed even though on his last day, he was found in a Baltimore bar. He was delirious and talking to spirits he claimed where looming from the walls. Just before he died, he asked a friend to shoot him to put him out of his misery. His last words were—*Lord, help my poor soul.* He knew he was cursed in this existence and begged for a better life in the hereafter."

The final remark made Renee shift uneasily. "How old was he when he died?" she asked.

"Forty," Schroen answered. "And his final resting place is here in Baltimore, at the Westminster Presbyterian Burial Grounds."

"About his death-wish," Elinger began, "do you think Poe could've projected it on to other people—to the point of killing them instead of himself?"

"Interesting you should mention that," Biggs replied. "While I was brushing up on Poe for this meeting, I found something I had forgotten about. Poe wrote a story called *The Mystery of Marie Roget*. It was based on a real crime, a rape and strangulation murder of a young woman named Mary Cecilia Rogers. Poe knew her. She worked in a tobacco shop he frequented. It was said at the time he was fond of her. The last person seen with her when she was alive was described as a swarthy gentleman. That matches a general description of Poe."

"Do you believe he killed her?" Elinger asked.

"Well, in your world, he had motive, means and opportunity," Biggs began. "Sex as the *motive*, for *means* he was a man who could have overpowered this woman to strangle her, and the swarthy gentleman was seen walking with her into some thick vegetation near where her body was found later for *opportunity*. And Poe was known for drug and alcoholic fueled rages against women. Sometimes they were violent. He physically abused an ex-girlfriend from Baltimore once, but I don't think he was capable of murder."

"Men under less stress have killed," Elinger said.

"I know, but it doesn't change my opinion," Biggs answered.

"I don't think he was a killer either although he usually lived on the edge of insanity," Schroen said.

"The very thin edge," Biggs chimed in. "He had several bouts of delirium. He said he saw visions and heard voices at times. He wrote about this, and I've got a copy of it."

"I'd like to hear it," Elinger said.

Biggs pressed a few keys on his laptop and found the screen he wanted. He read aloud for the others. "*For more than ten days I was totally deranged, although I was drinking not one drop; and during this interval I imagined the more horrible calamities. All was hallucination, arising from an attack of mania-a-potu.* That's the Latin term for delirium tremens."

"But hallucinations from alcohol withdrawal last only about forty-eight hours," Elinger said. "Not for ten days."

"That's right," Biggs said. "Poe wasn't suffering from *mania-a-potu.* He was delirious without alcohol. Poe himself assumed he was crazy at times. He once said—*I became insane with long intervals of horrible sanity.* On his last day, while he was being rushed to a hospital, the attending physicians weren't sure if his violent ranting were from inebriation or deliriums? His death was listed as *congestion of the brain.*"

"Recently, here at the Medical Center, physicians speculated that Poe really died of rabies," Schroen said. "They said he had the classic symptoms. He was delirious with tremors and hallucinations, then he lapsed into a coma—then emerged from the coma and was calm and lucid—then he became delirious again and combative in the final stages of death."

"I think it was his short, tormented life that gave him his cerebral food," Biggs said. "He drew from those dark complexities and wrote the most horrific stories in American literature."

"What do you make of these taunting notes I receive from time to time," Renee asked.

"That's pure Poe," Biggs replied. "He loved that kind of stuff—the mental games and challenges that come from a fanciful mind as he would have put it."

"So be it," Schroen said, setting his empty cup on the table.

Biggs riveted his vision on Renee. "Well, this has been an informative and scintillating conversation, but why don't you just admit you've cloned Mr. Poe?"

Renee stared hard at Biggs for a moment.

Elinger watched Renee, knowing she would like to slap the arrogant expression from Biggs's face.

"You'll never know how much I wish that were true, Mr. Biggs," Renee finally said.

Once Biggs and Schroen had left, Elinger, Renee and Professor Winfield resettled on the sofa and informally discussed the meeting. All three were amazed by the similarities between Renee's writing and Poe's and had concluded Edgar Allan Poe was writing through Renee.

"Psychologically, Poe was a mess," Renee said. "I wonder if he was really insane or a borderline sociopath in control?"

"Or an addict or drunk out of control?" Elinger added. "Or suffering from rabies?"

"Whatever he was or whatever he had, he did possess the imagination to commit murders as macabre as what's been happening," Winfield said. "But what's his motivation in the modern world? An insane anger caused by an unfulfilled life?" Winfield asked no one in particular.

"Or maybe he wants to write the ultimate horror story?" Elinger guessed. "A Gothic tale full of gore with a life of its own, happening in reality as it is written?"

"But how could he claim authorship?" Winfield asked.

"I would think his first move would be to get rid of me," Renee guessed. Her own words seemed to put her on edge.

Elinger sensed Renee was right about this and could see the tremble in her body. He put an arm around her, and she buried her head on his shoulder. Elinger placed a finger under her chin and tenderly lifted her head until their eyes met. "I'm not going to let that happen," he promised.

"You can't be everywhere all the time," Renee replied.

Elinger allowed Renee's head to rest on his shoulder again. The remark worried him. Even having her under police guard was no guarantee she would be safe. He knew his adversary was cunning enough to slip through his net.

● ● ●

Outside, at that very moment, Leonard Ravnik was crouched in the lush growth of the Holland estate. He studied Renee's house through the bushes, undetected by the policeman in the squad car. The light of a full moon lit the earless side of his head, reflecting dully on the lumpy, scarred flesh uncovered by his hair.

Ravnik had watched the professors leave but he wasn't interested in them. He wanted Renee Holland—to possess her, to control her, and to kill her.

"Go home, Mr. Ravnik. And spank along about it," the voice whispered coarsely. "You will not dispatch Miss Holland on this night. When the time is right, I will inform you. You must arouse yourself from this situation. Too many eyes are out on this lunar evening. They would spoil our work and terminate my purposeful undertaking before it is completed. There will be another time when I can put you more safely up to my task."

Ravnik knew the voice was right. It wasn't a good night to kill Renee Holland. Ravnik could stretch his patience. A week, a month, it didn't matter because he knew the time would come when the voice would allow him to have his way with Renee Holland—the voice had promised that a long time ago.

FORTY-EIGHT

● ● ●

"Edgar Allan Poe may have been dead for over a hundred and sixty years, but apparently his consciousness still lives, Ms. Holland," Dennington said. Wearing a bright dhoti, he sat on a rattan chair behind a folding table that served as a desk inside his retreat's main Quonset hut.

Sunken in a faded, sagging couch, Elinger and Renee faced Dennington, sipping herbal tea from garage-sale tea cups.

Elinger glimpsed at the photos on the wall behind Dennington. They displayed the images of several metaphysical philosophers including Aristotle, Saint Thomas Aquinas, Immanuel Kant, Descartes, Spinoza, and the Maharishi Mahesh Yogi.

"I'm glad you could make it on such short notice," Dennington said in a tone of gratitude.

"You said it was important," Elinger replied.

"Yes, the mystery and astral complexities of Renee's situation has more than peaked my professional interest. In fact, it has turned some of my convictions upside down and many of my philosophies inside out," he admitted. "I have some new ideas that might help Renee against the killer and the entity."

"I'm all ears," Renee said, sipping more tea.

"Well, let's start with the scope of eternity," Dennington began. "A century or two happens in the blink of an eye. Think of Poe passing from this existence just seconds ago, and you'll understand why he's still charged with the karma of his past physical life," Dennington clarified, leaning back in his chair and setting his tea cup on the table.

Renee raised her cup with a shaky hand and sipped some tea before she spoke. "So, without question, you think it's really Poe?"

"The experts say so," Dennington replied. "That's good enough for me. Remember, authors cannot help but leave mental signatures in their writing. The murders in your pages are as bizarre as anything Poe ever created."

Studying Dennington over the rim of her cup with a look of uncertainty, Renee didn't respond.

"The first time we met, you said you thought a freak of nature had caused all this," Elinger reminded Dennington. "You have any more thoughts about that?"

"I think about it all the time, in terms of cause and effect," Dennington summarized. "Cause, of course, being the catalyst. But we ask ourselves, what kind of catalyst could cause Ms. Holland's trances and connect her to a murderer and a consciousness we think to be Edgar Allan Poe? If anyone knows, it should be her."

"Me? But I don't remember anything when I go into these trances," Renee interjected in a tone of surprise.

"I'm talking about before the trances started," Dennington said. "Believe me, there was a catalyst that triggered your trances. Just ask yourself—did anything unusual happen to you just before your first trance? Anything out of the ordinary?"

Elinger watched Renee for a moment as she mulled over the question before she answered.

"I remember fixing dinner the night before Alex found the first set of pages," Renee reported. "After Alex went to bed, I went to my den to work on my novel—but the next thing I knew, it was morning, and I was in bed. Alex showed me the pages. That's all I remember."

"Just keep thinking about that night or the day before," Dennington urged. "Some kind of an event started your trances. That's always the case. An injury, a medical problem, an accident, an emotional shock, the sudden death of a loved one, anything like that. Feed your subconscious. You ask it questions and it will provide the answers."

"Yes, I use it that way when I write," was Renee's reply. "That is when I write normally and not in a trance."

Dennington shifted his eyes toward Elinger. "I called this meeting because I think I've come up with a better way to break the entity's connection to Renee."

This statement grabbed Elinger's attention. He placed his empty tea cup on the table. "I'm listening."
Dennington leaned forward in his chair. "I've been giving this some serious consideration, and I can't get it out of my mind."

Dennington rose from behind the table and began to pace the hut while he spoke. "And I keep coming back to the basics. Entities exist on a magnetic plane on a different level than our physical life. Nonetheless, all magnetic planes can be altered or disrupted. If we could do that, then Poe's consciousness could be sent back to its rightful place in the universe. When we first met,

I was sure simply ending the life of the killer would accomplish this."

"And now you think you're wrong?" Renee asked.

Dennington took a few steps without speaking. His face was rigid with purpose. "I'd like to think I just took half a step in the right direction instead of a full step. I was thinking that when the killer dies, his brain, of course, ceases all electrical activity. That means it can no longer host the consciousness of Poe. But as I've revisited this scenario, I realize this would not guarantee that we have rid ourselves of Poe. His entity could very well remain connected to Ms. Holland because if we end the life of the killer, we have merely removed a breaker or conduit in the connection. The key to this is how you kill this Leonard Ravnik."

"What do you mean?" Elinger asked quickly.

Dennington continued to pace the hut. "Well, we know Poe's consciousness is a collection of powerful thoughts made up of electricity, light, and energy. We also know they exist on their own electromagnetic field that can be diffused by a high voltage jolt," Dennington said. "I'm sorry I didn't think of this at our first meeting—but I'm now sure a blast of high-voltage electricity at the killer while he's trancing would stop Poe's entity. Not only would the electrical activity in the killer's brain cease but the plane of Poe's existence would change as well—sending him back to the astral plane. This would guarantee Ms. Holland's return to normal life."

Dennington approached his table desk and sit back down in his chair.

Elinger was quiet at first, considering the information, then: "It sounds logical, Kirk, but it's a tall, if not impossible order," Elinger said. "I have no idea how to juice my suspect with a large dose of electricity. As you know, my taser had almost no affect on him."

"A taser is high-voltage, low amps, right?" Dennington asked.

Elinger nodded.

"You want high-voltage, high amps."

Elinger considered Dennington's statement for a moment. "Okay, let's say I figured out how to electrocute Leonard Ravnik while he's in a trance—would that hurt Renee in any way?"

"No," Dennington replied. "Poe's consciousness is focused on the killer. Ms. Holland only receives an overflow of that power. If you electrocute the killer while he's being controlled by the entity of Poe, you will break its connection to Ms. Holland because you will have diffused and altered the magnetic planes of both the killer's brain and Poe's entity."

"So basically, I can't shoot this Leonard Ravnik when he's in a trance. I can only end his life by electrocution to save Renee?"

Dennington nodded. "It's my personal hypothesis based on what I know about these matters."

"And all hypotheses have to be tested to prove they're valid, right?" Elinger asked.

Dennington nodded. "Yes, all hypotheses need to be tested."

Elinger saw Renee straighten up in her chair with a look of sudden realization.

"My trances started near the time of the storm!" Renee blurted, throwing her words at Elinger and Dennington.
Elinger and Dennington shifted their attention to Renee.

"I was thinking about everything that happened before my first trance," Renee said. "I suddenly remembered the bright flash of light. It came from my bedroom window. The headaches started after that."

Elinger studied Renee's expression. He could see that she felt she was on to something.

"You said thoughts have the same properties as lightning, right?" Renee asked Dennington.

Dennington nodded.

"My trances started shortly after I watched a strange storm a few weeks ago. I was at my window," Renee recalled, slowing rising from the couch.

Elinger saw Renee's eyes haze over in remembrance.

"It was the weirdest thing I'd ever seen," Renee said. "The lightning was in one spot... hitting a small part of the city," she added, her words coming slowly. "I remember the lightning in the distance, hitting the earth... Then I saw a huge flash... like the sun exploding in front of me. I must have blacked out because I can't remember anything after that."

"You think you were hit by lightning?" Elinger asked, surprised.

"It's possible, I guess. I found a burn mark on the side of our house a few days later and that window was broken." Renee gave the men a look of curiosity. "But if I were hit by lightning, why can't I remember?"

"You can't recall something your mind has blocked out," Dennington assured her.

"Retrograde amnesia," Elinger said. "It happens to violent crime or accident victims. They can't remember being stabbed or shot or hit by a car, only the events leading up to it."

"But wouldn't I be dead or injured if I were hit by lightning?" Renee asked.

"It would depend on how you were grounded," Elinger said. "Some people survive lightning strikes while others don't."

"But I don't understand how lightning could start my trances?" Renee asked as she sank back down on the couch. Dennington suddenly chuckled humorlessly. "It's so obvious!"

"What?" Renee asked.

"My stupidity and the answer," Dennington volunteered in a chagrined timbre. He rose from behind his table desk and approached Renee. "With thoughts having the same properties as lightning, they should be compatible with lightning. One is just more powerful than the other. Lightning could have altered your brain's wave length, enough to tune it in to the killer's wave length," Dennington explained. There was rising excitement in his voice. "Lightning was probably the catalyst that set everything in motion. It makes sense."

"I remember the storm," Elinger started. "Citizens were scared. Our phones were jammed. The storm seemed to be focused on one spot. The—" Elinger suddenly interrupted himself. A thought hit him like an uppercut from a heavyweight champion. "The Westminster Presbyterian Burial Grounds. The lightning nearly destroyed it—and that's where Edgar Allan Poe is buried!"

"If lightning struck Poe's grave, the tremendous electromagnetic disturbance could have forced him to our plane of existence," Dennington said. "A consciousness usually stays close to its earthly remains, contemplating its earthly mistakes while waiting for its next life or its judgment day. It could've been there when the lightning struck."

"I don't want to dilute your enthusiasm, Kirk," Elinger interrupted. "But this would only prove part of the mystery, how Poe was brought back to this world."

"Yes," Dennington acknowledged. "And what do you think would be the logical explanation that connected your killer to Ms. Holland and Poe?"

Elinger had already conceived the answer. "What if they were all hit by the same bolt of lightning?"

Elinger could see the sudden look of revelation in Dennington's face.

"You missed your calling, Lieutenant!" Dennington said. "That would explain the three-way connection! One lightning bolt with a single frequency, in a split second, strikes the brains of your killer and Ms. Holland and the entity of Edgar Allan Poe and puts the electromagnetic planes and frequencies of their minds in sync." Dennington grinned at Elinger. "If Poe's entity was born of lightning, then I can guarantee it can be destroyed by lightning. Without question, you need to electrocute your killer while he's in a trance."

Part Three
Karmic Justice

● ● ●

Ye who read are still among the

Living: But I who write

Shall have long since gone my way

Into the region of shadows.

For indeed strange things shall happen,

An secret things be known.

Edgar Allan Poe

FORTY-NINE

● ● ●

It was past one o'clock in the morning when Elinger parked his vehicle outside the Westminster Presbyterian Burial Grounds. As Renee emerged from the passenger side, she noticed the humming and static sounds of the power station across the street.

Renee glanced through the wrought iron fence bordering the nineteenth century graveyard. The full moon rinsed the aged tombstones and crypts with a bluish hue, casting long, distorted shadows. She knew her view of the cemetery was a glimpse of history, almost the same panorama Edgar Allan Poe would have seen the day he was buried had he sat up in his coffin.

Carrying a long-handled flashlight, Elinger guided Renee through the darkness with the beam of light. He pushed open the iron entrance and ushered her into the cemetery. He panned the flashlight, highlighting marble and brick headstones, searching for the stony marquee of Edgar Allan Poe's burial plot.

Wherever Elinger's light rested, the storm's damage was still evident—cracked and shattered gravestones—split branches hanging from the hearts of trees—clumps of shrubbery brittle and brown—and the large cavities blasted into the earth by lightning were now filled with fresh dirt.

The storm's force was awesome, Renee realized, noticing many more headstones were in various stages of patching and repair.

"Must've been hell on earth," Elinger commented as he and Renee moved deeper into the damaged graveyard.

Finally, Elinger's flashlight flickered on Poe's grave.

It wasn't what Renee expected. Poe's tomb was untouched by the storm. The marble monument, with carvings of harps and leaves, was intact, and the bricks on the ground surrounding it were as solid as a London cobblestone street. The circular bronze relief of Poe's expressionless face stared hauntingly at Elinger and Renee.

"Quote the Raven Nevermore," Renee read the epitaph aloud.

Elinger let his flashlight rest on Poe's undisturbed grave.

"Sure blows a hole in Dennington's theory, doesn't it?" Renee said, a bit confused yet comforted Poe may not be her antagonist after all. "The lightning never hit his grave."

"Unless his grave has already been repaired," Elinger speculated, dampening Renee's last thought. "I'm sure Poe gets that kind of treatment around here."

"Can I help ya folks?" The twangy voice surprised Elinger and Renee. They turned, and in the shaft of the flashlight, they saw a rusty man in his eighties standing before them. Carrying a kerosene lantern and a Winchester 1873 replica lever-action rifle, the bow-legged man was wearing a wide-brimmed cowboy hat, faded jeans, cowboy boots and a red and black plaid shirt suitable for checkers. He approached Elinger and Renee. His stare was deadly serious. "I'm supposed ta be here, but you ain't! Graveyard's closed. I forgot to lock the gate."

Elinger withdrew his badge and held it up for the old cowboy to see.

The cowboy lost his mean look and grinned, exposing teeth as crooked as his smile. His years of horse busting under the sun gave his face the lines of driftwood. "Well, thank Gawd," he said in an easy drawl. "I was gonna call you folks about trespassers, but it's you folks who are trespassing. When it's ol' Edgar's birthday, people do funny things," he added, placing the lantern on the ground and extending his hand to Elinger. "Name's Elmo Thompson. I take care of these fine grounds," he explained, squinting in the flashlight beam. "What can I do fer ya? Neither one of ya looks like ya partake in graveyard birthdays."

"Well, we have become big fans of Edgar Allan Poe's lately," Elinger said, "but we're really here to look at the damage done by that storm a few weeks ago."

"You picked a darn funny hour to be doin' it, but you done asked the right person. I was here when it hit," Thompson offered. "I bunk over yonder by the church."

"Then you'd know if Edgar Allan Poe's grave was damaged by the storm?" Elinger asked.

Thompson chuckled, tightening the large rose agate on his string tie, snugging it below his bony Adam's apple. "That commotion ruin't just about everythin' but his grave! I darn near got ma head blowed off by them yeller bolts when I was runnin' fer the church!" he said. "That dern lightning tore up the whole place! It was like World War Two, and I oughta know. I was in the Two-hundred and Forty-First Artillery Division back then," he added in a tone full of pride.

Thompson lifted the front of his cowboy hat and rubbed his shirt sleeve across his forehead, a fidgety habit developed from years of wiping sandy sweat from his brow. His face saddened before he spoke again. "I wish I coulda done somethin' to keep this fine bone yard from bein' ruin't. Some of these tombstones will take six months to the far side of a year to get fixed. And they'll never be like they was. A hundred years ago a gravestone was a real monument to somebody's life. Nowadays, ya just get yer name on a plaque in the dirt."

Renee attempted to comfort Thompson. "I'm sure if these people were alive today, they'd thank you for taking good care of their last resting place."

Thompson lowered his head as though in self-imposed penitence. "Well, I sure couldn't do much for 'em durin' that storm." He withdrew a red scarf from a back pocket and dabbed the moisture building in his eyes. "And I couldn't do nothin' for the T-V people neither! I yelled at 'em to get out of the storm, but they couldn't hear me!"

"T-V people?" Elinger repeated.

"The young buck n' filly from the TV station," Thompson replied. "They was the one's that got electrocuted over yonder." He pointed toward a tree with a blackened trunk and limbs full of crispy brown leaves. "They did their job right up ta the end. I knew they was dead. So, I stayed inside the church 'til the storm was over."

"What do you mean, they did their job right up to the end?" Elinger asked.

"Their camera was still runnin' after they was dead!"

Thompson revealed, then his expression wrinkled with grief. "They filmed the storm, and they filmed them ownselves bein' kilt!"

"Do you know what station they worked for?" Elinger asked.

"They was local," Thompson replied. "K-R-T-V. They met their maker like they was comin' straight from hell, burnt and smokin' like that," he offered, glancing down at Poe's grave. "But I guess it's befittin' when something like that happens near ol' Edgar's grave."

Elinger handed Thompson one of his business cards. "If you think of anything else we should know, please give me a call."

Thompson took the card. "I surely will."

After being cleared by two gate guards, a security officer, a receptionist, and several secretaries, Elinger and Torres were finally led to the office of KRTV's news director Frank Williams—a fifty-year-old workaholic veteran of the media grind.

When Elinger and Torres entered his office, Williams had his overworked body humped over his desk, eyes locked on AP, UPI and Reuter's news feeds on his computer screen. He stopped and looked up at Elinger and Torres through dark encircled eyes that needed more sleep and less coffee. The thick gray hair on the sides of his head was long and bushy and swept back like the wings of the Greek god Mercury. He looked haggard for a man his age.

"Yeah, I remember the friggin' storm!" Williams answered Elinger's first question, loosening his tie. "How could I forget it? I lost Marsha Mayfield and Chuck Nash!"

"We were told they filmed the storm," Elinger said.

"Yeah, they did," Williams replied. "And their own deaths, too. Really stupid what they did out there."

"Could we take a look at the video?" Torres asked. Williams leveled a gaze at Elinger and Torres. "Is this official business or morbid curiosity?" he asked.

"It's police business," Elinger answered, ignoring Williams' remark.

Incomprehension registered on Williams' face. "How can a storm be involved in a crime?" he asked. "Was the wind going faster than the speed limit?" he chuckled darkly.

"We're not sure how it fits into our case," Elinger said, again ignoring Williams' attitude. "But if you cooperate, you won't be left out when the story breaks."

"Guess that means I have to take you at your word?"

"Or we can get a search warrant," Torres added with a shrug.

"No need for that. I don't want my office trashed," Williams said. "I copied the video to a DVD, but I keep it at home. I'll bring it in tomorrow."

Elinger and Torres exchanged a look. Elinger wasn't sure if he believed him.

"I almost threw the damn thing out," Williams said. "The network wanted to run the electrocutions for ratings during sweep's week. Can you fucking believe that? But I wasn't going to let them exploit my people. Next thing you know, the footage would be on the Internet. So I took the disk home and told them the electricity in the storm had erased it."

Elinger felt Williams was truthful, but his need to see the

video was still urgent. "We'd be happy to drive you home to get it," he offered.

"Look, guys," Williams began, moving from behind his desk. "I understand you're busy, but so is the rest of the world. I don't have time to go home. I've got half an hour of news to fill by noon, and I'm five minutes short. I'll bring the disk in with me tomorrow. That's probably just about as fast as you getting a search warrant."

Elinger knew obtaining a search warrant could take that long. But more important, a search warrant would be a document revealing the video's existence. More fair game for the press and Amos. Elinger handed the news director his card. "Okay, Mr. Williams. We'll do it your way. But don't forget to bring it in, or we'll drive you home whether you have the time or not."

"If I said I'd bring it in, I will," Williams said, tossing Elinger's card on his cluttered desk where it instantly disappeared into the pile of papers.

Elinger gave Williams an irritated look.

"Don't worry," Williams told them. "I know where everything is," he added, then gave Elinger and Torres a sad look. "Are you guys sure you want to see this video? I mean, it's the most terrible thing you're ever going to see—even in your line of work."

FIFTY

• • •

Elinger and Renee observed the jagged white arcs as they streaked through the dark sky and stabbed the Westminster Presbyterian Cemetery. Followed by peals of thunder, fountains of soil burst skyward and tombstones from a bygone era shattered as if hit by wrecking balls. Nature's *blitzkrieg* again raised the dead. Skulls rolled on the ground, bones and pieces of moldering flesh showered down with the torrents of rain. This time, however, the storm was a replay.

Elinger and Renee stood near Williams' desk watching the thunderstorm on a KRTV newsroom monitor. Elinger had asked Williams to give him the privacy of his office to view the video.

Elinger glanced at Renee. Her eyes were steadfast on the monitor. Elinger could tell she had not realized the true fury of the storm she had witnessed from her window a few weeks earlier.

Elinger's eyes searched the screen now, trying to find Edgar Allan Poe's grave but the lightning provided only fleeting glimpses of the cemetery. It was difficult to see in the deep shadows following each blast. Marsha Mayfield and Chuck Nash, the KRTV news people, suddenly ran into the shot to keep their appointment with death. When they stopped near a large tree, Elinger could see that Elmo Thompson, the graveyard caretaker, had proved himself right—Mayfield and Nash had recorded their own electrocutions. A lightning shaft struck the tree behind them. Bark popped and split as the voltage hissed down the trunk and shot along the ground in a wide, searing sheet. Mayfield and Nash were hit in the legs, and the force braised their flesh in a split second.

Although dead, Marsha Mayfield remained standing for a moment. Smoke from her poached brain curled from her ears. Her muscles, rigid as oak, held her upright for a moment. Then, slowly, she timbered to the muddy ground.
Thrown by the blast, Nash screamed as he went down. After a violent jackknife convulsion, he was lifeless. Golf ball sized water pockets bubbled up from beneath his skin on his face and neck, then burst into steaming red sprays.

Elinger and Renee saw another dazzling blaze of light. It was the mammoth lightning bolt. Wide as a car, and with a dozen splintering shafts, it rocketed toward earth and met a rising counter charge shooting up from a grave site. In a blinding flash, the grave exploded, spewing forth a geyser of earth. The bolt was too powerful to obey the basic laws of nature. Losing little power, it skimmed across the ground and soared toward the arched opening of the church's catacombs.

Elinger moved closer to the monitor as a shadowy figure in the distance stepped a few yards from the archway and was side-swiped by the main beam of voltage. The man reached up for the side of his head, then staggered and fell to the ground. The bolt remained as bright as the sun as it streaked off in a Northerly direction, slicing through the air toward a hilltop lined with homes.

"My God," Renee uttered, watching. "I live in that neighborhood. I was hit by the same lightning bolt as the murderer!"

"And it connected both of you to whomever was buried in the grave that was hit," Elinger added, studying the screen, hoping to identify the man felled in the archway as Leonard Ravnik. But the man was too distant in the shot to make a clear identification.

Elinger punched a button on Williams' keyboard to replay this lightning bolt on the monitor. "We need to know exactly where the lightning hit," he told Renee, his mind replaying the elephantine shaft striking the unidentified grave. He watched the strike again on the monitor but the lightning's exact contact point was lost in a maze of broken headstones.

Elinger and Renee slid into Elinger's car in the KRTV parking lot. Both of them looked numbed by what they had just seen.

Elinger wondered if Edgar Allan Poe's grave was not struck by lightning, then who was the force behind the killings?

Elinger drove from the lot into city traffic with something on his mind he needed to explain to Renee.

"I'm going to double the men at your house, Renee," Elinger said, breaking the silence. "And I'm going to spend a lot more time there, too."

"What are you expecting?" Renee asked in a nervous tone.

"I'm not sure—but you said once that the entity might want you out of its way," Elinger said, not wanting to alarm Renee but couldn't avoid it. "And in the last note, it said it was growing quite fond of you. Just in case it sends Ravnik for you, I want to be ready."

Renee reached out and touched Elinger's hand. "Thank you for caring. If there's anybody who can stop him, it's you."

Elinger shifted his eyes toward Renee. "I haven't done much to prove that yet."

Renee smiled. "I'd probably already be dead if it wasn't for you!"

Gazing thoughtfully at Renee, Elinger was glad she felt that way. There were many things he wanted to tell her. Sometimes to comfort her, other times to let her know how much he cared for her. "When this is over, I'm going to take you to some far-off, exotic place," he promised.

Renee smiled again. "As a celebration, if this thing ends?"

"I was thinking more of a honeymoon." Elinger was surprised at how natural and easy those words came from him.

"Is this a proposal?" Renee asked with a smile.

Elinger's answer was a glance at Renee with a loving grin. He hoped she could read his expression.

Renee moved over to the center of the seat and snuggled against the Elinger's shoulder. "I like the Bahamas."

"Is that a yes?" asked Elinger.

Renee lifted her head and kissed him on the cheek. "I love you. That's better than a yes."

FIFTY-ONE

● ● ●

Torres joined Elinger for a thirty-five-mile trip to Washington, D.C. Because the storm was recorded at night, the recording quality was grainy, Elinger explained to Torres. The graveyard images were dark and fuzzy except when flashed by lightning. The light on the news people's camera had gone dead, Elinger added. Image enhancement and the resulting clearer images would be the only way to pinpoint the grave decimated by the colossal lightning shaft. And perhaps, cleaner images would also confirm the man hit by lightning was Leonard Ravnik. To accomplish this, Elinger told Torres they were taking the video to the FBI's leading image enhancement specialists in Washington, D.C. He had seen their work when they enhanced BPD bank robbery photos. They were undoubtedly the best.

Elinger, alert as an owl at midnight, noticed every dip, curve, and line in the road as he steered South on the Gladys Noon Spellman Parkway. What kept him wide-eyed and fueled with adrenalin was a single thought. Who was the real consciousness behind the murders if it wasn't Poe? The answer, he hoped, would be revealed when he found the grave that was struck by the massive bolt of lightning.

After several security clearances, Elinger and Torres found themselves deep inside the FBI complex, in a computer lab as sterile as an operating room. They noticed the space was chilly, climate controlled to protect the delicate electronic equipment and servers that lined the walls. Elinger noticed several super computers with large high-resolution monitors sItting on a long table. He also saw a sophisticated projector system, a powerful file server, a video direct microscope system, other microscopes with digital cameras and camcorders attached to their eyepieces, and a high-end DSLR digital camera secured to a copy stand.

Thirty-seven-year-old Dr. Philip Zhang entered the lab and approached Elinger and Torres. Using a viselike handshake, Zhang introduced himself with great panache. He tightened his ponytail with a rubber band as he announced he was ready to begin.

Elinger handed him the DVD that contained the video of the storm.

Zhang nodded and took the disk from Elinger. He moved his short, thick body to a DVD player near him. After inserting the disk, he watched the rains and swords of light bombard the Westminster Presbyterian Burial Grounds on a nearby monitor. After several tombstones exploded, he turned to Elinger and Torres with a frown. "What is this? Where's the robbery?"

"There is no robbery," Torres said. "Didn't they tell you what we had?"

Zhang shook his head. "I was only told the assignment was different."

"That would be an understatement," Elinger said.

Dr. Zhang studied Elinger's serious expression. "Okay, you've got my interest," he said. "What am I looking for?"

"We think there's a man in the video that's a suspect of ours. We'd like to get a good look at his face if we can," Torres said.

"That's simple enough," Zhang said, turning back to the screen where more graves exploded like they were hit by mortar rounds. "Needs more light, but I'm sure you already know that," he mumbled. "I'm running the video through our modular image analysis system." Zhang's eyes returned to Elinger. "Do you want the enhancements in color or black and white, Lieutenant?"

"Color."

"Good," Dr. Zhang said. "I invented the program for that. I think it's the reason the FBI lets me keep my long hair," he chuckled with a tone of pride.

Zhang shifted his gaze back to the monitor where more rain washed the cemetery and several rods of lightning struck the church. "That's one helluva storm," he said. "I'll need to break it into the basic color components and put it through the frame buffer before it goes into my programs. But I don't see your suspect."

"He'll step out of that archway anytime. You can't miss him," replied Torres. "He gets hit by lightning."

"And we also need to know exactly where that particular bolt of lightning hits the ground first," Elinger said.

"You can't miss it either," Torres added. "It's the really big one."

"Okay, I'll histogram what you want and pass it through filters for sharpness and contrast improvement."

"In plain English, what are you doin'?" Torres asked.

"This is a real time video digitizer," Zhang explained. "Basically, I'll lift the pixels, sharpen their edges, adjust their shades and colors, and put them back where they belong. And presto, I've got a clearer picture that's easy to manipulate. I can make parts of it disappear or sections lighter or darker," Zhang said. "Give me a satellite picture of your neighborhood, and I'll give you the license plate number of a car parked in your driveway."

When Zhang finished enhancing the video, he removed a handkerchief from his pocket, held it over his nose and blew a B-flat. Elinger took it as a trumpeted announcement he had finished his work.

Zhang approached Elinger and Torres who had been sitting patiently among the computers. Zhang handed Elinger and Torres several enhanced photos. A few enlarged shots showed Leonard Ravnik emerging from the archway near the church's catacombs and being zapped by the lightning bolt. Sharply defined, the face was no longer faded or blurry. Without question, Elinger recognized Ravnik.

"If this is your suspect, he should be quite dead," Zhang said.

"But he's not," Elinger replied as he and Torres examined more photos. The resolution of the pictures was a vast improvement over the video. One shot was a frozen image of Ravnik's head as it was hit on the side by the huge bolt. In another, he was sprawled on the ground—his hands reaching for the side of his smoking head. His long-nailed fingers were drawn like claws.

Dr. Zhang handed Elinger and Torres more photographs. "Now here's the big zapper you wanted. Wide as a frigging car!"

Elinger and Torres examined the picture. The arc of the bolt side winded from the sky, touching the cemetery's grounds with its branches splaying outward.

"That's a standard enhancement," Zhang said. "I inverted the image with my program so you can tell exactly where it hit. I compared the geometric relationships of objects in the cemetery to establish their positions. This is what I came up with." Dr. Zhang handed Elinger the photo.

Elinger was taken aback with what was in his hand. The huge bolt stretched from the sky to a grave—but this time the angle Zhang created was straight down the side of the shaft from the sky. The graveyard below was squared into small sections like a grid map. Dr. Zhang had drawn lines from the thunderbolt to various locations in the cemetery. On the lines were numbers ranging from five to one hundred.

Zhang pointed at the numbered lines. "These numbers are distance in meters. I'd say the lightning hit about fifty meters inside the fence from West Fayette Street. It hit a grave dead center. No pun intended," Zhang added, smiling. "If you follow my measurements, you'll know exactly what grave was hit."

FIFTY-TWO

• • •

It was late when Elinger and Torres drove up and parked their vehicle at the Westminster Presbyterian Cemetery. After emerging from the auto, Elinger peered out at the graveyard, illuminated only by the faint spill of street lamps. The marble tombstones glowed dimly like distant lighthouses in a sea of ink.

Elinger and Torres moved to the cemetery's iron gate. Elinger pushed the gate but it would not open. When he saw the heavy padlock and chain wrapped around its latch, he turned to Torres. "Shit!" he growled. "The caretaker locked it up."

"Guess we're gonna have to go over the top?" Torres advised, quickly scanning the tall fence.

Studying the spear like points that crowned the iron fence, Elinger nodded with a definite lack of enthusiasm.

"Don't worry. It'll be no sweat!" Torres reported upon seeing Elinger's look. "I used to jump over these all the time when I was runnin' from you h*uff 'n puff boys*."

"Huff 'n puff? You got caught, didn't you?" Elinger countered quickly. "By a rookie if I recall."

Torres' smart-assed expression shriveled. "You know

what I really hate about you? You remember everything!"
Elinger nodded with a slight grin.

"But I'm also sure you remember the rookie was a college track star!" Torres added.

Elinger nodded again, then glanced at the top of the fence. "Looks like this is your chance to relive those yuk-filled days, Ralph," Elinger said, his eyes searching for hand and foot holds on the fence's vertical rails. "As a kid I could have flown over one of these, too."

"But now, it could make a *capon* out of you."

"A *capon*?" Elinger asked as he studied the fence for bent rails and foot holds.

"A castrated bird," Torres needled, then gripped the vertical bars of the fence and wedged his feet between them. He pushed outward with his legs and pulled himself up with his arms. When he reached the spikes, he swung up a leg on one, placing a thick leather sole on it, then pushed himself over. He landed in the cemetery as graceful as a cat.

Torres grinned widely. "If you'd like, I'll hold your flashlight. I don't want you weighted down for your flight."

Elinger waved off Torres' wisecrack as he walked to a nearby tree with a heavy branch growing over the top of the fence and into the graveyard. He climbed the trunk of the tree and pulled himself out onto the branch and walked along it until he was over the graveyard. He jumped down near Torres.

Torres looked across the street and suddenly scowled. "Well, look who's here."

Elinger glanced in the same direction and saw Mervyn

Amos' auto parked in the shadows between streetlights.

Amos studied the graveyard through his SUV's windshield. He knew if he approached Elinger and tried to grill him for case facts, he would get nothing in return and quite possibly spend the night in jail. He had already decided to be a quiet observer tonight, not to be seen, yet hoping to see something worthy for his exclusive.

Elinger mumbled an expletive under his breath. He had more important things to consider at the moment than to confront Amos. He pulled his flashlight from his pocket and turned his attention back to the graveyard. "Let's go!"

Using his flashlight beams to guide the way, Elinger and Torres moved through the burial grounds. Elinger's light penetrated the musty air, occasionally glinting off the marble and bronze headstones.

Elinger and Torres moved deeper into the burial grounds, nearing the fence near West Fayette Street as Dr. Zhang had instructed. After a few more yards, Elinger and Torres stopped. Elinger withdrew the top-view photo Dr. Zhang had given him. He studied the bright shaft that had burrowed into the grave and Zhang's lines and meter ranges written next to it. Elinger alternated glances between the photo and the tombs near him. "According to this, the lightning hit about thirty meters in that direction," Elinger surmised, pointing his flashlight into the night, its beam sweeping past several tall tombstones.

Elinger and Torres began walking, counting off their steps, until Elinger's flashlight illuminated a grave beneath their feet. They noticed the plot was an uneven mound of fresh, grassless earth—the obvious result of being refilled recently. A deep, ragged crack in the pearly headstone was patched with concrete. A corner of the bronze plaque was melted from the heat of the lightning.

Elinger shined his light on the marker and read its words:

RAYMOND PATRICK 1810-1860
Weep Not For Him

Elinger and Torres studied the grave. Elinger realized they had finally learned the name of the entity connected to Ravnik and Renee and causing the string of murders. It was true, Elinger deducted. The same lightning bolt had bonded their minds just as Dennington theorized.

Elinger and Torres moved quietly from the grave, heading for the street. Elinger didn't have any time to waste. He had to find out everything he could about Raymond Patrick, and why he'd become such a curse to Renee and the citizens of Baltimore.

FIFTY-THREE

• • •

Captain Robert Osborne was nestled in his bed under a brightly-colored patch-quilt. He snored himself into a deep sleep, but the ringing phone on the nightstand interrupted him. It was 2:00 a.m., and Elinger was on the line.

"This better be good, Kent," Osborne opened the conversation with a grumble.

"I need to get into the main branch of the Pratt Library," Elinger said instantly.

"Tonight?"

"Yeah, right now."

"What's so damned urgent?" Osborne asked.

"I'd only be telling you things you wouldn't believe. Just get me in, okay?"

"What makes you think I can get those doors opened at this hour?" Osborne asked.

"The Director of the library," Elinger answered. "What's his name? Simmons? You were both involved in the R-I-F program, remember?"

"Yeah, the Reading is Fundamental program," Osborne

recalled with a tone of regret.

"That was his pet project and you gave him full police support," Elinger recapped for the captain. "He'll do you a favor at any hour."

"Yeah, I suppose."

"Call him, Cap. I'll meet him there."

The line clicked dead in Osborne's ear. Osborne looked at the phone and shook his head.

●　●　●

Elinger and Torres reached the Enoch Pratt Free Library about the same time as the Director—a thin and withered seventy-year-old man named Edward Simmons. Simmons ushered Elinger and Torres across the flecked, marble floor and past the squared pillars near the circulation desk. The men climbed a flight of stairs and entered the Maryland Room. They passed several long wooden tables near a wall of old archival books and stopped at a row of computers.

As Elinger and Torres studied the index on the screen of one of the computers, Simmons repaired to a table with the thermos he carried and a first edition of the *Baltimore Sun*. He poured himself a steaming cup of coffee and began to read the paper.

Elinger and Torres scrolled on the screen, searching for references of Raymond Patrick. They discovered only one—in a book that recorded Baltimore's History during the years of 1810 to 1860.

After locating the book, Elinger leafed through its pages

and located a biography of Raymond Patrick's family. He read aloud, paraphrasing for Torres. "*He was born in Annapolis,*" Elinger began. "*His father was an Englishman, a craftsman from a bloodline of prominent shipbuilders. His mother was from a wealthy family of aristocratic tobacco farmers. His ancestors are traced back to the eighteenth century and considered founding fathers of Baltimore.*" Elinger paused, allowing his eyes to explore more words before continuing. "*When Patrick was young, his family moved to Baltimore, and he got his first job as an errand boy for The Baltimore Saturday Visitor.*" Elinger glanced at Torres. "*The Visitor* printed some of Poe's works."

"Where'd you learn that?"

"When I was reading up on Poe," Elinger replied, then dropped his vision to the book in his hand. "When Patrick was older, he became a typesetter it says here. Hmmm?" Elinger paused, still studying the page.

"Hmmm, what?" Torres probed.

"He became a literary reviewer and was the judge that awarded Poe a fifty-dollar prize for *Ms. Found in a Bottle.*"

"He must have known Poe personally," Torres concluded.

"It looks that way. Poe must've impressed the hell out of Patrick," Elinger added.

"Why do you say that?"

Elinger glanced up from the book. "When Poe was alive, his critics usually panned him. True respect for his work didn't start until a few years after he died," Elinger said as his focus traveled back to the text. "According to this, Patrick lavished Poe with praise while Poe was still alive. Here's one of his critiques."

Elinger read aloud, directly from the book: "*The 'Murders*

415

of the Rue Morgue'—Let me beg your notice that Edgar Allan Poe's latest tale of ratiocination is an extraordinary literary masterpiece! The main character, a policeman whose genius matches that of Poe's own brilliance of mind, possesses most keen deductive powers ever scribed in the literary field! Monsieur C. Auguste Dupin can investigate the most obscure clews and weave them into the tightest web to befoul the villain. No one has or ever will surpass Poe with the consummate wit he has bestowed upon his hypothetical policeman. You will marvel from the title page to the unexpected finale of this profound and entertaining mystery whilst it unravels before your eyes. And since I dare not be the one to reveal its conclusion, you must take it upon yourself to become aware to the pleasures of reading such a gifted, masterful writer as Edgar Allan Poe."

Elinger retracted from the volume and glanced at Torres. "Clue is spelled *c-l-e-w* here. Just like in Renee's pages." Elinger returned his gaze to the book. "This review was written for Graham's Magazine. Guess who else worked there?"

"Poe?"

"Yeah, about nine years after the award at *The Visitor.* So, what does that tell us?"

"That Patrick and Poe did know each other, and probably for a long time," Torres replied.

Elinger nodded. "There's other reviews in here by Patrick, all of them flatter Poe. Listen to this—*Do not deprive yourself during your toilsome journey through life. Wait for a moody storm and recline by the fire to rivet your attention on The Black Cat or my favorite The Premature Burial, all penned by Edgar Allan Poe. One must treat the innermost chambers of their soul by dunking*

*their brain in the literary drink of Mister Poe. The intoxication
is matched by no other earthly pleasure for no writer will ever
match the power of Mister Poe's pen—his imagination so vivid as
to create worlds on paper as real as the chair one sits on whilst
reading his astounding genius."*

Elinger lifted his eyes from the book. "What we've got
here is a sycophant. And sycophants sometimes emulate the object
of their worship."

Torres gave Elinger a questioning look. "Well, Winfield's
experts were right—it is a Poe copycat who's writing Renee's
pages and causing these murders."

"What they don't realize is he's just as dead as Poe,"
Elinger added. "But this makes sense. Patrick lived in Poe's time
so the spelling and writing styles of that era were natural to him.
His job was to review Poe's work, so he read Poe regularly and
probably mastered his vocabulary?"

Torres chuckled quietly but there was not a hint of humor
to it. "If we're chasing a nineteenth century groupie, a ghost no
less, what is he up to in this century?"

"Maybe he wants to impress Poe with his writing?
Something he couldn't do in his own lifetime," Elinger guessed.
"Maybe now he thinks he can do it through Renee by creating
a story based on the reality he creates? Who knows the logic of
a twisted mind?" Elinger added, thumbing through a few more
pages. His face reflected an unexpected surprise.

"What?" Torres asked.

Elinger handed the open book to Torres, exposing a
missing section.

Torres looked bewildered at the ragged binding.

"The information about Patrick's later years is gone," Elinger said. "Somebody ripped out the pages!"

Simmons could offer no explanation for the absent pages. He was perplexed and agitated as he assured Elinger the books in the Maryland Room were always under the scrutiny of several attendants. The rare book was the library's only copy and may not be replaceable.

Simmons suggested another place where Elinger might find the information he needed. He led Elinger and Torres down the stairs and into the Microfilm Center where old newspapers, magazines and historical documents were preserved on microfiche. The space housed over a dozen microfiche readers and printers near shelves and cabinets filled with hundreds of rolls of microfiche.

Following Simmons' instructions, Elinger pulled out a large drawer from a cabinet. Inside were dozens of cases of microfiche. He studied the labels listing the years and name of the publications. Elinger removed several boxes that chronicled 1850-1860, figuring these decades covered the last years of Raymond Patrick's life.

Elinger and Torres sat behind a reader as Elinger opened the first case. He discovered half of the microfiche rolls were missing. He lifted the lid of another box and found it only half filled with spools. Elinger turned to Torres. "The years we need are not here!" he said, giving Torres a look of intense frustration.

Elinger and Torres threaded the remaining microfiche rolls into the readers and studied their contents. Elinger hoped they would find anything about Raymond Patrick, something the history thief might have left behind. After an hour of scanning, however, he found nothing.

"His reviews aren't even in here," Torres reported. Elinger nodded, flicking off the equipment. "Someone's trying to hide the last years of Raymond Patrick's life."

When Elinger explained the missing microfiche to Simmons, the Director became livid. He despised anyone who would dare steal from the library and fragment the proud history of Baltimore. He promised a thorough investigation.
"Do you have any other copies?" Elinger asked Simmons.

Simmons answered by moving to a computer on a nearby counter. He clicked the mouse a few times then peered at the screen of information. Shaking his head, he told Elinger and Torres *The Baltimore Weekly American* and the other publications on the missing rolls have not been around for decades. The library does not keep extra microfiche copies, but he could order another set if they were still available.

""How long would that take?" Torres asked.

"About a month," Simmons replied. "But if I put a rush on it, I could probably get them in a week or so."

"I don't have that kind of time, Mr. Simmons," Elinger said.

Elinger pushed open the library's exit door and he and Torres stepped into the night air. "Why do you think somebody's hidin' his life, Kent?" Torres asked.

"Because he didn't die as a model citizen," Elinger guessed. "He must have done something his family wanted to erase from history." Elinger suddenly graduated a new idea. "I think a genealogist could help us."

"But we've already traced Patrick's lineage." Torres reminded Elinger.

"I want to go the other way," Elinger said. "I want to find a living relative. We might learn more from them than we could from an old newspaper."

FIFTY-FOUR

● ● ●

Elinger stood on Renee's front yard addressing a half dozen uniformed BPD officers he had recruited to guard Renee Holland. His concern for Renee's safety had increased. Besides being part of the triad connection with an entity and a flesh and blood killer, the entity's latest notes had become more personal. Elinger sensed an underlying threat in them—that having complete control of Renee was the underlying theme.

Torres and Sanders flanked Elinger, straight and erect, reflecting a military seriousness. As Elinger spoke, he noticed his mood reflected the afternoon weather. A gray, sunless sky had produced a frosty day. The officers were lucky their uniforms were made of heavy fabric. Elinger could feel the cold through his suit as though it were paper thin. He knew Torres and Sanders probably felt the same chill.

Elinger explained the security assignment and talked about the suspect, Leonard Ravnik. This man was dangerous, he explained, strong enough to effortlessly pin most any man to the ground. And now, because of the gun shop robbery, he was a one-man army. Elinger concluded by telling the men he wanted the suspect captured alive by any means possible.

A twenty-year veteran named Murphy took a half-step forward. He was a husky man with piercing dark eyes. Elinger knew Murphy and how Murphy's time on the streets had put real grit into his mannerisms.

"If this guy's so bad, how're we gonna take 'em alive. Lieutenant?" Murphy asked.

"With multiple hits from taser guns," Elinger began. "If several of you can taser him at the same time, you can disable him long enough to cuff him and hobble him. He's strong but he won't be able to break through steel handcuffs."

"We hear this guy is some kind of freak that doesn't feel pain," Murphy said. "We need to know what we're really dealing with."

Worried Murphy might unnerve a few of them men, Elinger made a quick announcement to everyone. "If you feel your life is in danger, you can use your weapon—but shoot him in the legs." Elinger turned to Murphy again and gave him a penetrating glare. "Anyone who feels they can't follow those orders, can leave now and return to their regular duties."

Elinger watched as the officers glanced at one another. He knew they wanted to see if anyone would break rank.

Elinger turned his attention back to Murphy and his defiant expression. He knew he could not intimidate Murphy.

"If our life is on the line, why can't we shoot this scumbag's balls off and hang them from our rear-view mirror?" Murphy asked.

The uniformed officers chuckled.

Elinger did not respond immediately. He knew he couldn't

reveal Ravnik's murdering spree was influenced by an unworldly consciousness and, he certainly couldn't explain he needed Ravnik alive so he could electrocute him! Right now, Elinger had to be a politician and field the question. "You're a tough guy, Murphy. You're not afraid of anyone. You shouldn't have any problem with this assignment."

Murphy nodded, appreciating the praise while in front of his peers. He stepped back into the ranks.

Elinger understood Murphy's point. Murphy was right. He was indeed fucking with the lives of the men, but he couldn't do a damn thing about it.

Elinger sat with Renee at her kitchen table sharing a lone cup of coffee. Renee had consumed several cups before Elinger arrived, and the caffeine had already inflamed her feelings of anxiety.

"Besides everything else, now you're telling me I'm a prisoner in my own home?" Renee objected, raising the tone of her voice.

Understanding, Elinger clasped one of his hands on hers. "You've been a prisoner of your body since this thing started, so being in here for awhile shouldn't be so bad."

"How would you know? No one's asking you to be locked up in your own home," Renee exclaimed, withdrawing her hand from Elinger's.

"There's nothing fair about any of this, Renee," Elinger shot back. "You think I like seeing you in danger? Or that I enjoyed watching Ralph get injured?"

Elinger's sharp reply surprised Renee. Sliding into an

introspective silence, Renee realized she wasn't the only one on edge. She leaned back in her chair, taking a moment to calm herself, then managed a grin. "Are you trying to tell me I'm being a bitch?"

"It's okay, you're well motivated," Elinger said in a softer timbre.

Renee rose from her chair and moved behind Elinger. She placed her hands on his shoulders and began to massage them. "I really do appreciate what you're doing, Kent. Forgive my lack of gratitude."

Elinger rolled his head side to side as Renee's fingers pushed into his flesh. "It's okay. You've earned the right to blow a fuse."

"I guess what's really bothering me is that I've forgotten what normal life is like," Renee said. "The wonderful feeling of being creative. How great an omelet tastes on a Sunday morning. Watching the hummingbirds outside my kitchen window. Playing baseball with Alex. Now it seems I can't go to the bathroom without an armed guard."

"It's just a matter of time before we get him and give you back your life," Elinger pledged.

"The only time I feel safe anymore is when I'm with you," Renee said, bending down and tenderly kissing the back of Elinger's neck.

Elinger stood and embraced Renee. Pulling himself tightly against her, he kissed her tenderly.

After a moment, Elinger withdrew gently. "I've got to go. I've got to follow up on something."

"Be careful, Kent," Renee said. "This monster said

Providence would be taking you soon."

"Better me than you," Elinger said as he kissed Renee, then headed for the door.

Later, Renee filled her bathtub with steaming water and soaked herself, hoping to dull her strained mind so she could have a good night's sleep. She was embarrassed by the attitude she directed at Elinger. He had been through as much as she had. She wished she could erase the day.

After the bath and slipping on a robe, she knocked on Alex's bedroom door.

"Yeah, Mom," Alex's voice filtered through the wood.

"I haven't seen you all day. Are you okay?"

"Yeah."

"Can I come in?"

Alex didn't answer.

"Alex?" Renee called out with concern. Her son was rarely quiet.

"Why do you want to come in?" Alex finally asked.

"Because you're my son, and I love you, and I want to talk to you."

"Okay. Come in."

Renee pushed open the door and entered the room.

Alex sat on the floor by the window, peering out at the policeman in the parked prowl car.

"What's wrong?" Renee asked. "This is the first time I've been in here without the T-V or stereo blaring?"

"Is that against the law?" Alex answered sharply without turning to face his mother.

"Honey, it's me, Mom. Why're you snapping at me?"

"Sorry," Alex said, keeping his focus directed out the window.

Renee moved to her son and placed her hand on the back of his head. "I know when something's wrong. You want to tell me about it?"

Slowly, Alex turned toward his mother, exposing a blackened right eye and a flame of embarrassment on his checks.

"My God, Alex! What happened?"

"I got in a fight with Tommy."

"Who started it?"

"You…"

"Me?"

"He said you were crazy," Alex said, his eyes filling with tears. "Like some of my other friends have said!"

Renee squatted down on the floor next to her son and placed an arm around his shoulder. "Honey, I'm sorry."

"You don't have to be. Tommy's got two black eyes," Alex said in a proud tone.

"You didn't hurt him, did you?"

"No." Alex returned his gaze outside the window. "I didn't hit him very hard."

"I'm sorry this has been so rough on you, Alex."

"Don't worry about me, Mom," Alex said. "I'm only called a geek at school. But your whole life is screwed up!" he added, his eyes suddenly sharpening. "I don't want anything to happen to you, Mom."

Touched by her son's feelings, tears glinted in Renee's eyes.

Alex pulled his shirt tail out of his pants and held it out to his mother. Renee dried her tears on it, then choked out a smile. "You know, Alex, I'm not going to say what you did was right, but I feel honored you stood up for me."

"You told me never to fight unless it was for a good reason, and I think you're a good reason, Mom."

"Thanks," Renee said. She stood and grabbed one of Alex's arms and pulled him to his feet. "C'mon, let's take care of that eye."

"You don't have to baby me."

Renee looked philosophically at her son, recalling his various stages of maturation. "You know, Alex, you're at an age when you're half-man and half-boy. Part of you wants your mom to fix your eye. The other part, Mr. Macho Man, says no. Why don't you be a boy for a few minutes and let me help you? I promise your friends will never know."

Alex grinned. "What friends? My crazy mother scared them all away!"

Renee and Alex shared a laugh as they headed for the bathroom. Renee felt fortunate to have a son who openly expressed his love for her. With her life in shambles, Alex and Elinger were the only people who kept her sane. If she lost either, she figured she would really go crazy.

FIFTY-FIVE

• • •

"I'm sorry this isn't what you expected, Lieutenant," Ms. Allison Van Buren stated in a blunt voice. Listening, Elinger looked across the linen covered table at the forty-something genealogist he had hired. Her hair was unkempt, her glasses were goggle-sized and her dress was the old-fashioned one-piece belted style. Elinger realized she looked out of place in DiSesso's, an Italian restaurant in Baltimore's Little Italy that catered to the city's young shakers and movers.

"Believe me, it isn't my fault I couldn't find much on this Raymond Patrick," Ms. Van Buren continued, wiping a streak of pasta primavera sauce from her lips. She pointed at the open folder on the table. "I've never seen anything like it. He's from a prominent family yet he seems to disappear from history when he hits forty."

Elinger frowned, scanning the papers in the folder. "You found nothing after forty?"

"I didn't say that, but I will say you're damn lucky you hired an expert like me," Van Buren boasted. "The Mormons give me special access to their records. They track everyone, even non-

Mormons so they can posthumously convert their souls. At least from them I learned where Patrick was buried."

"I already know that," Elinger said, twirling his fork in his clam linguini lunch. The mystery of Raymond Patrick's past had captured more of his appetite than the house specialty.

"But did you know about the bizarre codicil he added to his will just before he died?"

Elinger stopped coiling the pasta.

Ms. Van Buren sipped a mouthful of ice water before she explained. "It instructed his estate executor to buy a plot next to Edgar Allan Poe's."

This information lifted Elinger's eyebrows. "Did his will say why?"

"No."

"You know he's not buried next to Poe?"

"He was at one time," Ms. Van Buren counted. "Poe's body was moved a few years after he died and Patrick's was left where it was."

"What else did you find out?" Elinger asked.

"Not much. The guy turns middle-age and *poof!*, he disappears like a ghost."

If only she knew the irony of her words, Elinger mused. "Did you find a living descendant?" he asked.

"Of course," Ms. Van Buren answered, forking a piece of calamari from an hors d'oeuvres dish. She stuffed it into her mouth, sucking in the legs last. "I have a DAR contact in D.C."

"The Daughters of the American Revolution?" Elinger asked.

"Yes," Ms. Van Buren continued. "She found a

descendant in the lineage of DAR's members—but it's very odd local records didn't show that. Patrick was a Baltimore purebred from first generation Americans. There should be documents of his descendants right here in town."

Ms. Van Buren's words caused Elinger to put more hope in learning Patrick's past from a living descendant. "Does Patrick's descendant live in the area?"

"Right here in Baltimore."

Elinger perked again. "What's their name?"

"A widow. Virginia Walker. Raymond Patrick's great-great-great-great granddaughter," Ms. Van Buren replied. "She lives in Bolton Hill with other high-society snobs. Her smile is as wide as Charles Street, but she can be as cold as January snow. You say the wrong thing to her, and she won't talk to you for a year."

"You know her?"

"In a way," Ms. Van Buren said. "I do research for DAR so our paths cross occasionally. The less the better."

"Do you know if she keeps her own set of family records?"

"I would think so. Members have to document their lineage before they can join."

"Where does she live?"

Reaching into her purse, Ms. Van Buren withdrew a piece of paper and handed it to Elinger. "Here's her address."

Elinger drove into the turn-of-the-century Bolton Hill area, considered the most elegant address in Baltimore. He remembered reading Henry James once described it as the *gem of the town* and, it was a place where F. Scott Fitzgerald and Gertrude

Stein once lived. Even today, few zip codes match its richness and reputation.

Curbing his auto on a tree-shaded street, Elinger parked near a two-story Greek Revival townhouse with shuttered windows and brick walls. He noticed the residence still had its original double doors and the Victorian scroll work carved in its entryway cornices. The paint on the trim was fresh, and the general maintenance made the dwelling pristine. Elinger imagined it looked as new as the day its first nineteenth century occupants took residence.

Elinger was looking at himself in the sheen on the massive wooden doors when Virginia Walker answered his knock. She stood before him as though she was on a stage waiting for the spotlight. Elinger guessed she was about seventy-five with her great shock of white hair and wrinkled face beneath her designer glasses. Her clear and alert eyes, however, told Elinger her mind was not dimmed by her years.

Ms. Walker spoke in a dignified tone. "May I help you, sir?"

Elinger studied the diminutive woman, remembering Ms. Van Buren's warning about her. But the Ms. Walker he saw didn't appear to be mercurial. Her smile seemed affable. She was dressed in an elegant silk sheath and wore diamond and ruby drop earrings and a two-carat diamond ring on her right hand. She looked as though she was ready for the opera.

Following Ms. Van Buren's advice, Elinger decided to carefully approach Ms. Walker's reputed unpredictable personality.

Showing his badge, Elinger introduced himself and said he was aware Ms. Walker was a descendant from an impressive list of Baltimore founders. He was interested in her forefathers, he claimed, because he was writing an article for the Baltimore Police Department's Newsletter. Besides focusing on the people who shaped the city's heritage, he wanted to connect them to their living descendants to promote a past and present theme to the story. More human interest, he explained.

"It sounds interesting, Lieutenant," Ms. Walker replied through a guarded expression. "What is it you require of me?"

"Just answers to a few questions."

Ms. Walker nodded but Elinger could see the suspicion in her expression.

"If you could be quick about it," Mrs. Walker said. "I have an appointment."

"Sure," Elinger agreed, managing a grin, trying to charm her. "First, do you personally keep records of your ancestors?"

"Yes."

"What kind of records?"

"I have a gamut of items. Letters written by eight generations of my family. Family Bibles, birth and death certificates, newspaper articles and photos," Ms. Walker said. "There are other people in the area who have ancestors like mine? Why did you select me?"

Elinger noticed Ms. Walker's suspicious look again. His mind scrambled for an answer. "Your lineage is more impressive than the others," he replied, hoping some flattery would buoy Mrs. Walker's mood.

The timbre of Ms. Walker's voice remained unchanged. "Why did you want to know if I had my own records? Our libraries are full of ancestral information," she asked in a distrusting tone.

"That's true, but I don't want broad generalities of their lives. I want a more personal level," Elinger said, hoping Ms. Walker would believe him. "I don't want my article to sound like an excerpt from an encyclopedia. What these people accomplished is far too important for that."

Ms. Walker contemplated Elinger's statement. "Yes, you're absolutely right."

Elinger sensed a crack in Ms. Walker's wall. He wondered if sympathy would open it further. "I guess I owe you an apology though," he said. "I didn't think it would hurt if I dropped by unannounced to ask you a few questions, but I think I've disturbed you. I'm very sorry."

Elinger noticed Ms. Walker's features softening a bit. He was sure she believed him.

"There's no need to apologize, Lieutenant," Ms. Walker offered. "I have too much respect for what you do—keeping our streets clean from the low-brow filth that's contaminating our country. I'm afraid I should be the one who is sorry. What specifically did you want to know?"

Elinger withdrew a small note pad and pen from his coat, eager to take notes. He thought he'd begin with an easy, non-threatening question. "Well, for instance, how is it you became the keeper of your family's history? Why not another family member?"

Ms. Walker smiled before she spoke. "When I was a little girl, my great-grandmother gave me old photos and letters of our ancestors," she explained. "I became interested in my family's past right away. Whenever my family and I visited other relatives, I'd ask for old letters and photos. Pretty soon I had a trunk full and all of my relatives considered me to be the keeper of family records."

"How far back do your records go?"

"To the Revolutionary War," Ms. Walker replied. "It's a collection that brings me great pride. I have things you'd never find in the library. You were right about that."

Ms. Walker glanced at her watch. "Oh dear, I really must be going, Lieutenant."

Elinger smiled, trying to camouflage his disappointment. "Seems like we just got started. I had a few ancestors of yours I wanted to ask you about specifically. Perhaps we could continue tomorrow?" Elinger asked.

"Perhaps," Ms. Walker replied.

"Maybe you'd let me look through your records?" Elinger suggested gingerly, trying to make the request sound reasonable and innocuous.

Elinger could see a shadow pass over Ms. Walker's expression.

"I respect the dead, and I respect them even more when they're my family," Ms. Walker said. "I don't think they would want anyone reading their personal letters."

Elinger didn't want to antagonize Ms. Walker any further. "I can see your point."

Ms. Walker eyed Elinger for a long moment without saying a word. "Lieutenant, I have this feeling you haven't been honest with me," she finally said. "What do you really want?"

Since little else worked, Elinger decided to follow Ms. Walker's lead and be more direct. "Well, you do have an ancestor I'm particularly interested in. He was a literary critic? Possibly a friend of Edgar Allan Poe's?"

Elinger could see this question disturbed Ms. Walker. She seemed to shrink back from him.

"I think you've been misinformed. There's no one in my family like that," Ms. Walker answered quickly.

Elinger knew the conversation had ruptured. Now he decided there was no harm in being as strong-willed as Ms. Walker. "Hmmm, that's strange? The documents I've found say you have a great-great-great-great grandfather named Raymond Patrick. He was a literary critic."

"You're in error, Lieutenant," Ms. Walker said in a chilled tone. "I have no ancestor by that name. Good day!"

With that, Ms. Walker slammed the door shut in Elinger's face.

"Shit!" Elinger mumbled. He started to ring the doorbell again but knew it would be futile. He moved down the steps and headed toward his auto. He was satisfied he had established three important things—that Ms. Walker had ancestral records that could be important to his investigation—that Ms. Walker was responsible for the missing pages in the Enoch Pratt Library—and her overly defensive reaction to Raymond Patrick indicated Patrick had done something terrible. If he had committed criminal acts, Elinger reasoned, they could be found in Baltimore's police records. He remembered there were old police files stored in the basement of Headquarters. Maybe he could find something there.

Stepping from the Headquarters' elevator, Elinger moved quickly down the basement corridor. He entered the storage area and moved past a single table with two chairs and a computer on top. A microfiche reader rested on the tabletop. Elinger stopped at a wall of shelves and old filing cabinets where he found dozens of boxes of microfiche that chronicled the history of the Baltimore Police Department.

Elinger studied the labels of the microfiche boxes, searching for the 1800s—but the dates began in 1905.

Elinger moved to the computer, keyed in a few commands and scanned the index appearing on the screen. He learned that no 1800's files existed. They were destroyed in the Baltimore Fire of 1904.

Elinger leaned back in the chair, recalling the blaze. He had read about it. The fire had raged for three days, devouring eighty city blocks, including the police department. Fire companies were summoned from New York, Boston, and Philadelphia, but by the time they arrived, Baltimore's fate was sealed. Very little withstood the 2,800-degree heat, especially paper records.

Elinger rubbed his forehead, frustrated by his fruitless search. He wondered what forces were preventing him from finding Raymond Patrick's history. He asked himself where he might find other historical police records. One person might know, he realized, the museum curator for Headquarters.

When Elinger met with the curator, he learned that some old police ledgers had survived the flames of 1904. An alert sergeant had spirited them away in the early hours of the blaze. Elinger learned those records were kept in another part of Headquarters' basement.

Elinger entered a small basement room that resembled a concrete bunker. He found an old crumbling box and inside it: three large, timeworn, police ledgers. He placed them on the table. After blowing dust from the cover of the first book, he turned its brittle pages carefully. The entries were neat, handwritten in the scrolled penmanship of the era. Each report contained the date, name of the arrested, the suspected crime, and information concerning the suspect's bail.

Elinger checked the dates in each ledger until he found the one that chronicled the 1850s and 1860s. He scanned each page until a name leaped at him from the page. Raymond Patrick was scribed clear and distinct. Next to his name was the arrest report.

Elinger's eyes became transfixed on the words. After a moment, however, he realized he shouldn't be surprised by what he had just read.

FIFTY-SIX

* * *

When Elinger exited Headquarters and walked toward his auto, he was still digesting what he had discovered in the police ledger. Now he understood why Ms. Walker would not admit her ancestral link to Raymond Patrick. A nineteenth century policeman had described Patrick as a vicious murderer who suffered from *congestion of the brain* like Edgar Allan Poe. Patrick had been arrested as the prime suspect in a spate of cold-blooded, gruesome killings. Patrick was probably Baltimore's first serial killer, Elinger reasoned. He was disappointed there were no more details in the ledger. Although he was lucky to garner the few threads of Patrick's later years, Elinger knew he still needed Ms. Walker to weave the full fabric.

Moving across the parking lot, Elinger recalled how Ms. Walker was adamant in denying her lineage to Patrick. He figured she was hiding family records with secrets about Patrick. Elinger wondered if Ms. Walker would destroy those records if he pressed her to see them. He also wondered if he could make Mrs. Walker talk freely about Patrick. Elinger knew that wouldn't be easy. If she admitted she had a mass murderer in her family, it would ruin her sterling reputation in DAR and the other lineage conscious organizations.

By the time Elinger reached his auto, he noticed Mervyn Amos sitting in his auto across the street. *The bastard looks tired*, Elinger thought. He wanted to be angry with the reporter but for the moment respected his determination.

Elinger moved to Amos' car and leaned in the open passenger window. "I told you to stop following me, *Anus*," Elinger reminded in a semi-friendly tone.

"It doesn't matter what you tell me anymore, Lieutenant," Amos replied frankly. "If I don't get this story, I'm fired. So, if you want to lock me up, it's okay. At least it would make me look like I was trying."

Identifying with the reporter's aggravation, Elinger considered cutting Amos some lack. "You look like shit," Elinger said, changing the subject.

"I feel like shit. I've been living in my car since I started following you. Don't you ever sleep?"

Elinger shook his head and chuckled. "I don't think you're cut out for this, Amos."

"I haven't done too badly. I've been on your ass like a bean-fart since day one."

"And you're beginning to smell like one."

"Just tell me why you're looking for your suspect in a graveyard, and I'll take a shower."

Elinger wondered if Amos was ready for the truth. Instead of answering, he looked off, down the street.

"There's a whole lot of shit you're not telling me," Amos accused. "You've been jerking me off—but everything won't be totally lost," he added, casting an enigmatic smile at Elinger. "I already have a great story. I think I can go column one, page one with it and buy some time. It's about famed police lieutenant Kent Elinger and his lack of progress with the city's worst serial murder case. But that's only the hook," Amos warned. "The real meat is in your investigative methods—they'll make great kickers and subheads. Midnight swimming in the harbor, graveyard prowling in the middle of the night, trespassing in Sidney Harrison's backyard, opening the Pratt library after midnight, lunching with an overpaid genealogist on the police budget, and using our tax dollars to post police officers at your girlfriend's house. And let's not forget the slaughterhouse. Your perp brings a knife to a gunfight and he still wins! That's only off the top of my head. Wait until I really think about it."

Elinger gave Amos a hard look then opened the auto's door and slid onto the passenger seat. "You don't have the balls, *Anus*."

"You want to find out?"

"I wanted to be nice to you tonight," Elinger said in a gentleman's tone. "Because I respect your diligence and resourcefulness." Now Elinger's voice assumed a combative edge. "But you've threatened me. Makes me want to find a cub reporter at the *Sun* who needs a break."

With a sudden look of exasperation, Amos slammed the palm of his hand on the steering wheel. "Jesus, Elinger! Just give me something! Anything!"

"You were only bluffing about the article, right, *Anus*?" Elinger asked. The reporter shrugged, then nodded in agreement.

"I'm glad to know that. It makes me want to help you

again," Elinger said. "But first you've got to help me."

Amos' eyebrows dropped. "You never ask for anybody's help."

"I've never been this desperate," Elinger confided freely.

"You're serious?"

Elinger nodded. "I've got a lead that looks promising, but it needs flushing out. And I don't have the time. That's where you come in."

"What do you want me to do?"

"Some research. Dig into the *Sun's* records and find out everything you can about Virginia Patrick-Walker. She's a social maven from Bolton Hill. I'm sure your paper has done stories on her. She mingles in high society."

"You think an old woman is the killer?"

"What are you into now, *Anus*, cretinism?"

Elinger could see Amos' expression redden with embarrassment as he shifted his vision out the driver's window for a moment.

"When you're done with her, see what you can find about a guy named Raymond Patrick," Elinger continued. "You'll be up to your ass in cobwebs with him though. He's her great-great-great-great grandfather. He's been dead since the beginning of the Civil War."

Amos' eyes suddenly deadlocked on Elinger. "What's going on, Elinger? An old woman? A dead man? What do they have to do with your case?"

"I'll let you know when I know," Elinger replied truthfully. "Just do the research and see what you come up with. I'll be at the *Sun* first thing in the morning."

"I'm not sure I can have it done by then."

"It's just a little library work, *Anus*. Don't disappoint me," Elinger warned as he climbed from the auto. "I'll be there at dawn."

As Amos drove off, Elinger smiled. He appreciated the irony of his new involvement with Amos. Of all things, he and Amos were becoming allies.

● ● ●

Leonard Ravnik was asleep on a large horizontal grave slab on the ground. He rolled, then awakened and sat up, staring into the black space surrounding him. He was deep in the catacombs beneath the Westminster Presbyterian Burial Grounds Church. He arched his back to stretch. When he did, his diaphragm compressed and forced air through his mouth, making a guttural sound. He could smell the fetid odor of his own breath.

Rising from the stone, Ravnik stepped over a stack of rifles and several boxes of ammunition. He walked through the inky space, passing dozens of shelved dead people. He breathed the musty odors until he reached the archway. He peered out and sucked in the fresh air outside. He could see the sun lingering on the horizon, yellowing the clouds above the Baltimore skyscrapers before it withdrew its final colors and sank from sight. A light breeze swept over the graveyard, sweeping dead grass and dust across the old graves. He watched a nimbus of fog creep in and shroud the grave markers.

Ravnik was glad the cemetery had become his home again. The voice had suggested it when Ravnik's neighborhood was overrun with policemen obsessed in their search for him. Ravnik agreed it was a wise decision, knowing it was unlikely the police would search for him in the catacombs. And living there wasn't so bad. He was comfortable in the darkness. After all, the newspapers were calling him the Shadow Man. And, so far, he had been undetected by the old caretaker of the grounds. And if he bumped into him, he would kill him anyway.

As Ravnik's eyes still grazed the cemetery, he remembered the night two detectives had probed the area with flashlights. They moved from grave to grave, reading the names on the tombstones. Ravnik burned with rage when he saw them. He knew who they were. They had torn up his bicep, shot at him, zapped him with a Taser gun and made his face look like a pizza. Feeling like a wild dog, he wanted to rip the flesh from their bones with his bare teeth, but the voice told him not to kill on that night. It would only bring more policemen. But once their mission was complete, the voice promised Ravnik he could turn the detectives into corpses. Ravnik counted the time impatiently, waiting for his moment.

Watching the fog rise to knee level, Ravnik reminisced that being struck by the awesome lightning bolt had given birth to the voice in his head. He and the voice had different personalities, but during acts of violence—they were one and the same.

Ravnik recalled the night the voice had told him it had once lived on earth as a man named Raymond Patrick. And like Ravnik, Patrick loved to kill. Now he could murder again through Ravnik. *It was a good relationship*, Raymond Patrick said. They shared a powerful bond—the passion for killing. Patrick admitted, however, that he had a second passion—a craving for fame. The kind of fame that brings respect and admiration. Patrick also told Ravnik he was nearing the completion of his goal.

FIFTY-SEVEN

● ● ●

Waiting for Elinger's arrival, Mervyn Amos stood outside the *Baltimore Sun's* offices at 6:00 a.m. He glanced at his watch, feeling his lack of sleep. It had taken him all night to locate the information Elinger wanted. Amos was too tired to pay attention to the rising sun. It angled over the high-rises and lighted parts of Baltimore in gold and shadowed other areas, covering the city with black and gold patch-work. It was through heavy lids when Amos noticed Elinger roll up in his black car.

"This Ms. Virginia Patrick-Walker's a real muckety-muck all right," Amos reported quickly. Being in the presence of Elinger again had renewed his excitement for the elusive, exclusive story. It gave his body the jolt of adrenaline it needed to wake up.

Amos handed Elinger a folder of articles through the open driver's window. "And her ego must be as big as a blimp. She's never let one of our photographers take pictures of her. She submits her own retouched pictures. Wait until you see them. It's the only time you'll ever see a seventy-five-year-old with a face as smooth as my two-year-old nephew's ass."

Elinger pinched the one-inch thick folder. "Looks like

you've got a lot on her."

Amos nodded. "She's been in our Features and People sections several times. We've covered her career in DAR and The Maryland Historical Society."

Elinger opened the folder and scanned a few pages, learning Virginia Walker has an impressive record as a matron for Baltimore's historical preservation. Some articles touted her as the maven of Maryland heritage.

"I didn't do so well with this Raymond Patrick guy though," Amos said, wondering how a dead man fits into the case. "Our archives went up in smoke in the 1904 fire."

"Shit," Elinger mumbled, glancing up from the papers.

Amos raised his hands. "Hey, don't get a hemorrhoid! I've got a contact at the Library of Congress. Even at the ungodly hour I called her. She went to her office and worked the files for me. She found some heavy shit on this Raymond Patrick and faxed it to me."

Elinger's vision shot back to the pages in his hands.

"Level with me, Elinger. What's a dead man got to do with these killings?" Amos asked again.

"You wouldn't believe me if I told you right now. Just trust me and wait, and I will give you the biggest story of your career."

"I love my options. None."

"If it's any consolation—you can follow me, and I won't complain."

"Thanks for the big favor," Amos replied with a slightly cynical tone. He was thinking about his nose-diving career as Elinger put his vehicle in gear and drove off.

Elinger cruised slowly down the street. With one eye on the road, he thumbed through the pages. When he found archival records about Patrick, Elinger curbed his auto. The information he read was sketchy but enough to prove Patrick was the prime suspect in several 1800s murder cases and was indeed Ms. Walker's ancestor. Elinger hoped this proof would loosen Ms. Walker's mouth so she'd fill in the blanks of Patrick's life. Anything that might stop the killing spree that bloodied Baltimore's streets would satisfy Elinger.

Elinger turned more pages, finding newspaper articles about Ms. Walker. According to the *Sun*, she belonged to several organizations besides DAR. She was Vice President of The Baltimore Society and held high-ranking memberships to The Maryland Historical Society, The Society of Colonial Wars, The Society of the Arc and the Dove (named after the two ships that deposited early settlers in the Maryland area), The Society of the War of 1812, and The Society of Colonial Dames, (dames in the British sense of baroness). With famous ancestors, Elinger was sure Ms. Walker would fear social disaster if her contemporaries discovered her great-great-great-great grandfather was a serial killer. This was real leverage, and he would use it.

Elinger closed the folder and considered his options. He could obtain a court order but then that makes everything a matter of public record. That would be his last choice. Elinger considered using a woman-to-woman approach to soften Ms. Walker. If he brought Renee with him when he confronted Ms. Walker, perhaps she would sympathize if she knew Renee's predicament. It was worth a try, he thought.

Within a couple of hours, Elinger drove Renee to Bolton Hill. He parked his auto under a thick-trunked tree as old as the neighborhood's townhouses.

"We're only going to get one chance," Elinger reminded Renee as he unbuckled his seatbelt. "I want to hear violins when you tell your story."

"That won't be difficult," Renee assured Elinger, opening the passenger door. "I should sound like a Stradivarius."

Carrying the folder of the *Sun* articles and archive files, Elinger and Renee approached Ms. Walker's front porch. Elinger rang the bell.

Dressed elegantly at a time when most people were still washing breakfast dishes, Ms. Walker opened the door. She recognized Elinger immediately. "What are you doing here? I told you I couldn't help you!"

Ms. Walker started to push the door shut, but Elinger wedged his foot in the jam. Ms. Walker leaned on the door anyway, pinching Elinger's shoe.

Elinger latched his eyes on Ms. Walker's and saddled his words with a harsh edge. "I could come back with uniformed men and a search warrant. I don't think handcuffs would go well with your dress, Ms. Walker."

Elinger could see his words had pumped fear through the socialite. "What do you want from me?" she asked.

"A chance to save someone's life."

"What kind of nonsense is that?"

Renee peeked through the partially opened door. "It's my life he's talking about, Ms. Walker," she explained, her voice wavered with emotion. "You have information that could save me and others. All you've got to do is tell us about Raymond Patrick."

"But I don't know anyone by that name," Ms. Walker insisted.

Elinger's fuse had sputtered during his first visit, but now it was burning again. "He is your ancestor, Ms. Walker, and I've got records to prove it!' Elinger pushed the folder through the narrow opening of the door and into one of Ms. Walker's hands. "If you don't talk to me right now, I'm going to call every newspaper in the state and invite them over while I serve you with a court ordered search warrant!" Elinger bluffed. "It would make great headlines for the next DAR newsletter."

By Ms. Walker's reaction, Elinger knew he had her. She was rendered speechless by his threat. Bad news would certainly devastate her noble career and put a kink in her ancestral linkage.

Elinger watched as the flustered Ms. Walker locked her vision on the pages in the folder and thumbed through a few of them. She saw the copies of newspaper clippings and photos of her climb to the top of her social strata. She was smiling, dressed in several thousand-dollar gowns at many dinner parties and awards ceremonies. Ms. Walker flipped over more pages and saw the Library of Congress faxes about Raymond Patrick. Elinger noticed her face had turned almost bloodless.

"We know Raymond Patrick was a vicious killer," Elinger revealed. "You can't hide it anymore."

"With your affiliations, we know your ancestors are a touchy subject for you," Renee interjected. "But you can save some lives if you help us."

"Save lives? I don't understand?"

Renee leveled a serious and honest look at Ms. Walker.

"Ms. Walker, the recent killings have something to do with him."

"If you'll tell us about Patrick, we won't press charges against you for stealing records from the Pratt library," Elinger added.

Ms. Walker seemed to swallow with difficulty as she looked up from the folder. "You know about that?"
Elinger nodded.

"Oh, dear," Ms. Walker muttered in a fearful tone, pulling open the door and freeing Elinger's foot. "Please come in…"

Ms. Walker led Elinger and Renee into her living room. Renee noticed Ms. Walker's mélange of exquisite antiques. Each piece, decorative and furniture, was meticulously hand crafted, spanning several generations of American design. Everything in her home seemed to reflect aristocratic American history.

Although rattled, Ms. Walker attempted to be gracious. She served a silver tray of coffee, tea, and pound cake in her living room. She sat on a hand carved chair while Renee settled next to Elinger on a sofa. Pouring for Elinger and Renee, then herself, Ms. Walker was ready for a conversation she was sure would not bode well for her future.

After a dainty bite of cake, Ms. Walker confessed to her theft of the library records. She did it, she explained, at a time when she vigorously pursued respectable social status. As she rose in the ranks of her heritage conscious organizations, it became more important the killer in her family remained undiscovered. Her lineage was more prestigious than most of her peers, and she wanted to protect that distinction. Tarnished ancestors guaranteed a ground level rung in the hierarchy of the organizations, Ms. Walker clarified. And her beloved memberships had been the focal point of her life since her husband died twenty-five years ago.

When Ms. Walker finished, Elinger detailed the murder case for her. He talked about the odd storm over the graveyard, Raymond Patrick and Leonard Ravnik's involvement, Renee's trance writings and the strange personalized notes.

Drinking her tea, then staring over the rim of the cup, Ms. Walker listened, never suggesting she thought Elinger was a lunatic. She did react, however, when Renee explained how she feared for her life—how she could be a victim of the serial killer believed to be under the control of Raymond Patrick.

Ms. Walker placed her tea cup on the table and delicately wiped the crumbs from her lips. "From what my grandmother told me when I was younger, and from what I've read in my family's old letters and records, I realized Raymond had a troubled spirit that would never rest. I suppose none of this should surprise me." Ms. Walker took a deep breath, hoping to calm the nervousness she could feel rising in her body. "Most people wouldn't believe your story, Lieutenant. But I read a few weeks ago the grave of Hiram Berenson was desecrated at the Westminster Presbyterian Burial Grounds. His tombstone was found shattered in the catacombs. It was the only tombstone broken into pieces by what appeared to be a vandal and not by the storm. That told me something."

"What did it tell you, Ms. Walker?" Elinger asked, his curiosity suddenly roused.

Ms. Walker drew in another sip of tea before she spoke. "Hiram Berenson and Raymond lived at the same time. Raymond hated him with an unrelenting passion."

"Why?" Renee asked.

"Mr. Berenson was a literary critic, and he spent an inordinate amount of time condemning the works of Edgar Allan Poe. Raymond loathed him for that—and murdered him because of it."

Ms. Walker stopped for a moment, then gazed at Renee in a soft, grandmotherly way. "You, my poor dear, do not deserve to be hounded by that cursed ancestor of mine." Ms. Walker reached for her napkin and dabbed a tear in her eye, then spoke quietly in a heartfelt tone. "You remind me of my daughter. God rest her soul. She died just before her thirtieth birthday. We were picnicking, and she went for a swim in the bay. She was caught in a current and—we never saw her again."

"I'm sorry," Renee consoled.

"It's grief I'll carry to my grave," Ms. Walker said, her eyes misting again. She turned to Elinger. "I'll tell you what I know about Raymond, Lieutenant, if it'll help this young lady and stop these terrible killings. But first you'll have to go down in my basement and bring up my trunk. It's too heavy for me to lift anymore. That's where I keep the family records. There are letters in there about Raymond. They're the most telling."

Elinger retrieved a large, gold-leafed trunk from the cellar and placed it near Ms. Walker's feet. The socialite opened the trunk and exposed stacks of letters, tattered Bibles, and yellowed documents. She reached in and withdrew a bundle of letters and browsed through them as she spoke. "My ancestors have been Baltimore Mayors, Maryland Senators, founders of educational systems, war heroes, famous inventors, police chiefs, railroad presidents, and confidants to George Washington. But then there's

Raymond Patrick, the genealogical cancer that's blackened my family for generations."

"We've been curious about his relationship with Edgar Allan Poe?" Elinger said. "Do you know anything about that?"

"Oh, yes," Ms. Walker replied. "Raymond met Poe while he was a typesetter—before he became a literary critic. He admired Poe's stories, but admiration doesn't really explain Raymond's feelings. It was something much more powerful. A godlike worship," she added as she retrieved a letter from the bundle in her hand. "This might help explain it. This was written by his mother when Raymond was about forty."

Ms. Walker settled back in her chair, holding the delicate letter with care and read it aloud:

My Dear Sister,

I received your letter of last Tuesday and with much pleasure read it three times. All is well with us except for dear Raymond. I do worry about him and watch over him as if he were still an infant. During the night whilst we sleep, Raymond's mind reaches a terrible fever as he reads the stories of a deceased writer he used to be under the same employ—a fellow named Edgar Poe. I know this to be true because often times, when I rise for a drink of water in the wee hours, I find Raymond awake, studying the works of this man. I have warned Raymond about the ruination of his health fore the lack of slumber, but he becomes agitated and tells me Edgar Allan Poe was the greatest writer who ever walked the earth! He says sleep be damned! Raymond claims these tales give him inspiration to live although they portray horrible deaths and human misery. Can you imagine that? It is mortifying to me, but I don't approach the subject anymore. I don't know when my poor boy sleeps. His shoutings still interrupt our life. He bellows at the top of his lungs talking to this dead Poe fellow. It chills me deeply. Of recent, I caught Raymond in our church's cemetery wandering about with a keen interest in the graves. For some time, he has favored a morbid fascination with death. He tells us that when he passes on, we shan't worry fore he will come back! I am at a loss but will keep him at home as long as I possibly can.

I do not wish for him to be locked up in one of those filthy houses for the insane. Although he is a man, he is still my boy. He was my first born who brought much joy to my life, and I cannot forsake him now or ever!

Ms. Walker folded the letter and slipped it back into its envelope. "It was after Raymond met Poe that he began to act strange," she said. "He followed Poe from periodical to periodical. No matter what magazine Poe wrote for, Raymond would find a job there as a printer or typesetter. He wanted to be Poe's friend and confidant, and I'm sure it made Poe uneasy. You can imagine, someone following you from job to job like that. Raymond went to great lengths to impress Poe, but it didn't work. When Poe shunned Raymond, Raymond started creating his own reality. At family picnics and social gatherings, he bragged that he was good friends with Poe and described the many things they did together. Raymond relived those moments in his mind, though they never existed. By the time Raymond was in his mid-forties, he was completely obsessed."

"What else did he do? The crazy stuff?" Renee asked.

"He quoted Poe's works in public like a village idiot,"

Ms. Walker replied. "He also impersonated Poe's voice and mannerisms and tried to master Poe's extensive vocabulary. But this was nothing compared to what he did later."

Reaching into the trunk, Ms. Walker grabbed another bundle of letters. She removed a rubber band and found the letter she wanted. "This will give you an example of how awful Raymond became. This was written by his younger sister, Julia, who still lived at home with her parents to help take care of him. I'll just read the part about him."

Ms. Walker opened the fragile letter carefully then read aloud:

We have really become worried about Raymond's untiring single mindedness of Edgar Poe. At our Halloween picnic, he shaved the hair from the top of his head to match Poe's receding hairline. This was horrifying enough, but then he dyed his beautiful red hair as black as the night sky with shoe leather dye so he would look like this deceased writer who was so obsessed with death! We can no longer care for Raymond, but Mama will not admit it yet. We are at wit's end not knowing the proper care for him, and I fear he will be put in a house for the insane. There are times when Raymond is most agreeable and sharp of mind, but there are periods when he is ungodly and more frightening than the devil himself! Sometimes he goes into the city for days at a time and returns in bloodied clothes. When he is at home, his behavior is ghastly. On Wednesday last, we found him in the cemetery digging up the remains of our recently dear departed neighbor, Mr. Hubbard. Raymond said he only wanted to ask Mr. Hubbard if he was cold. I'm afraid Raymond's brain has turned as sour as buttermilk left in the sun. I wish we could do more for him, and I pray for the wisdom to help him, but God does not answer me.

Ms. Walker folded the letter gingerly and slipped it into its envelope. "Raymond took his obsession to the grave," she added, placing the letter back into the trunk.

"How did he die?" Elinger asked.

"Pneumonia. While he was in an insane asylum," Ms. Walker explained. "He thought he was Poe and recited Poe's lines constantly. He slept very little and his body weakened. He got a cold that turned for the worst. His last words were: *Quote the raven nevermore.*"

"Right from Poe's grave marker," Renee commented.

"Raymond used to visit Poe's grave regularly," Ms. Walker said. "He even bought the plot next to Poe's and wanted to be buried there. He put it in his will."

Ms. Walker refilled her cup before she continued. "Raymond's mind was brilliant when he was young. Poe's stories seemed to release hidden fantasies in him. The civilized man in him was blotted out—only demons surfaced."

Leaning forward in her chair, Ms. Walker put the letters back into the trunk and closed its lid. "You said something earlier that made me know for sure that Raymond is involved in your case."

"What was that?" Elinger asked.

"The writing that comes through Ms. Holland," Ms. Walker replied. "You see, shortly after Poe died, Raymond decided to write. Not short stories or poems like Poe, but a Gothic novel about a series of killings, more horrific than Poe wrote—but he never finished it. He was almost done when he was caught and arrested for doing his ghastly research," she added, her eyes dulling with repulsion.

"Research?" Renee repeated.

"It's the reason he killed all those people," Ms. Walker said. "He was bringing more reality to the murders in his story by observing violent death first hand. He went out and killed people so he could write about each death more accurately."

Renee glanced at Elinger with a queasy expression. "Oh, my God…"

"He chose people similar to characters in his book and murdered them in ways that fit his story," Mrs. Walker continued. "And sometimes the killings were similar to the murders in Poe's works."

"How many people did he kill?" Renee asked.

"Twelve according to a police ledger I found," Elinger replied for Ms. Walker.

"You're a trifle short, Lieutenant," Ms. Walker countered. "It was closer to twenty-three."

"Twenty-three?" Elinger repeated in a tone of amazement.

"I know what the official records say, but the truth is in there," Ms. Walker confided, pointing at the trunk. "My family knew about the murders that were never connected to him. He took his book very seriously."

"Do you have a copy of it?" Elinger asked.

"No, his mother destroyed it. She didn't want it around for fear it would only bring more shame to her family."

"How long did Raymond research his book?" Renee asked, drinking the last of her coffee.

"About a year. The killing ended one night when the

police caught him disemboweling a young man with a butcher knife."

Ms. Walker set her tea cup on the table. Her lips began to tremble. Up to this moment, she had held in her emotions. "Raymond's murders were atrocious. He mangled and maimed his victims in horrifying ways. He killed children, teenagers, the middle-aged, and the infirmed. He shot them, stabbed them, hanged them, axed them, buried them alive, smothered them, strangled them and sliced them open. He beat one poor woman to death with a blacksmith's hammer." Ms. Walker stopped, waiting for her deep feeling of disgust to subside.

"Why didn't anyone know about the other murders?" Elinger asked.

"My ancestors were very influential, Lieutenant," Ms. Walker replied candidly. "They had connections with the press and government." She shook her head with a sad thought. "All those poor dead people and their families never knew who killed them."

"What was the outcome of his trial?" Elinger asked. "We couldn't find that."

"It never finished," Ms. Walker answered. "Being incarcerated meant Raymond couldn't finish his book. It was more than he could bear. He became a raving madman and was committed to an institution with my ancestors' blessings. Then he died shortly thereafter."

"May I borrow your records Ms. Walker?" Elinger asked. "I want to learn everything I can about Patrick."
Ms. Walker had expected the request. "Yes, especially if they can help you save Ms. Holland's life and others. That's far more

important than my rank in social circles."

The officer in the prowl car nodded dutifully as Elinger drove past. Renee, sitting on the passenger seat, felt secure knowing armed policemen were parked outside her house. She was confident he and the other officers would protect her should Leonard Ravnik come to her home.

A cigarette dangled from the corner of veteran officer Murphy's mouth as he paced Renee's front porch. A taser stun gun was clipped to his belt and a shotgun leaned against the house near him. Alert, he scanned the front yard, thinking of survival should the killer make an appearance.

In the living room, Elinger and Renee found Alex asleep on the couch. The room was lighted only by the television screen that played a vintage episode of *Hawaii Five-0.* Renee unfolded a comforter that was lying on the back of the couch and spread it over Alex.

"I want to read the letters and more stories by Poe," Elinger whispered, clicking off the television. "I want to find out if Poe and Patrick had anything in common."

Before Renee could respond, her head jerked backward and a searing bolt of pain shot across her skull. Her eyes fluttered, and Elinger slipped his arms under Renee's shoulders. But she pulled away and walked in a stupor toward the staircase.

Renee's guttural moans awakened Alex. He jumped up from the couch. "What's going on?"
Elinger didn't need to answer. He simply pointed at Renee who was half way up the stairs by now.

Elinger and Alex followed Renee into her den and watched her sit in front of her computer. She was a mindless puppet again, her eyes cocked toward the ceiling. Renee turned on the system and began to tap the keyboard rapidly.

Powerless to stop the trance, Elinger and Alex could only observe and hope Renee would survive this one. Words rocketed across the screen as Renee's finger's zigzagged across the keyboard.

In a few seconds, Renee slumped in her chair as though someone had suddenly yanked her spine from her body. Her milky complexion began to color as a steady flow of blood nourished her brain again. She regained consciousness and unlocked her sightless gaze.

"You okay, Mom?" Alex asked.

"I think so," Renee mumbled weakly.

Renee steadied her hands on the arms of the chair and stood on wobbly legs. She hugged Elinger with one arm and placed the other around Alex, pulling them close to her. She managed a feeble smile with her pale lips. "What would I do without my two big strong men to protect me?"

The printer suddenly powered up and printed out what Renee had written. It was a note from Raymond Patrick.

After easing Renee back into her chair, Elinger took the sheet from the printer and read it aloud:

Good Evening, Madam Holland and Detective Elinger:
I have learned something very unexpected from Madam Holland's mind. You have broken the will of my great-great-great-great granddaughter. I must commend you for that. It does prove you are not fortuitous in your investigation, Detective Elinger. I

fancy you are as worthy of praise as Edgar's C. Auguste Dupin, but fore now I have a more extra-ordinary test for you.

Every respectable mystery requires a sterling policeman such as yourself to represent the virtuous—and, of course, every tale requires a demoniac creation of evil such as myself. The moral opposing the feral—add a dash of melodrama and the excitement of the drama regards no boundaries. I am fully prepared for the finale where it is much predisposed that good defeats evil. But, ere long, this will not be the result of our engagement. It is you who will be at my feet, Lieutenant. Fore you, like every soul trapped in flesh, possess character flaws; the curse of the mortal—a weakness that will destroy your ability to defeat me—and I fancy that will disturb you immensely. By now you must know I am about to finish my book. I will dedicate it to Edgar Poe, and he will be extremely proud of me when he learns of my success.

Would you dare not agree my story is more realistic than his? I shall call it THE DEVIL'S KILLER because to most mortals my work will be remembered as that of the devil! I look forward to meeting both of you when I bring you to the gulf beyond where you can join Edgar Poe and me.

> *- Your devoted adversary, Raymond Patrick.*

Elinger's vision scraped the words from the page like a razor. He dissected every syllable, every sentence, searching for a hint of a flaw that could betray him—but the note yielded no Achilles' heel.

A balloon of worry crowded Elinger's mind. He did not want to fail Renee again. And his concern was with good reason. Many predictions in earlier messages had already come true.

FIFTY-EIGHT

• • •

It was a few minutes after midnight when Elinger looked through Renee's large living room window. Some of the house lights shined through other windows, illuminating the front yard. The outdoor bulbs surrounding the lawn also glowed brightly, resembling floor-mounted theater lights. The yard looked like a green felt stage ready for a play to begin. It was fitting, Elinger reasoned, with his case being like surrealistic theater. Elinger recalled what Shakespeare had once written—*all the world's a stage and all the men and women merely players.* He hoped he was close to the final curtain of the play that involved him so he could stop the loss of more innocent lives.

At the rear of the house, a young officer finished patrolling the grounds and approached his duty station on the back porch. Like Murphy, a stun gun was attached to his belt. He called the prowl car out front with his shoulder mounted radio and reported everything was normal.

Elinger closed the living room window curtains and returned to the dining room. He sat on a chair where a few of Poe's books were stacked on the dining table. Ms. Walker's trunk was on the floor nearby. Its contents, the ancestral letters, were scattered near the books. Elinger had read many of them and learned of more atrocities committed by Raymond Patrick. Patrick's consciousness was far more evil than he originally thought, even more wicked than Leonard Ravnik. He was combating two cunning, vicious killers in one body.

Elinger picked up a book and began to read. Since Patrick was writing to emulate Poe, Elinger hoped Poe's works might reveal clues to the case. He was searching for character actions similar to Ravnik's behavior or Patrick's recorded behavior. He also probed for story incidents that matched anything in the current spate of killings. It was a long shot, he knew, but he would try anything that might help him outwit the killer.

Elinger read several stories. As he finished *The Pit and the Pendulum*, his cell phone rang.

"You're gonna love this!" Torres reported in an excited tone through the phone. "Tyler came through! We're gonna get Harrison tonight!"

With the case's latest developments, Elinger had temporarily thrown the unscrupulous attorney into the backyard of his mind. But when he took a moment and considered all the reasons he wanted to put Sidney Harrison behind bars, he was elated.

"That's great, Ralph," Elinger said, charging his words with zeal.

"Can you meet me at Headquarters?" Torres asked.

Before Elinger replied, he glanced through the kitchen rear window and watched his officer patrolling the grounds at the rear of Renee's property. Then he peered through the kitchen and watched Murphy's shadow ripple across the living room curtains. Satisfied his men could protect Renee if Ravnik came after her, Elinger decided it was safe to leave. The idea of nailing Harrison gave him a gung-ho-rookie-rush he hadn't experienced in a long time.

"I'm rolling now, Ralph," Elinger said.

Torres paced in the Headquarters' parking lot, glancing at his watch when Elinger's auto moved toward him. Elinger parked near Torres and emerged. "What's the setup?" he asked.

"Tyler wants us to hit the streets and give him a call on his cell," Torres replied.

"What's his plan?" Elinger asked.

"He just said he could make things happen tonight, but we needed to hurry."

"Okay, let's go," Elinger ordered enthusiastically.

Once Elinger and Torres were cruising city streets, Torres dialed Tyler's number, punched the speaker icon and handed his cell phone to Elinger.

"Yo, Lieutenant," Tyler's voice suddenly squawked from the phone.

"What's going down?" Elinger asked pointedly.

"We still got our deal?"

"Nothing's going to change unless you screw up."

"Chill out, man. We'll get 'im," Tyler promised. "I got some uncut *China White*. Lots of it."

"No doubt, but we're missing Harrison. He should be with the heroin," Elinger said impatiently.

"I know, man. I tried tellin' him he'd have to take the load hisself 'cause I was sick. But that didn't fly," Tyler said in a reluctant voice. "He said he didn't care if I was going to die—I still had to do the job myself."

Elinger was in no mood to play games. "Tyler, you better not be fuckin' with us!"

"I ain't' fuckin' with ya. I'm the one who's got everything to lose. Remember? Where are you?"

"Madison Street," Elinger said.

"I'm on Cathedral. I'll meet'cha where they cross. You already know what my ride looks like."

Elinger wove in and out of traffic and within minutes, he and Torres spotted Tyler's black 60s sedan. Elinger pulled out onto Cathedral and cruised about twenty yards behind Tyler's auto.

Elinger tapped the horn to draw Tyler's attention and pulled ahead, closer to the Tyler's auto. "Give him a call," he asked Torres.

Torres dialed and handed the cell phone to Elinger.

Tyler's voice came through the phone speaker. "Hey, back off, man. You're steppin' on my tail."

"What's your plan to put Harrison with the heroin?" Elinger asked, impatient again.

"I'm still thinkin' on it."

"Then we're going to have to do it my way," Elinger warned without hesitation.

Elinger hung up the phone, stepped on the gas, and pulled alongside Tyler's pristine auto on the passenger side. He began to edge his auto toward Tyler's vehicle until his tires were on the line that divides the lanes. The whites of Tyler's eyes grew large when he saw the fender of Elinger's auto was only inches from the side of his classic car. He leaned over his seat and rolled down the passenger window. "What the fuck are you doin', man!?" he shouted in a nervous voice.

Elinger smiled lopsidedly. "We can either have an accident or you can have car trouble. Either way, Harrison won't want his load parked on the street."

Elinger steered his sedan even closer to Tyler's car. Tyler steered further away from Elinger's auto and started to cross the double yellow line into oncoming traffic.

"Fuckin' up my wheels wasn't part of the deal, dog!" he yelled at Elinger from inside his vehicle.

"Accident or car trouble. You call it," Elinger shouted back at Tyler.

"Okay, okay, car trouble!" Tyler yelled.

Elinger pulled into his lane and slowed his auto, giving Tyler room to steer his shiny car off the street and park. Elinger pulled in behind him.

Elinger emerged from his vehicle and moved to the front of Tyler's car. He opened the hood, reached in and yanked out the coil wire. He moved to the driver's window, looked in at Tyler and tossed him the wire.

Tyler put the wire in the glove compartment. "Okay, I'll call Harrison," he said. "Just go hide yourselves and lemme get to it."

Elinger climbed back into his car and inscribed a U-turn across several traffic lanes. He parked across the street under a large tree that shadowed his car from the street lamps.

Elinger and Torres watched as Tyler dialed his cell phone

and began a conversation. In less than fifteen seconds, he was gesticulating wildly, obviously embroiled in a furious argument.

"Guess they have a warm and understanding partnership?" Torres said in a wry voice.

When Tyler finished his call, he extended a hand from the driver's window and gave the detectives a thumbs-up sign.

Elinger nodded. "Harrison must be on his way. Let's get Tyler on the line."

Torres dialed and passed the phone to Elinger.

"He's comin', man," Tyler reported through the phone in a nervous timbre. "What if he finds out what you did to the car?"

"He won't have time," Elinger replied.

"Why?"

"Because you're going to tell him you already called for a tow truck," Elinger said. "He'll have to take the dope himself. He won't want it towed off with your car."

Tyler's eyes lit up. "That'll work, but he's sure gonna hate my ass!"

"It's about time you got a new set of friends anyway," Elinger said. "Leave your cell line open so we can hear what's going on."

"Yo, anything you say, Lieutenant. I just wanna be done with this and start my new life. I also wanna get the fuck away from you!"

Minutes later, Harrison's expensive auto glided to a halt behind Tyler's vintage auto. Sidney Harrison emerged from his car and glanced cautiously down both ends of the street. Once he was sure he was not being watched, he moved to the rear of Tyler's vehicle. Tyler slid out from his car and met him there.

"What's the matter with your car?" Harrison asked, studying the Tyler's auto.

"You got me," Tyler replied. "One minute she's purrin' like fine pussy and the next minute, she's as dead as road kill."

"Let's take a look," Harrison said. He started to move to the front of the vehicle, but Tyler stepped in front of him.

"We don't have time," Tyler warned. "I called for a tow truck. It should be here any minute."

Harrison's face twisted with anger. "We've got a hundred grand worth of shit in the car, and you called for a tow truck!"

"I was afraid a cop might come by," Tyler lied. "You know I've got a rap sheet. They might search the car." Harrison clinched his fists. Although he was angered, he knew Tyler made sense.

"Look, just take the stuff and get it out of here. No fuss, no muss, man," Tyler said.

Harrison hesitated, shooting a worried glance up and down the street again, then finally nodding. "It's going to be a long time before we do business again."

"I understand, bro," Tyler replied, then removed a large briefcase from his auto's trunk and passed it to the attorney.

Harrison opened the case and studied the heroin-filled plastic bags jammed in the case.

Tyler began to strut away, like a rooster with a cork up its ass. "Go on, man. Get that shit outta here!" Tyler said, throwing the words over his shoulder.

"Where are you going?" Harrison asked, closing the

briefcase. "What about your car? You've spent thousands on it and you're just going to leave it here?" When Tyler didn't answer, a look of sudden regret tightened Harrison's face. He realized he had been set up.

From across the street, Elinger and Torres could see what was happening.

"He's dirty, Ralph. Let's take him!" Elinger ordered.

"*Vamos, amigo!*"

Elinger started his car's engine and punched the accelerator to the floor. The auto lunged from the curb and screamed across four lanes of honking and swerving traffic.

Harrison whirled in the direction of the sounds and squinted into the headlights zooming toward him. Glimpsing the no-frills unmarked police sedan, he shot a quick look of murderous animosity toward Tyler who was now sprinting up the street. Now he looked down at the briefcase full of bagged heroin in his hand.

Harrison's eyes darted about wildly, looking desperate. He saw the open mouth of a flood drain at the curb. The bars that prevent objects from dropping into the city's subterranean drainage system were bent and broken, leaving a gaping hole. Harrison's face brightened. He swung the case and pitched it toward the drain. The briefcase hit the pavement and skidded toward the opening.

Elinger watched in mortified silence. If the case dropped into the sewers, he knew it would float away and probably never be recovered. Harrison's culpability to a drug deal would be literally down the drain.

"No, dammit!" Elinger shouted, steering his auto and gluing his eyes on the briefcase sliding toward the sewer.

The briefcase skidded onto the edge of the metal grating and stopped only inches from the opening.

"There is justice in the world after all," Torres said through a breath of relief.

Harrison hustled to his auto and swung open the driver's door. At the same moment, Elinger drove his car into the side of Harrison's car, slamming the door shut on one of Harrison's hands.

Harrison screamed. His fingers were crushed in the door jam. Pain streaked up his arm like shafts of high voltage. He froze at the door, unable to move.

"This is the second bit of justice you've seen in your career, Ralph," Elinger said as he and Torres jumped from their car.

Elinger and Torres moved to Harrison whose face was a mask of agony.

"Guess this means you'll have to cancel your piano lessons, Sidney," Elinger said dryly, looking at the attorney's hand stuck in the door jam.

Harrison stood there, shaking and glaring through a bloodless expression at Elinger. "Back up your fucking car, Elinger!" he raged. "You sonovabitch!"

"I didn't hear please," Elinger said.

Harrison didn't comply.

Elinger knew Harrison was not about to surrender his pride. Elinger looked into Harrison's face that seemed to be on fire with hostility.

"You're going to burn for this!" Harrison shouted.

"Just say please, and I'll move the car." Elinger repeated, not giving an inch.

Harrison's vision shifted to his hand. The first two joints

of his fingers disappeared into the door seam. Blood trickled down and began to pool on the street.

"Don't worry about it, Harrison," Torres said in a nonchalant tone. "Doctors do miracles with plastic surgery these days."

Harrison knifed Torres with his look. "I'll have your scrawny brown ass, too, you fucking spic!"

Elinger approached the attorney with an amused look. "I can't believe you said that, Sidney. Most of your career you've been fighting for the rights of minorities, and now we find out you're a closet bigot."

Harrison gave Elinger a smoldering look, and then spewed out his words. "Right now, you can abuse your authority and defile my civil liberties—but when we're in the courtroom, I'm going to wipe that smirk off your face and shove it up your ass along with your badge!"

Elinger smiled confidently. "Don't place your bets yet, Sidney."

Torres moved to the storm drain, retrieved the briefcase, and opened it in front of Elinger and Harrison. Looking at the bags of heroin, Elinger smiled in total victory. He knew Sidney Harrison would be dead meat in the courtroom.

Elinger glanced up at the attorney. What he had to say would bring him great joy. "You're moving a lot of weight, Sidney. You get extra years for that."

"This is entrapment," Harrison countered in a feeble tone.

Elinger smiled triumphantly again. Harrison's argument had no spine. "Wrong, Sidney. This is the most righteous bust of my career. And any judge in the state is going to give you the max because they all hate your fucking guts like I do."

Elinger turned to Torres. "Read him his rights, Ralph. Make sure he gets the full benefit of the law. Something the innocent people who've been murdered, conned and robbed by the scum he's put back on the streets never had!"

After sucking in a few breaths, Harrison fired his thoughts at Elinger. "You're no better than they are, Elinger!" he sneered. "You are breaking the law! Police brutality! Use of excessive force! You're out of control under the color of authority! This thing you have for me is an obsession!"

Elinger's face clouded suddenly. Harrison's words became seeds in his mind and grew quickly. His fixation on Harrison was indeed an obsession, he realized. And slamming the attorney's hand in the door jam with his vehicle was indeed excessive force and could be considered police brutality. Maybe he was screwing up his career over a few minutes of personal satisfaction? Then a lone thought soared through Elinger's mind and blocked out all others. Raymond Patrick's note warned him that a character flaw would cause him to lose his battle with Patrick. Was it his fixation on Harrison? Had he mindlessly left Renee and Alex vulnerable to an attack by Ravnik and Patrick because of it?

Elinger bolted for his car. Snatching the police radio mike, he called the police sentries at Renee's home. His worst fears began to materialize. At first, he received no response, then Murphy came on line. His words were staccato gasps, the sounds of a dying man. "He's here, Lieutenant… I heard screams in the house…" After a few more raspy breaths, the line became quiet.

Slamming down the mike, Elinger was overcome with

personal condemnation. He ignited the engine of his vehicle, backed its nose out of Harrison's car and freed Harrison's hand. The vehicle barreled into traffic, leaving behind a billowing roll of smoke.

Choking on the fumes of exhaust and melted rubber, Torres watched Elinger's sudden departure with a look of bewilderment.

Harrison studied the first joints of his fingers that looked like hamburger. He withdrew the silk scarf from his suit coat pocket and wrapped his fingers, grimacing with each twist of the cloth.

FIFTY-NINE

● ● ●

When Renee heard gunshots shatter the night, she was adjusting the burning logs in her fireplace with a poker. She thought her police guards had killed Leonard Ravnik. But when she heard someone trying to kick-in her front door, she panicked, fearing the nightmare that stalked her was now breaking into her home. Renee bolted up the stairs and into Alex's room. She pulled her sleeping and suddenly startled son from his bed. She clamped a hand over his mouth then placed a finger across her lips to let him know to keep quiet. Alex nodded that he understood.

Renee quickly ushered Alex out of his room and into the den. As they went, they heard the front door give away and crash down into the living room. Renee pulled Alex into the den closet with her, hoping it would be a safe place to hide. They burrowed deep behind the hanging clothes. Renee hugged her son, wondering why the police guards hadn't stopped Ravnik.

And where was Kent? She had awakened when she heard him drive away earlier that night. Probably a new clue to investigate, Renee had guessed. Unable to sleep after that, she had gone downstairs and started a fire in the fireplace. She wanted to read by its warmth with hopes it would make her sleepy. Her concentration was thin and unfocused, however. With Elinger gone, Renee could not relax.

Renee's nostrils were assaulted by the harsh odor of naphthalene from the mothballs in the closet. This, mixed with the smell of cedar, caused Renee's stomach to churn. She swallowed hard, hoping she wouldn't vomit in the small space.

The sound of footsteps plodding up the stairs struck more terror in Renee. She heard Ravnik entering her den and walking its parameters. The steps halted outside the closet. Trembling, Renee knew she needed a weapon to protect herself and Alex if they were discovered. She groped in the dark and found a wire coat hanger. She turned it into a crude weapon by straightening its hook, bending it in half for strength and stretching its body like the shaft of a spear. When the closet doors suddenly flew open, she was ready.

Renee lunged forward, stabbing at Leonard Ravnik's cold, emotionless expression. The hanger pierced Ravnik's cheek and bored into his tongue. He snarled, cursed, then spit blood on Renee's face as he yanked the wire from his mouth. He grabbed Renee's hair and yanked her screaming from the closet. As she went, she pushed Alex deep into the closet with her foot, hoping Ravnik would not notice him.

Struggling in the powerful grip, Renee dug her fingernails into Ravnik's cheeks, filling her nails with flesh.
Snarling again, Ravnik pitched Renee to the floor.

Renee watched Ravnik as he wiped the blood dripping through the hole in his cheek and licked it from his fingers. She could see by the look on this face that his pain seemed to be diminishing. It was like he was suddenly strong and pain-free.

Catching her breath, Renee jumped up and bolted for the door, wanting to draw Ravnik farther from her son. Ravnik dove at her, reached for her ankles and tripped her. Renee stumbled into the hallway and started a long fall down the staircase. Screaming as she tumbled, her head and limbs bounced on the wooden stairs. Racked with pain, she crumpled on the living room floor. She glanced around the room, frantically searching for something she could use to protect herself. She saw the fireplace poker she had left in the fire. Its tip rested in hot ashes, glowing an amber-orange.

Though sharp pains knifed through her back, Renee lifted herself from the floor and crawled toward the hearth. She looked up in time to see Ravnik throw Alex over the second-floor hallway railing. Alex landed on the couch and bounced onto a nearby coffee table. He hit the solid walnut with his right shoulder, then dropped to the floor groaning and holding his arm.

"You son-of-a-bitch!" Renee shouted at Ravnik as he bounded down the stairs toward her.

Renee glanced fearfully back at Alex. Although Alex's face was stretched tight with pain, his hands were clutching his shoulder where it had hit the table.

"Are you all right, Alex?" Renee asked urgently.

Alex looked at his mom and nodded slowly through the anguish contorting his face.

Satisfied with Alex's answer, Renee turned from him and crawled closer to the fireplace.

Ravnik rushed Renee from behind as she reached the fireplace. Ravnik grabbed her by the hips just as she lurched forward and curled her fingers around the handle of the hot poker.

She spun around in Ravnik's grip and jabbed the sharp iron into Ravnik's crotch. The hot tip burned through Ravnik's pants and stabbed his scrotum.

Growling with pain, Ravnik yanked the poker from Renee's grip and pulled it from between his legs. He cast a murderous look at Renee while blood trickled from his cheek and smoke curled from his pants.

● ● ●

Across town, Elinger's mind revved like the engine of his car as he sped recklessly across city streets. He couldn't believe he had jeopardized Renee's and Alex's safety because of a scumbag like Sidney Harrison! Why didn't he heed the warning in Patrick's note? His flaw was so obvious now.

Elinger, still wrestling with his thoughts, shot through a red light at a crowded intersection. When he realized what he'd done, he jerked the steering wheel to the right and skidded to avoid a collision with another car. A discordant orchestra of blaring horns and screeching rubber greeted his errant maneuver. When he finished his sweep through the crossing, he zigzagged through a spread of scattered cars and resumed his fear-fueled journey to Renee's home.

When Elinger reached Renee's street, he slid to a scudding halt next to the prowl car parked in front of Renee's house. He jumped from his vehicle and looked inside the prowl car. The officer was slumped sideways on the seat. His head was in deep shadows. Elinger slid his hand under the policeman's arm and pulled him into a sitting position. Now, under the glow of a street lamp, Elinger could see the officer's head was limply cocked to the side. His neck had been broken.

Elinger didn't see brutality like this often. Outrage roiled through his body. The feeling confirmed his intense hatred for Leonard Ravnik.

Elinger sprinted across the yard toward Renee's darkened home. When he reached the front porch, he saw Murphy sprawled on the steps. Murphy's chest heaved with short, choppy breaths. A pale tone painted his face.

Kneeling at Murphy's side, Elinger noticed a large hole in Murphy's chest near his heart. It was a close-range shotgun blast. He knew the wound would be fatal.

Murphy slowly opened his eyes and focused his blurred vision on Elinger. "Jesus, I'm cold," Murphy sputtered weakly through blue lips. "I've never been so fucking cold."

"I'm sorry," Elinger offered in a low, remorseful tone, feeling responsible for what happened.

Murphy shook his head slightly. "If I could've, I would've blown away that sonovabitch no matter what you told us to do."

Elinger glanced at Murphy's wound that now oozed a pink bubbly froth. He was torn between two emotions. He wanted to kill Ravnik for what he'd done to his officers—but another part of him needed Ravnik alive so he could destroy Raymond Patrick and break Renee from his control.

"Where's Renee?" Elinger asked, fearing what the answer might be.

"Never saw her," Murphy replied, his voice a whisper now. "He jumped me—from the roof—before I could do anything."

Elinger looked across the lawn and saw the body of the officer who patrolled the rear of Renee's house. Two fist-sized shotgun wounds had decimated his back. This officer was young, Elinger knew, just beginning his career. A wife and young kids left behind. More reason to loath Leonard Ravnik.

Murphy's eyes closed and his chest stilled. With a determined and sorrowful look, Elinger stood up and glanced at Renee's house. He looked at the puny .38 revolver tucked in his holster, knowing it was no match for Ravnik's arsenal. Elinger moved to the young officer's body and retrieved his shotgun. Elinger pumped a round into the chamber. He was ready for war.

Moving toward the front door, Elinger recalled his previous encounters with Ravnik. His suspect's ferocity and uncanny strength made him wonder if he could survive another confrontation.

Elinger jumped over the splintered front door and dove into the living room. From a crouching position, he surveyed the blackened interior. The moon, shining through a large window, silhouetted overturned furniture, evidence of Renee's struggle with Ravnik. Elinger stood and flipped on a light switch, but the room remained dark. Ravnik had obviously cut the power.

After searching the rooms on the first floor of the house and finding no one, Elinger moved toward the staircase, praying Renee and Alex were still alive should he find them. He mounted the stairs, thinking each step could be his last if Ravnik was hiding in the dark.

Entering Renee's bedroom cautiously, Elinger pointed the shotgun at the room's darkest corners—but no one was there. He threw open the closet's double doors and pushed the barrel of his weapon into the clothes, probing, but found no one.

Elinger headed for Renee's den next. Hugging the door jam, he slid into the room. Renee's computer was on, its glow spilling light into the space. After a cautious patrol of the room and inspection of the closet, Elinger discovered no one.

As Elinger walked down the stairs, his mind was a tumult of emotion. What had happened to Renee and Alex? Did Leonard Ravnik kill them? The last question was self-recriminating. If he had been here instead of pursuing Harrison, Elinger reasoned, maybe he could have saved them.

When Elinger reached the living room, he heard a whimper from a closet nearby. With his heart pumping pure adrenaline, he yanked open the closet door and leveled the shotgun at the closet's interior. There was movement behind the hanging clothes and Elinger quickly tightened his finger on the shotgun's trigger—but he eased up when he saw who was in the closet.

Sobbing, Alex walked toward him, with his left hand holding his right shoulder. When Alex opened his mouth to speak, there was no sound. Elinger realized terror had paralyzed the boy's vocal cords.

SIXTY

● ● ●

With a dazed and frightened look on his face, Alex took a few steps toward Elinger. In a few seconds, his complexion began to pink and his tense eyes relaxed slightly.

Elinger lowered the shotgun and studied Alex's tear streaked cheeks. It made him feel worse about leaving Alex and his mother. "Are you all right, Alex?" Elinger asked.

Alex opened his mouth to speak, and this time his voice worked. "I think so, but my shoulder hurts really bad."

Elinger placed a fatherly hand on Alex's head. "Where's your mother?"

"The one-eared man took her away," Alex replied, his face twisting into a mold of incredulity. "Where were you? Why weren't you here to help us?"

"I was on a call. I'm sorry, Alex," Elinger replied, hoping he was spared further questioning.

Pulling his cell phone from his pocket, Elinger called Headquarters and reported to Jay Sanders that Leonard Ravnik had kidnapped Renee Holland, and that he wanted every officer alerted, even those off duty, to conduct an all-out search to find Renee. He also requested an ambulance for Alex.

"You need to tell me everything you can remember, Alex," Elinger said, pushing his cell phone back into his pocket.

Before Alex spoke, an emotional shadow eclipsed his face. "If you had stayed here my mother would probably be okay," he accused in a harsh tone.

Alex's words echoed Elinger's own thoughts and it pained him deeply. "You're right. I shouldn't have left. I thought you and your mother would be safe with my officers."

Alex stared at Elinger for a long moment, his features softening a bit. "I'm really worried about my mom," Alex finally admitted, hearing sirens approaching.

"Don't worry, Alex. I'm going to find your mother," Elinger vowed. "Now tell me everything that happened."

Alex drew in a breath and explained the events of the evening. The muffled cry in the night, heavy footsteps on the roof, shotgun blasts from the front and rear of the house, his mother fighting Ravnik and how he was thrown over the balcony railing.

Jay Sanders stepped into the living room with six uniformed officers and two paramedics. Also at his side was Detective Brown, a middle-aged balding man with thick rimmed glasses.

Elinger ushered Alex to the medical team and asked them to check Alex's shoulder.

"Toss the house and see if there's anything here that might tell us where he took Renee," Elinger told Sanders.

"You got it," Sanders replied and turned to Detective Brown and the officers behind him. "Vacuum cleaner mode, guys.

Let's do it!" Sanders, Brown, and the men spread out to begin their search.

Elinger turned toward the broken-down front door as Captain Osborne walked in. At his side was Willard Montagna.

Elinger had not seen Montagna for almost a year. It was rare for him to appear on a crime scene. Elinger didn't remember him being as short as the five-foot seven he was. His thick blond hair was combed straight back and slicked down with styling gel. The graying on his temples added extra years to his youthful thirty-six. Elinger couldn't help but think that Montagna looked like an aging California surfer who was stranded on the East Coast.

"We need to talk, Kent," Osborne said, motioning for Elinger to join him and Montagna in a corner of the room.

"I've been briefed and everybody's rolling on this, Kent," Osborne reported. "A BOLO will hit the streets within minutes. Every available man is pounding the pavement to find Renee Holland. We found Leonard Ravnik's place a little while ago. Over in The Block. Doesn't look like he's been there in a while though. We've got the place staked out just the same, and we're knockin' on every door in the area."

Montagna pulled expensive kid gloves from his hands. Their caramel color matched his long-tailed cashmere overcoat. "What I want to know, Lieutenant," Montagna began in a cynical tone, "is how can this guy slip through you and your men? The Captain won't tell me much. He's been covering your ass but now his dump truck is out of gas. So, you tell me. How could this scumbag kill three of your best and get in here?"

"He's not your typical bad guy," was Elinger's simple answer.

"I need details, Lieutenant," Montagna said, slapping his gloves sharply on the palm of his hand. "I want a full report. Now!"

"You think I'm going to stop what I'm doing to write you a report?"

Montagna's voice was as icy as Canadian snow. "You don't have any choice. That's an order!"

"Not until we find Renee Holland," Elinger argued, his voice bristling with anger.

"Yes, I understand your special concern for her," Montagna commented in a condescending tone. "Very unprofessional."

Elinger's face stiffened. "You know, I've always wanted to tell you what a putz you are. So, let me take this opportunity. You are a fucking putz!"

Montagna's face became a menacing frown. "You better tell me everything you know. I'm tired of your little secrets. I don't have the patience of your Captain and neither does the Mayor. Now what the hell is going on?'

"You'd have me measured for a net if I told you," Elinger said curtly.

"You'll be measured for a blue uniform and put back on the street if you don't tell me—right here—right now!" Osborne gave Elinger a sobering stare. "The point is, Kent, Montagna and the Mayor want the truth. And you know something, it is their right to know. Go ahead and tell him."

Elinger evened his gaze at Osborne. The Captain was right about one thing. It was time for the facts. He was tired of keeping secrets. "Okay, Cap, I'll tell the Mayor's little errand boy

the truth. But there are some things you don't know about either."
Elinger rolled his look toward Montagna. "Leonard Ravnik is
being mentally controlled by another murderer named Raymond
Patrick. The kicker is—Raymond Patrick has been dead for over a
hundred and fifty years. Call it channeling, possession, whatever,
but this Raymond Patrick is killing people through Leonard
Ravnik. He's writing a book and the killings are his way of doing
research, to make his grisly descriptions of the murders more real."

Montagna stared sharply at Elinger. "What are you—
fucking nuts? I can't tell the Mayor this kind of nonsense!"

"No shit," Elinger agreed, studying Montagna's stupefied
expression. He also noticed Osborne's face had become equally
disbelieving.

"I warned you, Cap," Elinger reminded Osborne. "I
didn't believe it at first either but that's what's happening," Elinger
explained. His face became immobile to make sure both men
understood what he said was no joke.

Montagna gave Elinger a sidelong glance. "You've
obviously been overworked, Lieutenant," Montagna surmised,
shoving his gloves into his coat pocket then turning to Osborne.
"Take him off the case and get him to our shrink before he loses it
completely."

Elinger cocked his brow at Montagna. "I'm going to
follow through on this whether I'm a police officer or a civilian,"
he warned.

The Deputy Mayor's face glowed with growing fury.
"You'll be in jail if you fuck with me, Lieutenant!"

Elinger removed his badge and handed it to Captain
Osborne. "I'll make it easy for you, Cap. This will take the heat off

your ass for a while."

Osborne stared balefully at the shield in his hand. "This isn't what I want, Kent."

"Well, I don't want to screw-up your retirement," Elinger replied as he retrieved the Colt 2-inch from his belt and handed it to Osborne. "No telling what this prick will do to you if I don't obey his precious orders."

Montagna snatched the badge and gun from Osborne's hand and put them in his coat pocket. "I'm glad you have enough sense to cooperate, Lieutenant."

"This makes me feel lower than an asshole in a Tokyo crapper," Osborne mumbled to Elinger.

"Don't lose any sleep over it, Cap," Elinger said. "We've been through too much for me to take this personally."

Osborne started to respond but was distracted by a sound from upstairs. Renee's computer had suddenly started printing. The sounds of the printer were unmistakable.
Elinger spun from Osborne and Montagna and dashed up the stairs, knowing whatever was printed might contain new information from Raymond Patrick and possibly details of Renee's abduction.

Alex pulled himself from the paramedics nearby and followed Elinger with his right arm in a sling.
Osborne and Montagna hurried up the stairs on the heels of Elinger.

When Osborne and Montagna stepped into Renee's den, they halted suddenly. Words were flying across the computer screen without an operator at the keyboard. The keyboard keys were clicking down on their pads, pushed by invisible hands. As Osborne and Montagna watched the phenomena unfolding before

486

them, their expressions became frozen with disbelief.

Accustomed to the strange occurrences in Renee's den, Elinger watched in reserved awe, aware the computer's electricity was triggered by a physical manifestation of Raymond Patrick's thoughts.

Elinger then gave Montagna and Osborne an over-the-shoulder, wise-guy look. "I hope you're beginning to understand the reason for my little secrets," he said, looking at the men's expressions, noticing they had quickly become believers.

The printer suddenly turned on by itself and two pages emerged from the printer.

Elinger removed the sheets and read the newest message from Raymond Patrick:

Dear Detective Elinger:

If I may beg your notice, it appears I have fatigued you and that staggers my senses. All this time I have regarded you as indefatigable. Perhaps I have unstrung your sinewy nerves with my fanciful mind? Ha! Like you, I am remiss about your character flaw, but I did fairly caution you. Such a pity! But alas! I am desirous to give you one final opportunity to participate in the thrilling conclusion of my little tale.

I suppose you are wondering why I have created this fanciful narrative from the gulf beyond? You see, I have an insatiable craving to impress my mentor, Edgar Poe. And I am sure you agree that I will be successful. My work is every bit as horrifying as anything he penned. I have conversed with Edgar over here, you know, but his time away from his pen has weakened his fiery spirit. He had so much more to write. His premature demise robbed your world of literary riches it will never know. Methought I would brighten the inner chambers of his soul by dedicating my book to him. Hence, when I receive my proper accolades, Edgar will have no choice but to respect me! And that, Detective Elinger, brings to mind a paramount problem. I must insure that Madam Holland does not infringe upon my destined right of authorship of my work. In your world, my writings may be misunderstood as a work resulting from the passionate efforts of Madam Holland! That is why I must bring her to me and assist her with a hasty retreat from your world. I have become very fond of her and want to be close to her.

I am truly apologetic about having my accomplice abduct your love—but all is fair in matters of love. Now don't tarry, Detective Elinger, fore we will make a game of your torturous demise. I have littered your path with clews and many have already passed before your very eyes. If you can unveil their secrets before the sun's first light, you might have a chance to save your precious love. But I must warn you, there will be a hell bound struggle of life and death betwixt you and me. And I will have the distinct advantage—fore I am already quite dead!

-Happy Hunting, Raymond Patrick

Elinger, Osborne, Montagna, and Alex took a moment to digest the information. Montagna was rendered speechless by what he had seen.

Elinger consulted his watch. "The sun's first light," he repeated from the note. "That only gives me about three hours," he said, reaching into Montagna's coat pocket and retrieving his badge and revolver.

Osborne gave Montagna a hard look, then smiled at Elinger. "Don't worry about that report, Kent. You've got more important things to do right now, and I'm sure the Deputy Mayor agrees with me. Regardless, I'll back you a hundred percent," Osborne added, shaking his head and chuckling. "Christ! We're both gonna be walkin' the bricks in uniform again. It'll be like the ol' days before we were invaded by the starched shirts and pressed suits," he added, glancing at Montagna who was still speechless by what he had seen. "Let's go, Montagna. If the Mayor finds out you're here, you may have to explain all of this to him. And if you do, I want to be there," Osborne added with another chuckle.

Torres bounded up the stairs and scurried into the den as Osborne and Montagna exited the room. "Got here as soon as I heard, Kent," he said, out of breath. "I'm really sorry, man."

"I should've stayed with her," Elinger replied, handing Torres Patrick's note. "Here, see what you make of it?"

While Torres read the note, Elinger turned to Alex and saw his arm was in a sling. "Is your arm broken?" he asked.

Alex shrugged. "They said I need an X-Ray. They said it might be a cracked collar bone."

"Okay," Elinger said. "After your hospital visit, I'm going to send you to your father's while we look for your mother."

Alex flexed his brow with a look of indignation. "I can't go to my father's. He's in Europe."

"Then we'll take you to your grandparents."

"But I want to help," Alex pleaded. "She's my mother."

"I know, Alex," Elinger agreed. "But your injury would slow us down. I can't afford that and neither can your mom."

Alex nodded slowly in agreement.

"Detective Brown," Elinger called out, looking at a group of policemen not far from him and Alex.

"I need you to take Alex to the hospital for X-Rays, then take him to his grandparents," Elinger instructed quickly.

"You got it," Brown replied. "C'mon, son."

Alex followed Brown's lead to the door, then stopped and turned back toward Elinger. "Please save my mom," he asked with tearful eyes.

"I will Alex," Elinger pledged.

"Hey, Kent!" Sanders' voice boomed through the den window from the backyard. "We got something out here!"

With that, Elinger and Torres hustled out of the den, heading for the downstairs' back door.

Elinger and Torres emerged from the house into the back yard. Sanders was bent over, holding his flashlight beam on a piece of clothing. He lifted it from beneath a shrub and handed it to Elinger. It was a torn, blood spotted sleeve from Renee's night clothes. Elinger studied the blood stains and wondered how badly Renee was hurt. If she were bleeding, it meant she was alive at least. But this thought did little to comfort him.

"I'll take charge here, Jay," Elinger said with a pained expression.

"Okay, I'll check on the men inside," Sanders replied, moving off toward the house.

"This isn't your fault," Torres told Elinger.

"But Patrick was right," Elinger replied dismally. "My obsession with Harrison got in the way! My character flaw."

"We had armed officers here," Torres reminded Elinger.

"What could you have done that they couldn't?"

"Some of the blame is still mine."

"It'll be a lot easier for us to find Renee if you clear your head. You've always told me not to let my emotions interfere with my job."

Elinger knew Torres was right. He couldn't allow his thinking to impair his ability to search for Renee. It wasn't easy, but he gave himself a temporary pardon, hoping to wash the guilt from his mind.

A cool breeze skimmed across the property, fluttering leaves on the lawn. Elinger and Torres lifted their lapels to deflect the chill.

Elinger looked up and noticed the moon and stars were obscured by a fast-moving cloud front. The weather's murkiness reminded him that he hadn't generated any ideas on how to find Renee. Elinger felt like his brain had sprung a leak. Now when he needed it to be most creative, it was failing him.

"What'd you make of the note?" Elinger finally asked, blowing warmth onto his cupped hands. "You see anything in it that might tell us where to start looking?"

"Well, it says clues, spelled c-l-e-w-s, have passed before our very eyes. I haven't noticed any," Torres said as the men began to walk the boundaries of the property, probing the grounds with their eyes, searching for any physical clues that would be important for finding Renee.

"Dennington said these murders are every bit as morbid as anything Poe had created," Elinger began. "After what I've read of Poe, I agree. And Ms. Walker told us Raymond Patrick's M.O. and murders were similar to deaths in Poe's stories."

"I haven't read all of Poe's stories yet," Torres said.

"Well, I've been on a crash course the last few days. I've tried to compare the shipyard murders to Poe's works for similarities but couldn't find any," Elinger said.

"Yeah, the shipyard thing doesn't seem like Poe," Torres said. "I mean, a group of workers crushed by a huge block and tackle."

Elinger's thoughts suddenly rear-ended one another. He halted and turned to Torres who also stopped. "Wait a minute, Ralph. You said crushed. The men weren't crushed. The block and tackle weren't dropped on them. They were hit from the side."

Torres nodded. "What are you getting at?"

"Didn't a witness say the block and tackle was swaying back and forth just before it hit the men?"

"Yeah."

"Like a pendulum maybe?" Elinger speculated.

Torres' face took on an insightful look. "You mean pendulum as in *The Pit and the Pendulum?*"

"Did you read it?" Elinger asked.

"No, but I saw the movie on DVD."

"Well, there's no swinging block and tackle in the story, but there is a swinging axe. It swayed back and forth, closer and closer to the intended victim."

"I think you're stretchin' it a bit, Kent."

"Maybe, but Poe did a lot of stretching in his stories. Some critics think he was on the edge of farce," Elinger rebutted. "In one of his stories, a husband digs up his wife just for her teeth."

"Okay, he was a little weird."

Elinger moved on to his next thought. "Let's talk about

victim number two. The hooker. Can you think of a similar death in a Poe story?" he asked, walking again with Torres at his side.

"I don't remember anyone getting hit over the head with a bottle or being carved up with broken glass," Torres answered as a light gust rustled through his hair.

Elinger grinned. A revelation had just struck him. "I think this one has more to do with how and what she was buried with."

"She was buried in concrete."

"With a battery in her mouth," Elinger added pointedly.

"We never did figure out what the battery meant."

"It's the logo, Ralph," Elinger said, suddenly realizing. "The logo on the battery contains a black cat."

Torres felt the knowledge traveling from his brain to his mouth. "Jesus! In one of Poe's stories a woman was buried behind a brick and concrete wall with a cat?"

"*The Black Cat,*" Elinger said, knowing he was on to something.

"So that's why he left the battery in the hooker's mouth," Torres said. "Patrick made Ravnik mimic Poe in his own strange way."

Elinger nodded.

"What about the couple in the underground channel?" Torres asked. "Did Poe ever write about drainage systems?"

Elinger considered it a moment. "I don't think so, but he did write *A Descent into the Maelstrom*. It's about a ship trapped in a whirlpool."

"Interesting," Torres said. "If we hadn't saved the young couple, they would've drifted down the tunnel and into that big whirlpool we found."

"Right. And it could've killed them just like the sea captain in Poe's story."

"So why were we able to save them?" Torres asked. "I keep thinkin' Patrick let us. I mean, he's a friggin' ghost, and ghosts can do all kinds of weird things, right?"

"He can't control us or what we do," Elinger replied. "He can only influence Ravnik and Renee and use them to slow us down. And he can't always do that. That's why we can stop him."

Accepting Elinger's point-of-view, Torres returned to the original subject. "Okay, that's three murders down. What about Richard Smith?" he asked. "Poe never wrote about slaughterhouses or meat butchers, did he?"

"Not that I'm aware of."

"So how does that one fit the M.O.?"

Elinger stopped walking, suddenly aware of something. "Shit! It's so obvious. You read Smith's file. There was another attempt on his life."

"Yeah," Torres agreed, remembering. "Smith called Headquarters about a week before he died. He said somebody tried to kill him."

"With a mattress," Elinger finished for Torres. "Somebody—no doubt Leonard Ravnik—broke into Smith's house one night, yanked him from bed, threw him on the floor and covered him with his own mattress. Smith said the mattress was pressed on his face by someone very strong. A neighbor had seen the intruder break into the house and called the police. The sirens must have scared off Ravnik before he could suffocate Smith."

"A mattress was the murder weapon in *The Tell-Tale Heart*!" Torres suddenly clarified. "I read that one."

Elinger nodded his agreement.

"So, what about Renee? What's the story for her?" Torres asked.

"This last note said Patrick is fond of Renee and wants to bring her to the gulf beyond," Elinger began, his mind sorting through the message.

Torres nodded.

"Dennington said a consciousness likes to remain close to its last earthly remains until it's reborn. So, I'm thinking if Patrick's going to roam the graveyard where his body is buried, he'd want Renee there, too."

Torres nodded again. "Yeah, the Burial Grounds."

Elinger's face began to pale. His mind painted a grim picture. "Then there's only one story that fits that. Patrick, in one of his critiques, said it was his favorite—*The Premature Burial.* He's going to bury Renee alive!" Elinger said, the shock of it numbing him for a moment.

"The note says Patrick wants Renee close to him—so he's going to bury her in his grave with his own remains?" Torres concluded.

"Nothing else could make them physically closer," Elinger said just as his cell phone rang. He put the phone to his ear and listened as the voice on the other end.

"Mr. Elinger, this here's Elmo Thompson. The caretaker at the Westminster Burial Grounds. Ya gave me yer card. Do ya 'member me?"

"Yes," Elinger replied, surprised by the unexpected call.

"There's a guy in the cemetery with yer purty gal friend," Thompson said. "She's knocked out cold, lying by a grave. The sonovabitch dragged her there by the hair."

"Did you call nine-one-one?" Elinger asked.

"Nope. It's yer gal. I figured ya'd like to handle this yerself."

"You're absolutely right, Mr. Thompson," Elinger agreed quickly. "Please do two things for me. Unlock the cemetery's gate and stay in your quarters. I'll explain everything later."

"I'll do that fer ya," Thompson replied. "Glad I can help ya."

"That was the cemetery caretaker," Elinger told Torres as he shoved his cell phone back into his pocket. "Raymond Patrick's got a character flaw, too. His obsession for Renee Holland!"

SIXTY-ONE

• • •

"We got a plan?" Torres asked as he and Elinger trotted urgently across Renee's front lawn, heading toward their autos parked on the street.

Elinger was still adrenalized by the call from Thompson. "You know what Dennington told us to do."

"Yeah, electrocute that sonovabitch while Patrick's controlling him," Torres replied. "All we need is a lightning bolt," he added in a tone that implied the impossibility of the task.

Elinger's mind hatched an idea as he took in a deep breath from running. "There's a power station across the street from the cemetery, right?"

"Yeah, a substation," Torres answered, then grinned with some hope. "Plenty of electricity there to make a crispy critter out of Ravnik!"

"When we first became partners, you said you used to work for a power company," Elinger said, sucking in more air as he ran.

"Yeah, in Frederick," Torres replied, not breathing as heavy as Elinger. "I could get us a hot wire from the station to juice him," Torres replied, then hesitated. "I mean, I think I can. It's been awhile since I've been in a substation."

"You're all we've got," Elinger said. "Do you have your night-vision binoculars in your car?"

"Yeah."

"Take 'em to the graveyard and keep an eye on Ravnik and Renee. I'll be right behind you."

"No backups, right?"

Elinger nodded. "We can't chance scaring off Ravnik, and Osborne would never approve what we need to do."

"You got it," Torres started to peel away from Elinger, but Elinger grabbed him by the coat.

"One more thing, Ralph," Elinger said, running alongside Torres. "It's okay to be a hero tonight—for your brother, for Renee, for me, for you, for whomever. Let's just get rid of this sonovabitch!"

Torres replied through a smile of bravado. "You can count on it." With that, Torres picked up his pace and ran toward his nearby parked auto.

Elinger turned from Torres and reached his auto. He jumped in, started the engine and burned rubber from the curb.

As Elinger accelerated down the street, he noticed the headlights of Amos' SUV in his rearview mirror. He sure as hell didn't need Amos on his ass while he broke every law, and moral code, he had ever known to try to kill Ravnik and save Renee. Maybe he could lose him on the ride to the cemetery.

● ● ●

Earlier that night in the tenebrous catacombs below the church, Ravnik had breathed in the musty odors ingrained with death and decay. He stood at the archway and looked out at the Westminster Presbyterian Burial Grounds, noticing scores of tombstones breaking through a tight belt of mist. Miniature skyscrapers in a city of the dead, he mused. His eyes twitched and fluttered, and an unnatural smile warped his face. He was under the control of Raymond Patrick again, and Patrick had ordered him to begin the final phase of Patrick's agenda—to bring Renee to the gulf beyond.

Ravnik retrieved an AK-47 assault rifle from a pile of weapons he had hidden in the catacombs. He slammed a loaded clip into the weapon and shoved another one into his coat pocket. He felt comfortable with the rifle. It was powerful enough to punch holes in telephone poles. He bent over and retrieved a shovel from the ground and moved outside.

Ravnik approached Renee who was lying on the ground behind a row of marbled crypts. He realized Renee was also under Patrick's spell. Her eyes wobbled deep in their sockets, expressing her mindless condition. Ravnik also noticed her bottom lip was split, and her cheeks and arms were marked with bruises—injuries from his punches. It took more blows than he expected to knock her out.

Ravnik grabbed Renee by the hair and dragged her limp body along the row of graves. He looked at her, noticing the gray tones of her flesh reflecting in the moonlight even from beneath her blood-flecked nightgown. Although she was alive, Renee Holland could easily pass as a corpse.

At Raymond Patrick's plot, Ravnik released Renee's hair

and her head hit the ground with a thud. He leaned his assault rifle against a nearby tombstone, then, with a mighty thrust, slammed the shovel into the earth that covered Patrick's grave. He placed a foot on the spade's heel and stepped down. Driven by Ravnik's strength, the shovel cut deep into dirt. Repeatedly, Ravnik shoved the spade downward with his weight and scooped out the soil, piling it next to the grave site. At this rate, he knew it wouldn't take him long to reach the remains of Raymond Patrick.

● ● ●

Driving like a stuntman, Torres rocketed over the nearly vacant night-shrouded city streets. He was pushing his auto to its limit in his journey toward the graveyard. A dense fog had moved in and patched the streets. The poor visibility, however, didn't slow Torres. He sped through several intersections against red lights.

During the ride, Torres considered his next confrontation with Ravnik. He was a knot of nervous energy—his chest was barrel tight and his heart pounded against his ribs. He was aware he and Elinger were coming full circle with their adversary. The battle would mean victory or death for them. Either way, he was sure it would end tonight.

As Torres's auto squealed around another corner, Torres rummaged through his mind, trying to plan what he needed to do at the substation. He had been in various substations in Frederick when he worked at the power company. Some functions he remembered, others he had forgotten. He figured he could create a powerful surge of electricity but he wasn't sure how to direct it into Leonard Ravnik. He hoped his memory would revitalize itself once he was at the substation and could examine the equipment. Renee Holland's life would depend on it.

Torres's auto suddenly emerged from a dense cloud that hugged the street. Torres' face twisted with shock at what was before him. A clanging bell rang in his ears as he jammed both feet on the brake pedal. His wheels locked, his tires squealed, and his car fishtailed out of control, crashing into something very large, metallic, and unyielding.

Torres' face struck the steering wheel, crushing and splitting tissue. Blood gushed from his nose and spattered on his shirt and the dashboard. A black haze tried to engulf Torres' brain, but he fought it off. He glanced in the rearview mirror and gaped at his face. It was bleeding from a dozen cuts and swelling rapidly. His nose was lying sideways on his cheek.

Torres opened his glove compartment, rifled through its contents and withdrew a pencil. As a cop, he learned emergency room doctors sometimes used pencils to realign broken noses. Torres pressed the pencil against the center of his forehead to the cleft in his top lip. He gripped his nose and jerked it from his cheek, aligning it with the pencil. Stifling a yelp of pain, his nose spurt a fresh torrent of blood. After Torres applied pressure to his nose and stopped the bleeding, he withdrew a handkerchief. He tried to wipe his face clean but it only became a red smear.

Torres was still light-headed when a middle-aged man in greasy coveralls opened the car door and helped him from the auto. "You okay, mister?" the man asked, his friendly expression partially covered by a dark beard.

"I think so," Torres replied, staring into a wall of fog. Beyond the mist, he could barely make out the stalled freight train stretched across the street. The line of railroad cars seemed endless, both ends disappearing in the fog.

"My engine's dead. I'm waitin' on a tow," the engineer replied. "Sorry you didn't see me." He lifted his hand to show Torres the burning emergency flare he held. "I was just startin' to put these out on the road."

Torres only nodded, his mind back on Ravnik and Renee. He slid back into his auto and started its engine. He threw the car in reverse and stepped on the accelerator. The rear tires shrieked, burning away half their treads, but the auto didn't move.

"You're not goin' anywhere, son!" the engineer shouted, pointing at the front of Torres' auto.

Torres withdrew his foot from the accelerator and stepped out of the car. He glanced at the front end of his auto. Through the mist, he could see it was crumpled beneath the train and wedged firmly there.

"Shit!" Torres muttered at the same moment his car's engine sputtered and died. He snatched the night-vision binoculars from the seat and looked up the road for an auto to commandeer. The street was empty. He knew there was only one way to reach the cemetery—on foot!

Draping the binoculars over his neck with their cord, he climbed between two railroad cars and vaulted to the other side. Torres sprinted away, his head throbbing with every step. He could run and jog the two miles to the cemetery in about fifteen minutes, he hoped.

Torres' pores gushed perspiration, soaking his shirt and changing the deep crimson stains of his nose bleed to a pinkish tint that spread across the front of his chest. His legs pumped a strong, determined rhythm, carrying him across town with graceful strides. Over sidewalks and pavement, his youth did not betray him, but guided him and drove him like an arrow toward the cemetery.

Once at the graveyard, Torres stopped and leaned against the fence while he caught his breath. He lifted the night-vision binoculars to his eyes and scanned the cemetery. Though he didn't see Ravnik, he heard a shovel working the earth. Torres continued to look through his binoculars hoping to pierce the fog and darkness. When a slight gust parted the mist, he saw the greenish image of Ravnik scooping earth from Raymond Patrick's grave. Ravnik worked like an efficient machine, Torres noted, with single minded, tireless precision. Ravnik was already waist deep into Patrick's grave.

Torres panned the binoculars to the right and spotted Renee. She was lying motionless in the dirt near Ravnik; her chest heaved with choppy breaths. Torres was thankful Renee was alive and wondered if he was being foolish to wait for Elinger. What if Patrick decided to kill Renee before dawn? Torres didn't want to think about it. There was only one way to kill Patrick and Ravnik to free Renee and put an end to the killings. Electrocution. With that consideration, Torres knew he must wait.

Torres pulled his eye from the binoculars and noticed the Eastern horizon was a shade lighter than the rest of the sky. Day break was approaching, reducing the time left to save Renee. Regretfully, Torres was missing the two most important things for her deliverance—Lieutenant Elinger and a lightning bolt.

SIXTY-TWO

• • •

Elinger peered through his windshield and noticed the veil of light rain that had unexpectedly descended upon Baltimore. The drizzle had saturated the pavement and rinsed much of the fog from the air. With slippery streets, Elinger realized he was driving too fast. He slid around corners and fishtailed back onto the straight-aways. Occasionally, a motorist pumped their horn in angry protest but Elinger didn't care. He had one goal—to save Renee Holland's life.

After careening around another curve, Elinger drove upon the stalled train that suddenly loomed from behind the curtain of misting rain. Elinger braked sharply, sending his vehicle into a broadside skid. Once he stopped, he looked through the water-beaded driver's window. Several emergency flares hissed near his car, sparkling on the road like thirty-carat rubies. At the tracks, a half-dozen railroad workers waved lanterns, signaling more railroad men in the distance. Other railroad employees inspected the couplings of the train's cars.

Elinger shook his head, realizing it would take the rest of the night to clear the road. Then he saw Torres' wrecked car.

Elinger drove through the flares and pulled alongside the vehicle. The driver's door was open, exposing the blood-spattered steering wheel and dashboard.

Elinger realized Torres had been hurt. He wondered how seriously and pondered the grim consequences if he had been taken to the hospital and didn't make it to the graveyard. If so, Renee could be alone there, totally vulnerable to Leonard Ravnik and Raymond Patrick.

Elinger rolled down his window and shouted to the railroad men. "Does anybody know what happened to the driver of that car?"

An engineer turned toward Elinger. "Yeah, he's one crazy fella! Never seen anybody in that much of a hurry to get somewhere. He took off runnin' that way." The engineer thrust a finger into the wet night air.

Elinger's lips cocked into a half smile. Renee was not alone.

Needing a quick detour to the graveyard, Elinger yanked down on the shift lever, dropped his auto into reverse, then accelerated up the street backwards. Twisting the wheel, he spun the car into a one-eighty spin, then shifted into drive and sped from the area.

Amos, sitting in his auto parked on the street, watched Elinger as he zoomed away from the scene. Amos stepped on the gas and quickly followed.

● ● ●

In the glow of street lamps, Torres stood next to the graveyard fence and tilted his face upward toward the light rain. It resembled falling snow. The gentle drops drifting like dandelion seeds, offering cool relief that drew the heat and pain from his swollen features. He wanted to linger, but knew he couldn't. The rumbling of thunder brought him back to the job at hand.

Torres opened the cemetery gate and crept into the graveyard. Step by step, he moved from one tombstone to another, using them as cover to hide from Ravnik who was still digging up Patrick's grave. After inching forward a few more yards, Torres stopped and sat on the wet grass behind a monolithic tombstone some forty feet from Ravnik. When he looked up at Ravnik, a streak of lightning shot through the sky in the distance. He considered how easy all of this would be if one of those bolts hit Ravnik while he was entranced.

Leaning against a marble tombstone, Torres focused through his night-vision binoculars. He still maintained a clear view of Renee who was sprawled on the ground near Raymond Patrick's grave. Her vision was unseeing, her eyeballs yawing in their sockets. Raymond Patrick continued to dominate her. Torres knew he could intervene should Ravnik suddenly decide to bury her. But right now, Ravnik seemed engrossed in his task of digging deep into Patrick's grave. His sweat and rain slicked muscles bulged, and Torres guessed Ravnik was being fueled by excesses of adrenaline. His strokes were smooth and rhythmic. He watched as the soft earth crumbled easily against the shovel driven by the powerful Leonard Ravnik.

Across the street from the cemetery, an auto pulled up and parked. Its headlights blinked off.

Torres peered through his binoculars and recognized Elinger's vehicle. Although his swollen nose prevented a full curve, he managed a flicker of a smile. Using grave markers as cover, he moved cautiously from one tombstone to another, working his way back toward the street.

Elinger was standing next his auto when he saw Torres, in the distance, running across the cemetery grounds toward him. Torres was in the shadows as he jogged past the open gate and moved closer.

"Ralph, I saw your car. I thought you were hurt," Elinger said.

When Torres stepped under the hue of a street light, Elinger noticed Torres' bloodied clothes and the blood drooling from his mouth and bulbous nose. "You're right. I do hurt," Torres replied in an unceremonious timbre. "But my night's still better than Renee's. Ravnik's digging up Patrick's grave. Renee's not movin' but she's breathing." Torres lifted the night vision binoculars from his neck and handed them to Elinger.

Elinger pointed the night glasses toward the graveyard. He saw Ravnik's ghostly green image in the distance standing in Patrick's grave, spading more dirt from the plot. He also saw Renee on the rain-soaked ground, noting her short, stilted breaths. Elinger handed the binoculars back to Torres.

Elinger swept his hand toward the large substation near their cars. "Okay, Ralph. We need a lightning bolt."

Torres took a long moment to carefully study the substation. It was surrounded by an eight-foot chain link fence topped with razor wire. Behind the fence were several rows of eight-foot high metal canisters mounted on a wide platform. Torres knew these transformers lowered high voltage, making it suitable for use in homes and businesses.

He studied the dozens of thick power cables that linked the transformers to the saucer-like porcelain insulators stacked above them. Other conductor wires were stretched eighty-feet across the length of the substation to a fifty-foot pylon tower at the street.

Elinger moved to his auto and opened the trunk. He removed a pair of channel locks, then walked to the substation's gate with Torres. Elinger placed the jaws of the bolt cutters on the gate's padlock. As he snipped its hasp, a large bolt of lightning slammed into the graveyard across the street.

When Elinger and Torres entered the station, they were caught in the glare of headlights. The auto slowed, then parked behind Elinger's car. Its lights died.

"It's Anus," Elinger said dolefully.

Elinger handed the channel locks to Torres and hurried toward the auto as Amos climbed from it. The reporter gave Elinger a shrug. "You told me I could follow you."

Elinger's stare on Amos was corrosive. "Not now, not here."

"I've been on your leash long enough, Lieutenant. This is a public street!" Amos countered. "I'm not going to leave."

With no time to waste, Elinger was aware he'd have to be quick and brutal. "Okay, Anus. If you're going to stay, you can use my on-road office to take your notes."

"On-road office? What the hell are you talking about?"

Elinger grabbed Amos by the arms, spun him around and flattened his left arm behind his back into a Half Nelson.

Amos struggled, but Elinger's hold was tight. "What the hell are you doing?" Amos protested. "Let go of me!"

Ignoring Amos, Elinger pushed him toward the rear of his car where the trunk lid was still open. Elinger shoved the reporter into the small space.

"No time for the First Amendment tonight, Anus," Elinger quipped. "If you need any air, just push the valve on the spare," he added, then he reached in and grabbed his shotgun. He thrust the stock of the weapon at the emergency truck release handle inside the trunk and bent it, making it inoperable. Elinger slammed the trunk shut.

"You bastard!" Amos' shout was muffled but his mood was quite clear to Elinger. "I'm going to sue you for this!"

Elinger ignored Amos' threat when he heard the rumble of another bolt of light from the sky. Elinger opened a rear door of his car and tossed the shotgun onto the back seat.

Elinger hustled to the substation's gate and re-entered the electrical station with Torres.

Torres stopped in front of the transformers and studied them and their connecting electrical cables. Details he had forgotten were coming back to him. He had more confidence now that he could create a large charge of electricity and send it into the graveyard.

Elinger glanced at the paling eastern horizon. "We've got less than half an hour," he said grimly. "What do you need, Ralph?"

"A chain, some tape, wire cutters and a lot of electrical cable," Torres replied like an electrical power expert. "We'll probably find them in the storage room over there," he said, leading Elinger to a small, tin building.

Using the bolt cutters again, Elinger snipped the pad lock from the building's door.

Inside, Torres found a wall switch and flipped on the lights. His eyes canvassed the walls that were crowded with voltage gauges and control dials. A stand of shelves was stacked with tools and a storage bin was in a corner of the room.

Torres grabbed heavy-duty ratchet cutters and a roll of duct tape from a shelf. He opened the storage bin and found a coil of chain. "Perfect," he muttered, retrieving a thirty-foot length of light chain. Torres then approached a large wooden spool about as tall as a wagon wheel. It was tightly wound with quarter-inch aluminum wire wrapped in heavy black neoprene. "And we'll need this," he said, kicking the spool with his foot. "We can use it to run the electricity into the graveyard. It's underground aluminum cable. The insulation will keep it from shorting out."

Torres tipped the spool on its side and rolled it from the room, carrying the chain.

"How're you going to juice the wire, Ralph?" Elinger asked as he followed Torres outside.

"From the load side of the breakers," Torres replied, pointing at a power cable fifteen feet above them. The bare cable was strung tautly from the power pole outside the station to a transformer labeled 16KV. "That line carries sixteen-thousand volts," Torres explained. "It's a conductor wire. It takes electricity from the transformers and carries it into the city. I'm going to short it out. And when I do, it's gonna explode. I'll tape the end that's still connected to the transformers to the aluminum cable you'll be rolling into the graveyard until I join you. When we get near Ravnik, we cut the cable, peel back the insulation and somehow we stick him with it before he kills Renee."

"But you said you were going to short out the wire. Won't that cut off the power?" Elinger asked.

"Only for two minutes. When the conductor wire blows, an automatic reclosure will read it as a fault and open the main breaker," Torres said. "That kills the power. The breaker is over there." Torres extended a finger toward a large gray box near the transformers. "Works just like a breaker at a house. But it only breaks the power for two minutes. Then the juice automatically kicks in to retest the line."

"Once the circuit is open, we have only two minutes, right?" Elinger asked.

Torres nodded. "So, all we gotta do is waltz up to Ravnik and ask him to hold the wire while we blow up his ugly ass?" Torres remarked, accenting the implausibility of it. "And while we're at it, why don't we give an enema to a grizzly bear?"

Elinger glanced at Torres, his expression was grim. Torres knew from Elinger's look that he was very aware of the implausibility of their task. He could tell Elinger's mind was racing through a hundred scenarios, trying to come up with a fail-safe way to put the electricity into Ravnik's body.

"Are you all set here?" Elinger asked Torres.

"Almost," Torres replied, carrying the chain toward the transformers. Torres glanced down at the transformer platform and found what he was looking for—a nickel-sized copper wire. He knew it was the grid wire that grounded the substation's equipment. Torres ripped a piece of duct tape from its roll, then tapped one end of the chain to the grid wire.

Torres moved back to Elinger, stretching out the chain as he went. He pulled several feet of aluminum cable from the wooden spool and withdrew the ratchet cutters from his pocket. He trimmed the cable's end, peeling back the insulation to bare wire.

"When the overhead conductor wire blows, I'll splice it into this," Torres said, holding up the stripped end of the spooled cable wire. "Then I'll catch up to you in the cemetery. We'll have two minutes before 16,000 volts shoots goes into the wire. We just have to stay clear of it when that happens—and somehow have it connected to Ravnik.

"I'll need some tape and the wire cutters." Elinger said.

"You got a plan?" Torres asked with enthusiasm.

"I think so," Elinger replied, his mind in high gear.

Torres tore off a foot of tape and pressed it against his jacket, then handed the roll and ratchet cutters to Elinger who pushed them into his belt.

Torres picked up the free end of the chain and set himself to toss it over the conductor wire above him. "I'm ready when you are. All you need to do is signal me from the cemetery—but what's your plan? How are we going to get the current into Ravnik?"

"Follow me," was Elinger's curt reply.

Torres dropped the chain on the ground and followed Elinger who was rolling the spool from the substation, leaving a snake of cable behind him.

Back at Elinger's car, Elinger and Torres halted. Elinger shoved his key into the trunk lock.

Confusion curled Torres' brows. "What're you doin'?"

"Getting what we need."

"Amos?" Torres' eyebrows twisted further as Elinger opened the trunk.

Amos suddenly bounded forward, flailing at Elinger like an amateur featherweight. But Elinger grabbed the reporter's arms and shoved him back into the trunk.

"Let me out of here, goddammit!" Amos yelled with an indignant voice as Elinger's hand spread across his chest and pinned him down in the cramped space. "This is illegal custody and excessive force, Elinger!" Amos shouted. "Have you lost your fuckin' mind?"

Elinger withdrew a large plastic case with his free hand, then slammed the lid shut, muffling a fresh burst of obscenities from the reporter.

Elinger put the case on the trunk of his auto and opened it so Torres could look inside.

Despite the pain from his injuries, Torres managed a full smile this time. "Damn! You're brilliant!" he blurted, ogling Elinger's European CO_2 spear gun, its cabled reels and long metal spears.

"We'll connect the underground cable to the spear gun reel which is metal and filled with fifty feet of stainless-steel line connected to a spear," Elinger explained. "You get the idea."

"Yeah, we'll shoot that bastard with the spear, and it will carry the current directly into him," Torres replied through a brightening expression.

"Now all we've got to do, is do it," Elinger said, closing the gun's case and grabbing it by the carrying handle.

Elinger gave Torres a somber look. "Ralph, I don't want to come back without her." Elinger had already vowed to himself that he would save Renee even if it cost him his life, and he knew the inevitable and unavoidable confrontation with Ravnik could be that expensive.

"I'm with you, partner," Torres replied simply.

Elinger began to roll the spool of underground cable across the street with one hand while he carried the spear gun case with the other. Torres followed him. They crossed the street and moved toward the cemetery. The cable unwrapped from the spool and laid a trail behind them. Elinger and Torres rolled the spool into the cemetery through the open gate.

"I got it from here, Ralph," Elinger said.

Torres nodded and sprinted back into the substation and picked up the chain, ready to loop it over the overhead power wire.

Elinger trotted deeper into the graveyard, carrying the spear gun case in one hand and pushing the spool of wire with the other, laying out more cable behind him.

Crouching low, Elinger quietly continued to roll the spool of cable farther into the cemetery. He used the larger grave markers to conceal himself from Ravnik as he moved forward, row by row. As he went, his clothes became soaked from the soft rainfall.

When Elinger reached a tall and wide tombstone about forty feet from Ravnik, he stopped and slid down on the wet ground behind it. As he went, a jagged light flashed through the sky. Besides hearing the resulting thunder, Elinger noticed the rainfall was increasing.

Elinger glanced back toward the street and saw the cable laid out on the ground the entire distance of the graveyard.

Satisfied it would carry the substation's electricity, he turned back and looked at Ravnik. Ravnik was up to his shoulders in Patrick's grave, shoveling out more earth. His face was cold and savage, streaked with mud. And his eyes quivered, telling Elinger he was under the control of Raymond Patrick and only aware of his immediate task of digging up the grave.

Renee twitched helplessly on the soggy ground near Ravnik. The rain peppered her face, then dripped down her cheeks as her eyes twitched in their sockets. A bolt of lightning streaked across the sky above her and flashed her face with harsh light.

Elinger opened the spear gun case and pulled out the spear gun. He attached a reel of metal line to it and then the large CO_2 cartridge.

● ● ●

Ravnik's shovel chipped the top of Raymond Patrick's casket. After another shovelful of dirt, Ravnik tossed the shovel aside, bent over and began brushing the earth from the coffin's worm-eaten lid with his bare hands. When the last clod of dirt was gone, Ravnik yanked loose what was left of the coffin's lid. Only a yellowed skeleton and moldy shreds of a Victorian suit had endured over a hundred and fifty years. From the dark confines of the earth, Raymond Patrick's skull stared hauntingly at Ravnik. Ravnik was glad to finally be face to face with a person whose soul was as murderous and hateful as his own. And this man's ghost was the most powerful force Ravnik had ever encountered. His eyes steadied for a moment as he gazed into the black sockets and smiled.

Patrick's voice suddenly reverberated in Ravnik's head. *"In my youth, I was a most handsome lad, Leonard. But alas, the years have taken their toll. I have not done well by the earthly creatures that have feasted upon my mortal flesh. Bring Madam Holland to me at once, and place her in my grave chamber so we can share a life in the gulf beyond. I have so much to show Madam Holland. Every day will be a wedding day for us when she is finally with me for all of eternity. But spank along about your task, Mr. Ravnik! There are those nearby who wish to halt this glorious undertaking. But their arrival is far too tardy to stop us now. Once Madam Holland takes her final breath, our mission cannot be reversed no matter what counter actions are taken!"*

Ravnik nodded his head in answer to Patrick and reached up from the hole. He grabbed Renee by the hair, and pulled her into the pit. She fell face down on Patrick's bones, causing the ivory arms and hands to bounce upward. They landed on Renee's back as though Patrick was passionately embracing her.

Ravnik threw a leg up and pulled himself from the hole. He grabbed the shovel and began to spade earth into the grave, dropping heaps of suffocating dirt on Renee.

Still crouched behind the tombstone, Elinger unrolled a few feet of the aluminum underground cable from its spool. Using the ratchet wire cutters, Elinger cut the cable and peeled back its neoprene insulation. He ripped a strip of duct tape from the roll he carried and taped the end of the cable to the spear gun's reel. Next, he slid a spear into one of the barrels of the gun. Elinger then attached the stainless-steel line in the spear gun reel to the tail of the spear. Elinger studied his weapon for a moment. As he had planned, when the current came through the cable stretched across the graveyard, it would travel into the spear gun's reel, then through the steel line connected to the spear that would hopefully be stuck in Ravnik's chest. Ravnik would be electrocuted and the terror that plagued Renee and the city would end.

Satisfied he was ready, Elinger glanced at Ravnik and confirmed Ravnik was still in a trance. His eyes were slightly shifted upward, resembling Renee's spaced look when she was being controlled. Elinger twisted toward the street, lifted his hand and raised a thumb.

At the substation, Torres saw Elinger's cue through the lenses of his night vision binoculars. He glanced at the 16,000-volt overhead cable then looked at the end of the chain taped to the copper grid below the transformers. Satisfied it was secure, he began to whip the free end of the chain in a wide circular sweep over his head. Faster and faster, then Torres threw the chain skyward and retreated from the area beneath the overhead cable. The chain dropped on the cable, and the cable exploded with a loud pop and blinding flash. In that instant, the current from the overhead cable shot through the chain and into the grid wire below the transformers. The distinctive metallic clunk of the automatic reclosure opening the main breaker was unmistakable to Torres. The power was dead. The crucial two-minute countdown had just begun.

Torres rushed to the length of overhead wire connected to the transformers. He carefully lifted its smoldering end from the ground, then picked up his end of the aluminum underground cable Elinger had wheeled into the cemetery. He peeled the duct tape from his jacket and taped the two wires together. Torres knew when the reclosure tested the wire in two minutes, it would send 16,000 deadly volts into the cemetery.

With his work done at the substation, Torres pivoted on his heels and sprinted from the substation. He crossed the street, bolted into the graveyard and ran as fast as he could over the muddy burial grounds to join Elinger.

In the graveyard, Torres reached Elinger in less than thirty seconds. He joined Elinger behind the tombstone that concealed them from Ravnik. Elinger carefully aimed the spear gun at Ravnik who continued to shovel dirt into Patrick's plot.

Ravnik worked tirelessly, pushing the shovel deep and pitching dirt into the grave rapidly. He looked down into the hole at Renee. Although she was half-covered with earth, she seemed to have an involuntary primal survival reaction. She struggled for breath and tried to lift herself from the coffin, but the weight of the dirt on her back held her down.

Ravnik tossed another shovel full of muddy dirt on the back of Renee's head, forcing her face deeper into the soil and Raymond Patrick's skull face.

Elinger locked Ravnik in the spear gun's sight and began to tighten his finger on the trigger. But Ravnik suddenly noticed the glint of aluminum from the spear gun and saw Elinger and Torres. He threw down the shovel and snatched up his assault rifle. He aimed it at the detectives and yanked the trigger. The weapon spit fire and lead.

The spray of bullets peppered the tombstone protecting Elinger and Torres. The marble splintered like wood, shooting glass-like shards in all directions. The muddy earth erupted as a dozen more slugs pounded the area. Fragments of stone and wet earth spattered Elinger and Torres, clouding their eyes. With little choice, they started to withdraw from behind the grave marker. But Elinger's left shoulder and arm went flaccid at the same moment he heard the pronounced *thunk* of a bullet hitting flesh. The impact knocked him down on the wet ground, causing him to drop the spear gun.

Torres bent over Elinger and examined his wound.

"Never mind me! Shoot him!" Elinger ordered, holding his shoulder tightly to stop the blood flow and pushing the spear gun toward Torres.

Torres glanced quickly at his watch. Thirty more seconds had lapsed. He aimed the spear gun at Ravnik as more of Ravnik's bullets ricocheted off the pieces of marble that shielded him.

Having heard the gunshots, Elmo Thompson trotted across the slippery cemetery grounds as fast as his old legs would carry him. Weaving in and out of the tombstones for cover, he carried his trusted Winchester rifle. When he saw Ravnik in the distance holding Elinger and Torres at bay with another volley from his high-powered rifle, he ran to a large grave marker and crouched behind it. He rested his rifle on the marble for a steady shot at the crazy man who was trying to kill Lieutenant Elinger's woman.

But Ravnik had seen Thompson's movement. He pivoted toward the old cowboy just as Torres fired the spear gun. The shaft traveled directly for its target, but when Ravnik had turned toward Thompson, he moved a half step—enough for the spear whistle past him, missing him only by inches.

Ravnik unleashed a stream of bullets toward Thompson,

creating an exploding trail across a row of graves. Thompson shrunk behind the grave marker but not before a bullet chipped off a large piece of marble. The marble fell and hit Thompson in the head, knocking him out cold.

"Shit! I had him!" Torres yelled at Elinger, glancing at the spear that had embedded itself in a tree behind Ravnik. Its stainless-steel line trailed across the ground back to the spear gun.

Elinger quickly assessed his left shoulder injury. It was painful and bloody but not life threatening. As long as he could use his right arm to pull the trigger—that was all he needed.

Using his uninjured arm, Elinger reached into the spear gun case and withdrew another reel of line and handed it to Torres. Torres removed the first reel from the spear gun and attached the new reel. Elinger grabbed another spear from the case and pushed it down a barrel of the spear gun. Torres handed Elinger the gun.

Last chance, Elinger thought. This shot needs to be perfect. With his right arm, Elinger steadied the spear gun on the tombstone and beaded its sight on Ravnik who had just stopped shooting at Thompson. Elinger placed his finger on the trigger.

Torres glanced at his watch again. Only thirty seconds left.

Ravnik whipped his rifle toward Elinger and Torres again and released a new wave of gunfire. The projectiles chipped stone and broke the earth, devastating everything in their trail.

Elinger's line of vision was clouded by the flying mud and increased rainfall. He couldn't hold the sight on Ravnik. With no other option, he ducked down, pulling the spear gun with him.

Suddenly, Ravnik's gun clicked empty. Ravnik punched the magazine release, dropping the empty clip to the ground. He pulled a loaded magazine from his pocket and slammed it into his weapon. He yanked back the slide bolt, cocking, and chambering a round in the rifle.

Elinger steadied the spear gun on the tombstone again and aimed it at Ravnik. He looked directly into Ravnik's quivering eyes, realizing he had about twenty seconds remaining before the substation reclosure would retest the main line and send 16,000-volts of electricity through the spear gun.

A tranced grin lifted the corners of Ravnik's lips as he took a few steps toward Elinger and Torres. His mouth moved with eerie locution as he spoke in a low, guttural tone. *"Lieutenant, I was shamefully in error. Perhaps you do possess the wit of C. Aguste Dupin to find me in this final chapter. But do not laud the success you will never claim. Your gallant final hour efforts have failed. Madam Holland has passed. Now she is mine!"*

Although the voice came from Ravnik's throat, Elinger realized he was listening to Raymond Patrick. This is what he really wanted and needed, absolute proof Patrick was in control of Ravnik when he released the electrical blast, the only way to scatter Raymond Patrick's consciousness from this realm of existence.

"Just a few seconds left, Kent," Torres reported above the din of a new burst of automatic rifle fire that made him and Elinger withdraw behind the tombstone.

"He's got to be distracted so I can get off a shot," Elinger said, coughing dirt from his mouth.

"Then I guess it's time for me to play hero," Torres said quickly. "Don't miss, dammit! I'm only gonna do this once!" With that, Torres leaped from behind the cracked and chipped tombstone with a wild look in his face. He sprinted into the open and shouted at Ravnik, "Hey, dumb ass, I'm over here!"

Ravnik trained his rifle on Torres and shot a streak of lead at him. The bullets pock-marked the earth, ripping up a path behind Torres who was now running for cover.

While Ravnik's attention was on Torres, Elinger beaded the speargun's sight on Ravnik again. As Ravnik paused to survey the damage he had inflicted, Elinger began a smooth pull on the trigger, hoping and praying Patrick was still in possession. Last spear, he reminded himself, as he shifted one eye toward his watch. Four seconds left. "Good bye, you sonovabitch!" he muttered, tugging the trigger until he felt the click.

Time froze for Elinger. It seemed like forever before the spear shot from the weapon. The shaft split the air, gleaming in the cloudy moonlight, glistening in the rain and towing its steel line. And true to Elinger's aim, the shaft found its target, hitting Ravnik in the center of his chest.

Even Ravnik could not withstand the impact of the powerful spear gun. He staggered backward, involuntarily pointing his rifle skyward and shredding branches from a tree with an erratic sweep of shots. He faltered, dropped his weapon, and reached for the shaft protruding from his chest.

Elinger gaped at the spectacle. Suddenly, he realized he still clutched the spear gun, and it was taped to the aluminum cable. He threw the weapon aside.

Behind a thick slab of granite, Torres's eyes were riveted on his watch. The second hand had just passed the two-minute mark.

Elinger was still in awe as he locked his eyes on Ravnik.

He knew the automatic reclosure at the substation had probably just retested the line and had fired its 16,000-volts into the conductor wire he had rolled into the graveyard. Elinger glanced back at the cable laid out across the grounds. He could see the power surge through it, causing the cable to jump from the ground. Elinger turned back to Ravnik, hoping the cable would stay speared in his chest for a few more seconds.

Ravnik tugged at the spear in his chest, but its barbs were snagged in his ribcage. Raymond Patrick, through Ravnik's mind, noticed the steel line connected to the spear was also linked to a long cable stretching across the cemetery grounds. Suddenly aware of Elinger's plan, Patrick screamed in Ravnik's head, ordering Ravnik to pull the cable from the spear. Ravnik reached for the end of the spear and began yanking on the cable, but it was too late. The electricity suddenly fired through the spear gun cable and traveled into the shaft embedded in Ravnik's chest.

With the same fury of the lightning bolts in the night sky, the electricity hit Ravnik mercilessly. His limbs flailed violently as he danced a jig of death. The voltage spiked his hair and the intense heat caused smoke to billow from his one ear and the auditory hole in the other side of his head. His body fluids simmered, his flesh baked, and his brain boiled. Ravnik's hands exploded first, then his feet, leaving him with stubbed, smoking appendages. As the heat intensified, Ravnik's eyes melted in his head and poured from their sockets like strawberry preserves. Patches of his body began to explode, sending chunks of flesh in every direction. The pieces fell to the ground, steaming on the cold, wet soil.

Elinger jumped out from behind the tombstone and rant to

Patrick's grave pit. He jumped in, and Torres quickly joined him. Together, they dug frantically with their fingers to reach Renee. Once they uncovered her, Torres grabbed her by the shoulders and pulled her from the grave and clutches of Raymond Patrick's skeleton. Elinger steadied Renee with his right arm while Torres jumped from the plot, then pulled Renee's limp body free.

Torres placed a finger under Renee's jaw, feeling for a pulse in her carotid artery. He felt none and shook his head at Elinger who was just climbing from the grave.

Disbelieving, Elinger crouched at Renee's side and cleared the dirt from her mouth with his fingers. With steady counts, Elinger pushed her chest with the heel of his hand. A minute passed and Renee didn't respond.

Elinger trembled inside, fearing he may not be able to revive the woman he loved. But Elinger doggedly continued the chest compressions. More seconds passed and the reality of what he might have to accept became more evident. He fought his emotions and refused to acknowledge Renee's fate.

With a grim expression, Torres watched Elinger continue to push on Renee's chest with the heel of his hand. Elinger stared sadly at Renee's lifeless form. Suddenly, Renee made a strangled sound. She coughed and spat dirt from her mouth, then heaved for air in violent gasps.

Elinger rolled Renee over on her side while she gagged and pulled for air. After a few seconds, she breathed more steadily. And when she opened her eyes, they were clearly focused. She was looking at the world from her own mind again. Her first sight was Elinger. She put her arm around Elinger's neck.

Elinger bent down, and with his right arm, lifted her into

a sitting position. He hugged and kissed her tenderly. This was the best moment of his life. "It's over, Renee," he said softly. "It's over."

Torres had turned away to give Elinger and Renee a moment of privacy. But he saw something in the cemetery that turned his expression cold. "Oh, shit!" he muttered, pointing a finger where Leonard Ravnik last stood.

Like Torres, Elinger and Renee saw the misty shape. Slightly larger than a football, it floated about six feet above the ground over the bloody and charred remains of Leonard Ravnik. It pulsated, beating like a heart.

Watching the strange apparition, Elinger feared Raymond Patrick had survived. In a few seconds, however, the mystical form wavered. Its rhythm glitched, then it thinned and dissipated into the rainy air.

Torres gave Elinger a grin of victory. "You're right, man. It is over."

Tears flooded Renee's eyes, streaking the dirt on her cheeks. She sobbed and buried her head on Elinger's chest. Elinger and Torres exchanged a glance when they heard sirens in the distance.

"I'll clean up here," Torres volunteered.

"Yeah, even with self-defense, it would be difficult to explain the spear gun and the substation cable," Elinger said quickly, then reached in his pocket and removed his car keys. He tossed them to Torres. While you're at it, let Amos out of the trunk and tell him he'll get his story tonight."

"Do you think the Sun will print it?" Torres asked with surprise.

"Not the real story. But they'll print the version I give Amos," Elinger replied.

Torres nodded, pocketed the keys and started to move off. He stopped, however, when he glanced at Leonard Ravnik's bloody and charred body parts. "What about him?"

Elinger had already considered that. "Don't worry. I think Ozzie will be glad to know lightning can strike the same person twice."

Torres could only grin. Without another word, he picked up the spear gun, its cables and its discarded reels. Torres pulled the spear he had shot from the tree. He removed the substation cable from the reel on the spear gun and put all of the gun's parts in the case. As he headed for the street carrying the spear gun case, he grabbed the end of the substation's underground cable. He pulled it with him as he trotted toward the substation in the distance. In less than a minute, Torres knew there would be no evidence of what really happened to the murdering one-eared man named Leonard Ravnik—except that he was struck by lightning a second time.

As for Raymond Patrick, Torres knew his name would never come up again.

Elinger gently pulled Renee to her feet and hugged her. He looked into Renee's eyes, thankful for her survival and their second chance to live and love together.